ONCE BITTEN ...
CLASSIC MONSTERS ANTHOLOGY 5

YeOldeDragonBooks.com

Ye Olde Dragon Books
6909 Ackley Rd.
Parma, OH 44129

www.YeOldeDragonBooks.com

2OldeDragons@gmail.com

ISBN 13: 978-1-969197-07-9

Published in the United States of America October 15, 2025

Cover Art designed by Jessica Tanner. © Copyright 2025 Ye Olde Dragon Books

TABLE OF CONTENTS

FOREWORD

It's the anthology-that-almost-wasn't.

I was down to the wire and hadn't finished my story yet. Most of the edits were done. (except Michelle's!) I was processing an online order—or rather, trying to process it—and my cursor vanished. I tried tabs. Nothing. I smacked the keyboard a couple of times. Nothing. Laptop ceased to function. Huge deflated sigh. I trudged to the corner to fire up the desktop, which is a few days older than dirt. After a couple of hours of updating, I finally got it up and running. Paid my bills, finished my orders, and opened the author bio page to get it ready to send to Michelle.

Click! Click! The whirr of the motor shutting down. Screen fades to black.

NO!

It wouldn't let me reload because it said I had "logged in too many times." I left the desk before the temptation to put a brick through the monitor became too overpowering. I tried again the next morning. I actually had the bio page almost finished when… click! Click! Whirrrrrrr… Fade to black again.

Long story short… I had to arrange a trip into town to snag a new computer, because none of the electronics in my house were going to get the job done. By the way, it seems my computers never die UNLESS we're on a deadline for an anthology. (This is the second time I've been forced into a large purchase in order to finish a book!)

So please DO enjoy! I'm not a vampire, but some of my blood, sweat, and a LOT of tears went into this volume. When all is said and done, I believe it's worth it!

This marks the end of our fifth year in business. Our wonderful authors make all these collections possible, and we are blessed beyond measure to be able to join their creative efforts. Laugh at some tales, cry over a few, and feel that little shiver in your spine over all the rest.

Deborah Cullins Smith
September 2025

I'll admit it, vampires are not my "thing," and I kind of cringed when Deb decreed that anthology 5 would be Dracula. What the heck was I going to write?

Then I remembered that gee, some of her dark influence had prompted me to put a vampire in the first full-length Enchanted Castle Archives novel. So you all get to meet 'Na's "Uncle Morris." How he becomes "Uncle Morris" will be covered in an upcoming Smedley & 'Na novel.

But I digress ...

This is a BIG baby. There were so many stories we couldn't say no to, and a handful of others we very reluctantly said no to. A wide variety. Some really clever twists on the whole vampire mythos. Some giggles, some "Huh ... interesting" moments.

But I still recommend that for those of you with hyperactive imaginations ... better read this before moonrise. You know. Just in case ...

Enjoy!

Michelle L. Levigne
September 2025

THERE GOES THE NEIGHBORHOOD
Jordan Campbell

I died more than 250 years ago. Or I almost died, I should say. I was minding my own business, fighting for my life somewhere in Europe. I do not remember where, precisely. The borders changed so often that I honestly have no idea where I was or who currently holds that territory. I shot my musket at an enemy soldier just as he fired at me. I missed. He didn't and his round went through my lung. I lay there for hours, even after the battle halted, bleeding from a gaping wound and waiting to die. Nobody ever told me how bad dying hurts or how tedious it is. But then a vampire found me, and I became a very easy meal.

The vampire drank his fill of my blood without my permission, and he wound up keeping me from dying altogether. I did not go to the White Throne for my judgment. I did not don a white robe and pick up a harp. I stayed on Earth, neither fully alive nor truly dead. I was trapped in this state, never aging, incapable of feeling scorching heat or bitter cold. I could no longer experience mundane pleasures, not the warmth of a hearth or the scent of freshly baked bread. I existed without joy…but not without rage.

All vampires must learn to control bloodlust, lest they attract too much attention from humans. I was stronger than any one man, but I weakened near holy items. I saw many vampires destroyed over the years and I feared sharing their fate. So, I tamed my temper as best I could, and I became very choosy when it came to finding people to feed on.

One thing that did not change after my becoming a vampire was my disposition toward my neighbors. All through my mortal life, I hated my neighbors, and I saw no reason to change this as a vampire. A neighboring nation had started the war that cost me my human life, and even in peace, my hatred grew. I utterly despised my neighbors. They were nosy and annoying and never shut up, and I craved silence more than anything else. I killed a neighbor within a day of returning to my village.

Once I started, it became difficult to stop and were it not for a particularly frigid winter that caused many to starve, I suspect I would have been detected. A human life sustained me for weeks, one neighbor after another drained of blood down to the last drop. But after that winter, I ran out of neighbors entirely and had to move on.

Through the years, I moved from one village to the next, taking care to only feed upon the most unsavory of neighbors, those who would not be missed. Often, I transitioned from neighbors to lone wanderers and vagrants, so as to better keep my presence unnoticed. I drank the blood of more than one thousand souls without being detected. Humans have a remarkable ability to be incredibly ignorant of what might be happening right under their noses. They will convince themselves of any lie, no matter how convoluted, to maintain a false sense of security.

I no longer remember the name I was born with, but that does not matter. When I crossed the Atlantic Ocean, I took a new name for myself. Call me Wagner.

~~~~~

Three heavy moving vans barreling down the street ripped me from my slumber, nearly driving me into a frenzy of fury. How dare they interrupt my rest! Five months before, three college-aged humans had fancied filming the forest near my dwelling—a vain attempt at fame and fortune. I devoured them to the last drop and had been practically hibernating since the search parties had been called off.

I did not truly *need* to sleep as humans did, but that did not mean I did not appreciate it. Deep within my own house, I could cut myself off from the noisy outside world, a world so full of neighbors. I had eaten enough to sustain myself for at least a year, and now my rest had been interrupted. I would have vengeance for this!

I dangled much like a bat, but it was fruitless to attempt to sleep any longer. I leapt from the ceiling to the floor, landing silently and stalked to the nearest window. My teeth ground together louder than my footsteps. Moving vans were among the loudest vehicles allowed on residential roads and I found their sound quite distinctive. I hadn't had any neighbors on this stretch of road in some time—the college students had been trespassing. Irritation burned hot in my belly, and I knew I would not be able to reorient myself for a second round of hibernation.

I stalked down the narrow staircase to the ground floor. Most vampires who survive their first year prefer similar constructions: High ceilings, narrow hallways and staircases, furniture arranged to cast shadows on every corner. I had few windows, so as to keep out as much sunlight as possible. Sunlight would not kill me, but it would weaken me and dull my normally superior senses.

The air was warm with the heat of late summer, so I donned my thickest pair of sunglasses. I preferred wearing a duster jacket as well, but that would likely attract unwanted attention. The sunglasses would
~~~~~

shield my eyes from the worst of the sun's beams and allow me to observe this newest batch of interlopers.

I walked soundlessly toward the neighboring house. Three moving vans and an enormous passenger van that might as well have been a bus parked in front of it. A family then, judging from the stickers and toys strewn across various seats in the van. Neighbors were bad enough on their own, but a family was worse. Families meant too many eyes to observe my actions and a lot of visitors. Families attracted attention by merit of their own existence. Before that batch of trespassing college students, my previous neighbor had been a single, self-important, egotistical young woman who had scoffed at family. Still, she had cried for her mother as I drank her blood down to the last drop.

Carefully observing the various family members and assorted workmen, I discerned the patriarch and matriarch of the family with ease. They were the two eldest people present and carried an air of authority about them. They would be the first ones to target then—turn the parents, or at least lower their defenses, and the remainder of the family would be child's play.

"Salutations," I said as I drew near enough to speak without raising my voice. "Glad tidings and welcome to the neighborhood. I am Wagner."

Was it unnecessarily archaic to greet them so formally? Perhaps, but it had been a long time since I had had proper conversations with people. Usually, I struck silently, but being awakened in such jarring a fashion had made me feel rather theatrical. The response was immediate.

"Well, how about that?" the patriarch boomed. He was a big-bellied man with graying hair and mustache. "Less than an hour and we've already made a friend!"

The man seized my hand with both of his own. His hands were everything my hands were not. Wide and tanned, warm and soft from familial affection while calloused from work. His grip was nothing compared to my own strength—I could break stones with no more effort than an average man would use to snap his fingers. I turned my attention from the patriarch to his wife. She stepped forward and embraced me.

"Why, aren't you sweet?" The woman beamed, her smile stretching from one round cheek to the other. She was ruddy, and I could not help but think of drinking her blood. She took my staring and hunger for confusion and cleared her throat to introduce herself. "It's lovely to meet you. My name is Victoria Cazadora-Cacciatore and this is my husband, Andreas."

Before I could respond, we were interrupted by a strapping young man carrying a very large box. His muscles bulged and he walked slowly, with deliberately long strides. But from the way he kept rearranging his fingers ever so slightly, his grip had to be weakening. Ah, the arrogance of youth, the desire to show off one's strength! Clearly it must be universal throughout the ages. I remembered that all too well, though I was now exponentially stronger than I had been at that awkward age. I moved swiftly, taking the box from the young man's hands and setting it aside.

"I could have managed that myself," the young man said, his expression a mixture of bravado and relief. He was altogether in denial of his own limitations.

"Niccolo!" Victoria snapped, putting her hands on her hips. No doubt, she was Niccolo's mother. "Where are your manners?"

"Sorry, Mamma!" Niccolo blushed and flashed me a sheepish grin. "Thanks for the assist, neighbor. There's still more boxes down in the vans. I bet I can lift the heaviest one!"

I was nearing my three hundredth year of existence and accepting a teenager's challenge to prove myself was something I had no desire to do. Nevertheless, I found myself following him to the vehicles. Two girls, one a slender teenager and the other at the awkward age hovering between childhood and adolescence, struggled to maneuver a heavy bookshelf between them. Sweat dripped down both their brows.

"Helena! Luccia!" Andreas called. "Need a hand?"

The girls smiled, their eyes shining at the sight of their father. I paused, perplexed. Teenagers were a relatively recent cultural phenomenon, but most adolescents I had seen over the last few decades tended to be chagrined at best at their parents' presence. How peculiar indeed.

"Hi, Papa!"

I sidestepped the girls and took the bookshelf in my arms. I lifted it without the slightest effort and the children gasped in wonder. Part of me wondered whether my actions were too conspicuous but given that Andreas and Victoria were so openly amicable, it was doubtful I'd be able to maintain an especially low profile.

Several other children darted about in front of us, greeting their parents and mingling with the movers. One boy stood taller than Luccia and Helena, but was not nearly so large as Niccolo, and two girls nearly danced about, small and slight. One boy about Luccia's age carried two bicycles, one under each arm.

"Leave it to ol' Salvador to have to carry the bicycles," the boy muttered. "Not Isabella and Noella, oh no, even if these are *their* bicycles, all girly and ribbony. No, they get the easy boxes full of aprons."

I disregarded the boy's grumbling about his sisters. If he truly disliked having to carry the bicycles, he could easily choose something else. I moved on to help carry furniture. The second oldest boy came to help me move a table and introduced himself as Enrique. Apparently, he had the best manners of all his siblings, no doubt using Niccolo as an example of how not to behave. He chatted on and on about how he and his family had lived in a dozen states in the last twelve years, but he hoped that this year, they would finally stay in one place. I considered the implications of everything he said but did not reply.

One tiny boy carried a box in his hands, desperate to emulate his siblings. He promptly dropped it on my foot, though I barely felt the impact.

"Giovanni!" Victoria spoke sharply and crossed her arms. "You apologize to Mr. Wagner right this minute. That landed on his foot!"

"It is of no concern," I soothed. When vampires want to, we can convince humans of just about anything. "I am completely uninjured and an apology given under duress is no apology at all. Curiosity dictates, however, that I ask what is in the box."

"Cookbooks!" Giovanni piped up. He was no older than five and he took the opportunity to turn his declaration into a cheer. "Cookbooks! Cookbooks! Cookbooks! Looky, looky cookbooks-y!"

As if on cue, the box burst open, though that notion was nonsensical. There were no such things as sentient boxes. But the box did contain cookbooks…many cookbooks. More cookbooks than even a family of this size had any business owning. The sight of the books caused the family to congregate. Each member of the family chose a volume, and in so doing they arranged themselves in a row, ironically by age. The full scope of the family's size struck me as fiercely as any broadsword. Victoria and Andreas had *eight* children: Niccolo, Helena, Enrique, Luccia, Salvador, Isabella, Noella, Giovanni.

I wrenched my glance away from the family and focused on the books they held. Cookbooks can reveal many things about people: their preference for one cuisine over another, their inclinations to experiment with many recipes or cling to a select few. For the most part, the family held recipes of Italian and Mexican cuisine. However, Noella held up a tome catering entirely to garlic-based recipes and Luccia held a book called *Meals from the Holy Land.*

I turned my attention back to the family members themselves. Most of them wore cross necklaces and Niccolo's forearm bore a tattoo of Scripture verses penned in Italian.

"We've nearly moved in," Andreas said. He beckoned to the workmen. "So, everyone gather 'round. We must pray, to thank the Lord for granting us a safe journey and allowing us to find such a lovely home."

Dread filled my entire being, down to the last cell. I excused myself as quickly as I could, brushing past family members and moving van workers alike, just as the Cazadora-Cacciatore family bowed their heads in unison. I had to flee. I could not risk exposing myself just yet. The moment I crossed my threshold, I slammed the door behind me and locked it securely.

I paced, leaping up to the ceiling so I could prowl without tripping over the furniture. I had to take stock of the facts. The new neighbors were, in effect, the physical manifestation of everything that was anathema to me. Garlic was bad enough on its own, due to its ability to grow wild. But this family served the Creator. By my own nature as a vampire, regardless of what I did when I was human, I now opposed the Creator in all aspects.

I did not have a heartbeat to pound and my hands were perpetually cold so they would not be discernibly clammy. It was difficult to ascertain when I managed to calm myself down without these symptoms to act as a measure. But in time, my apprehension ebbed, and I allowed rage to take its place. How dare these humans come to my territory, bringing so many of their toxic habits with them! The very nerve! I was Wagner, was I not?

I had lived the life of a vampire since before this blasted country was founded. I had drunk the blood of hundreds of souls through the centuries, and I was not going to stop now, by thunder! I would spill every drop of blood in the Cazadora-Cacciatore family if it was the last thing I ever did.

~~~~~

I avoid revenge under most circumstances. Revenge attracts attention and attention leads to complications. I wanted to taste blood and I did not seek to ensure retribution, but my neighbors were the type of people I needed to destroy, root and stem. Whittling them down one by one would be the least conspicuous option. In truth, I doubted I could take more than one or two, but as I watched the family, my hunger grew alongside my hatred of all they stood for.

I approached the eldest child first. Niccolo was nineteen, and not so much a boy as a young man. He walked with purpose, and I learned that he planned to leave home soon, as he had no talent for the kitchens his parents so loved.

They ran a small restaurant devoted to the cuisine of their ancestral lands, but Niccolo sought the life of a soldier. There was a brutal irony in that, given my own youthful misadventures in an army that had led to my becoming a vampire in the first place.
~~~~~

Niccolo sat on the stoop to his family's home. At his side was a large pile of sticks, branches and other pieces of wood. He glanced up at me as I approached and gave a polite smile.

"Good morning," I greeted, though I did not believe it was a good morning at all. I could already tell it was going to be a bright, sunshiny day. I despised bright, sunshiny days. "Where is everyone?"

"Here, there, and everywhere," Niccolo replied with a shrug. "It's hard to keep track. The little ones run so fast."

That was true enough, from what I had observed. For almost a fortnight, I'd witnessed the children run every which way. I glanced over my shoulder, but for the moment, Niccolo and I were alone. How long that would last, I had no idea. As strong as he fancied himself, I could overpower Niccolo without straining a muscle, but I preferred to take my food in solitude. This was not a private setting.

Niccolo took one of the larger sticks from his pile in one hand and with the other, he pulled a pocketknife from his trousers. With swift slashes, he carved the stick into something sharp, and all too familiar.

"What are you doing?" I asked, the question barely more than a whisper on my lips, for I already knew the answer.

"Whitling stakes," Niccolo replied. "It's the best form of busy work I know when there's nothing else to do. My friends like to go camping, so I always make sure they have plenty of stakes for their tents and hammocks. Maybe after my turn in the Guard, I'll start my own business with these. Wood makes much better stakes than plastic."

Wooden stakes...I took a step backward without meaning to. However many myths about vampires that have sprouted up over the centuries, one legend that is absolutely true is that a stake impaled through the heart will paralyze a vampire. Especially a wooden stake. Niccolo had already finished a second stake and moved on to a third. For him, they were no more than a means to stay busy, but to me, they were weapons. If I were to come any closer, how difficult would it be for Niccolo to take any one of his stakes and drive it into my chest? He would sap my strength and drain my powers...I would surely be destroyed.

"It's not just my friends, of course. My family likes camping too," Niccolo continued. "We've been to Yellowstone, Glacier, Zion, Denali, you name it. Maybe you can come with us on our next trip. Mamma and Papi were just saying that you need more sun, Mr. Wagner."

That was more than I needed to hear. What I needed more than anything was to flee. Camping? Not an option. To think I had scorned the trespassers in the woods! This was far worse. Humans, by and large, had forgotten most sorts of weaponscraft as technology had advanced.

But the skills that came with camping were the exception. Stakes, axes, knives…all of them could spell disaster for me.

I resisted the urge to turn my back. It would be best to keep my eyes on Niccolo, and his many, many stakes. I walked backward, in quick, steady strides, until I was at my threshold. I fairly leapt up the steps of my porch, my eyes locked on the young man and his weaponry. I shut the door and twisted every lock into place, letting go a breath I had not realized I'd taken. Given that I cannot actually breathe, that was certainly significant.

The *stakes* for my survival had risen dramatically.

~~~~~

Niccolo may have been the eldest and theoretically the easiest of his siblings to pick off, as he was the one most often left to his own devices. But he was hardly the only child in that house. Given that Niccolo was so heavily armed—he carried the stakes with him nearly everywhere— I turned my attention to the second child, the eldest daughter Helena.

Helena sat under the shade of a large tree, her nose in a large book. I reflected on how many trees might have been cut down to provide the paper for that volume, but decided it wasn't worth dwelling on. I stepped closer and closer, one foot in front of the other. Helena was none the wiser and when I was within arm's reach of her, I extended my fangs. Helena was a very pretty young woman, with skin and hair a shade darker than her siblings, and she carried herself with grace. I had eaten many such women over the years.

"Hi, Mister Wagner," Helena said, looking up. I had no idea what had caught her attention but when she squinted at me, I retracted my fangs lest I alarm her.

"Good afternoon," I replied as evenly as I could while frustration stormed in my gut. I had gotten so close. "Why are you reading outside? Is that not uncomfortable?"

"Not really, no," Helena answered. "I like reading outside. When my family's at home, it's so noisy in the house I can't concentrate. And when I'm alone, the house is so quiet, I can't enjoy the peace. Being outside is the best of both worlds."

A touching sentiment, and one I even understood to some degree, though I did find greater enjoyment when I had a victim to feast on, listening to them become quieter and quieter as I drank their blood and consumed their life.

"Well," I said with a nod. "I see where you're coming from there. What is it that you're reading?"

"Oh!" Helena smiled. "This is my absolute favorite book. It's the first book in the *Tomas, the Handsome Neighborhood Vampire* series!"
~~~~~

I knew all too well what that book was. It was as farcical a depiction of my kind as any ever written. The very idea of a vampire becoming a hair stylist and enjoying his neighbors' company! Pah, that was a mockery of every aspect of my being! I could have bitten Helena then and there and shown her what a true vampire is capable of. More to the point, I despised and detested that book from a technical standpoint. The grammar was poor and the spelling bad, and not from a colloquial sense that fit the setting either. But striking Helena here and now would be far too conspicuous. Her parents would notice her absence eventually and a bloodstained book would be evidence as to what had happened.

"You want to borrow it? We could form a book club!" Helena exclaimed, looking years younger and far more earnest than she normally did. "Nobody else in the family reads these books and that's so frustrating!"

And for good reason! Whatever hatred I felt toward Andreas and Victoria, I could not and would not fault them for their discernment in literature. I took a few steps back and stared at Helena again. She turned page after page, reading rapidly. There was no way that such a volume could be so engrossing.

"Ouch!" Helena muttered. "Paper cut. Hold on, I'll be right back! I have lots of *Tomas* books, Mr. Wagner. I can loan you one!"

The scent of her blood nearly drove me into a frenzy. The desire to seize Helena and bite down on her neck—siphoning out every drop of blood—nearly consumed me. It would be nothing to overpower her. But just as I moved forward to grab her, she leapt to her feet and darted inside, closing the door behind her. I blinked rapidly and shook my head as my senses slowly returned to normal. Helena had left the book behind. I knew it would be better not to touch the book, for I despised it and I loathed the author. But Helena's blood had stained one of the pages. My instincts, my desire for blood, overruled everything else.

I seized the book and lifted it up, ready to bite into it, but I could not help but recoil. The plotlines of the *Tomas* books were nonsensical at best, but this passage featured the vampire taking part in a musical, and the lyrics were printed on the page! A love ballad between the lonely, jaded vampire who sought to be friendly and his lover, a she-werewolf! Gah! I tossed the book to the ground and fled, my desire for sanity overriding my desire to feed.

I was safely over my own threshold before Helena returned, calling out that the offer to loan me a book still stood.

~~~~~

It was days before I ventured out of my house following that incident. My desire to feed had grown with each passing day. Niccolo
~~~~~

and Helena were not options, but they had more siblings, and I turned my attention to Enrique.

Enrique took long walks every morning and every afternoon. Perhaps this was an attempt to best his elder brother at something, for as strong as he was, Niccolo rarely participated in this exercise. Due to his relative isolation, it was easy for me to track Enrique down when he was far out of sight of his family.

"Early riser!" Enrique greeted cheerfully. He kept pace at a steady jog, which I matched easily. "Care to join me?"

"But of course."

I should have thought of this sooner. The neighbor who had turned up her nose at families had had a similar habit of jogging frequently. Enrique and I ran together in silence, which might have been companionable if I were not planning to eat him. At last, it came to this. I would be able to feed upon Enrique and nobody would be the wiser. I pressed my footfalls down harder, cracking the tiny rockers of the earthen road beneath my feet.

"You're good!" Enrique grinned, his round face eager and excited. "I never have anybody to run with. Most of my family is slow! Running snack!"

He reached into his pocket and pulled out a bag filled with sunflower seeds. Enrique's hands slipped as he fumbled with the bag, and it dropped to the ground. Seeds spilled out in all directions as the bag burst.

"Ah, man! How many spilled?"

Blast it! He just had to ask the question! It is not strictly a weakness in the sense that it harms me like garlic or wooden stakes, but as a vampire I am often unable to resist counting items. Enrique's question only worsened the obsession, for now I *needed* to know how many seeds spilled to the ground. I do not know the reason for this, since I never felt such compulsion when I was alive. I halted and crouched down in front of the spilled seeds. Enrique skidded to a halt and began jogging in place.

"I wouldn't bother with anything but the bag," Enrique said. "Littering is wrong, but raw sunflower seeds aren't really litter. The seeds aren't worth salvaging and this way the birds and squirrels can have a snack."

I did not reply. I *could* not reply. I could do nothing but count seeds and listen as Enrique's footsteps grew fainter and fainter. He ran the rest of the way back to his house alone. I had been so close to devouring him. But the seeds…the seeds…the seeds.

I counted 625 sunflower seeds. I swore 791 times.

<div align="center">~~~~~</div>

Taking Enrique proved to be too tricky. He was clumsy and spilled seeds and nuts three more times before I gave him up for a lost cause. I moved on to the next two children in the family. How bothersome these neighbors were!

Luccia and Salvador were twins. Twins were always a challenge when it came to my needs as a vampire. In my experience, there were not many twins who followed the example of Esau and Jacob, continually at odds during their childhood. If only that were the case! Nay, most twins I had met clung to each other and were difficult to separate at the best of times. As a result, I would have to prey on them both at once.

Salvador and Luccia frequently bickered, as siblings were wont to do, but they didn't tolerate anyone else picking on them, even their siblings. They hovered between childhood and adolescence, perhaps twelve years old. One day, I watched the twins march out of their house. Salvador clutched a collection of comic books, while Luccia held a book under her arm. I shuddered involuntarily before I recalled that Helena had told me that nobody in her family shared her interest in dreadful paranormal romance literature.

Luccia crouched down in front of several potted plants while Salvador sat under a tree, reading his comics in silence. I took a few steps forward, looking from one child to the next, trying to decide which to lure away so that I might feed. But I was aware that I might need to snatch both in one fell swoop. Neither twin stood out as less desirable than the other. Before I could deliberate further, Salvador apparently grew bored and pulled from within his comic book a single straw. He inhaled sharply and blew out—a small piece of paper rolled into a ball struck his sister in the back of her neck.

"Gah!" Luccia squeaked. "You jerk!"

"I didn't do anything," Salvador claimed, though his smirk betrayed his actions.

"You did too!"

"Did not!"

"Did too!"

"Did not!"

"You just stay on your side forever, you big jerky jerk!"

Salvador responded to Luccia's latest rebuttal by shooting another spitball at her. Luccia's squeal pierced my ears as the spitball landed on her forehead. Something smelled peculiar about the spitball, but I couldn't quite place it. In any event, Luccia elected to ignore her brother's taunts and she tended to a row of potted plants. I counted to two hundred thrice, waiting to make a move, when Luccia stood up and stomped over to Salvador. It might have been more intimidating if she weren't wearing bright blue flip-flops.

"Come and see my plants."

"I thought I was a big jerky jerk," Salvador teased. "What's so special about your plants that they need a jerk's attention?"

"Just come and see!"

It was blatantly obvious that as much as they bickered and despite him being less than forty feet away and they hadn't actually been apart for more than a few minutes, Luccia had missed her brother. Twins could be very strange.

"Why should I?"

"Because!"

"Because why?"

"Because I'm older and I said so!"

I had to admit that was rather pitiful, but Salvador only laughed as he rose to his feet. He was taller than his sister and that was enough to make his point. Even standing on tiptoe, her feet nearly sliding out of her flip-flops, Luccia could not match her brother's height. Luccia stomped a foot in irritation and Salvador responded by wrapping an arm around her neck, trapping her in a headlock.

Luccia shrieked in protest as Salvador dragged her over to her plants, her feet sliding out of her flip-flops. For a moment, I thought he might snap her neck, which would make my own task of isolating them and feeding all the easier. Actually, I might be doing his family a favor. But rather than harming Luccia, Salvador merely rubbed his knuckles against his twin sister's scalp and her shrieks dissolved into a peal of giggles.

I paused, unsure what to do next. By now, I was only a few paces away and the children finally noticed me. That was another idiosyncrasy of twins, often so blind to their surroundings.

"Hi, Mr. Wagner!" Luccia called, pausing in front of her plants. "My brother is a big jerk."

"You started it!"

"Did not!"

"Did too!"

"Never mind," Luccia said. "So, Salvador, since you like spitballs so much, I figure this is a birthday present. Your own garlic cloves."

Wait, what? Luccia had been pestered continuously by her brother, and she was *helping* him figure out ways to tease her? Or else they had cut a bargain, and their bickering was part of a game for their own amusement? And worst of all, *garlic*? Bad enough the family cooked with it constantly, but to grow it themselves?

"Would you like one of my plants, Mr. Wagner? It's actually quite easy to cultivate."

I did not bother giving a reply. I forced myself not to scream in terror as I retreated into my own house and slammed the door. I underestimated my own strength and broke off two hinges.

~~~~~

By this point, I had run out of patience and my annoyance with the neighbors grew with each passing day. The family had long overstayed their welcome and every action they took seemed designed to antagonize me personally. I no longer cared about discretion and for good reason! I was a vampire. Mightier than any human had ever been or ever would be. I would grab the first child I saw, whatever the consequences.

I walked soundlessly to the neighbors' house. A single child paced the driveway, looking miserable and grumpy — all too easy to abduct for my meal. I recognized the child at once: Isabella.

"Nobody wants to play with me," Isabella whined, in the nasally tone of a spoiled brat. She blinked large brown eyes at me. "Will you play with me, Mr. Wagner?"

Isabella was around the tender age of nine, too young to keep up with her older siblings, but not so young as to enjoy playing with the still younger Noella and Giovani. That made her the perfect prey, and I should have chosen her from the beginning.

"Why, certainly," I answered. I reached out one long, pale hand and she took it in her own small, tanned one. "Why don't we go back to my house? We can play hide-and-go-seek there."

Isabella's eyes shone at the opportunity to play at another person's house. As we crossed my threshold, I extended my fangs. A single bite would be enough to subdue Isabella, and I would have my feast. And then, in turn, her family would come looking for her and I would feast again and again and again.

The child oohed and aahed at my furnishings, which to her must have been quite the novelty. With my high ceilings and various hooks and ledges upon which I rested, my home resembled a castle to a young mind. Her fascination was ironic, of course. Isabella was small enough that binding her to one of the hooks would likely cause her to bleed out before I could drink my fill. It was tempting though, as she darted this way and that, irritatingly curious. But I would hold off for now.

"Hide and seek!" Isabella squealed. "I can start counting! I'll count to one hundred. Is that okay, Mr. Wagner?"

She covered her eyes and began counting. I moved soundlessly until I stood directly behind her. Isabella wore her hair in two braids,
~~~~~

exposing her neck. I bit down hard, but instead of soft flesh and tasty blood, my fangs pressed against something hard…a thin chain of metal. My mouth caught fire and I screamed silently, wrenching my neck back and taking the metal chain with it. Isabella, ever an oblivious child, did not seem to have noticed.

I pulled the horrible metal from my teeth and gripped it in my hands. It was a small, silver cross.

My body turned to dust a moment later.

~~~~~

Isabella uncovered her eyes and looked around. Mr. Wagner was gone. She hadn't peeked when she'd been counting, but she hadn't even heard him move. Giovani and Noella were much noisier when they played hide-and-seek because they were pretty much babies. But Mr. Wagner was a really big grown-up, so it didn't make sense for him to be able to move so quietly. She would have to find him and fast!

She looked in every single room that had an open door. She looked under the beds and behind the curtains. It was kinda strange that Mr. Wagner had so many curtains and so few windows. She looked in the funny box that smelled real bad, but she couldn't find Mr. Wagner. Isabella searched some more — under the tables and behind the couch and underneath the rug. But there was still no Mr. Wagner. All she found was a big pile of dust. Oh, and her necklace, but Isabella wasn't worried about that too much because the chain was busted and it always fell off with even a teeny-tiny tug.

After she searched everywhere a third time, Isabella got scared and she ran all the way back home to get Mamma and Papi and all her brothers and sisters. They all hurried back to Mr. Wagner's house. Isabella tried to explain what happened, but she didn't think she did a very good job, since she didn't understand it herself.

"He went away," Isabella whined. "I closed my eyes and counted to a hundred and then he was gone. We gotta find him!"

They all searched the big house that Mr. Wagner lived in all by himself. Mamma and Papi even checked the basement and the attic and all the closets. But they didn't find Mr. Wagner at all. Isabella felt like crying. She knew, she just knew, she was never, ever going to see Mr. Wagner again. Her siblings all gathered around her in a circle and that made Isabella feel a teeny bit better. But then, she started to cry.

"He was so nice!" Isabella bawled. "He was going to play hide-and-seek with me!"

"I was hoping he'd go camping with us next summer," Nicollo said sadly. "I planned to surprise him with his own tent and stakes."

"Maybe he has a cold and needed to run to the store for medicine,"
~~~~~

Helena suggested. "I think we can make him some nice garlic and onion soup to fix him right up. If he does come back…"

"We really don't have very much luck with neighbors, do we?" Enrique asked. "Remember what happened to Mr. Talbot when we got him that genuine silverware for his birthday? And the monkswood Mamma planted for the gardening contest? He sneezed so hard, I thought his house was going to fall down!"

"Oh, Mr. Talbot! I miss him too!" Luccia exclaimed. "Him and that nice Dr. Victor. And Mr. Griffin, too. But I don't remember what Mr. Griffin looked like. Do you think we'll ever have neighbors who stick around?"

"I'm not sure," Salvador piped up. "But I suppose all we can do is pray for Mr. Wagner, the same way we pray for Mr. Talbot and Dr. Victor and Mr. Griffin."

Noelle and Giovani hugged Isabella and she felt a little bit better. She looked around and began to think. If Mr. Wagner ever did come back, it might be nice to surprise him by tidying up a bit. If they could find a vacuum, they could get rid of that pile of dust.

After all, Isabella wanted to be a good neighbor.

The End

MOONMIST EVE
Cortney Manning

Three Months Before Moonmist Eve

"Minna, come see!" The needle in Minna's hand narrowly avoided piercing her skin when exuberant young Agathe tugged at her sleeve. "That rakish vampire, Doros, is strolling down *our* promenade."

"Look at his graceful walk," another seamstress sighed. "Have you ever seen a person more dapper?"

"I hear he's splendidly wealthy!"

Minna glanced warily from the silken folds of the dress she'd been sewing over to the window the other seamstresses had rushed to fill. Beyond the glass, she could see the moonlit park with its usual surfeit of vampires strolling where they could see and be seen by the best of vampire society.

Minna blinked bleary eyes and rolled shoulders that had grown stiff from hours of concentrated labor. Resisting the urge to call the girls back to their work, she instead gently laid down the resplendent crimson gown, which had consumed her thoughts all night, and joined them for a moment of ease. After all, it was a slow night with no vampire patrons currently in the shop.

Only half-listening to the human girls around her, Minna narrowed her gaze on the coterie of vampires meandering from the other side of the park. Though all wore the finest cut suits and gowns, Minna recognized at once which vampire must be the infamous Doros.

He did indeed move with a languid grace, his every gesture magnanimous to his doting assembly. With each step, his blue cape swished around his well-tailored frame. An intricately knotted cravat spilled from his throat across his chest and down to an embroidered waistcoat. Minna squinted a little, imagining what she would have done differently with his ensemble. A longer cloak perhaps, to better swirl against his muscled legs, and a fabric in a different shade of blue—dark enough to really contrast his long, silver-gold hair.

One of the girls sighed to her left. "Could you imagine if he stopped here?"

Minna gritted her teeth. As little as she savored the idea of hosting new vampire clientele, their shop could use the money and attention so notable a client would bring.

"He's so handsome," Agathe murmured, leaning her forehead against the window's glass. "I almost wouldn't mind if he made me his thrall."

A shiver iced down Minna's spine at the girl's reckless words, and she stalked back to her seat, though still positioned to glance at the window and gauge any new ideas from the clothing worn by the famous trendsetter and his entourage.

"What's the matter, Minna?" Agathe called from the window.

Minna glanced at the young girl with her wide brown eyes. She was so innocent, so… naive.

Minna plucked up a needle, which she began to thread, and chose her words carefully. Agathe was still so young and, as the daughter of Minna's business partner, Lucia, the founding seamstress of this house, she had lived a sheltered life. Unlike most of the other seamstresses, Agathe had never lived without the safety of her trade, fully vulnerable to the whims of their vampire overlords.

"Nothing, Agathe," Minna replied at last. "I have work to do, and unless that dandy miraculously deigns to patronize our shop, I'm sure we've no need to wish him anywhere except far away from here."

"Aye," Janet, one of the older seamstresses chimed in. She had not risen with the others, and the wrinkles on her face were testament to the years of survival she had endured. Janet was one of the few in the room old enough to remember the days before their kingdom of Whitby had been overtaken by the Dracula and his vampires. "No matter how handsome, that monster's as dangerous as all the rest. He'd as soon snap your neck and throw you across the room as keep you as a little pet. At least here we have work and value."

Agathe pouted at the rebuke and crossed her arms. "Don't forget, it's *because* of vampires like him, buying new clothes and jumping on every new trend for their revelries, that we even have this job."

"We may be lucky, girl," Janet snapped back, "but this is not half the life we could've lived before."

Minna cleared her throat and cast a meaningful glance at the night sky where several bats flitted about. Both Janet and Agathe heeded her warning and ended their bickering. No one could guess which bats were regular animals and which were informants for the vampires who enslaved them.

Just as Minna pulled the crimson dress back onto her lap, a new movement caught her attention, and she bit back a groan.

"Those halfer children are back again," one of the seamstresses muttered as Minna hopped from her seat and scooped up the basket that held her midnight meal.

"Where are you going?" Lucia asked as Minna marched to the door.

"Those half-blood children are outside again," Minna explained, "and they're sure to receive nothing good from those they beg from. I'll give them what I can and hopefully send them on their way before they can cause trouble again."

"Minna wait," one of the girls called.

"They're just halfers, Minna, leave them be!"

"Minna!"

Ignoring the voices of her seamstresses, Minna swept out the doorway of her storefront onto the cobbled street beyond with its grotesque statues and crystalline fountains. She stepped quietly, careful to avoid any passerby.

Having once been part of a grand human-made park, the trail was ever-curving rather than direct, but Minna could not step off the path. After two decades of the Dracula's reign with its mist-shrouded days, all the lush greenery and flowers had withered away, so the plants had been replaced by shattered glass in jewel tones, arranged in swooping patterns. One misstep beyond the trail, and Minna's blood would be a beacon for every vampire within the mile. Not even her gray seamstress sash could protect her then.

Instead, she picked her way across the uneven path. Doros's vampires had paused beside one of the older statues, a relic of the old days, before Minna was born, when humans still ruled Whitby. Carefully, she angled herself just beyond their eyesight and gestured enough to catch the attention of one of the half-blood children. A girl with reddish human curls and only slightly extended incisors lifted her eyebrows in eager expectation at the bread Minna offered.

The child hurried over, grunted, and hopped excitedly as she swallowed the treat. From the thinness of her limbs, it seemed many days since she'd had a proper meal, and she released cheerful little sounds like, "bloof, bloof, bloofer," as she chewed. Minna wondered if the child even knew how to speak. She ground her teeth with suppressed rage and gestured as serenely as she could to another child. This was what came from favored human thralls and careless vampire masters. As soon as a human lost their worth, their blood was drained and any unwanted children of impure blood were cast out to the streets without care. Or worse, they were shipped back across the magical divide to Vania, the vampires' homeland, where they were sold as food to the vampires too poor to afford the passage to Whitby or to those who would not turn up their noses at less-than-pure blood to drink.

While Minna seethed at the cruelty, more children swerved her way, and she urged them to leave the park rather than fawn after the vampire elite. They were more likely to receive anger than aid from that front.

Minna swallowed, recalling the last night a group of these children had upset a vampire. The seamstresses had been forced to barricade themselves in the storage room until the morning mists returned, and the cobblestones had been stained red for nights after.

With much gesturing, Minna finally convinced most of the children to leave the park, but then dread encased her heart at the sound of a boy's voice raised in song. The notes were high and melancholy as he poured his soul into a human ballad.

The world seemed to hold its breath. Crickets grew silent, and even the swooping of bat wings overhead began to slow. Minna swallowed as she looked from the half-blood human who sang with his cap held out before him to the unmoving vampires gathered before him.

He had talent but wore no tradesman's sash to protect him. Perhaps he hoped to gain a vampire patron or at least some coin with his song, but Minna knew the vampires were just as likely to revile his music as value it for its primitive charm.

Several in the group turned to Doros as if awaiting the charismatic vampire's response, but a different lone figure cut through the dark park from the opposite direction, slamming his heavy boot into the child's back. Minna winced as the child tumbled to the far side of the trail, almost into the shards of artistically laid glass.

Minna's fingers tightened around her basket. If the glass drew even a drop of his blood, this entire street could quickly transform into a bloodbath. As silently as possible, Minna urged the remaining children to flee as the monster shouted at the stunned singer.

"What gives you the right to raise your voice among our grand race and sully these ladies' ears with your wretched human songs?" The hulking brute growled with a sadistic curl to his lip, pale face almost red with fury.

Despite the panic pounding through her veins, Minna edged closer, her mind whirling, seeking some way to diffuse the situation without loss of life. As a tradeswoman, she had some protections, but not many. Any vampire who harmed her would have to repay the shop's chief vampire patroness for damages. However, judging from this brute's jewel-tipped cane and imperious tone, he appeared wealthy enough to afford it.

Minna cast a quick glance at the shop as the large vampire raged. Surely Lucia and the girls would be wise enough to lock the doors and shelter in the back if worse came to worst.

She turned back to the crisis in time to see the half-blood child raise a hand in supplication toward the brute. In that moment, Minna foresaw all that would happen. The vampire would lift his walking stick like a club and slam it down on the child, beating him into silence or worse, drawing blood and stirring the others into a frenzy until none of the humans or half-bloods around were left unharmed.

With no other hope, Minna swooped between the monster and child, scooping the half-blood boy into her arms and intentionally turning her seamstress sash into the vampire's view. His stick paused midair.

"Good sir," Minna rushed to speak, her head bowed low as if in reverent respect. "I thank you for your wise words. I will see to it that this child learns from his mistake."

For several heartbeats, no one moved. Though Minna did not lift her head, she felt the gazes of a dozen vampires trained on her and the brute she'd dared to challenge.

"Is there no end to the gall of these humans and half-breeds?"

Minna flinched as the cane swung down again but stopped mere inches from her body. She blinked in confusion to see the vampire wrenching himself free of Doros's grip.

"What do you think you're doing, you fool?" The brute snarled at the dandy who restrained him. "These creatures need to be taught their place!"

"At the end of your rod?" Doros spoke with an easy drawl. "Good sir, do you really think your brutality is any more reassuring to these refined ladies you sought to defend?" His lace-festooned sleeve gestured lazily at the cluster of vampire ladies around them.

The aggressive vampire wrenched free of his grip, and Minna swayed with relief as his attention swiveled from her and the child to the finely dressed vampire.

"I know you," the brute snarled. "You're Doros, the popinjay so newly arrived from Vania." His white fingers tightened on the cane, and Minna shrunk back at the sight of him straightening to his full height to loom over Doros. "You may cut a fine figure in your capes and sharp waistcoats, but someone like you doesn't belong here, any more than those humans, less so even, for they at least provide us with blood to sustain us while you are nothing but an unknown from the homeland. You have no noble blood, only money to recommend you, and one day that, along with your favor, will be spent."

His dark words were met by the gathered vampires with uneasy silence. Minna gripped the child who clung to her, preparing to leap to her feet and sprint from sight if the tide should turn against their unexpected protector. But he simply turned to his entourage with a gleeful laugh.

Is he mad? Minna wondered.

"Did you hear that, my friends?" Doros practically skipped with delight toward the brute. "This good fellow thinks I cut a fine figure!" Without warning, he draped an arm conspiratorially over the vampire's shoulder, rendering him speechless. "You don't know what that means to me, my friend! I *do* strive for excellence."

The brute twisted and tried to rip himself from Doros's hold but nearly tripped instead, clearly not expecting the strength of Doros's arm.

"I did not give you permission to touch me!" he shouted, making the child in Minna's arms quiver. "Do you even know who I am?"

"Of course!" Doros grinned. "A fine gentleman who recognizes quality when he sees it, though I dare say you could use some help with your own wardrobe." The other vampires snickered at this as Doros waved his free hand over the vampire's dark and crumbled coat. "I must say, you are looking worse for wear. And," he gasped, "just look at the state of that cravat!"

The vampires laughed, and the brute's face burned red with rage.

"Who do you think you are, insulting me and protecting a human and a halfer, too? Are you the Wolf's Bane himself?"

Minna blinked at the unexpected insult.

"I say, good sir," Doros guffawed, lifting his hand to the corner of his eye to wipe at a mirthful tear. "The Wolf's Bane indeed!"

Minna's heart lurched with the irrational hope that somehow that very human hero could appear and whisk her and the child away from this threat, the same way he had spirited away countless human thralls beyond Whitby's borders to the safety of kingdoms whose kings had not been foolish enough to invite vampires into their lands.

"If—" Doros continued after struggling to rein in his laughter. "If that dashed fool is going round gathering all the most talented humans for his service, mayhap I *should* see if he's got any openings for a vampire like me in his ranks. It'd be dashed upsetting to lose all the fine singers in this town to your lead foot."

The vampire glared such hatred at the dandy, Minna half feared he'd burst into flames. "You are nothing but a lowlife of unworthy blood who could only join this colony in the human realm because of the size of your treasure chest."

"Indeed." Doros wistfully lifted the full coin pouch from his belt. "I really should do something about all my extra coins lying about." He spun around to place both hands on the vampire's shoulders. "I know! Perhaps I could make you my next special project. What do you think, friends?" Doros called to the vampires behind him. "Would he not look magnificent in a pink frock coat with peacock trim?"

"Or perhaps a well-placed corsage," a gentleman vampire heckled from the back of the group, drawing more laughter.

"Even a properly tied cravat would do wonders," a lady opined.

The brute broke free then, as Doros loosened his grip enough to nearly send him sprawling. The monster's hands tightened into fists, and Minna prayed the dandy had not pushed him too far. But the laughter of the other vampires proved Doros had won the fight, and the brute pushed past them, muttering obscenities and threats beneath his breath.

Slowly, Minna allowed herself to breathe and soothingly rubbed the back of the sniffling child in her arms. They only had to remain in place a little longer. As soon as the other vampires continued on their way, she could get up from her knees, and—

"Allow me to help you, lass."

Minna blinked to see Doros's pale hand outstretched before her face.

Her gut churned, and she refused to lift her gaze above his hand. As much as she hated to accept the aid of a vampire, even one who had saved her life, she could not afford to offend him now. Lightly, she touched only the tips of her fingers to his cold hand while rising to her feet. She caught his gaze snap to the sash thrown over her shoulder.

"Why, you're a seamstress?" he exclaimed. "What a coincidence! I was just on my way to find the lovely little shop I've heard so much about. What was it now?"

Minna shifted awkwardly as he tapped his chin in thought. Her legs felt weak, and she longed to be anywhere but there, on display before so many vampires.

"Lucia and Minna's?"

Her spine tightened as his words met her ears and the ladies tittered behind him. "Doros," one of the ladies simpered, rolling her eyes flirtatiously. "The shop is right here." She pointed behind Minna. "You need only read the sign to remember the name."

The vampire craned his neck to look around Minna. "Ah, but it is!" His steel-colored eyes flashed down at her. "Surely you're not one of the seamstresses of this esteemed establishment?"

Minna bobbed into a low curtsy. "I am Minna, sir."

"Ah!" He bounced back onto his heels. "Then what a pity indeed it would have been to see you clobbered into the cobblestones." He swiveled to the lady on his left and explained in a loud, theatrical whisper, "Why, this is the very lass who designed Delina Scythe's lace-lined bustle and Timoth Honour's waterfall cape!" He spun toward the others. "Such talent is not to be wasted!"

Eager eyes inspected Minna from all around, but the vampire stepped back to the front of the crowd.

"Would you happen to have an opening in your schedule today for a consultation with the ever-so-dashing vampire who saved your life?"

Minna felt like her mind was spinning but forced her chin to duck into a small nod. "I'll see what I can do."

"Then lead the way, my dear!"

Doros gestured her forward and placed a hand at her back. The touch felt almost reassuring, but Minna stiffened her spine, forcing herself to step with strong, measured steps. At the door of the shop, he turned to the other vampires.

"Alas, my friends, here we must part, but I will see if any openings can be found for you as well."

The ladies pouted while the gentlemen assured him they'd see the ladies safely home. Doros turned to look between Minna and the shop's doorway with a raised brow.

She nodded. "Do come inside." The invitation burned in her throat each time she found herself forced to speak it to their vampire clients. For no vampire could enter a home or land without invitation: a mistake their last king learned too late.

Seamstresses stared as Minna led him inside and left the half-blood child with Lucia. She knew she could trust the mother to be sympathetic to the half-vampire child. "Please find him some food and a space in the back to catch his breath. I'll handle our new client."

Lucia's eyebrows lifted close to her hairline, but she took the child and ordered the girls back to their places. Minna's head pounded as she strove to ignore their curious glances, still unsure what was happening herself. How had she gone so suddenly from almost dying in the street to instead ushering in the finest clientele she'd ever served?

Stepping to her worktable with Doros beside her, she took a moment to eye the fine jewels on his fingers and the quality of the fabric on his frame. Her heart thudded. Perhaps with him, she could finally set aside enough funds to help her team escape from Whitby into the still free human realms beyond.

"Thank you for this impromptu consultation." His lilting voice startled her from her thoughts, and she caught him eyeing the crimson gown she'd clearly set aside. "My name is Doros, by the way."

He gave a lopsided grin as if awaiting her response, but Minna did not speak. She only nodded and tucked away the other patron's gown. As if unable to endure the silence, he continued at last, "It means 'gift,' in the ancient tongue of vampires."

Minna nodded again and pulled out her measuring tape. No vampire could be a gift to humans. Though perhaps this one *could* bring some benefits if he brought more commissions to her shop. She smoothed her skirt and gathered the last of the items she needed from her desk. Either way, she had long since learned silence was best when it came to these creatures whose every whim could threaten her life and livelihood.

"And you said your name is Minna?" He continued to press as she led him toward the private chamber used for consultations. "After the ancient human heroine, perhaps?"

Her gaze flickered to him for an instant, jarred that a vampire would know such a thing.

"Ah," Doros sighed as they stepped into the room. "Her ballad is my favorite, I think."

Minna eyed her client curiously from beneath her lowered lashes. Surely, he must patronize a singing guild if he knew the old human songs.

"How about you?" he asked before sprawling on the waiting sofa. Minna blinked, unsure how to halt his barrage of questions. He threw back his head with a light chuckle. "Come now, lass, you can't fool me, for I know you can speak. I heard you out there with my own two ears."

"Most clients *prefer* I don't speak," Minna blurted before she could rein in her thoughts.

His head tilted. "And you prefer it that way, as well?"

Minna bowed her head. "I will do as you wish, sir."

He crossed his arms as if sulking. "I believe you would."

Did he truly care what she preferred? Minna cleared her throat uncomfortably. "What would you like to speak of, my lord?"

"Doros." He met her eyes from where he sat. "Please, call me Doros if you truly do wish to please me."

Minna bit back any irritation in her tone. After all, this was an important client, and he'd done nothing but help her thus far. "Very well, then, Doros, what do you want to speak about?"

He sat forward on the edge of his seat, a bright smile transforming his sharp features. "What interests you?"

Minna sighed. "At the moment, sir, your measurements and to know what will please my client best."

He hopped to his feet at once. "In that case, how would you like me to stand?"

Minna directed him and stepped to his side with her tape.

More silence followed and sweat trickled down her back. She could feel his eyes on her, watching every movement. She could feel her heart thudding against her chest and imagined he must, too, with his focus so trained. Finally, she opened her mouth, needing to know.

"Why is it you wish to speak with me?"

Another smile brought a dimple to one of his cheeks. "I wish to know those I hire."

Minna bit her lip and made a note in her mind of the latest measurement. "Few vampires would care. After all, a human's life is fleeting, even that of a tradeswoman."

"All the more reason to take the time to learn about you while I can."

Minna frowned at his words.

He fiddled with the buttons on his sleeve in a human-like gesture. Was he nervous, too? "I realize my reputation is quite well-known around Whitby. Given your generosity in providing me with this immediate consultation, I can guess you've heard something of me. I know you heard I hail from Vania." His hands clenched into fists and a pained expression crossed his face. "It is not a land of luxury, and I know better than to take pleasures in this world for granted, certainly not beings of such talent as yourself."

Minna ducked her head, unsure how to respond. "Th-thank you, sir."

"So, I will sit in silence the rest of this meeting if that's what you prefer," he continued in a gentle voice, quite unlike his theatrics from outside. "But, *if* you don't mind, I truly would still like to hear your thoughts."

A blush heated her cheeks, but she somehow felt less flustered now. "Very well." She took a breath. "*The Ballad of Minna* is indeed what my mother named me for."

"Ah yes, the daring heroine who stood against the lord of death himself and walked back home alive. I always found something truly inspiring in that tale, in all your human ballads, really. Do you have a favorite?"

Minna folded her measuring tape slowly. A part of her felt guilty sharing so much of herself with this strange vampire. But could he really use these small facts to harm her or her shop?

"I'm partial to *The Impossible Tasks of Florian Figgs*." Minna glanced up at him from beneath her eyelashes, wondering if he would recognize so obscure a song.

"Hah!" He slapped his hand against his leg. "An uproarious comedy if I've heard one, though not what I would've expected from so serious a human as yourself."

Minna crossed her arms over her chest. "The story is about far more than its jokes and wordplay. Florian's true strengths lie hidden deep beneath the surface, and his loyalty and unswerving determination are truly admirable."

Amusement lit his eyes, and she could not look away. "Indeed. I wonder what more one could learn about *you*, deep beneath the surface."

Embarrassment heated Minna's cheeks again, so she asked him instead about the type of clothing he wished to commission. He listed several minor pieces before adding that he had one very special project in mind.

"What precisely are you hoping for?"

"Something show-stopping." He grinned again, and the light of the hearth glinted off his fangs.

Minna tilted her head. "And where will you wear this show-stopping ensemble?"

"At the Moonmist Eve ball."

Minna's jaw dropped. "But that's impossible." Moonmist Eve was the night the noblest of the vampires gathered to celebrate their entrance to Whitby, when the last human king had fallen for their deception and invited them to use the Moonmist stone to open the portal between the two realms. It was the night that paved the humans' destruction. "Only the highest-ranking vampires with the noblest bloodlines are permitted to attend the Dracula's ball, and you... well..."

"And no one knows my lineage?"

She nodded, but he merely winked.

"I have my ways, but I'll be needing an outfit truly worthy of the evening, one which will wipe away the very stench of the Vanian cesspits that cling to my name. And I believe *you* can make it for me."

Minna considered his earnest expression. For someone as popular in society as he was, he'd arrived in Whitby only very recently, and it was the mystery of his past and wealth paired with his inherent charm that drew so many to his side. In a social world where everyone's life was endless, nothing felt truly new under the moon, so the vampires latched onto anything and anyone that could offer a bit of thrill or liveliness into their existence.

And as Minna met his sincere gaze, she couldn't help but wonder if he truly could achieve the impossible.

"Very well. Let me fetch my sketchbook, and we may begin drafting ideas. But do know that you *will* pay for my efforts, regardless of whether you wear the design to the ball or not."

He bowed. "You have my word, m'lady."

Minna shook her head even as her heart skipped a beat and turned from him to the desk with her writing supplies. The drawer stuck, and Minna tried again. It was locked.

Minna sighed. One of the girls must have been extra zealous in their tasks that evening.

"Forgive me, Doros." She turned to find his attentive eyes still trained on her. She swallowed. "It appears I will have to leave you a moment to fetch the key."

He stepped in front of her. "Please, allow me. Do you happen to have a spare needle or pin?"

Unsure of his intentions, Minna drew one from a pincushion nearby. He lifted it deftly and knelt before the desk. Within seconds, he'd used the pin to pick open the lock with a resounding clink.

"Uh, thank you."

"Of course." He handed the needle back into her waiting palm, and Minna pulled out her pencil and paper. For several minutes, they dove into a discussion of fashion trends and possibilities. He wanted something in theme with the night that no one else could rival. They considered several designs, which she sketched as they spoke, and he finally settled on her most dramatic piece. Styled after a moonbeam, it included a double-breasted coat crisscrossed with intricate braids, closely fitted trousers, varied tones of silver, and a swooping cape that would stretch nearly to his toes—perfect for drawing attention on the dance floor. He promised to directly supply some of the richest fabrics she'd ever worked with. To each suggestion she made, he responded with respect, as if he valued her ideas and skill. Soon, Minna found herself matching his excited grin as she pieced together the details and planned how exactly to bring his vision to life.

Near the end of their meeting, she even found herself comfortable enough to return his jokes.

"With so much silver, I could almost be the Melanthian Miser from the *Tale of Aris and Anita*."

Minna shook her head, marveling at his knowledge. "Do you know all the human songs?"

"Not as many as I'd like." He laughed. "I've always been fascinated by your heroes and the names they make for themselves—names that are remembered and sung far and wide. It's your own form of immortality." He sighed and rested his chin in his hand before flashing his eyes back at her. "It's such a charming notion. Do you think they'd ever consider singing about a vampire like me?"

Minna nearly choked on the air in her throat. "Never."

He looked as if he'd laugh at her response but painted on a pained expression instead. "Even if I'm as dashing as can be?"

Minna forced her lips into a serious line but feared her eyes would sparkle with the merriment she hid. "Even then, I fear."

At this he laughed at last, and Minna felt emboldened to ask the question that had weighed on her mind since they'd first met an hour before. "Why did you help us — that half-blood child and me? Surely you did not know who I was, and there are plenty of other seamstresses who could help you, no matter what you claim. So why did you come to our aid?"

She half-expected him to laugh off her question with a joke about the rarity of fine singers or skilled designers, but his face took on an expression of solemn sincerity. "A half-blood's life is not easy. You humans suffer enough, but those children... they did not ask for such lives either. And it's rare to see anyone, vampire or human, lift a finger to help them. Yet you did. I could not stand idly by in the presence of such bravery."

Minna felt pinned beneath his gaze. "It was nothing," she breathed.

One of his brows quirked upward. "Nothing? I highly doubt a knowledgeable and capable woman such as yourself has lived in this land completely sheltered from the dangers you willingly stood against this night."

A strange warmth settled into Minna's chest at his words. She'd received compliments before, of course — at least her work had, but something about this unexpected acknowledgement set her emotions fluttering off-kilter. Suddenly, she felt truly seen by another soul, and for once, that was not a bad sensation.

Two Weeks Before Moonmist Eve

"Do you think it was the Wolf's Bane who spirited the halfers away? I heard his trademark glass flower with its blue petals was found in the alley near here."

Minna sewed away at a gentleman's waistcoat, idly listening to the conversation of two vampire ladies who sat waiting for a fitting with Lucia. Her interest piqued at their mention of the hero. It *was* true there'd been fewer half-blood beggars in recent weeks.

"I'm only glad to not have to worry about them getting under foot when I walk by. Though —" She leaned her head conspiratorially close to her friend. "I did hear he used their half-vampire blood in some human ritual to bring curses against the vampires he plans to strike against next."

Minna bit the inside of her cheek to keep from laughing and met Janet's glance across the room. The older woman rolled her eyes. If humans possessed such magic, the king would have never seen fit to invite vampires into Whitby from the start.

Minna glanced out the window, tuning out the gossiping vampires, not doubting that a hero like the Wolf's Bane would only wish to help such children, even in spite of their half-vampire blood.

Outside, the park was packed with onlookers, both wealthy and servant vampires, all hoping to be among those lucky enough to see the mighty Dracula in his scheduled parade. Minna tensed at the sight of so many vampires. Not only would the crowds likely delay Doros for his scheduled fitting, but it also brought back troubling memories of another parade she'd witnessed as a child, back when the last princess still lived.

She'd witnessed it quite accidentally, sent on an errand by the vampiress she'd served at that time. She'd gone to the specified shop only to find herself surrounded by a sea of vampires as eager as the ones gathered now. The Dracula, ruler of all vampires, had been carried by a litter of human slaves, and at his side had sat a dainty woman with golden hair and sorrowful eyes. She had looked pale and drained but determined, too. Her poise and dignity had struck Minna's mind, so she'd asked the other servants that night to learn more about the woman who had been the human princess.

Minna shook her head, thinking of the tragedy of such a noble light snuffed out too soon, but the princess had been the human king's gift to the Dracula. She had been offered as his bride, a symbol of peace and goodwill between their peoples, along with flocks of sheep, in exchange for knowledge of vampire magics cultivated over centuries of use. To the king, it had seemed a small price at the time.

Minna pursed her lips. Of course, there would be no princess in today's parade. The Dracula had drained her until she died, and the hope of the nation died with her, for only the blood of the king's line and the Dracula's shed upon the Moonmist stone could force the vampires back to Vania, and the princess had been the last of that line.

Minna tapped her foot and looked at her watch to clear her mind of such dark thoughts, wondering how late Doros would arrive today. Even on ordinary nights, he had rarely been punctual, struggling to break free from his gaggle of sycophants to check in on his smaller orders and discuss updates on his Moonmist Eve design.

"Are you waiting for the handsome Doros?" Agathe's voice whispered in Minna's ear, and she snatched her attention back to the waistcoat in her lap.

"I'm sure the crowd will slow him today. Besides, his appointment is not for another ten minutes."

"True," Agathe sighed. "But I do so adore seeing his face."

Minna shook her head and swallowed back a smile. Her heart gave a small flutter, and she realized she, too, had come to anticipate his visits.

Of course, his persona shifted depending on the audience. With other vampires, his conversation was grandiose, theatrical, even. With the other seamstresses he was kind, complimenting even matronly Lucia and wary Janet. And alone with Minna, he seemed to open up completely, and every visit brought with it an unexpected glance into the person who was Doros.

Minna smoothed out the embroidery of the waistcoat she held and thought of the countless moments they'd shared: him humming a half-forgotten human tune he hoped she could help him recall, him muttering a sour word or three about his fellow vampires, his perfect imitation of a particularly buffoonish client, the respect he showed for her work, which he recognized as both real labor and true art, the way his eyes lit up when he saw her doodles of a dress designed like sunshine to compliment his moonbeam suit, the small flower he had plucked from the cobblestones, saying its tenacity reminded him of her.

Minna shook her head to clear it. Surely, she was just surprised to find a vampire with kindness in his heart, nothing more. She looked toward the window again and blinked in surprise to recognize Doros's wide shoulders and silver-gold hair bent in conversation with a human who wore a gray tradesman sash.

Minna squinted, trying to get a better view of the brown-haired man with a thin nose. But then they parted. Doros seemed to glance about himself warily before marching to the entrance of the shop. The bell jingled, and seamstresses and vampires all hopped to their feet, but Doros did not heed them, walking instead to Minna's station.

"Good evening, Minna. It appears I'm here early for once, and your showroom is busier than ever."

Minna shot him a grateful smile. "Thanks to your generous endorsement."

He lifted her hand and pressed a kiss to it, and Minna feared some of the ladies might swoon. "Truly, it's all due to your own ingenuity and talent, and the hard work of your ladies." He cast a wink at the girls, and even old Janet's cheeks blushed pink.

"Shall we go to the showroom?" Minna asked, hoping to escape the perusal of so many eyes, both human and vampire.

"Please, lead the way." He held out his arm, and she took it lightly, directing him to the private room.

"I thought you'd be late again," Minna teased, "until I saw you out there talking to that tradesman. Who was he?"

Doros's gaze shifted from her face to glance about the room, and the tension in his shoulders tightened. "Oh, no one special," he answered, his tone evasive. Minna narrowed her eyes. "He crafts little trinkets of glass, and I had half a mind to order an ornate headpiece. But that is of no matter. Shall I try on the coat again?"

He began unbuttoning his current coat, and Minna hurried to fetch the requested garment, though she still wondered what he was hiding. Their fingers brushed as she handed him the piece she'd been adjusting all week, and Minna ignored the tingling sensation in her hand.

He buttoned the intricate braids with expert skill before stepping in a slow circle. "How does it look?"

"Excellent." Minna nodded, observing the fit and how the fabric molded to his frame as he moved. "Very good, only —"

"Yes?" He paused mid-step.

"Your hair." She gestured to the long silver-gold strands still tucked into his collar. "May I?" she asked, and he stood unmoving as she reached to pull the silken locks free.

She began to draw back, but his hand reached up toward her own face.

"May I?" he asked, and she nodded, though her brain could not decipher what he intended to do. For a moment, she thought his palm would cup her cheek, but his fingers slid instead to tuck her own hair behind her ear.

"Your hair's come loose from that strict bun." He exhaled slowly, his breath heating her face. "I've wondered what it would feel like," he murmured, his brow puckered in thought. "Your hair is quite soft."

Minna felt the fires of a blush blaze across her face and half-considered leaning into his touch, wondering how he would respond.

Instead, she wet her lips and replied, "My drab hair? It's nothing compared to yours with its unique color."

A gentle smile curved across his features, and he shook his head. "No, it's *your* hair color that's rare to me."

"Brown?" Minna chuckled uneasily, her breath light. "That's nothing special."

"No," he insisted. "Among the vampires, I see black and white aplenty, but your human shades are all unique. And yours is the most special of all."

Minna gazed at his eyes so close to hers. "And how is it special?"

"It's like sweet, dark honey, and I can't help but wonder what it would look like in the sunlight if the mists would ever pass."

Minna tilted her head at his strange words. Why would a vampire wish for the passing of the mists? How would he know the taste of honey? And why did his eyes look so sincere as he tucked the strand of hair behind her ear?

She wanted to ask him, to learn everything about him and savor his kind touch. But then her gaze slipped down to his teeth, sharp enough to drain the life from a human.

For a moment, Minna just breathed, unmoving, yet longing to trust him fully. Slowly, she turned her face against his open palm, leaning into his calloused touch. His steel-colored eyes widened, and his mouth opened to speak when shouting sounded from outside.

An expression firm with resolve tightened his features. With a gentle pat to her cheek, he let her go and rushed toward the ruckus beyond the door.

Minna trailed behind him, wondering both at her actions and at the sounds that had disturbed them.

In the shop, seamstresses and vampires pressed their faces to the windows, but Doros dashed past them through the open door, and Minna shadowed his steps.

He pushed through the gathered crowd of now agitated vampires. Minna eyed them with caution but followed close in his wake, trusting he'd not let harm befall her. She could only pick out a few words from the throng.

" — attack — "

"How could a human dare?"

" — punishment will be severe."

"The Dracula doesn't tolerate — "

Suddenly, they pushed past the last of the crowd and stood directly before the Dracula's parade, which had stopped mid-progress. Minna tried not to gasp at the closeness of the vampires' monarch, as stern and terrifying as he had been when she last saw him so many years ago.

This time he stood in a phaeton drawn by two massive wolves, a sharp whip clutched in one hand, and his silver hair reflecting the light of the moon. His metallic eyes remained latched on a single human, pinned beneath the paw of one of the wolves. Minna gasped to recognize the same craftsman she'd seen speaking with Doros before.

"How dare you impede my progress?"

The whip drew back. Minna winced in sympathy for the poor man, but Doros's loud drawl rang out over the din, "In this instance, a sound lashing may not be the best punishment, my liege."

All eyes, including the Dracula's, snapped to Doros as he bowed. *Has he gone mad?* Minna wondered, making herself as small as possible to escape similar notice.

The Dracula's eyes narrowed as if trying to place the daring vampire before him. "Who are you?"

"Doros, lately of Vania," he replied smoothly, as if speaking to the Dracula in front of a simmering crowd was an everyday occurrence for him.

"And tell me, *Doros*, why I should listen to a word you speak, let alone spare both this human and yourself from my judgment."

"Oh," Doros waved his hands before him. "By all means, mete out your justice! I merely hoped to ensure this human had not completely succeeded in his ruse."

"What nonsense do you speak?"

"If I'm not mistaken, Your Majesty, you intend to whip this man for impeding your progress today, but he holds at least three secrets from you, our great Dracula."

Unease settled over Minna's skin as she wondered what scheme Doros was playing at and whether or not the stakes were too high, even for him.

"And what, precisely, do you claim to know that I do not?"

An ominous light crept into Doros's eyes, and Minna tried not to shiver. He lifted one finger dramatically. "One. That he's distracting Your Majesty so your human attendant can slip away."

The Dracula spun to his left, jaw tightening as he faced empty air where a servant must have once stood.

"Two." The Dracula whirled back to Doros's second lifted finger. "Under his coat, you'll find a leather and metal plate built to withstand the sting of your whip."

The Dracula gestured to a pair of vampire attendants who held down the human, tearing back the coat. Minna watched in confused horror as the man gazed defiantly at the crowd. Her gaze fixed back on Doros, wondering how he could know such things and why he'd reveal them to the Dracula.

"And three?" the majestic vampire growled, moonlight glimmering off his sharpened incisors.

Doros's lips tipped into a wicked grin, and Minna's mind was struck by how much he resembled the vampire ruler in that moment. "That in his pocket, you'll discover indisputable proof that this man is none other than the Wolf's Bane himself."

The strength leached from Minna's spine, but she forced herself to stand upright, watching as the vampire she'd come to trust tore the mask from her image of him. As the attendants snatched a small glass flower with mournful blue petals from the struggling hero's pocket, Minna's mind could only repeat a single question: *Why?*

The attendant lifted the flower above his head, catching the light of the moon in its twinkling glass. The crowd roared to life, jostling each other to view the notorious human pinned to the cobbled street.

Then the Dracula raised his arms, and the crowd fell silent. "The blood of the humans' hero will flow, and we will enjoy our vengeance at last." His whip cracked down an inch from the human's eye, but the hero did not flinch. "It will be a most delectable treat to savor at my ball on Moonmist Eve."

Cheers and taunts rang out from the crowd. Minna wanted nothing more than to disappear into the night, but she'd not be able to pass them so easily as she had when following Doros.

Her gaze flicked to his traitorous form, just as he stepped closer to the Dracula. Others saw him, too, and the crowd's attention swung back to him. "What a splendid conclusion, Your Majesty." He bowed again. "I'm overjoyed to have been of service to my great liege. No other rewards could ever equal my pleasure in this moment."

The Dracula turned hard eyes to him once more. "Of course, a reward is in order for your part in this victory. What boon would you request for such valuable insight?" His tone was cold and unyielding, as if commanding the grasping dandy not to demand too much.

"For one as *simple* as I?" He flourished his lacy sleeves, and the nearest vampires laughed. Once again, he'd won over a crowd. Only his steely glance at the Dracula revealed they both understood the game he was playing. Minna swallowed, her traitorous pulse accelerating as she considered all the horrible ways his dare could fall through, but the Dracula merely inclined his head.

"Why," Doros exclaimed. "I could think of no higher honor than an invitation to the Moonmist Eve ball where I can view the execution of the criminal myself." He turned to whisper theatrically to the assembled crowd. "Perhaps I could even set a new trend or two."

Nervous chuckles filled the air, though most held their breaths, eyes glued to the Dracula, wondering if he would strike the dandy for his impudence or break tradition to allow a vampire of unknown origins to join the sacred revels.

Disgust and loathing roiled in Minna's gut, and she feared she might be sick.

"*I have my ways,*" Doros had claimed on that first night when he'd ordered his moonlit suit despite the impossible.

And she'd made it for him.

Minna felt her body sway as she gazed down at the Wolf's Bane being tied hand and foot by the vampire attendants. Her ears rang. As if from a great distance, she heard the Dracula speak.

"Very well. As reward for your invaluable aid, you will be granted entry to the Moonmist Eve Ball. But—" His tone turned sharper than a blade. "—do not forget too soon your place in our world."

Three Nights Before Moonmist Eve

Minna stared at the raindrops sliding like tears across the windows of the store, her mind numb, and her body sore.

"Are you sure you'll be all right?" Lucia asked, standing at the door with her umbrella in hand.

Minna nodded and tapped the red tube attached to the vein in her arm. "It's my turn to replenish our customers' refreshment supply, and the storm will keep any vagrants away."

Lucia nodded, concern and understanding mingled in her eyes. "Just be certain to leave before dawn. Even with the dark storm clouds, the curfew is still in place."

"Of course." Minna smiled sadly and watched as Lucia stepped from the store at last. In her absence, the room felt colder.

She had been the last to leave, so now Minna sat listening to the dripping of her blood into the magic-imbued glass jar with no company but her thoughts and the carefully tied parcel on her desk.

All night, she'd kept her attention elsewhere, ignoring the package that held Doros's completed ensemble, but now she could not tear her eyes from it. For eleven days, her mind had been consumed by the events of that night, the night Doros transformed into a monster she could not recognize.

Minna thought of the girls and her own modest savings. If something happened to her and the shop, if the funds she'd set aside so carefully failed to help them escape, who would be left for them to turn to? Minna's heavy eyes burned with the need to weep, but she obstinately kept them trained on that package instead.

Why would he do it? Why would Doros hand over the one hope humans like her had left?

Those were the questions that haunted her thoughts as she tried to sleep each morning.

He was a vampire of course, and a few months ago, Minna would not have doubted any vampire would shy away from an opportunity to take down the Wolf's Bane. But that was before she met Doros, before she saw his kindness to humans and half-bloods, before she felt the warmth of his regard.

No matter how she looked at it, the vampire he'd been in private could never align with the monster she'd seen stare down the Dracula that night for the mere gamble of a night among the nobility.

Minna chewed at the nails of her free hand, ignoring the suction of the tube draining away at her blood. Something did not add up.

She could not deny his betrayal had stung her heart and her pride, but could she have truly misread his character so thoroughly? Minna rubbed at the budding ache behind her temples. It was not as if she was naive like young Agathe, prone to trusting anyone with a handsome face.

Thunder rumbled, and Minna's gaze dipped again to the tube in her arm. Of all the tasks for keeping this shop, the bloodletting was her most abhorred. She hated how weak and tired it left her, but she still recalled the years in her youth when she'd not been protected by her seamstress sash — the time when she'd been at the mercy of her vampire masters, whimpering with fear when she wondered if one night they would not stop themselves before draining every drop of blood from her veins.

Minna shivered and carefully pulled the tube from her arm. The glass would have enough blood for the week's customers, and she had no wish to dwell on those dark times, never knowing which breath would be her last. At least now she had some semblance of control, if not freedom, deciding when to stop that dreadful tug at her veins.

But no one who'd lived that life could lower their guard as she had with Doros without good reason.

In her heart, she still believed she'd seen more to him than that selfish monster in the park.

"I'm a fool," she groaned, gazing at the parcel of clothing he'd been scheduled to pick up that night. Half of her had hoped he'd send a servant, though that foolish side still longed to see his face again, to pretend the mirage she'd painted in her mind had not been false.

She ground her teeth, for that was where the true trouble lay. Her heart she could doubt, but her mind? Somehow it kept urging her to think deeper. She could not doubt the truth of all she'd seen and felt, yet her own experiences could not fit together, like a puzzle missing its most vital pieces.

Minna's head spun as she rose from her seat, preparing to leave before sunrise.

Lightning scored across the sky, illuminating a figure outside the door.

Minna stumbled back against her desk as the door swung open, and Doros strode in, his cloak drenched, and his features tense.

"Good, you're still here." He rushed to her side, reaching as if to take her hand in his, but Minna drew back.

His fingers curled, then his hand swung back to his side. "Of course, you would not trust me now."

Minna blinked, watching as water dripped from his hair and cloak to the floor. He shook his head. "Minna, I need your help."

She tightened her jaw and slid the parcel across her desk. "I've completed your order. You'll be the best dressed vampire at the ball."

Ignoring the package, he stepped closer, and lightning lit the desperation in his eyes. "Please, Minna, I don't have much time. I fear I'm being watched, and you're the only human I can rely on."

She lifted a sarcastic brow. "I wonder why that is."

He winced. "I deserve that and worse, I'm sure, from your perspective. But Minna, I promise, that human, the Wolf's Bane I turned in shall not be harmed, not if you help me on Moonmist Eve."

Minna felt a line furrow between her brows. "You intend to help him? How?"

His face turned into the shadows as thunder rumbled. "I cannot tell you now, but if you accompany me as my attendant on Moonmist Eve, then I promise that heroic man will go free."

Minna's heart thudded. Was this all some elaborate trap? But to what end?

"Believe me, Minna, there is no one else I can turn to. No one else I can *trust* as I trust you."

Minna bit the corner of her mouth. "You trust me?"

"With my very life and so much more."

The room around Minna seemed to spin. Perhaps she'd given too much blood.

"What more is there?" she muttered, yet the pieces of her puzzle seemed to be realigning themselves in her mind at last. She'd seen Doros with the Wolf's Bane before his capture, and they'd seemed to be working together, planning something. And now, when he claimed to be in need, it was not a vampire he sought but a human. The challenging glare he'd cast at the Dracula passed through her mind, and she began to wonder how many secrets Doros still hid.

Pressing her palm onto the desk, Minna met his steel-colored gaze. "What exactly do you seek?"

A morose grin lifted the corner of his mouth, and he pressed a hand to his chest. "Didn't I tell you I crave the immortality you humans make with your songs? After that night, I believe even this humble vampire will have an eternal name in your human ballads."

Despite his joke, Minna sensed the fortitude of truth in his voice.

Lightning flashed as she gazed at the stranger she almost felt she knew. "You promise the human hero will not die."

Solemnity washed over the planes of his face. "Not if I can help it, not if I have *your* aid."

"And I will learn the full truth then?"

Sadness and regret shimmered in his eyes. "Everything will be revealed that night, so Minna—" He cautiously slipped his hand over hers. She let him. "Will you join me at the Moonmist Ball?"

"I will go."

Gentle rain washed against the window as he pressed his lips to the back of her hand in a dozen kisses of relieved thanks.

"What must I bring?" she asked, her voice low.

"Come prepared with a sewing kit of odds and ends—anything you'd use for fashion emergencies," he replied. "And prepare something suitable for yourself to wear." He reached into an oiled satchel he'd carried with him through the storm. "I'm sorry to give you such short notice, but I'd hoped this might work."

Minna laid the parcel he offered on her desk, opening it carefully to reveal the gauziest fabrics of golden yellow and melon orange.

"No," she gasped.

"Yes." He grinned. "These felt like the perfect cloth for your sunshine design."

Minna rubbed the light fabrics beneath her fingers. "Moonlight and sun."

"The perfect match," he murmured.

Minna gritted her teeth, struggling to keep her mind focused and clear. "And you're certain you cannot tell me more tonight? Not even what I'll be doing?"

His finger traced over the back of her hand. "In truth, I desire nothing more than to tell you, but it is too dangerous, and I will not place any more risk on your life than is absolutely necessary." His gaze bored into hers with an earnestness she could not deny. "Please, Minna, put your trust in me."

"I will."

Moonmist Eve

"Remind me again." Doros's breath stirred the carefully arranged curls around Minna's face as he whispered into her ear. "Have I taken the opportunity to tell you how magnificent you look tonight?"

Minna inhaled slowly, striving to ignore the stares of the vampire guests who filled the great hall of the palace.

"Only three times," she muttered.

"Ah!" Doros exclaimed, tightening his grip on her hand as it rested on his escorting arm. "Then that's a hundred times too few, my darling."

Minna shook her head, grateful at her foresight in covering her sunlight gown with a mist-like cloak. Even so, she felt like a candle in a darkened room.

Doros pressed his lips close to her ear to whisper. "Relax, love. You're doing splendidly."

Though what exactly she was doing, Minna still could not guess. Rather than trailing Doros like a proper servant, he'd insisted on her taking his arm as they ambled through the moodily-lit room with its black chandeliers, vaulted ceilings, and wisps of magical blue light. Thankfully, Doros steered them well away from the tables laid with bowls of blood where various vampires paused to feast.

Along one wall, a gathering of human musicians stood in their tradesman sashes, pouring their talents into the tightly constrained notes of ancient vampire melodies. In the center of the room, couples twirled to the sound beneath the watchful gaze of the Dracula on his throne. Beside him, bound in chains, knelt the Wolf's Bane.

Minna swallowed, wondering what torture was planned for him this night.

And before the throne, lit as if from some inner power, glowed the silver Moonmist stone.

Minna swallowed and looked to Doros, resplendent in his own silver robes, with a silver-hilted rapier at his hip.

"The sentencing will be soon. I think it's nearly time," he murmured, and Minna felt her pulse accelerate.

"What do you need me to do?" she whispered.

"We must get closer to the Dracula."

Minna gazed across the shifting sea of revelers "How?"

Doros swiveled to stand before her, hand outstretched. "Dance with me."

Minna feared her jaw would not be able to return to its closed position.

"Doros, I'm a human attendant. What would these nobles think?"

"Forget them." His gaze locked on her with unadulterated admiration and focus, making her heart thud. "Look at me, Minna."

She did and found herself instantly carried away in the notes of the song, following his lead in great circles across the room.

And it was just Doros and her, vampire and human, caught up in the thrumming beat, capes and skirts swirling with dizzying momentum, his silver fabric blending with the gold and gray of hers.

Without shifting focus, she knew all eyes in the room were trained on them. She felt the waves of emotion from the throng: admiration, jealousy, intrigue. *Had the meteoric vampire fallen for his human tradeswoman,* they surely thought, *and would she bring him crashing down in a blaze of light?*

But Doros and Minna did not stop. They danced. They spun. They practically flew across the room, hair and fabric tossed about like banners in the wind. And she looked at his eyes locked on hers and knew that come what may, she could never regret this night.

Almost without warning, the music stopped, and Minna found herself catching her breath with Doros beside the Dracula's throne. The vampire leader stood with his hands upraised, and the room fell silent. Only then did his voice boom out.

"Welcome, my children of the night, to this, the greatest of all evenings, when the magics of the moon are at their strongest, and we gather to celebrate our entry into this fertile land."

Applause sounded from around the room before the Dracula continued. "And now, the time has arrived for what you all came here so eager to witness." He tugged at the chain binding the prisoner at his feet. "The execution of the human that has plagued our great land."

A vampire servant approached the Dracula, a jagged ceremonial knife balanced on his silver tray, but Doros chose this moment to step between him and the throne.

"Oh dear," he called out, loud enough for the crowd to hear. *So his show begins*, Minna thought, anticipation prickling over her skin.

"Such unfounded assumptions," Doros exclaimed, clicking his tongue at the Dracula himself.

The silver-haired ruler glared at the unwanted interruption. "Ah, Doros of Vania," he growled. "I believe we had an understanding. Why do you interrupt our judgement again? Was it not you who led us to this traitor?"

Doros's ordinarily light voice hardened like steel. "And it was you who trusted the word of your foe, as little *human* as he may truly be."

In an instant, Doros drew his sword and swung its point against the Dracula's chest. Vampires gasped across the hall, but none dared move, lest the blade end the Dracula's ancient life.

"Allow me to reintroduce myself." Doros swung out his free arm, sending his cape swirling, as he cut a quick bow. "The true Wolf's Bane at your service, this evening."

Minna inhaled sharply as the vampires hissed around her. Suddenly, the pieces of the puzzle named Doros were fitting together at last.

"Traitorous fool!" The Dracula's voice rumbled like thunder deep within his chest. "You think you've vanquished me?" His roaring laugh bellowed through the ballroom. "You just revealed yourself to all the noblest blood in our land for nothing." A taunting sneer curled his crimson lips. "It's not as if a lowly vampire of your unknown origins could claim a place on my throne. Even if you slay me here, the others will tear you down the moment they have a chance."

Doros did not shift his stance, keeping his blade poised to strike. "You think it's your throne I seek?" He clicked his tongue in disapproval. "Always so short-sighted, my liege." His free hand stretched out from his side, palm upward. "Minna, my dear, a spare pin, if you please."

Minna rushed to his side, plucking a pin from the reticule at her waist and placing it in his outstretched hand.

He smiled without taking his gaze from the Dracula as he directed his voice to her. "You always have just what I need, love.

"Now," he continued, "Minna, my dear, would you hold this?" Shifting his stance, he handed the sword into her grip, showing her how to stand. "There you go. Just like that. It won't be for long. If anyone so much as stirs, plunge this silver blade into his chest. Even he can't survive a silver stake through the heart."

Minna swallowed, imagining starch to stiffen her spine. She could do this. After all, Doros believed she could.

Doros lifted the needle he'd given her, letting it catch the dimmed lights of the hall as he spun back to the vampire nobles.

"Now..." He tapped his jaw as if in thought. "Where are my manners? Here I am, interrupting an elegant speech with so many esteemed figures assembled here. There's nothing else for it! I simply must continue where the great Dracula left off."

Minna felt sweat drip down her arm as she clutched the sword, feeling the Dracula's eyes swivel between her and Doros as if awaiting their first misstep. The other vampires scarcely moved, torn between unease for their leader and their ever-present desire for dramatic flare.

"What was it he said?" Doros continued, "Ah yes, the blood you all came to see!" He turned to pat a heavy hand against the Dracula's back, bringing him closer to the blade and reminding him not to stir. "You wished to watch the blood of the hero spill this Moonmist Eve? Very well. Let it be known that Doros Wolf's Bane is nothing if not accommodating."

Minna's hands shook around the handle of the sword as she watched Doros slam the point of the pin into his hand. Blood pooled there and began to drip. He flipped his hand, letting the dark red drops cascade like rubies over the Moonmist stone.

All around, vampires inched in closer, drawn to the scent of blood, but then a silver-white light shone from the stone. When the light struck their eyes, the nearest vampires fell to their knees, covering their faces and snarling. At the end of Minna's sword, the Dracula's eyes squinted, and his pale face became whiter than snow as his mouth fell open in horror.

"Impossible."

Doros looked from the Dracula to Minna, shooting her a wink. "I'm known for doing the impossible." He shook his hand and more blood fell.

"You wanted the Wolf's Bane's blood, did you not?" He shouted. "Here I am. And with my blood, the blood of the most ancient line passed down by my father, I cast you out!"

"No." The Dracula hissed, and the sword at his chest drew blood but stopped him from lunging forward.

Father. Father? Minna glanced between Doros and the Dracula, taking in their strong chins, metallic eyes, and aquiline noses, her mind whirling.

The Dracula had no consort—everyone knew that—and he'd kept no human slave alive for longer than a fortnight... except for one.

Wind roared around the room, spiraling from the stone, and Minna's eyes snapped to Doros, seeing him as she never had before: his unusual hair—a mix of silver like his father's, but also gold like his mother's. The set of his jaw, just like the Dracula's, yet those determined eyes so like the human princess's.

Minna saw it now, and so did the Dracula beside her, his face mottled with realization, horror, and fear.

But Doros did not stop. He yelled over the crowd that groaned and groveled before the growing light of the stone. "As blood heir of the royal houses of both Vania and Whitby, I revoke the invitation that opened the portal between these lands and cast all vampires in Whitby back into the realm from whence they came."

A whirlwind of silver flames blazed out from the stone. The nearest vampires vanished into the light while those who tried to flee did not get far, though the human attendants scattered among them stood wholly unscathed in the barrage of powerful magic.

In front of Minna, the Dracula's metallic eyes flared red with dark magic, and she barely had a moment to breathe before he flung himself forward, piercing his own flesh on the sword in his rage. One of his pale hands stretched toward his rejected son, but the flames overtook him too.

Minna stumbled back as the Dracula howled into the wind, "You were supposed to die in Vania like all the half-bloods."

But Doros did not flinch at his words. He merely stood with his hand above the stone, feeding it more of his blood as the Dracula vanished in a burst of light.

But then the flames shifted, swirling next around Doros's feet and tugging him to his knees.

"Doros!" Minna cried, dropped the sword with a clang, and stumbled to his side.

"What is happening? Why is the magic on you, too?" She bent to grasp the magic, tear it away if she could, but her hands merely slipped through its light.

Doros reached for her hand, stilling her desperate movement. "This is what's meant to be, Minna."

Meeting his steely eyes, Minna understood at last. There was still one more piece of the puzzle yet to fall… It was more than Doros's pseudonym or his heritage… He had not told her the cost he intended to pay.

Silver light snaked up his legs, pinning him in place, though he did not struggle. Minna bit back a sob. The magic was claiming him as it had the others. It was dragging him back to Vania where he'd be forever imprisoned with the monsters he'd betrayed, and he'd known all along that it would.

He'd chosen his own death in exchange for the humans' lives.

His unharmed hand lifted to wipe the tears from her cheek, and a wry chuckle rumbled from his throat. "I always hoped I'd go out in a blaze of glory. From the time I was a small lad at my mother's knees, listening to her ballads of prestige and valor." His hand angled her face toward his. "You will tell my story, won't you, love?"

Minna pressed a fist against his shoulder. "Only if you tell it with me!"

Doros leaned his forehead against hers. "I'm afraid that won't be possible."

Minna did not remove her brow from his but shook her head, unable to surrender yet. She thought of his mother and stared at the golden undertones of his swirling hair. "Why is the magic taking you with them? You're half-human aren't you? *This* is your home."

His hand squeezed hers gently, and the magic had climbed above his waist. "But I'm half-vampire, too. It's only taken this long to claim me because of my mixed blood, but I cannot escape that half of who I am. I'm just glad to have sent the other half-bloods I could find beyond Whitby's border where they can be safe."

"It *was* you who helped them," Minna whispered. "You've truly rescued everyone but yourself."

He winced, and Minna wondered if the magic coiling around his chest brought pain.

"It's too late to worry about me, Minna. This is how it must be."

His eyes looked resigned, as if he'd already gazed upon death itself and found nothing to fear. Minna clenched her fists around the fabric of his coat. If he could glare death in the eye, then what had she to fear?

She trusted him, she knew that now, and the feeling lent her strength.

"Let me go, Minna," she heard him say, as if from a distance, though his hold on her did not loosen, as if he could not be the one to release her first. "Please, Minna," he whispered, as threads of light began to choke around his throat. "Let me go, or I fear we'll both be destroyed in this gale."

"No." Minna ignored the light and gripped his shoulders all the more tightly. "I will not leave you, and *we* will not fail. Did you not say you would trust me?"

Confusion enveloped his face, and his eyes looked like those of a child—like the young half-bloods she'd seen on the streets, alone and abandoned to the caprices of the world, lit by the tiniest spark of hope.

"More than anything," he breathed.

And his trust, so innocent and pure, gave her the will to weather the rising storm.

Minna released her hold on his shoulders to pluck another needle from her reticule and lift her hands above the stone. She took a breath. All her life, she'd feared losing her blood and losing a part of herself, but now she could choose how and when her blood was shed. This was the freedom he had given her.

Minna pressed the needle into her thumb and watched the droplet form, refracting the silver light in shades of red as it wavered above the stone.

"Minna?" Doros asked, and Minna could barely see him in the light.

"Doros Wolf's Bane," she declared as the blood dripped down at last. "With my blood and my trust, I invite you to stay in my land with me. Make my home, your home. Stay and see the world you've set free.

The wind and fire froze, around the hall, like particles of silver light. Then another surge burst from the stone, this time sweeping Minna from her feet, but she did not tumble to the floor.

Instead, strong arms clutched her against a warm chest. She blinked and realized the light had gone out. She stood in the nearly empty hall, free of vampires. The remaining humans gazed about in wonder, but most reassuring of all, Minna lifted her chin to see Doros holding her tight.

She flung her arms around him. "You're here!"

A sheen like tears passed over his eyes, but he seemed to swallow them away. His hand tangled in her hair, pulling her close as cheers began to rise around them.

He cleared his throat with a chuckle. "After all my planning, I should have known to expect the unknown from you, of all people."

Minna grinned up at him. "Is that a compliment or an insult?"

He threw her another of his breathtaking winks and then drew his features into a wistful pout. "Considering that you've robbed me of my tragic, heroic sacrifice and doomed my chances of ever being remembered in the great ballads, I fear it cannot be a good thing."

Minna gave his cravat a playful tug. "I can assure you, Doros, mighty Wolf's Bane, nothing could ever rob you of your great triumph or the ballads the people will sing in your honor."

A bashful glint flashed over his eyes. "Even with my own clumsy, half-vampire self forever a present reality rather than a fondly remembered past?"

"Oh Doros." Minna rose on her toes to press a kiss against the dimple on his cheek. "Surely, if I can put up with you, then all the others can as well."

They stood together for a time before checking on the remaining human attendants. The glass tradesman, Minna realized with some embarrassment, had been waiting for them to remember to unchain him and set him free. He spoke to Doros teasingly, and Minna learned he had long been his partner in crime, casting glass Wolf's Bane flowers and aiding in missions to relocate humans to safer climes.

After ensuring the tradesman remained unharmed, Minna and Doros left the palace on foot. Even in the streets, the light had spread, overcoming every vampire that had staked a claim across the land. Humans stepped cautiously from their homes and shops, as if not daring to believe the magic they'd witnessed with their own eyes.

Many stared at Doros with his sharp teeth, but the word of his identity and deeds seemed to travel fast. Countless strangers ran up to thank him for their freedom. By the time they reached Lucia and Minna's, the stars were fading, and the edges of the night sky had begun to dissolve into faint color. But no mist rose against the sky.

Minna and Doros stopped before her shop, embracing the seamstresses who raced to greet them, and turned their faces to the horizon as a swath of colors Minna had only ever imagined painted their way across the sky. Warmth heated her skin as she leaned into Doros's arm and watched her first sunrise, at last.

The End

THE PALE NEW KID
Jessica A. Tanner

Natalie van Helsing tried not to stare at the new kid in school. Gavin Dracula was pale—as pale as a fresh sheet of paper, his hair darker than a black marker, and his eyes reminded her of dark chocolate.

She hid her face behind the door of her locker. It was better than continuing to stare. But she also needed to get her books for her next class. What was her next class?

The bells rang and she startled, dropping what she still held in her arms from her last class—art. Pencils and notebooks scattered in every direction as they hit the floor. She bent down to grab her things.

"Everything okay?"

"Yes!" Natalie hurried to straighten and smacked her head on the door of her locker. Her fistful of rescued pencils dropped to the floor again as she rubbed her bruised head.

"Are you sure?" A dark-haired head peeked around the door offering pencils and papers—one of which was a sketch Natalie had recently done of *him*.

"Uh huh." Natalie wanted to melt and hide under the locker. Heat rushed to her cheeks.

"Okay." The new kid handed over the recovered items. "Those are really good."

"Thanks." Her cheeks had to be as bright red as a ripe tomato.

Gavin headed down the hall.

She shoved everything into a corner of her locker, grabbed whatever books were next, and ran in the opposite direction while praying it was the right direction for her next class.

~~~~~

With school finally over for the day, Natalie crossed the open field behind the brick building and found the trail leading home. Pine trees towered over her and birds scattered at her approach. She shifted her heavy school pack into a more comfortable position, pulled out her cellphone, and flicked on her favorite playlist. Her headphones filled with the familiar notes of the 1940s blues singers she loved.

A tap on her shoulder caused her to scream and yank off her headphones.

Gavin stood a few feet from her, raising his hands and his black
~~~~~

eyebrows. "Whoa. Sorry."

One hand on her chest, the other flicking off her music, she said, "What'd you scare the Beetlejuice out of me for?"

Gavin lowered his hands. "I didn't mean to. I was just trying to ask if you'd mind company."

Natalie minded company very much ... except this was Gavin ... so she said, "No, I wouldn't mind."

"Cool." He offered a half-smile, only the right side of his lips tugging upward but not revealing his teeth. There was kindness in his dark chocolate eyes.

She tipped her head to him and turned around.

He stepped up beside her. "So ... where do you live?"

She cringed. She wanted to lie, but it wouldn't take much for him to figure out the truth. "The other side of the graveyard." Her father was the groundskeeper for the town cemetery and the job provided housing — a small stone house that leaned to one side.

"Cool. So do I."

Natalie's brow furrowed. "What do you mean?" There was an ancient stone mansion beyond her home, but it'd been empty and for sale for forever. Besides that, she wasn't aware of any other home close by. Although there was that empty lot across from the cemetery, but it was empty, and she doubted he lived in the bushes.

"I think it's called the Carmichael Mansion. The realtor told my dad it was built in like the seventeen hundreds or something."

A chill crept up her spine. "No way you live there."

He raised an eyebrow. "Yeah, we do."

"I mean you totally can." Natalie felt her tongue trying to trip on itself as she hurried to cover for her shock. "I hadn't realized the place had sold. Hadn't realized there was anyone there."

Gavin shrugged. "My dad just signed the papers for it last Friday and we haven't had a chance to get a car since moving here — just borrowed a friend's a couple times. No worries you didn't realize we were there."

"Last Friday?" That meant he'd probably caught her humming and watering her plants yesterday — as in Sunday — while wearing her baggy — but not baggy enough — *Save the Penguins* shirt and her ragged cutoff capris. And, what if he saw her trying to keep Taz, her family's dog, from chasing something into the woods? That would be horrible! She'd landed in the mud big time diving after Taz. Natalie wanted to melt again.

"Yup."

They reached the far side of the woods, where the dirt road wound alongside the cemetery to the Carmichael Mansion and her home.

He pointed to the cemetery and its rusting wrought iron fence. "Know anything about that?"

"A little. It used to be part of the Carmichael estate. The town bought it around the time the Carmichaels went bankrupt and left town. That was maybe a hundred years ago." She knew more than that but didn't want to admit it.

"How come?"

"They needed some place to move the bodies when this developer bought the land for the previous cemetery to build housing for the average family. He paid a bunch for that. The town paid pennies on the dollar for this."

Gavin nodded. "How do you know?"

Natalie felt heat rush to her cheeks again. "My dad's the groundskeeper — and he loves local history."

"Cool."

They reached where the road split, one narrower lane heading off to the Carmichael Mansion and one slightly wider arm heading toward her home and the entrance for the cemetery.

Gavin paused. "See you tomorrow?"

"Sure." She'd rather crawl in a hole and never speak again, but she doubted her parents would tolerate her missing school. She'd barely managed to get to stay home when she came down with the flu even worse than her friend Kendall Rogers had last year.

~~~~~

For a week, they walked to school and home together. Getting to know Gavin Dracula wasn't bad … it was actually super fun. She wondered though, why when he smiled, he never showed his teeth.

~~~~~

A week after the incident where she dropped her pencils and papers, Natalie bumped into Kendall Rogers.

"Hey, Nat," said Kendall, "what's the four-one-one on tall, dark, and handsome?" Her eyes gleamed as she leaned against the lockers.

"Not much. Why?" Natalie squeezed the last of her homework into her backpack and slammed her locker closed before she adjusted her headphones around her neck and tried not to look at Gavin. He didn't need two girls ogling him like he was a candy bar. Thankfully, he was busy with his phone.

Kendall shrugged and followed her toward the back of the school. "You seem to be spending a lot of time with him."

"I guess." Butterflies fluttered in Natalie's stomach. Not the kind like a boy was about to kiss her, but the kind that told her that her friend was up to something and wanted her involved, and she wasn't sure she'd be able to say no.

They reached the doors to the back exit and stopped.

Kendall turned to face Natalie. "Nat ....?"

"Yeah?" Here came trouble. Natalie's insides tightened into a nervous coil.

Kendall's voice softened. "Be careful with the new kid. There's something ... strange about him."

Natalie tried to keep her jaw from hitting the floor. That was not what she expected her recently turned boy-crazy friend to say.

Kendall adjusted the strap of her satchel. "Please, Nat."

"I'll be careful."

"Good." Kendall hugged her quickly. "I gotta run. One of the twins is supposed to pick me up for dance practice at the front." She jogged off.

A moment later, Gavin stepped from the shadows. "Ready?"

"Sure." She hoped he hadn't overheard any of the conversation with her friend.

They walked home like normal, parting ways where the road split. Nothing weird happened—until she reached home and her dad wanted to talk with her.

<p style="text-align:center">~~~~~</p>

Natalie left her pack in a cubby by the front door before following Dad over to the tool shed. Along the way, he glanced at the kitchen window. Music played on the old radio and her mother hummed while kneading bread.

Dad hustled her inside the shed and pulled the string for the overhead light. He gestured for Natalie to take a seat.

She moved over a couple of garden rakes and climbed up on a tall, dusty stool.

He sat across from her on the seat of his lawn mower. "You've been hanging out with that Dracula kid a lot."

"I guess." Natalie fidgeted. She was thirteen—her dad wasn't about to give her the you're-not-dating-'til-you're-out-of-the-house talk, was he? She'd been hoping she still had a year until that conversation.

He rubbed his stubble-covered chin. "There are some things I need to tell you."

So not the dating talk. "Like what?" she said while wishing Kendall was with her. Her best friend always knew how to give her courage—even if it was sometimes for the wrong thing ... like how they'd picked mercilessly on Lizzie Jones for visiting her mother's grave last year.

Dad pulled up a trapdoor and grabbed a flashlight from a drawer

52

in his workbench. "I think it'll be easier for me to explain if I can show you."

"Oooo-kay." Natalie trailed her father down a wood ladder and into a room she never knew existed.

Dad flicked a switch and lights clicked on all around the room, illuminating a space full of weapons—both modern and medieval.

Her eyes widened. "Whoa. What is all of this for?"

"To protect monsters."

"What?" Her eyebrows reached for the top of her forehead.

"Well, the ones that mean no harm. That just want to live their lives in peace." Her father sat on a chair. "Sort of like our new neighbors."

Her brows lowered and her eyes narrowed. "What do you mean?" Could Kendall be right about there being something weird with Gavin?

"Didn't you wonder about the pale skin and their last name?"

"Not really."

Dad smiled. "Should I be having a different talk with you?"

Heat filled her cheeks. "No." If she could have kept from blushing, she'd have been in the clear.

He chuckled. "We'll table that discussion ... for now." Then he turned toward the weapons lining the walls.

Buzz. Buzz.

Dad stepped toward the door and hit a button on the intercom. "Yes, honey?"

"The Draculas are here."

"We'll be up in a minute."

Butterflies fluttered frantically in Natalie's stomach. "The Draculas are here?" Hanging out with Gavin on the walk home was one thing, but seeing him in her home? Sweat slicked her palms.

Dad nodded. "Your mother thought it would be good to have our neighbors over for dinner."

With dinner over and the adults talking about adult things like how Mr. Dracula lost his title of count, Natalie and Gavin headed for the back door. Taz darted between them, barking like a maniac.

"Taz!" Natalie dashed after him. "Taz, come back here!" The little dog had been fine during dinner—in fact, he'd set himself up by Mr. Dracula during the meal and earned himself several scraps, the conniving chubby furball.

Gavin chased after them, calling the dog's name.

Taz disappeared behind a bush. His frantic barking turned to a surprised yip.

Natalie didn't like that.

She and Gavin slid to a halt on the far side of the bush. Taz lay in a crumpled heap with what looked like a dart in his neck … and standing over him was a guy who looked like a vampire slayer from TV—long trench coat, a wooden stake strapped to his thigh, dart gun in his hand, and long hair whipping about his face in the evening breeze.

The stranger grinned.

She glanced at her dog, hoped he wasn't dead, and grabbed Gavin's arm before trying to make a run for the house.

But Gavin shouted as he was jerked from her grip and Natalie lost her balance, falling to her knees.

"Not so fast," the creepy stranger said in a deep voice. "You're forgetting your dog."

She stood and faced him. "Let go of my friend."

Gavin struggled to break the hold on his neck.

"I don't think so." The stranger holstered his gun and pulled a bulb of garlic from his pocket.

Gavin turned a bit green. "Let me go!"

Natalie picked up a fallen tree branch. "Don't you dare hurt him!" She wasn't sure what good her branch would do her, but she had the deep suspicion that even if vampires could strangely walk in the daylight like Gavin did—they were still allergic to garlic. No wonder Mom had served rice, broccoli, and pork chops with rolls for dinner instead of her famous lasagna.

Taz shuddered behind the man, almost like he was slowly waking up.

The man waved at Gavin with his handful of garlic. "He is a monster, child."

"Maybe," said Natalie. "But he's never hurt anyone—and last I checked, a real monster is one who attacks without a good reason." She was impressed her voice didn't waver, because she wasn't really feeling all that brave.

Taz wobbled to his paws before shaking like he did after a bath, flinging the dart from his neck. His gaze still a bit out of focus, he turned and bit the stranger in the ankle.

The man hollered, releasing Gavin and reaching for Taz.

Natalie raised her branch and smacked the man over the head.

He sprawled on the ground, cussing worse than she'd ever heard anyone cuss.

Natalie grabbed Taz, the dog coming away with a mouthful of pants, and ran after Gavin in the direction of home.

The threesome reached the yard—but not the backdoor—before the stranger caught up with them. He yanked Natalie back by her ponytail.

She screamed and dropped Taz. The dog yipped as he hit the ground.

The backdoor of the house swung open—almost smacking Gavin in the face.

"Dessert is ready." Mom stood there, her smile faltering, and her eyes lighting with anger. "Release my daughter."

"Give me the monster," said the man, "and you can have your daughter."

Natalie kicked at the man and tried to reach his hand to scratch it. "Mom, don't let him have Gavin!"

Dad barreled out behind Mom. "Mina, what's—Carter." Dad glared. "Let her go."

The man shook Natalie—she yelled, her scalp felt like her hair was being pulled out by the roots—and then he brought an arm around her middle, pinning her arms. "Van Helsing."

If the guy had been a little shorter, Natalie would have thrown her head back against his nose just then. But he wasn't. He was nearly as tall and buff as her dad.

The stranger—Carter, her dad had called him—said, "Give me the monster and I'll release your daughter."

Gavin moved a step toward them and away from the safety of her parents.

Dad pulled him back. "The boy stays with me—and you will release my daughter."

Mr. Dracula squeezed his way past Natalie's parents and his son. "Carter."

Dad watched Mr. Dracula, but even though the new neighbor had addressed the stranger, he wasn't looking at him—he was looking at the sky. Natalie wondered why.

"You know," said Mr. Dracula, "your time is running out."

Carter scoffed.

Natalie tried as best she could to get a glimpse of the sky. What did dusk turning to night have to do with anything? What time was running out?

A growl, like something from a monster in a thriller movie, came from the trees behind her and the stranger.

Natalie felt the hairs rise along her neck and arms. Where was Taz?

Carter stiffened behind her.

"You'd better release the girl," said Mr. Dracula, a terrifying glint in his dark eyes revealed by the porch light someone—probably Mom—had turned on when coming out earlier.

Dad pulled something silver from his pocket. "Let her go, Carter."

Another growl. Deeper this time.

Mr. Dracula spoke but still did not face Carter. "My son and I are not the only monsters, as you call us, in this town. Nor are we the only ones to befriend the van Helsings. If you wish to live another day, release the girl and leave."

Carter's grip tightened, then he shoved Natalie away. "I will be back."

She fell forward, landing on her hands and knees.

Mr. Dracula finally turned toward them. His eyes flashed red and he revealed fangs. "If you're smart, hunter, you'll never return."

Natalie shivered, frightened, yet thankful the terrifying display wasn't for her but for Carter.

The sound of running feet moved away, probably into the woods, and a bone chilling howl greeted her ears as Natalie eased her feet under herself and brushed the dirt from her palms onto her shorts.

Her mother dashed down the porch steps and wrapped her in a hug. "My baby." Her eyes glistened, like she was on the verge of tears.

Natalie returned the embrace, inhaling deeply of her mother's bread dough scent.

Another set of arms encircled her. "My little girl." Dad.

Someone cleared his throat.

The family loosened their hold on each other.

Mr. Dracula waved to himself and Gavin. "I suppose it's time for us to head home. Thank you all for the dinner—and the friendship." He smiled without showing his teeth.

Gavin glanced into the woods. "What about—"

"The hunter?" Natalie's father interrupted. "I doubt we'll have any further trouble with him."

Natalie glanced up at her dad, one of her eyebrows climbing toward her hairline. A million questions danced on the tip of her tongue, but she didn't ask even one in front of Gavin. He was as unsettled by everything as her—and he still had to walk home in the dark.

Mom hustled into the house and brought out a flashlight. "To keep you from tripping on your way home."

Mr. Dracula thanked her before turning on the light and leading the way to the Carmichael Mansion.

Once the Draculas were out of earshot, Natalie said, "What did you mean about that Carter fellow not being any more trouble? And what was that thing that growled? And where's Taz?" She recalled dropping him, but not where he went afterward.

Her father handed her a dog whistle. "Go call for him. I doubt he's gone far."

The whistle glinted the same silver she'd seen Dad pull out of his pocket earlier. Weird.

Everything felt weird lately, if she were being truthful.

And why hadn't Dad answered her other questions?

~~~~~

The next day, Saturday, as Natalie was pulling on a particularly nasty weed, someone said, "Hello," behind her.

She screamed—from the weed unexpectedly releasing and her falling back as well as from the "hello." She collided with someone and they landed in a pile on the ground.

Taz yipped and ran around them. The dog's little tail waved fast as a hummingbird's wings.

"Sorry for scaring you," said a familiar voice.

"You're forgiven. I scare easily." She rolled off the poor sap she'd landed on and offered a hand up.

A pale hand accepted.

A familiar heat inched into her cheeks. Natalie slowly met the dark chocolate eyes of her neighbor.

Gavin pulled a flashlight from his pocket. "I was just trying to return this."

She bobbed her head once and took the light with muddy fingers. "Thanks." Maybe her dad did need to give her a certain talk. And where was a locker for her to hide in? Or to melt and hide under?

Taz jumped on Gavin, the chubby little furball barely swaying him.

Gavin reached down and scratched Taz behind an ear. "How's the little hero?"

Excited yips answered.

Gavin chuckled. "I'll take that as really well."

He straightened and smiled at her, showing a little bit of his teeth. "I, um, also wanted to ask if you'd like to check out the arts and crafts fair this afternoon ... with me?" There was a slightly pink tinge to his cheeks.

"Sure." Her whole face had to be on fire and her heart thundered in her chest while butterflies danced in her stomach.

"You'll have her home by six," called her dad from the porch.

"Yes, sir," said Gavin. His cheeks turned even pinker.

She was totally getting the talk before Gavin came back to take her out.

The End
~~~~~

SCREECHED
Stoney M. Setzer

Technically I could have sent any of my deputies on the call that Thursday afternoon and stayed in the office. In light of all the weirdness that I had encountered as sheriff of Sardis County, however, I wasn't about to farm this out to anybody else. I had to satisfy my own curiosity, so I drove my patrol car out to what had once been Janus Labs.

The facility sat secluded near the outer limits of the Sardis County line, a massive wall and a plethora of NO TRESPASSING signs forbidding intruders from entering. Nevertheless, somebody had been here. Old Mr. Malone lived about a mile away, nothing else between him and Janus Labs, and he had reported a white van making multiple trips up and down the road leading to the abandoned facility.

"Don't rightly know what they doin' out yonder, but it can't be good," he had said.

I agreed wholeheartedly, although I'm sure he was thinking in terms of much more conventional skullduggery. While I would keep an eye out for that as well, the mere mention of Janus Labs opened a completely different avenue of suspicion in my mind. Sardis County had long been a hotbed for cryptic events, long enough that not everything could be blamed on Janus Labs. However, some of it was tied to whatever had once gone on here before whatever disaster had gotten this place locked down. Mutant frogs, invisible men—directly or indirectly, those could be traced back to scientific experiments that had once gone on here.

Speaking of invisibility, the white van was nowhere to be seen. I could see some dirty tire tracks on the asphalt, but nothing particularly distinct. Somebody had been out here since this place had been locked down, but there was no way to tell how long ago. It could have been a few days or a few weeks. What I was sure of was that even in its abandonment, this place held more secrets than I could fathom.

"One day," I muttered under my breath, even though I was alone in the car. "One day I'm going to find out the truth."

For just a moment, I thought I heard a sound in the distance, a high-pitched screech that made my hair stand on end. My first impulse was to floor the gas pedal and get out of there as fast as I could. Fighting my fear, I looked around to see if I could ascertain the source. Nothing, which was somehow even more disconcerting.

Although I didn't dare shut my eyes, I prayed aloud. "Lord, I don't know all the answers. You've put me here in Sardis County at this time, and I know I'm supposed to serve and protect this community. Please help me, because I can't do it otherwise."

Listening intently for what felt like forever, I didn't hear the screech again. Instead, my phone went off, alerting me of a new text message. It was from my girlfriend, Dr. Staci Bridges. *Are we still on for dinner, Mr. Sheriff?* Her question was followed by one of those kissy-face emojis that she loved to send me.

I checked the time in the upper-left corner of my phone screen. Her veterinary clinic had just closed about three minutes ago, but Staci was probably still inside, as she was always the last to leave. Her reddish-brown hair was most likely pulled up in a ponytail, and she was no doubt clad in scrubs and sneakers—maybe the green ones that matched her emerald eyes. Best-looking veterinarian on the planet, in my humble opinion.

"Absolutely, Dr. Gorgeous," I replied aloud, letting my phone transcribe it into text. My hands were suddenly shaking, and my voice had a tremor that thankfully would be lost in translation. Hiding my nerves tonight was going to be a challenge, and another prayer item altogether.

OK, pick me up at 7. Gotta get ready. Another kissy emoji, followed by a couple more: A shower and lipstick.

"See you then." Assuming I wasn't a basket case by then. I drove away, taking a long look at Janus Labs in the rearview mirror.

~~~~~

We were sitting in a corner booth at Maria's Mexican, situated so that I was facing the door. Since I had started my career in law enforcement, I had always hated to sit with my back to the door in a restaurant. The place was at maybe three-quarters capacity tonight, but that part didn't matter to me. I could only pick at my beef chimichanga because my stomach was already full of butterflies.

Either I wasn't hiding it very well, or Staci was reading me like a book. "Are you okay, baby?" she asked, setting her fork down on her taco salad. She placed her hand on top of mine gently as she looked at me with concern.

I hesitated, not sure what to say. Staci and I had been a couple for a while now, long enough that I shouldn't have been nervous on an ordinary date with her. However, this wasn't going to be an ordinary night. My pocket held a little black clamshell box from McCrary Jewelers in town, and inside it was a diamond ring—a tiny item that held all my
~~~~~

hope for future happiness.

Nobody knew about my plan. If I had told Mom or my sister Carla, they would have both been somewhere in here along with my niece Michelle, all trying to act like it was just a coincidence and no doubt failing miserably. They would have tipped Staci off immediately, and I wanted to surprise her.

We had talked about marriage before, but that wasn't helping right now. There is a level of self-doubt that is probably unique to divorcees contemplating remarriage. My ex-wife had cheated on me multiple times, but was any one person truly one hundred percent responsible in a divorce? If we're all sinful and imperfect like the Bible says, wasn't it reasonable that the other person carried at least some of the blame? Or to put it another way, would Jennifer have ever cheated if she had been happy? And if I had contributed in any way to the disintegration of our union, then how could I be sure that I wouldn't mess this up too?

For her part, Staci had been widowed instead of divorced. She and Brad would still be together if not for his wreck, and even that had been someone else's fault. Maybe she deserved better than me. Yet here we were. We had been friends in high school, harboring secret crushes on each other that apparently everybody else knew about but us. Both of us had been through a lot since then, and now I was planning to pop the question.

I was going to wait until after dinner, but maybe I needed to just go ahead, right here. I reached into my pocket, touched the rough felt covering the jewelry box and started to pull it out, keeping my eyes locked on hers...

The ringtone that I used for the deputies shattered the moment. I started to ignore it, but Staci raised her eyebrows. "You'd better see what it is. Might be important."

It had better be, I thought as I took the call. "Yeah?"

"Sheriff, this is Gonzalez. I hate to interrupt you, but we have an issue over here at the jail, and we need you."

My heart sank like a stone. Why did this have to happen right now? Trying my best to maintain a poker face, I couldn't help cutting my eyes toward Staci. "Are you sure that this isn't something that you could handle without me?"

"I think we really need you for this one. It's...well, significant. We have somebody over here about a missing person. She keeps asking for you, by name."

"Me? Why?"

"I dunno. She's pretty worked up though, and..."

"Fine." I hung up and sighed. "Baby, I'm sorry, but they need me downtown. They wouldn't give me details, but…"

"I understand, honey," Staci said, lightly squeezing my hand. "You're the sheriff. I get it. Especially here in Sardis County. Sometimes things get, well, weird."

"Yeah, but I really wanted some time with you tonight." *Uninterrupted,* I added mentally.

Staci perked up. "Well, what if I went with you? And then if it doesn't take too long, then maybe the night can still be salvaged."

"But what if it can't? What if it turns into something big that takes longer to unravel?" *What if my plans are totally shot?*

Staci raised an eyebrow at me. "Come on, Dane. We've faced some crazy Sardis Couty stuff together, remember? I'm with you, end of discussion, I win." Before I could stop her, she had already motioned for our server. "Could we get the check and two take-out boxes, please?"

~~~~~

Deputy Javier "Javy" Gonzalez met us at the front door. Ordinarily he was calm and collected, but now he seemed ill at ease. "I've never seen her before, but she insists on speaking to you. I think I'd prefer that as well."

"Tell Dane to hurry up!" a female voice shouted from inside. "Time's wasting!"

As much as I would have liked to have forgotten that voice, I'd have recognized it anywhere. While it may have sounded normal to anybody else, it could have decalcified every bone in my body. It belonged to none other than Jennifer, my ex-wife.

"You've got to be kidding," I muttered as I walked in, probably with all the enthusiasm of a prisoner heading to his execution.

Since we had no children together, there had been no reason for Jennifer and me to interact in the years since the divorce. Surprisingly, she didn't look much different than I had remembered. Same short height and medium build, maybe a few extra pounds. Same dirty blonde hair, just cut in a different style now.

Most notably, her demeanor hadn't changed a bit. Jennifer was narcissistic, believing herself to be generally better than everybody else and better looking than any other woman around. It showed in everything about her—the way she dressed, the way she moved, and most of all the way she looked at me, looking down on me despite my being almost a foot taller than she was.

"Aw, sh—shoot," Staci muttered behind me, an expression of instant recognition and displeasure at the sight of Jennifer. Although she had never been one for using foul language, she just barely kept her tongue from slipping that time. Even if she had failed to catch herself, I
~~~~~

couldn't have blamed her.

The diamond ring in my pocket felt as if its weight had doubled. Not that I wanted our paths to ever cross again at all, but why did it have to happen tonight, of all nights?

No matter what, I had to keep my tone professional. "What brings you to Sardis County, Jennifer?" I inquired.

"Don't play dumb, Dane! I heard your flunky telling you that I was here to report a missing person!" Her eyes burned with anger. "Believe me, I'm not any happier about this than you are!"

"Why don't you fill me in on the details?" Keeping my voice neutral with her was difficult. I tried not to think about how her attitude toward me had changed shortly after we had gotten married. How she decided that I wasn't good enough for her anymore, how being married to a cop was suddenly beneath her. That eventually led to her having affairs — yes, plural — with men whom she thought were a little more worthy of her. Jennifer's lack of remorse and indifference toward my pain had only added insult to injury. Maintaining my professionalism was becoming tougher by the second, but I couldn't let myself take the bait, especially not in front of Staci.

"It's Lee, my nephew. Do you remember him?"

"I do. How old is he now, about eighteen?"

"Nineteen," she replied, seeming to relish correcting me even on such a small detail. "And he's sick. Rare form of blood cancer. He was told a couple of weeks ago that the treatments aren't making a dent in it and that he doesn't have much longer."

"I'm sorry to hear that," I said. Lee had still been in elementary school when Jennifer and I split up. It was a sad fate for someone so young. "But what brings you here? I thought he lived in Memphis. Why not report it there?"

Jennifer's eyes cut away from me, in Staci's direction. "Staci Riley? Is that you?"

"It's Dr. Staci Bridges now." She was behind me but now stepped in much closer, placing her right hand on my chest. I was accustomed to her showing affection through her touch, but this was different.

This was Staci marking her territory — ironic for a veterinarian. Why couldn't Gonzalez have called after I proposed? No doubt Staci would have made the same move, but maybe with her left hand instead, to make sure that the ring was fully visible. If only....

Jennifer's eyes widened for just a second before narrowing. "Oh, I see," she hissed, her voice dripping with contempt.

I'm no stranger to intense, threatening confrontations. Back in my days as a Memphis cop, I faced off against plenty of criminal types. Since becoming the sheriff of Sardis County, I had dealt with a number of more supernatural threats, from mutated monstrosities to invisible men. I'd seen a lot.

Even with that varied of a resume, nothing could have prepared me for the tension of having my ex-wife and current girlfriend together in the same space as they glared at one another with instant contempt. I could understand Staci's end of it. They had known each other slightly in high school but hadn't been friends by any stretch of the imagination. Since we had gotten together, nothing she had heard me or my family say about Jennifer had been positive. It made sense for her to hold Jennifer in disdain.

Jennifer's contempt made a lot less sense to me. Her chronic infidelity while we were married was proof enough that she wasn't committed to me, so what did she care if I was with someone else now, especially this long after we had gone our separate ways?

"I guess I should have figured," Jennifer said. "Heaven knows you gawked at him enough when we were in high school."

"You should know. As I recall, you were something of an expert on gawking at guys," Staci countered.

Jennifer's brown eyes widened. "Excuse me?"

Somehow, I had forgotten how much hearing her say those words could grate on my nerves. A common phrase, sure, but there was something about the way she said it, all haughty and superior. As if anything said to her that didn't sit just right with her was automatically some kind of an affront.

Staci's fingers dug into my shirt, and I knew she was about to say something else. Trying to diffuse the situation, I said, "Let's get back to why you're here. Your nephew?"

Trying to help, Gonzalez cleared his throat. "Ma'am, weren't you telling me that you had tracked his phone here?"

Jennifer's eyes flashed in an expression that I recognized all too well. Ladies always seemed to take a liking to Gonzalez anyway, and Jennifer seemed to take a liking to most men.

"That's right. It's showing a location not too far from here," she said, batting her eyelashes at him. I don't know if she had been trying to flirt with him before or if this was just some weird reaction to Staci's presence. For his part, Gonzalez's comportment didn't falter. He was either oblivious to her goo-goo eyes or utterly disinterested in them. Spitefully, I hoped for the latter.

"Why would he have come out to Sardis County?" I asked.

"He said something about this last-ditch treatment he wanted to try," Jennifer said. "Some place called Janus Labs."

Staci and I immediately exchanged glances. Neither of us said it out loud, but we both knew enough to think the same thing: *Not good.*

"If you've tracked him here, why did you want to report him as a missing person?" I asked, trying to keep my voice as neutral as possible.

"Because when I went to that spot, I found Lee's phone, but I didn't find him," she said, as if it should have been the most obvious thing in the world. "I wouldn't have even known you were the sheriff here if it hadn't been on the sign at the county line. If I could have done this without having to fool with you, trust me, I…"

I took a deep breath to regain my composure. "So, he's this far from home, he's never come to Sardis that I'm aware of, and you found his phone abandoned. Those are suspicious circumstances, I'll admit."

"About time you saw that," Jennifer huffed. "Now are you going to help me or not?"

"Where is his phone now?"

"I left it where I found it. We may have split up a long time ago, but I haven't forgotten everything about cops. I know not to mess with what might be a crime scene."

"Did you learn that from me, or from Roy?" I asked, unable to resist the urge. "How is old Roy Boy doing these days, anyway?"

Jennifer's cheeks turned scarlet. "I don't know. I haven't talked to him since we split up. I'm with somebody else now, or at least I was…"

I cut my eyes toward Staci. I had never given her much detail about any of Jennifer's indiscretions other than the fact that they had happened, but the look on her face told me that she had no trouble filling in the blanks here. However, there was also something else in my girlfriend's gaze, something that told me I had gone too far.

"Okay, never mind that," I said. "Can I see where you tracked his phone to?"

"Yeah." She fumbled with her phone and handed it to me.

Carefully I looked over the map as Staci leaned in to get a better view. I turned it toward her, partly because I trusted her and partly because I wanted to reinforce to Jennifer that Staci and I were together. For once, Jennifer was speechless. It was a good look for her.

I tapped the screen at Lee's marker. "Near the 6th Street Bridge. South end."

"Really? That close?" Staci asked. The bridge in question was only a couple of blocks away, walking distance. We were even on the right end already.

I handed the phone back to Jennifer. "Okay, I'm heading out there," I said. To Gonzalez I asked, "Is Nitro in the kennel?"

"Yeah. Why?"

"I'll take him out there with me. Maybe he can get the scent and help us find Lee's trail."

"Wait up. I'm going with you," Staci said.

"I'm not sure that's a good idea," I began. "If there's really something dangerous out there…"

The look in Staci's eyes stopped me cold. "I wasn't asking."

~~~~~

"Good old Nitro," Staci said, smiling for the first time since Jennifer's arrival. She scratched the dog behind his ear. "Your canine wingman when you thought you needed to make an excuse to talk to me."

"Yeah," I replied as I put the leash on him. I wanted to say more, but with everything going on, my head was spinning.

"Little did I know what I was getting myself into. Of course, who knows where I might be right now if you hadn't been there with him at the time that lizard bit me."

"Yeah, but I'm not sure you're safe coming out here with me," I remarked as we walked from the kennel toward the back door. "You know how things are here. If there really is any level of danger, I'd rather you be safe, and you have to go to the nursing home later to see about your dad, and…"

"Look, Dane," Staci said in a tone that brooked no argument. "Dad will be okay. As for you keeping me safe? First of all, I feel safer with you than I would anywhere else, even if it means following you right into the eye of the storm. Second, I rode with you, so I don't have any way to go to the nursing home or anywhere else except with you, which leads me to the third point."

"Which is?"

She smirked just a little. "If you had left me at the jailhouse with your ex, Gonzalez would have had to put one of us *in* the jail before it was all said and done, either me or her. You follow me?"

"Yeah." I gripped Nitro's leash tightly, vaguely aware of how sweaty my palms were. All the tension of the night was building up within me, making me feel that I might explode. The ring felt as heavy as a boulder, and I couldn't fathom that Staci hadn't noticed the shape of its box in my pocket yet. My impulsive side wanted to go ahead and pull it out right now, just to have it on her finger before we encountered Jennifer again, but I knew it would be too rushed. I wanted it to be exactly right, even though I now wondered when that might be.

Ahead of us, Nitro trooped along, knowing he had a job to do and totally focused on it, either oblivious to the human tension around him or simply ignoring it. Lucky dog.
~~~~~

"So, when did y'all get together? How long after graduation?"

"About two years. After you had already left for college."

"I would ask you what you ever saw in her, but I was there in high school, so I've got a pretty good idea," she puffed. "Younger Dane was no match for Little Miss Flashy-Trashy once she set her sights on you, were you?"

Sometimes, the hardest thing in the world is to admit the mistakes that you've done your best to forget. "Not much sense denying it, but I was young and stupid then. Too stupid to know that she wasn't going to be the faithful kind." I glanced over at Staci. "I'd like to think that I'm older and wiser now and that my taste has become a good bit more discriminating. Maybe if I hadn't been so stupid in our high school days, maybe I would have asked you out back then and saved myself a lot of heartache."

She didn't say anything, but her little half-smile suggested that maybe my response was satisfactory — maybe.

We stepped out the back door of the courthouse and into the night, our destination looming directly in front of us. The 6th Street Bridge was a steel truss structure spanning the railroad and the two side streets flanking either side of the tracks. It was on the side streets that the bridge's most well-known features could be seen. Maybe a hundred feet before going under the bridge, on either side, were huge signs with flashing amber lights hanging above the street at the same height as the clearance under the bridge. The signs bore a simple message: IF YOU HIT THIS SIGN, YOU WILL HIT THAT BRIDGE — a last-chance warning for truckers with high payloads. For as long as I could remember, it had been one of Sardis' most distinctive features.

On this side, there wasn't much else to see except the overflow parking lot for the courthouse and a small brick church, situated right at the base of the bridge. Well over a century old, it had been left behind as its former congregants had moved on to a newer facility in greener pastures. As with so many other abandoned buildings in Sardis County, obvious signs of decay pocked the exterior. Vandals had broken a few of the stained-glass windows. Nevertheless, its steeple and belfry still pointed up toward heaven, as if in defiant refusal to succumb to the ravages of time.

Off in the distance, I thought I heard a screech — one eerily similar to the one I'd heard back at Janus Labs. It made my skin crawl, not just because of the sound itself but also for the fact that I had heard it twice now. "Did you hear something?" I asked.

"High-pitched, far off?"

"That would be it."

Staci nodded. "Yeah. Sounded like a bat to me. It's nighttime, after all. Maybe that's all it was."

"Maybe," I said, pressing forward. "Thing is, I was checking out something at Janus Labs earlier and heard it then, too."

"I would have been a whole lot happier not knowing that part," she remarked.

Beneath the bridge sat a metal shopping cart with some rust spots peppering its frame. It was overflowing, not with groceries but rather with all of someone's meager possessions. On the sidewalk beside it, a dilapidated sleeping bag was stretched out. Clearly somebody had decided to camp out here for the night, but nobody was around right now. I wished that Mayor Collins was here, just so he could see the evidence of the homeless population that he constantly tried to deny.

"Man," Staci whispered beside me. "Sometimes you forget."

"Forget what?"

"But for the grace of God, there go I. All it would take is a few bad breaks, and any one of us could be right here. I read somewhere that the average household is about two paychecks away from destitution."

I ran numbers in my head, thought about where I might be if I was suddenly without income. "Makes sense."

"Oh, please! You'd agree with anything she says."

We spun around to see Jennifer walking up behind us.

"Seriously?" Staci blurted.

"What are you doing here?" I asked, barely able to keep my frustration in check. "You need to be back there at the—"

"No, this is my nephew. My responsibility. I want to know what's going on."

Fighting the urge to roll my eyes took a herculean effort. "And what if you interfere with the investigation?"

She laughed. "Excuse me? It's not like your little girlfriend there is a cop herself."

"There are things about Sardis County that you don't know," Staci said indignantly.

"You don't have to defend yourself to her," I said, shaking my head. That was classic Jennifer, taking any situation and somehow making it all about her. "And arguing with her is about as productive as arguing with that bridge over there. Trust me."

"If she can be out here, I can be out here," Jennifer said sternly.

Not taking the bait, I turned away from her and let Nitro sniff the area. As soon as he got the scent, he began to pull at the leash. "Did he get the trail that fast?" Staci asked.

"He's a good tracker."

"Is he, now?" Jennifer sneered, if for no other reason than to hear herself speak.

This time Staci didn't say a word back. She learned quickly.

Sweeping my flashlight toward Nitro, I saw he was heading past the deserted church, toward an equally forsaken house. Back in Memphis, I would have worried about this being a crack house. Here in Sardis County, it could be anything.

As we approached, Nitro whined, signaling he had found something. He led us to a man lying face down on the ground. He wore the tattered clothes of a homeless man, no doubt the owner of the shopping cart.

Staci gulped. "Is he...?"

Checking his pulse, I shook my head. "He's gone."

I was just about to call it in when someone shouted, "Aunt Jennifer! What are you doing out here?"

Looking up, I saw a man walking toward us from the house. My eyes were adjusting to the dark, and I could see the resemblance between him and the kid I had known so many years ago.

"That's what I'd like to ask you!" Jennifer countered. "What is going on?"

As Lee approached, Nitro growled deep in his throat. Even in this poor light, I could tell his hair was standing up on end. Never a good sign.

"You need to get out of here, Aunt Jen—Uncle Dane, is that you?"

According to the divorce laws of Tennessee, I technically wasn't his uncle anymore, but I didn't correct him. Something felt off.

"He's gone," Staci called out. "Lost too much blood. Bite marks on his neck, I don't know what from, but..."

"Y'all need to get out of here! All of y'all!" Lee said, still walking toward us. He was moving slowly, as if every step required a herculean effort. There was something strange in his eye, an almost haunted look.

Nitro barked loudly, a warning of imminent danger. I had the leash in my left hand and my flashlight in my right, but I quickly moved the flashlight to my left so I could have a hand free to draw my Glock if needed, all while keeping an eye on Lee. This would have been so much easier in daylight, or at least with better streetlights.

"Do you know anything about that dead man over there?" I asked.

Lee covered his ears. "Why is that dog carrying on like that? Can't you do something about him?"

Like all our other K-9s, Nitro had been trained in German to defend against conflicting commands in crisis situations. I ordered him to settle down, but I might as well have been speaking Greek or Swahili for all the good it did. Something had him on high alert.

"So you can't shut your stupid dog up?" Jennifer complained. Without even having to look at her, I was sure she was covering her ears melodramatically, acting as if Nitro's barking was a bigger annoyance to her than it was to Lee.

"Can't you shut yourself up?" Staci countered. I felt certain her ears were uncovered, partly because she was used to barking and partly to show Jennifer up.

"Oh, my head! If that dog doesn't stop barking...!" Lee cried. He was visibly agitated now, and all my experience told me to be ready for anything. He began walking forward again. "Seriously, y'all had better..."

"Freeze!" I commanded. "No sudden moves!"

"Oh, how original," Jennifer groaned from behind me. "I would have thought a real cop might—"

"Who asked you?" Staci snarled. "Dane, have you called it in about the body yet?"

Lee looked behind me, taking notice of the two of them. "Both of you shut your traps!" he demanded, his voice becoming shrill. "You're worse than the dog!"

"Excuse me?" Jennifer demanded. "I come out here to this hick town to find you, have to deal with one of my exes, and you're gonna talk to me like that?"

My muscles tensed, and I wondered if anyone had ever explained to her that silence was golden. For her part, Staci held her tongue.

"I said shut your trap!" Lee screamed. He dropped his hands from his ears to his sides, as if he was about to reach for something in his pocket. "That treatment at that lab...it was bad. And all of y'all need to run!"

"Put your hands where I can see them!" I commanded.

Lee stopped walking, but he kept his arms by his sides. Violent tremors shook his gaunt frame. "Careful what you wish for..." he said through clenched teeth.

He raised his arms, but not in the way that countless others would if confronted by the police. Instead, he lifted his arms straight out to the sides, like a bird stretching its wings. A bird—or a bat.

A screech filled the night air, just like what I had heard a few minutes ago—and just like at Janus Labs earlier. It was much louder now, much closer. Closer, as in coming from Lee's throat.

And here we go, I thought. I tried turning my thought into a prayer, but I didn't know what to pray beyond, *Lord, please help me...*

Under the beam of my flashlight, brown fur erupted all over his skin. His shirt ripped apart at the sides without falling off completely. As he raised his arms, I saw membranes running from his wrist to his waist that bore an uncanny resemblance to wings—bat wings. Staci screamed behind me, and Jennifer cursed. Part of me wanted to run, but I knew I couldn't. I had sworn to serve and protect and I had to do it, no matter what, even if I was facing an escapee from a nightmare.

Janus Labs strikes again, I thought.

He threw his head back and screeched again, a cry to curdle the blood and pierce the eardrums. His teeth became sharp like fangs, like something out of a vampire movie. Nitro finally stopped barking and started whimpering, but true to his training, he stood his ground. I stepped back, pulling him with me, until I stepped on Jennifer's foot and bumped into her. Ordinarily she would have snapped at me, but this time she didn't say a word.

Staci came in closer. "Dane, what is that?"

"You tell me, and we'll both know." I was doing my best to keep both my flashlight and my Glock trained on what had once been an agitated young man. "Looks more like a bat than a man now."

"A really big bat, but yeah."

"I don't suppose you'd want to take him to your clinic and do an examination?"

Staci didn't miss a beat. "If you figure out how to get him there, we'll talk about it."

"How are you two so calm about this?" Jennifer demanded, barely speaking above a whisper. "You act like you see stuff like this all the time!"

"Who said it's an act?" Staci countered.

The Lee-Bat threw his head back and screeched again, reminding me of how Lee had objected to all the noise. He spread his wings and coiled his leg muscles. In the blink of an eye, he leaped straight up. Wings flapping, he took to the nocturnal sky, screeching continuously.

Finding his boldness again, Nitro barked his head off at the airborne nightmare. Lee-Bat was going straight up, climbing higher and higher. I tried to keep the flashlight beam on it as best I could, but I couldn't keep pace. Before long, I had lost him. The cries faded, sounding more distant by the second. With my other hand, I tightened my grip on the Glock, just in case.

"What happened to him?" Jennifer squeaked.

"Let's just say that Janus Labs isn't exactly endorsed by the American Medical Association," I answered.

"Do you think Lee did that over there?" She gestured toward the corpse. "Do you think he...?"

"If he didn't, then I'd hate to know what else we have to deal with," Staci said.

Jennifer was shaking like a leaf. "Do you think he's…gone? Flown away?" She gulped.

"I doubt it," I said. "Nothing is ever that easy around here."

As if on cue, the shrill cries from above became louder again. Lee-Bat was back and closing in fast. And I had lost track of it…

"Everybody down!" I shouted. Had my hands not been full, I might have grabbed Staci and dived to make sure she got out of harm's way. I didn't dare do that with the Glock in my hand for fear of an accidental discharge. All I could do was hope they followed directions.

Lee-Bat darted past at about eight feet above the ground, judging that it passed less than two feet over my head. It flew too fast for me to draw a bead on it, with the same erratic pattern as a normal bat, making him an extremely difficult target.

Both Staci and Jennifer had hit the dirt. I had half-expected my ex to stay on her feet just for the sake of defiance. While understandably frightened, Staci seemed to be holding together all right—this wasn't her first rodeo. Something in Jennifer's expression unsettled me. Hers was the look of someone whose terror was just about to overwhelm their brain.

Nitro went ballistic, barking up at the sky. The creature arced upward again, no doubt gearing up for another pass at us. We had to find cover somewhere, because staying out here was just going to get us killed.

Other than the house, the nearest building was the abandoned church. Broken windows teased access to the inside, and even without them, a couple of porticos offered at least a little shelter. Even the underpass under the bridge was better than being out here in the open. Catching Staci's eye, I gestured toward it. If noise had set Lee off, then keeping quiet couldn't hurt. Staci nodded, picking up on it right away. She nudged Jennifer to get her attention and then pointed toward the church, even pantomiming running fingers to get her point across.

Jennifer looked at her blankly before finally nodding. They both got to their feet but still crouched down to move with as low a profile as possible. Looking upward, I could still see the creature, but he was at the zenith of his flight pattern now. I jerked Nitro's leash, and he came along without hesitation as I followed the girls.

Everything looked as if it would go off without a hitch—for just a second. Then another screech filled the night air from above, distant but still menacing.

Jennifer screamed, a long, distraught wail. Abandoning the crouch, she jumped up to full height and ran, still screaming like a banshee. Staci looked at her and then at me. I waved frantically toward the church as I mouthed the words, *Keep going.*

Looking up again, I saw Lee-Bat was diving down again, drawn by Jennifer's hysteria. *To serve and protect* felt like a punch in the gut. No matter how much misery she had caused me, I was duty-bound, and that oath included her.

The creature darted into the beam of a streetlight. I fired my Glock, aiming as best I could. With another ear-piercing cry, the bat lurched off his flight path. I couldn't tell if I had actually hit him or had just startled him, but I'd take it. Either way, it kept him from strafing Jennifer for the time being.

Lee had warned us to run, but Lee-Bat had tried to attack Jennifer. He had known the change was coming and apparently understood that his rational mind wouldn't be in control once he transformed. In this form, he was fully animalistic, with no ability to differentiate his own flesh and blood from anybody else.

And he had told us that Janus Labs was involved, despite all appearances of being abandoned. Maybe that was where Mr. Malone's call about a white van came in. Lee may not have literally sold his soul in an attempt to cure his disease, but what he had done wasn't far from it.

Lee-Bat was climbing into the sky again, no doubt getting ready to make another pass. There had to be a way to stop him — to stop this *thing* that he had become.

Quickly I looked around, trying to watch Staci and Jennifer as best I could. I looked toward the church just in time to see what looked like Staci's foot shimmying through one of the shattered windows. She was safe, or at least as safe as she could be under the circumstances. At least somebody listened to me.

Jennifer was still running blindly down the street, away from the church, still exposed. Thanks to her high-heeled shoes, she wasn't even making much headway. She would have done better kicking them off, but apparently she was too hysterical to think of that. All of which made her an easy target for Lee-Bat.

The only way to help her was to turn his attention elsewhere. Noise seemed to set him off. My Glock would be loud enough, but I wasn't about to waste any ammunition. I started to shout, trying to be louder than Jennifer.

"Hey, you! Hey, you ugly freak!" I shouted.

Nitro hadn't left my side yet. He started barking again, as if he was somehow attuned to what I was trying to do. A few seconds later, I saw

Lee-Bat swooping back down at full speed — straight at me.

I commanded Nitro to run, hoping he'd obey. Raising my Glock, I took another shot, but Lee-Bat's erratic flight pattern took him out of the way just in time. It also took him from coming at me head-on to swooping down from an angle, faster than I could pivot...

He slammed into me like a freight train, knocking me off my feet. The impact of hitting the pavement never came. It took me a moment to realize Lee-Bat had lifted me up and was flying with me, clutching me with his legs like talons. Not what I had in mind. Neither was the sight of those vampire teeth coming toward me.

I wouldn't say I have a fear of heights, but I do have a healthy fear of falling. I could have shot him at point-blank range, but then we would have both fallen. Barring that, I swung at him with my fists as hard as I could, using the Glock like a club. My attack kept him from biting me, but I wasn't sure if I was doing any damage.

A loud noise thundered through the air. Church bells. Somehow Staci was ringing the bell in the old, abandoned church. The noise made my captor's flight more erratic. Instead of trying to bite me, he used his mouth to screech loudly. Instead of climbing skyward, he came back toward the ground, then up again, then back down.

Right away it hit me. Bats navigate with echolocation, and the pealing of the bells disrupted him. Staci was a genius.

Up and down like a roller coaster, flipping upside down and right-side up. We had yet to drop low enough for me to feel safe in shooting Lee-Bat. I kept punching and yelling, hoping that would further sabotage him.

Lee-Bat flipped upside down again. Amber light flashed onto his furry face. Straining my neck, I looked to see we were heading for the warning sign about the bridge. Cables suspended it top and bottom on either side. The creature pivoted, wings almost perpendicular to the street. He was going to hit the sign. But maybe, just maybe, if he stayed turned this way, and if I could time it right, I'd go between the cables without hitting the sign...

I jammed my legs into his midsection and reached for the cables. They were taut as I grabbed them but went slack almost immediately. At his velocity, Lee-Bat didn't just hit the sign but went straight through it. The cable I clutched was now sagging to the ground, accelerated by my added weight.

Lee-Bat proved the sign's admonition to be true. He had hit the sign, and a second later he hit the bridge at full speed. Even with the church bell still ringing, I thought I heard bones breaking on impact. He seemed to hang there for a second before falling to the street below.

Cautiously I made my way over, Glock in hand. Nitro came up, growling a little. He sensed what I suspected, that the figure on the pavement wasn't long for this world.

Before my eyes, the transformation reversed itself. Lee-Bat was becoming Lee again, although in a much more broken form than he had been in previously. He looked up at me.

"Uncle Dane?" he wheezed.

I wasn't about to correct him this time. "Yeah. It's me."

"What did I do…while I was…?" Every word seemed laborious.

Sirens wailed in the distance now. The church bells finally stopped. Jennifer still screamed somewhere, over and over again.

"You didn't hurt anybody that time."

"I messed up…never should have gone to…" Lee was fading fast.

"Did Janus Labs do this to you?" I asked, hoping he would have time to answer. "But I thought they were shut down?"

"Building ruined…but the people…Dr. Lockhart…Searcy O'Dell…"

I didn't recognize those names, but I filed them away mentally. "So they did this to you?"

"Yeah…but…my fault…I agreed to…the caprinium…"

I recognized *that* word right away. "They dosed you with caprinium? Telling you it would help your cancer?"

"Yeah…didn't tell me…I'd have to drink other people's blood…"

"Is that what happened to the dead man over there?" I knew he was fading fast but wanted to get as much information out of him as I could. "You drank his blood?"

"Yeah…they hoped it would help them…"

"Help them? How?" Every answer made this feel more like a living nightmare.

"The Other Side…portal…Lockhart and his…want to fight them. But they don't know…don't know Searcy O'Dell is…" Lee wheezed. He opened his mouth to speak, but nothing came out. A second later, not even air was coming out.

~~~~~

The paramedics insisted on taking me to the ER at Bloom Memorial for a full examination. Like most people around here, that place made me nervous—it was nicknamed Doom Memorial, after all—but considering what I had been through, I couldn't argue with them. Other than a few bruises, I came out fine.

Staci was there, waiting for me. It was the first time I had seen her since she had ducked into the church. "Just to forewarn you, I already called your mom. She's probably gonna be here in about…" She looked
~~~~~

at the clock on her phone. "...Maybe fifteen minutes now."

I nodded, knowing what to expect. "How freaked out is she? Scale of one to ten."

Her eyebrow jumped. "What, only ten?"

"Got it." I looked at her and thought about how far awry my plans for tonight had gone. "Well-played with the church bells, babe."

She smiled. "Only thing I could think of to do. Thank God it was the old kind where I just had to yank on the rope, and not some electronic controls."

"Well, you saved my life. Thank you."

"You were pretty brave yourself." She looked at her feet for a minute and then back up at me. "They're saying Jennifer had a nervous breakdown. Like her mind just totally snapped. They were taking her to one of the big hospitals in Memphis and I think notifying somebody in her family."

I nodded. "I'd say that's understandable. What about Lee's body?"

"Morgue has it for now, but I've already heard that somebody with federal credentials is trying to commandeer it. I guess because of the Janus Labs connection. Same with the other body."

"Ain't even gonna ask how they knew. They have their ways." I was still wondering about that white van. Maybe they were feds, maybe they weren't.

Staci looked down again, and I suddenly realized that she had looked nervous this whole time. "Mr. Sheriff, I think you dropped something during all that melee."

"Dropped something? Like what?"

"Like this." She held out her hand, cradling the little black box from McCrary's Jewelers. She raised her eyebrows. "Look familiar?"

I started trembling, powerless to control it. I had no clue when it had fallen out of my pocket. "Uh, yes, it does."

One corner of her mouth turned upwards slightly, just barely enough to notice. "You're shaking, Mr. Sheriff."

"I was really hoping you wouldn't notice that."

"And this was something you were planning to do tonight, I take it?"

"Before everything else hit the fan, yeah. But then we got a little — well, sidetracked."

"That's one way to put it," she said, giggling in spite of herself. Regaining her composure, Staci put the box in my hand. "Well, it's still tonight, ain't it?"

I looked around at the hospital corridor. "This wasn't exactly where I had in mind..."

"So what?"

Nodding, I knelt on one knee. "Staci, will you marry me?"

"Gee, I don't know," she said in a teasing tone, tapping her chin and looking as if she was deep in thought. I could imagine what was going through her head: *Let's have a little fun with this. Make him squirm just a little.*

She couldn't keep the facade up for long as a huge smile broke out across her face. "Yes, Dane. Of course, yes!"

After I slid the ring on her finger and we enjoyed a round of kissing that seemed to last forever and yet somehow still not long enough, she cupped my face in her hands and looked me in the eye.

"One request, though."

"What's that?"

She leaned in and whispered almost conspiratorially. "You know, Sardis County is a pretty weird place, right? A place where pretty much anything can take a side trip through the Twilight Zone at any given point?"

"As a matter of fact, now that you mention it, I *have* noticed that..."

Staci raised an eyebrow. "Probably not the greatest setting in the world for our big day, right?"

"Right." Okay, so she wanted to get married somewhere else. That could be arranged.

Staci sighed. "And you know some of the crazy stuff that goes on around here, we never really know how long we actually have, right? I mean, you could have died tonight..."

I wasn't sure if she was thinking about Sardis County or if she was thinking about her first husband, how she had gone from happily married to widowed in the blink of an eye. Either way, she made a valid point. "True."

"So, a long, drawn-out engagement wouldn't really make a whole lot of sense if we're both sure...you *are* sure, right?" Staci bit her bottom lip nervously.

"Sure, I'm sure." I proposed, didn't I? And hadn't we talked about it countless times before this?

"Okay, then. You got anything planned for Friday night? As in, tomorrow?"

I don't know what I had expected her to say, but it certainly wasn't that. "Not that I can think of. Why?"

She smirked mischievously. "All right, Mr. Sheriff, here's my request. Let's elope. Tomorrow night."

After all we had been through, there was no way I was arguing with that. "Deal."

We kissed again, but this time she had her left hand held out from me, toward the door, as if to show the ring. I didn't understand why until I heard Mom's voice — not a screech, but a squeal of excitement.

The End

LOVE SUCKS
Rosemarie DiCristo and Pam Halter

Kedric Blackthorne stood on the doorstep of his parents' Romanian manor and took a deep breath. This was the last place he wanted to be, but he knew if he didn't tell his mother what had happened, he'd hear about it for the next two hundred years.

"Drat and blood curse," he mumbled. "Just get it over with."

He rang the bat-engraved doorbell, which was an actual bell in a widow's peak, and waited. After a couple minutes, he heard the slow, lethargic footsteps of Mother's hump-backed butler, Oleg.

Oleg had been ancient when Kedric was a boy. No idea how old he really was, since he never seemed to age, but he was a loyal servant. Mother often said she didn't know what she'd do without him after his father got beheaded by an angry mob a century ago. He shouldn't have gone to the rainforest on the other side of the world. But that was Father. "I'm faster than any Aztec," he had said. It was the last thing they heard from him until two members of the *Noctem Nostra* showed up with a bag of his ashes.

Kedric had to listen to Mother rant about Father's flaws nonstop for six months. She hardly spent any time in her coffin. Instead, she paced the manor and bemoaned her status of widow. Oleg, ever the faithful servant, brought her bags of blood from area hospitals the entire time.

The creaking door brought Kedric back to the present. Oleg peered through the crack for a moment, then opened the door wider.

"Master Kedric, we weren't expecting you."

"I know, Oleg," Kedric said. "Is Mother in?"

"She is, my master." Oleg closed the door behind them. "She's in her study. Shall I take your suitcase up?"

Kedric nodded. "Thank you."

He waited until Oleg had gone upstairs before heading to his mother's study. It had to be there, didn't it? Mother was the queen of that room. Everything in it reflected her tastes and strengths. He had never won an argument in that room. He bet Father hadn't, either.

The door was slightly ajar, so he tapped on it and went in. Mother looked up from her book and raised her eyebrows. "Home already?"

And here we go. "Yes, Mother. I'm home."

She stared at him.

"All right!" Kedric exclaimed. "I killed another one. I didn't mean to."

"That's what you say every time."

"I really didn't mean to. I *liked* this one." Kedric ran a hand through his hair. "Maybe I should try to find a wife in Iceland."

Mother threw the book on the floor and rose from the chaise lounge. She stood, hands on hips and nostrils flaring. "No, what you *will* do is find a vampire wife. No more human wives. You'll settle down and give me grandchildren!"

He tried another tactic, hoping to soften her. "Mama—"

"Don't you mama me!" she snapped, so miffed her fangs had dropped. "I've been barely living since your father got himself killed. I. Want. Grandchildren. And you will give them to me!"

"Fine," Kedric said through gritted teeth. "But at least let me stay a while and grieve my loss."

Mother snorted. "You are as sentimental as your father." She stared at the fireplace. "You know where your room is."

"Good morn," he said.

She never took her eyes off the fire as he left.

The next evening, Kedric came downstairs and entered the dining room. Mother kept traditional vampire hours, but she still enjoyed a meal of human food instead of a full blood diet. Many vampires her age and older kept the old ways, but not Mother. The one thing Mother liked about Father's travels was the food he brought home for them to try. Kedric didn't know how often she needed blood, but he knew she didn't go out for it anymore. She relied on Oleg for that.

Kedric enjoyed human food so much, he only needed blood once or twice a month. Less if he got fresh beef, cooked *bleu*. It wasn't exactly blood, but close enough to satisfy him. He was able to date to his heart's content, too, because human women loved going out to eat.

Patricia came to his mind. She was his latest wife and his favorite. He worked so hard to be careful with her during sex. But his feelings for her, coupled with the rich, delicious scent of her blood and one too many glasses of wine, got the best of him, and she was gone in just a few minutes. He didn't even have the chance to turn her, or he would have.

"I've been thinking all day," Mother said, gesturing for him to sit. "I think you should use a vampire dating site. Vivian uses them all the time. She can help set up your profile and get you started."

"Great, just what I need. Aunt Vivian's help," Kedric said under his breath as he buttered some toast.

Mother sniffed. "I heard that. But she really is an expert on dating sites. I'll call her later. She has plenty of room in her New York condo. I think we should go there. New territory and all."

New York City. Food capital of the USA. Kedric offered no opposition. And in a city that large, he just might be able to avoid all the women his mother and aunt wanted to throw his way.

Oleg came in with a tray of spinach quiche and raw beef ribs. His favorite. His mother was not even hiding the fact she was trying to soften him. He would just have to stay strong.

After Oleg left the room, Kedric filled his plate. "I really do need time to grieve, Mother. Patricia was the best wife I've ever had. I'll miss her."

~~~~

The one thing Cecelia Ignarra didn't want was a man with mommy issues.

She hunkered down into the comfy old sofa, her face buried in the soft pile hide of Mr. Juggins, her childhood teddy bear. Funny how she always cowered on *this* sofa, and quietly cried into *this* stuffed toy, whenever her heart was broken.

She listened to the rain beating on the patched-up, probably leaking roof, glad she was alone in the house, so she could scream the words, "*No Mommy issues!* Been there, done that, too many times."

Then she sighed so hard, she caused Mr. Juggins' tattered left ear to wiggle.

Why, she wondered, in her many years of dating, did she always-always-always latch onto the losers?

"Well, no more. Take a vow, girl. Show some gumption."

If she ever—ever!—dated again (and after the disaster with Niles, becoming a nun sounded good) she'd follow Cecelia's New Rules for Romance.

No preening metrosexuals. No smarmy egotists with penthouses on Manhattan's Upper East Side. And no, *definitely no*, swaggering jerks boasting of their castles or villas or forty-room mansions.

Unless it was a cool turreted job like that house—Tudor? Victorian? She couldn't remember—in Collinsport, Maine.

Okay, that old TV show was campy as heck, but Cecelia loved it.

Most of the actors on it were hot.

But Cecelia no longer wanted "hot."

She'd had disaster after disaster with men who were "hot."

She wanted an ordinary guy. Someone to stroll the beach with, hand in hand. True, she had the skin type that easily burned, but there were ways around that. *Twilight* strolls along the beach. Moonlight cuddles.

Cuddles. Some kissing. No S-E-X. At least not for a long time into
~~~~

the relationship.

So far, her relationships hadn't lasted long enough, or she wasn't in love enough, for it to happen.

Which was probably for the best.

"Losers! All of them," she growled.

Was it too much to ask for a weathered cottage down the shore instead of something that looked like a designer show-home? Seafood boils in a pit dug in the sand instead of being wined and dined at five-star restaurants? Simple things, like collecting seashells, driftwood, beach glass, with a nice guy? Humble, kind, fantastic sense of humor. The only gorgeous thing about him should be his eyes.

Cecelia loved gazing deep into her man's eyes.

But did such a man exist? Or was it forever the liars and cheaters and boasters and players and... and... and...?

She shouted to the empty house, "I want a soul mate!"

Yeah, right. You are setting yourself up for an impossible dream.

But was she? What if, this time, she took her time? Didn't go for the first guy that caught her eye. Didn't go for looks but for character. What if, for once, there was no rush?

The door opened behind her. She heard him enter, take a couple of steps into the living room, then huff in surprise.

"Yes," she said, "back again. And so soon since my last visit. Want me to cook supper, or will you?"

He didn't answer that, just said the two things he always said when he found Cecelia in his house. "What, again?" and "Cee-Cee, when are you going to give me grandchildren?"

Cecelia squeezed her eyes shut and groaned. *"Dad!"*

~~~~~

Kedric stared at his aunt and mother, who were intently working on his profile for the vampire dating app, *Love Sucks*. They had only arrived at his aunt's home an hour ago, and he was still feeling jet lagged. He mentally shook his head, sipped his brandy-laced coffee, and tried not to snort. Aunt Viv was well known on the vampire dating apps; all twenty-one of them. He sighed to himself. If any of his friends found out he was on one, he'd never recover his cool reputation.

"What's your favorite color?" Aunt Viv asked without looking up from the screen.

"I really don't want to do this," he answered, knowing it would be futile.

Viv snapped her fingers. "Color!!"

Kenric tried one more time. "I don't have one."

His mother and aunt glared at him. He glared back. Mother had
~~~~~

insisted that Oleg come with them, even though Aunt Viv had her own servant, Fenton. He slipped into the room with a charcuterie board and a bowl of steamed shrimp. More of his favorites. Okay, he'd play. He reached for a shrimp. "Now these, I like."

Viv quickly tapped the computer keys. "Good. Favorite food, shrimp. Now, about that favorite color?"

Kedric gave her a one-sided grin and lifted an eyebrow (his right one) which usually undid the human women. He knew it wouldn't work on his aunt, but it did make him laugh when she screeched her frustration at him. Complete with spittle and fangs. Oh, how he loved to make his mother's and aunt's fangs drop. And how he missed laughing with his father over it, as Father was the one who taught Kedric how to do it.

"Roxana," Viv said turning to his mother. "You're going to have to do something. If you want grandchildren at all, that is."

Kedric filled a plate with cheese and olives. He nodded to Oleg, who poured him a glass of Pinot Noir. After all the centuries, he still couldn't decide if his mother and her sister were engaging or annoying, but they were always entertaining. He really should take notes and try his hand at a novel.

He sighed. "Red, all right? Dark red, like blood."

"*Red???*" Aunt Viv screeched. "You're a hopeless case. I'm going to fill in what I know vampire women want."

Kedric took a sip of wine. He gazed at the firelight through it, sparkly and red. It really was his favorite color, but he wasn't going to tell Vivian that. "Whatever."

An hour later, Aunt Viv pronounced his profile finished. "And now we upload." A pause. "There! All done!"

Kedric looked up from the novel he hadn't been reading. "What happens now?"

"Well, you can either wait for women to contact you or you can do some searching of your own. I can show you how."

"No, I'll wait," he said. With any luck, he wouldn't get noticed or contacted.

Ping!

"What was that?" he asked, startled.

Mother and Aunt Viv both jumped up from their seats. "Your first contact!" Aunt Viv exclaimed. "Let's see." She touched the screen. "Looks like it's just a wink. That's a good start, though."

Before Kedric could ask ...

Ping!

Ping!

Ping!

"Oooooooooooooh!" Mother and Viv squealed together.

Ping!

Ping!

Ping!

It was going to be a long night.

~~~~~

Cecelia waited until her father was seated on the sofa opposite hers before saying, "I didn't come for a lecture."

Max Ignarra crossed his arms against his chest, his lips forming the same indulgent smile he used to wear when she was a child and raced to the mirror every morning, hoping her grown-up fangs had come in. "Let me guess. Another failed love affair."

"Dad! That's a lecture!"

"No. It's a statement. Okay, Cee-Cee. Then why did you come home again?"

Home.

Cecelia had lived, alone, in her townhouse overlooking the Long Island Sound in the Throggs Neck section of the Bronx for years now. Scattered throughout the working-class community were a small group of vampires who chortled at the idea of living in a place with "neck" in the name.

But Max had delighted in raising Cecelia in the Queens neighborhood called "Sunnyside." Their little home was typical of all city houses, laid out on an ordinary 25x100' plot of land, but with a large yard teeming with flowers. Cecelia loved every bit of it. It reminded her of her idyllic childhood… and her mom, whose presence still filled every room.

But there was only one reason she returned to stay, nowadays.

When she didn't answer her father, he smirked and added, "Did you come for a delicious meal and the fine company? I guess you didn't get that from Lance Romance. Oh! Maybe you wanted a good night's sleep in your comfy old bed, and a kiss from Mr. Juggins. Don't wanna *think* about what you got from Lance—"

Cecelia's lips tightened. "Aargh! Dad! If I didn't love you to pieces—and I'm seriously starting to wonder *why*—I'd never, ever put up with…"

But Max was grinning broadly, so Cecelia sighed and ducked her head.

He tipped his own head toward her. "Hah, I can see that smile you're trying to hide."

She gave up and let him see the smile. But it was partly wistful.
~~~~~

"I love you too, baby," Max said. "I want the best for you. And do you agree the guys you've been with are not even close to being 'meh'?"

She sighed again from the bottom of her toes, then nodded.

"That's why I'm taking the bull by the horns." He stood, then gestured for her to follow.

"Ugh, Dad, can you try not to use such ridiculously cliched—"

"You know it's one of the things you love about me. C'mon."

They entered his den, he fired up his laptop, typed in a URL, and stepped back.

She stared at the screen, then stared some more. "Okay, fine; I get it. You'd like me to try a dating site. It even might work, maybe. Weed out the rats, maybe. Help me find guys who are simpatico, maybe. But..." She looked at the header on the website again and barely kept the scorn from her voice. "*Love Sucks*???"

"Haven't you had enough of those human losers?" Max asked her. "It's past time you dated one of us."

~~~~~

Cecelia sat for nearly an hour, hunched forward, chin in her hands, elbows on her knees, scowling at her chuckling dad as he typed in what he thought her answers to the questions should be.

She was not going to give him the satisfaction of providing them.

Not that he cared.

Besides, he knew her so well, he could answer the questions exactly as she would.

"Done!" Max sat back and beamed his satisfaction.

She shot him her thundercloud look. "Doesn't mean I'm gonna get results."

His face softened. "Honey, why don't you like to date vamps?"

"Oh, I don't know; they're pale, they're mouthy—in more ways than one—they're flat-out, undeniably cold—in more ways than one."

Max sighed.

"And here's the biggie, Dad: most of *them* want human girls. It's rare for *any* vamp, let alone a halfway decent one, to respond to—"

Ping!

They looked at each other, then Max grinned a gigantic grin. "I hear Friday night the weather will be glorious. Perfect date night, and sometimes it's good to decide fast." He moved to tap the screen.

"Wait!"

He frowned at her. "C'mon, kiddo, no excuses."

"I will if you will."

"What?"

"Gotta get *you* a lady, Dad. You been alone way too long. Are you
~~~~~

having any fun?"

He looked down at his hands, and when he replied, his voice was unusually serious. "You know your mom was the only gal for me."

Cecelia nodded. "But it's been nearly a hundred years. And I know Moms would've wanted you to move on. Please, Daddy? Let me do a profile for you."

"If this is just an excuse to delay looking at your match..."

She shook her head. "I mean it. I will if you will." She gave Max a playful shove, then took his place before his computer.

It took her less time than it took him to do the profile, just like it took even less time for his profile to get the *ping!*

"What say, Cee-Cee, we check out *their* profiles, your match and mine?"

She huffed out a, "Sure, why not?"

Max looked at his potential vampire date first, then Cecelia (reluctantly) looked at hers.

"Not bad," she admitted. Maybe she would message the guy back. Maybe.

"Not like your Moms," he said about his match. "But no. Not bad." Then he grinned his face-splitting grin. "This might actually work out fine. If we go to dating events together — and there are a bunch, honey, in case this one doesn't work out — I can keep an eye on those losers you usually attract and give each one the heave-ho before you get enamored."

"Aargh! Dad! Why? Why do I bother? *Why?*"

"Because you said it yourself; you love me to pieces." He looked at his match again. "So, how about it? Friday night, first date for both of us? If they're willing, of course."

She had to un-grit her teeth before saying, "Fine. But *no way* are we double-dating or doing anything of the sort."

But Friday night when she entered the *Tad's* in Times Square (where the steaks were grilled right before you, so you could get one super-bloody-rare), she saw not her date (yet) but her dad and a chubby woman with bleached blond hair and a screaming-pink velvet jumpsuit, at the table along the rear wall.

~~~~~

Kedric paced the condo bedroom. He had put an old phonograph on but could still hear his aunt and mother talking over *Peer Gynt Suite*. Well, Aunt Viv shrieking louder than *In the Hall of the Mountain King*! The whole way up the staircase. He braced himself.

"Kedric Blackthorne, you come out of there this instant!"

With a loud sigh, Kedric turned off the music and opened the door.
~~~~~

"Aunt Viv! How nice to see you!"

She glared at him so hard, her eyes were practically red. From bursting blood vessels. He chuckled. He couldn't help it. She had been asking every day for almost two weeks, demanding to know which vampiress he was going to take out first.

"If you do not choose a date *right now*, I'm going to break all your wine bottles and slash all your suits!" she snarled.

Kedric shrugged. His suits and wine were safely in Romania.

She put her hands on her hips. "Did you even *look* at any of the women who winked at you?"

"Let's see," he said, stretching out his answer for ten seconds. "Nope. Not a one."

Viv gave him an even fiercer stink-eye, turned, and stomped down the stairs. "I'm booking a flight and heading to your wine cellar."

"Ha! As if you could."

She got a smug grin on her face. Just the tip of her fangs showed. *Uh oh.*

"Remember my friend, Elon?"

Drat! She would do it, too. "Wait," he said. "I'm coming."

Fifteen minutes later, Kedric Blackthorne, widower, had a date for Friday night.

~~~~~

Cecelia had gotten only that one *ping!*

Max had gotten twelve.

She tried not to let it bother her that a centuries-old vampire with a paunch and a receding hairline had gotten so much more interest than a ... what? A Cecelia-type?

She wasn't pretty. Every man she'd met made that clear, and she didn't need to see her reflection to know it was true. Making peace with that was a struggle, because who was she kidding? In a culture so focused on "beauty," making peace with "plain" was nearly impossible.

Her date—a vamp named Skye, with white-blond hair, ice-blue eyes, and astounding good looks—said only one thing when he slid into the seat opposite hers at one of *Tad's* orange plastic tables, "You look way different than your profile pic."

"Photoshop," she mumbled and cursed her father for his techie wizardry that had actually made her look stunning.

What was he thinking? What was *she* thinking? Didn't they realize that as soon as her date saw the real her, he'd vamoose?

Surprisingly, this one didn't. Skye Lafreniere stayed for the *Tad's* steak, salad, and baked potato, using his hunk of super-duper garlic bread (one good thing about him; he seemed to like garlic as much as
~~~~~

she did) to sop up all the blood escaping his super-duper-rare T-bone. Then he said he had to go.

"Previous commitment, can't break it, this has been nice, yeah, but you're not the one."

They'd agreed to Dutch treat. The last two humans Cecelia dated expected her to pay. Fool that she was, she did.

Maybe it was something in her face, because now Skye patted his pockets, then cursed. "I seem to have left the wallet at home. Could you possibly…?"

She shrugged and waved for him to go.

"I'll pay you back."

Yeah. They never did.

Maybe it was because it happened so often that Cecelia just shrugged again and chowed down the rest of her meal.

Or maybe it was because of *who* she chose that it happened so often. Guys named Skye? Niles? And then there was Allistair, Wynton, and Tybalt.

Who the heck was named Tybalt, outside of Shakespearean characters?

Maybe if I just once dated a Harvey or a Murray or a Fred, I'd find a kind soul.

What was in a name? Maybe everything. Maybe nothing.

If she ever got serious, it would be with a guy whose name was not so chi-chi.

<div style="text-align:center">~~~~~</div>

Kedric got to *Stoker's* fifteen minutes before the arranged meeting time with — what was her name again? Cloris something. Why did he let Aunt Viv pick? Because Pinot Noir. All his lovely bottles of Pinot Noir. He ordered a glass from the albino bartender.

He had only taken one sip when he caught sight of her walking through the entrance. Was it too late to run away?

Alas, she saw him. "Kedric!" she squealed. Her bright blue high heels clicked on the wooden floor as she walked in double-time toward him with her hands outstretched. "We meet at last!" She punctuated that with a giggle.

Gag.

He rose to his feet. "It's nice to meet you, too. Let's see if our table is ready."

They followed the host. Cloris walked in front of Kedric, who was now really wishing he could turn around and run for the door. He made the mistake of looking at her skintight dress. It was the same color blue as her shoes and had a very large copper zipper that went from the top of her neck to just above her backside. Dear bats and glory, could she be any more suggestive?

Gag, again.

Kedric was impressed by the menu, though. This was his first time at *Stoker's*, but he'd heard about it. The best new restaurant in Sunset Park, the vampire section of Brooklyn, although the humans had no idea. Too bad Patricia wasn't here with him. How he missed her company and her love. He smiled as he read the specials. Patricia would have ordered the shrimp scampi, just to tease him about the garlic. Which, of course, was a hoax many humans believed warded off vampires.

That decided it. Shrimp scampi it would be for him tonight.

Cloris ordered raw oysters, spicy nacho soup, a filet mignon cooked *bleu*, and a large tequila on the rocks. No, no. No lime for her. She drank her tequila (batting her eyes) *au natural*. She kept those eyes fixed on him as she slurped the oysters and the tequila. Then, after half a bowl of soup, she unzipped the zipper on the front of her dress (it matched the back) to almost her navel and fanned herself with the wine menu. "Oh my, that soup is *spicy!*"

And she *talked*. Kedric tuned her out after the first ten minutes. He ordered a second glass of wine and looked around the restaurant as Cloris slurped and talked and fanned. Most people were enjoying themselves. Except him, and maybe that young woman at the table to his left, diagonally. Poor kid. Her date had his back to Kedric, but he could clearly see the pained expression on *her* face.

Right before he looked away, she glanced at him. Her eyes widened and she flushed, which changed her plain face entirely into something quite lovely. He lifted his glass toward her. She gave him a small smile. Then they both turned their attention back to their dates.

~~~~

"No luck?" Max plopped down on the now-empty seat across from Cecelia.

"Where's Ms. Velvet P.J.'s?" she asked.

"Her name's Rhonda, and it was a whatchamacallit." He swallowed. "Gone."

"She didn't like you?"

Max's eyes narrowed. "*I* didn't like *her*. Oh, don't get me wrong. She's a sweetheart. But she's not your mom." He paused and asked again, "No luck?"

"No, Dad. Zilch. Zippo. Zero."

He squeezed her hand. "You'll find someone, honey. There's a cover for every pot."

In spite of her melancholy, she laughed at yet another cliché.
~~~~

"Listen, sweetie, we were both disappointed tonight. How about I treat you to a *Stoker's* chocolate mousse?"

Her lip twisted. The last three times her dad had treated her to that chocolate mousse — they served it with raspberry coulis — he'd wanted to cajole her into something. But she wouldn't be twenty pounds overweight if she wasn't a sucker for the fantastically rich, marvelously dense (more fudge-like than airy) hunk of dark chocolate topped with a splash of raspberry liqueur. Oh, and the house-made whipped cream.

Her mouth watered at the thought of it. "Sure, *Stoker's* it is."

After all, something had to go right tonight.

~~~~~

Stoker's was filled with its usual A-List wanna-be crowd.

At least Cecelia and Max were dressed for it.

Too bad the only times she'd been there were with her father.

"And speaking of pots…" Max's eyes lit up.

"Are you still on about covers and pots?" Cecelia had been glancing around the restaurant, seeing all the happy people and their dates… which made her voice sound sharper than she meant to.

At least the mousse was luscious.

Her dad had already finished his. But he always was a gobbler. "There's this new cooking-related dating thing-a-ma-jiggy that I know you'll love. *Zesty Bites — Hungry For Love*. It's on—" He stopped suddenly, scrutinizing her.

"It's on what?"

He shook his head.

"Dad!"

He said distinctly, "It's on target to be the funnest experience you've ever had."

"*Funnest?*" Max was hiding something, but Cecelia didn't care. "No." She looked away in disgust and caught sight of a man at a nearby table. He was staring moodily at the large crystal chandelier.

For a moment Cecelia's heart stopped.

He was gorgeous… and exactly her type.

Huh.

Gorgeous.

And exactly her type.

"No, Cecelia," she muttered aloud. *You've taken a vow.*

"Well, then, Cee-Cee, there's loads of *other* dating thing-a-ma-jiggies you can try."

She turned back to her father.

Max's eyes were merry. "I will if you will."

She had to look away again, before the ecstasy of the mousse *and*
~~~~~

her wussy-ness made her agree.

Big mistake.

Gorgeous Guy was looking at *her*.

She wanted to look away, but something in his eyes made her think, despite the Super Babe he was with, he knew something of her misery. And not just today's, but every day's.

What? How could that be?

He raised his glass to her. She gave him her usual weak smile—oh, yeah, that'll turn him on—and quickly looked away.

Max was waiting for her answer.

Her sigh was heavy. "How about I invite the next guy who responds to my profile to your place, where you can chaperone us while I cook for him?"

"I guess so. Maybe. Your cooking would be the way to any man's heart."

Cecelia nodded. "That way, I can *plan* how much I'll get stuck paying. And with coupons and sale items, I promise you, it won't be much."

~~~~~

"I want to hear everything!" Aunt Viv cried the second he walked through the door.

Kedric went to the sideboard and poured himself a cup of coffee. He splashed a bit of brandy into it.

"Well?" his mother added.

He took a sip, turned, and smiled at them. "It was horrific. Aunt Viv, I'll be making the choices from now on."

Viv gave him a smug smile. "That's fine, dear. Just fine. You keep me posted." She turned to her sister. "Roxana, what about lunch tomorrow? You haven't been out at all since you got here."

Kedric's mother gave her a tight smile. "As long as by lunch, you mean a midnight meal."

Viv laughed. "Of course, darling! It's New York City! Awake all night. Ta-ta for now! I have a date myself." She snatched up her purse and was out the front door before Kedric could take another sip of his coffee.

"Whatever you do," his mother said. "Do not let her get *me* on a dating app."

Kedric snorted into his cup.

~~~~~

After five weeks of wining and dining women from *Love Sucks*, Kedric rebelled. "I'm done!" he shouted at Aunt Viv. "Besides the wasted money, my time is worth something. Are there only voluptuous women on this app who are blatantly obvious that what they want is my money and my body?"

Viv sniffed. "Why is that a problem? Don't you like sex?"

Kedric rolled his eyes. "I can't believe you asked me that." He turned to his mother. "Don't you have anything to say?"

Roxana set her coffee cup down. "Well now, I have nothing to say about my son's sex life, if that's what you're asking. But surely, there's more to a dating app than taking women out to dinner."

"Yes!" Viv exclaimed. "Dating apps offer all kinds of opportunities."

Kedric groaned. "More?"

"You mentioned your time," Viv said. "I know just the thing. *Speed Dating!*"

"Speed dating? What kind of torture is that?" Kedric asked.

Viv gave a giggle. "It's *so* fun! I've done it lots of times. I can't believe I didn't think of it before." She scrolled quickly. "Here. I'll sign you up for tomorrow night!"

Kedric groaned again.

Viv raised her eyebrows. "What's wrong? Too soon?

"Definitely," he said. "Can't I wait a week?"

"Of course, darling. You can wait a week."

Kedric felt nauseous. Viv had given in way too easily. This was going to be worse than he could imagine.

~~~~~

Robb—spelled with two "b's," not one, but otherwise a blessedly ordinary name—liked Cecelia's profile and suggested they meet at *Golden Corral*.

Despite her plan to cook for Next Guy, Cecelia liked being able to easily binge-eat when this date went wrong, so she agreed. They paid in advance, separately, to her delight.

Robb-with-two-b's was nice—nice looking, nice personality, nice laugh—and he ate as much of the huge buffet as she did.

More, actually. When Cecelia got ready for dessert, Robb still chowed down on food.

"You're gonna finish that, right?" she asked. "They charge for everything not eaten."

"No problemo," he said through a mouthful of steak tartare.

She took her time pondering which of the many luscious desserts she'd choose, wondering if pigging out on four would turn Robb off.

Well, he has to know sometime.

When she returned with *five* desserts, he'd finished his food and sat there, hands folded on the table.
~~~~~

"No dessert for you, Robb?"

"No. I'll enjoy watching you eat."

That was odd, but not as much of a deal-breaker as the "No problemo" might be.

It was when they were leaving the restaurant that the actual deal-breaker came.

"Let's do this again," Robb said, just as the *Golden Corral* employee by the door stopped them.

"Ma'am? Can I look inside your bag?"

"Huh? Sure." Cecelia handed him her big cloth shopping bag.

Frowning, Door Guy pulled out *all* the food that had been on Robb's plate, now neatly contained in four plastic take-out tubs.

"I'm afraid we'll have to—" Door Guy began, but Cecelia hollered, "It was him! I've been framed!" Leaving the food (and bag) in Door Guy's hand, Cecelia dashed into the bus just pulling to the curb.

When it got to the next stop, her dad hopped on, out of breath, and tossed her now food-less bag at her. "Thanks to my cellphone pics of him stealing that food," Max puffed, "latest loser's in a kind of *Golden Corral* jail or—ha! corral."

"You were there?" Her words clinked like ice cubes falling into an empty glass.

"With my date."

"Sure." Her words were no warmer. "The same place as me. Again. And this one…?"

"I'm not like her Gregor; she's not like my Annie." He peered at her. "You plenty mad at me, or only a little?"

"I don't know," she said honestly. "But you gotta stop following me."

"I wanna make sure you're safe." He slipped an arm around her. "Chin up, Cee-Cee. There's someone out there for you. But ya gotta believe."

Catch phrase of the 1973 New York Mets. Cecelia and her dad were there for every game.

She shrugged away. "The Mets lost that World Series in seven games. After blowing Game Six."

They rode the rest of the way home in silence.

~~~~~

Cecelia got another response to her profile.

"Hoo boy, this one's a Mets fan," Max said, looking over her shoulder. "Is that a sign or what?"

She slammed shut the laptop and scowled at him.

"No, no, honey, you really gotta—"
~~~~~

"If you say 'believe,' I'll drive a shattered wooden baseball bat shard through your heart."

"Go." Max smirked at her. "What I was going to say was, go."

"Fine. Now *you* go. Out of the room. Leave me a little privacy."

The Mets fan's name was Steven—with a "v," not a "ph"—so, totally ordinary. He looked nice enough. Light brown hair, brown eyes, glasses. Preppy, not super-hot male-model. She agreed to meet him at Citi Field for Mets vs. Braves. A night game, of course.

Max got three more responses. Cecelia was so certain he'd take one to the game, too, that when he didn't mention it, she asked.

He sadly shook his head. "I think I'm done with this, Cee. None of them seem anything like your mom."

She was half glad, half sad he'd no longer follow her around. "You sure? I really want you to be happy."

"Who says I'm not?" he countered. When she opened her mouth to respond, he said, "Hon, if the lady's right for me, it'll happen, and yeah, maybe I'll be over the moon. But I'm not gonna force it. Now you go to that Mets game. Us versus the Braves? Yell your lungs out!"

Cecelia nodded. Yelling her lungs out would be a terrific test to see if this Steven person was the one.

He wasn't.

First off, he brought his food to the ballpark. Which was okay, considering the high prices and 'meh' quality. But Steven's supper was spinach leaves with cubes of leathery-looking tofu, plus some kind of mineral drink, both in green-reusable containers.

That wasn't a deal-breaker. Hey, Cecelia could do eating healthy. But Steven Sloane (Steven, not Steve) did not cheer once. Or boo. Or clap, yell, or react. He just sat silently through the hits and runs and errors *and* the between-innings games.

It was during Dance Cam that Cecelia, fed up and wanting to get *some* reaction from Steven, stood and danced her booty off, shaking it to and fro, pumping her arms, throwing her head back, singing a nonsensical "Yah-yah-yah."

The whole point of Dance Cam was to get enough applause from the fans to win a T-shirt, and the fans clamored louder for Cecelia than anyone… until the Cam focused on a paunchy, balding man who shook his gigantic booty even harder, tapped and bobbed and weaved and twirled, even doing that weird fingers-across-his-eyes thing that Adam West as Batman did on the old TV show.

Cecelia gulped and stopped dead, meaning her next shot on Dance Cam got only boos. But Max's next shot got an ovation worthy of a 9th inning Game 7 World Series walk-off home run. When he was declared the winner, *two* women rushed to his side and embraced him, each kissing a cheek.

Cecelia glanced at Steven.

His face was as impassive as ever.

"Aren't you going to say anything?" she asked.

He stood, brushing imaginary crumbs from his neatly pressed beige chinos. "I always leave in the 5th inning. Traffic, you know. Will you be okay going home alone?"

"I will be fine going home alone." *As long as we never see each other again.*

Vamps could sometimes mind-meld. Steven nodded. "It's not going to work, is it?"

Cecelia shook her head.

"I'm sorry," he said.

"Me, too."

And then he left.

When she met a newly T-shirted Max at the Home Run Apple outside Citi Field, Cecelia's voice was snarky. "Just had to take in a Mets game, did you?"

His smile was loving-Dad. "Had to make sure New Guy wasn't a creep."

She didn't smile back as she started toward the subway. "He wasn't."

"Just not the one?"

"No." She added tightly, "And please stop following me around."

"Okay, if that's what you want."

She still didn't put any warmth in her voice. "It is. I'm how many hundreds of years old? I don't need Daddy taking care of me."

His eyes said, *Maybe you do.* But he kept quiet as they climbed the subway stairs.

Finally she asked, "What happened to the Kiss-Kiss Twins?"

"Who?"

"Those women—"

"Oh." He said nothing else.

"Let me guess. Not like Moms?"

"Have no idea. I didn't try to find out. Do you really think I'd want ladies who kiss strangers from Dance Cam?"

The train pulled in.

"Do not get on the same train with me, Dad. I mean it. And I'm going back to my place. For good. I'm plenty mad at you this time."

As the subway doors closed, Max asked, "Who you really mad at, Cecelia?"

~~~~~

Kedric tried to pay attention to the instructions. He really did. But every woman he saw standing in the lines looked no different to him than the ones he had been meeting for dinner. Even the ones who weren't dressed to the nines.

He sat at a small table in a row of small tables, which was one row of several. Women had lined up on the right side of the rows. They gave off vibes like runners waiting for the signal to start a race.

A bell rang, jerking him out of his thoughts. The women sprang into action, sprinting to the tables where the men sat.

"Hi!"

A young vampiress slid into the seat in front of him. She wore cargo pants and a military style, death-green jacket over a white tank top. Kedric sat up straight.

"Hi. Hello." What was he saying? It didn't seem to matter to her.

"I'm Kally, well, Kallirena, but I don't really like that," she said in a huff.

"Kedric."

"Wow! Our names both start with K!" She pulled the band out of her ponytail and shook out her thick, dark brown hair. "That gives us a connection, don't you think?"

Kedric sat, not knowing what to do next. "Um ..."

No problem for Kally. "I like snails, *escargot*, riding roller coasters, and arm wrestling!"

"You arm wrestle?"

She gave a short shrill laugh. "No! I like going to arm wrestling *matches!*"

Again, Kedric sat silent. Then he jumped when the bell rang.

In two seconds, literally, another woman plopped down into the chair across from him, and it started all over again.

After about twenty minutes, Kedric was about to get up and walk out when a commotion started down the far end of the row of small tables behind him. The speed dating paused as everyone looked. A young woman, clearly distraught, had leaped up from her chair. Her face was flushed.

And familiar.

~~~~~

Cecelia was halfway through watching *The Shop Around the Corner* — in her opinion, the most romantic movie ever — when the phone rang.

"Speed dating."

"Dad. I'm pretty sure I stopped talking to you." She raised the TV's volume instead of muting it, but she could still clearly hear Max.

"Speed dating."

"Dad! I'm not talking to you!"

"You are, just by saying 'I'm not talking.'"

Cecelia gritted her teeth *and* huffed out her anger.

Max's voice was merry. "Is a sigh talking? To me, yeah, it's a form of —"

"Why?"

He replied without hesitating. "Because maybe speed dating's the modern version of finding someone like your favorite movie's 'Dear Friend.'"

"The far inferior remake, *You've Got Mail*, was the modern version... Never mind. *Why?*"

"It's three strikes until you're out."

"I've had my three strikes," she reminded him.

"It's four balls and you're on base."

She wanted to clonk herself in the head with the phone. "That doesn't even make sense. And my balls were all bad."

"If you're the pitcher. Maybe you're the batter. Ever think of that?"

She sighed. Again. "Will you be there?"

"Heck no; I gave it up, remember?"

"I meant as a nudge."

"No, pumpkin. Not even in the vicinity. Promise."

Cecelia agreed just to shut him up.

At least speed dating will be fast.

~~~~~

She entered the room with a positive attitude. What? Fifty guys to mix with? There had to be one with the potential to be The One.

She lined up with the other women, glancing around. But, holy hemoglobin! Most of the men seemed no different than the cocky, all-too-shallow types she'd been dating. Oh, and there were humans there, too. Well, why not? Her last few vamp dates had been disasters.

The moderators jabbered on about the rules, but only one seemed important to Cecelia: the gal picked the guy. So, she focused on an ordinary-looking human that might not get too much interest — shy-looking, with light-brown hair, blue eyes, and a slightly large nose — and quickly got in his line.

As Cecelia studied the other women, she felt glad it wasn't guys-pick-gals. Most of her competition had one lock of their long, slightly curled hair placed carefully over each shoulder. Most had eyelashes fluffier than caterpillars. Most wore eye shadow so thick, Cecelia figured it took them an hour to chip it off at night. And most wore mini-dresses
~~~~~

with pumps whose stiletto heels could double as stakes through the heart. *Not* a good image considering who most of the contestants were.

She wore just a coating of Avon Buttercrunch lip gloss and a flowery band to keep her wildly curling chin-length sandy hair under control. Her pale-blue denim skirt she'd picked for comfort, and her little beige fringed suede booties solely for style. But her blouse!

Cecelia moaned. The toothpaste dribble on her tummy that had *looked* washed off an hour ago had dried and was clearly visible against the maroon fabric.

She didn't think, *Could this get any worse?* Because it always did.

Then a bell rang, and the women hustled to the mini-tables.

So that's it? We charge to them? Ridiculous. Humiliating. But Cecelia did it anyway.

She sat before the guy she'd picked, then opened her mouth to say… what? She had no idea. "So…I…"

Human Guy #1 was staring open-mouthed at the gal at the next table—a tall, svelte blond in a skintight crop top and—what were they called now? Not hot pants or Daisy Dukes, right? No matter. Crop Top caught his gaze and dropped her fangs, coyly, for just a moment, and Human Guy gave out a soft yelp.

"Seriously?" Cecelia said.

Human Guy didn't react.

Let's see; I've already had my strike three, so what's left? Ball four as a batter? No. I'm done cooperating. She slapped both hands on the table and purred, "I vant to bite your neck."

That got Human Guy's attention, so she repeated it, adding, "And I vant you to bite mine with zee tiny leetle teeth in your human head." Then she stared a vampire stare at him.

His gaze dropped as he frantically looked at what was obviously his list of questions. "Um, what was the most daring thing you've ever done? Er, no, maybe not."

Cecelia *stared* at him until the bell rang.

Human Guy #2 had short dark hair, a muscle tee, and jeans that looked painted on. Ugh. But what the hey? She was taking Max's bull by the horns and driving it straight to the matador.

This guy *also* ogled a gal at the next table, and this gal was something else. Chalk-white skin that had to be makeup, black lips, long black hair with—no! a white streak in it!—and a shroud whose neckline plunged to the girl's belly. Not that any man was looking at her belly.

Cecelia cleared her throat, but that didn't get Human Guy #2's attention, so she leaned forward to say, "Bleh, bleh, bleh."

He blinked at her.

She pointed at Plunging Neckline. "I can't give you *that*, but you gotta be looking for vampire stereotypes, right? So, bleh, bleh, bleh."

She repeated it until the bell rang.

The third guy, a vampire, gazed—no, panted—at a big-breasted babe (she had to be a 46-Triple-D) who reminded Cecelia of that woman who charged onto baseball fields in the 1970s to literally throw herself at a player.

"What?" Cecelia asked The Panter. "You'd rather be talking to Morganna the Kissing Bandit?"

He cocked his head at her.

"Surely you're old enough to remember her. No? Google it. I am so done here."

She stood.

"Hey… the bell didn't ring," Panter said.

Cecelia got the feeling he didn't care she was leaving, he just didn't know what else to say. She did. In fact, she bellowed, "Ding!"

By now most everyone in the room was staring at her, but she got a shivery feeling that someone was watching her in a different way. She turned, then froze. It was Gorgeous Guy from *Stoker's*, and once again his expression made it seem he understood—no, *knew*—her misery. She felt her face soften. Then he nodded at her and lifted his right eyebrow.

Ugh.

What was he going to do next? Wink at her? Click his tongue? Do that double-pointing thing where he pretended both index fingers were guns?

"No," she snarled toward him. Then, louder, as she strode for the exit: "No, no, no, no, no." When she got to the heavy steel door, she turned and shouted back, "Cecelia has left the building!"

Whether he heard her over the noise of the resuming speed dating, she didn't know. Whether it would make him think her crazy, she neither knew nor cared. She hoped *all of them* thought her crazy. Maybe then they'd leave her alone.

Oh, wait. Most of them already were.

Love was hard.

~~~~~

The look the woman gave Kedric was pure loathing. What had he done? He felt her pain. He had never met her, yet he felt a kinship with her.

He had to shake it off. But as he turned back to the ancient vampiress sitting across from him, there was more commotion.

"Cecelia has left the building!"

The door slammed and the room went silent for about ten seconds.
~~~~~

Then the speed dating resumed. Granny gave him a toothless grin.

"No," he said. "No, no, no, no, no!"

He stood, pushed in the chair, and walked calmly to the door. Then he turned and said to the room, "Kedric has also left the building."

No one seemed to notice.

Once outside, he looked up and down the street, hoping to see "Cecelia" so he could catch up to her and apologize. Still no idea what he had done to earn a stink-eye that rivaled his mother's, but he wanted to apologize anyway.

She was nowhere to be seen, so he called Uber to take him back to Aunt Viv's condo. Sure, there would be questions to answer and hell to pay, but he was putting his foot down. No more dating app. No more speed dating. No more anything.

He needed a vacation.

~~~~~

Max took one look at Cecelia's face and gathered her in his arms.

"Daddy, no more, okay? If it's going to happen, it'll happen."

"Okay, pumpkin. No more. Let it happen." He kissed the top of her head. "Hey, what say we get away from it all for a bit, huh? How'd you like to take a cruise?"

~~~~~

"You didn't give it a chance!" Viv screeched.

"Kedric! After all Viv has done to help you!" His mother's tone echoed her sister's.

Kedric stared into the gas fireplace flames. He tightened his lips and refused to get drawn into an argument.

Oleg brought Kedric a tray of stuffed grape leaves while Fenton offered small skewers of marinated raw lamb with cherry tomatoes to Viv. It had turned out, Oleg and Fenton were old buddies and got along famously. And they had been cooking all kinds of food to the point where Viv had begged them to stop. "My figure, you know."

Kedric took a grape leaf and set it on his plate. "What do you think, Oleg?"

The servant just lifted his non-existent eyebrows.

Kedric sighed. "I need a vacation."

His mother huffed. "You're in New York City! Isn't this enough for you?"

But Kedric wasn't taking the bait. He was tired. Which was a rare thing for him. For any vampire. "I'm going to lay down."

He couldn't relax. Even through the closed bedroom door, he could hear Mother's and Aunt Viv's voices. What were they up to? He dreaded finding out.

~~~~~

The next evening, Kedric opened the door and listened. He heard noise coming from the kitchen, but that was Oleg and Fenton preparing the evening's break-fast. Ah, coffee. Kedric took a deep breath and stepped out of the bedroom.

Aunt Viv's condo was plush and comfortable. That meant thick rugs, as well as comfy furniture. Kedric walked silently through the living room to the dining room and poured himself a cup from the waiting carafe.

As he spooned a poached egg over his corned beef hash, his mother walked in.

"Good evening, dear," she said.

"What are you up to?" Kedric asked.

"Up to? I'm hungry." She asked Oleg for a cup of tea and a toasted English muffin and sat down with a bowl of fresh plum slices. She stabbed a slice and lifted it. "Viv and I talked most of the afternoon. We've agreed you need more time."

That surprised him. "Really? I'm glad." He pushed the sugar bowl toward her. "Thank you. I do appreciate it."

"Yes, well, I suppose I wouldn't want anyone forcing me to date and your father has been gone for decades." She shrugged as she sprinkled sugar over her plums.

Viv strolled into the room. "You need a vacation? I have just the thing! A cruise."

Kedric frowned. "Cruise? What kind of cruise?"

"Don't sound so suspicious, darling." Viv poured a cup of coffee. "It's an October themed cruise! The ship heads to New England where it will stop in Salem, Massachusetts for a witch hunt and trial reenactment. You can actually get in on the hunt, if you like. I went once, you know, and it was fabulous!"

"But—" Kedric tried to interrupt.

"And on the way back, it will go up the Hudson to Sleepy Hollow for some Headless Horseman fun!"

"Sounds perfect," his mother exclaimed.

"It does sound perfect … and suspicious," Kedric said. "What's the catch?"

Viv sat down across from him. "Tsk, tsk. Why would there be a catch? You need a vacation, this sounds fun, and I've already booked our tickets and rooms."

"Aunt Viv!"

"Now, now, my dear nephew. I'm not as unfeeling as you think. Let's just go and have some fun, yes?"
~~~~~

~~~~~

Cecelia wrenched away from her father. "A *cruise*? A Love-Boat, singles-magnet—"

"No, no…"

"—despicably-cliched, are-you-kidding-me *cruise*?"

"No, no. No. It's that small boat that goes up to Cape Ann."

Her suspicion was so strong, it nearly knocked him back five feet.

Max held up his hands. "But let's not talk about it on the doorstep, Cee-Cee. Let's go inside."

She didn't move one skinch.

"Cecelia." His tone was no-nonsense. "You came to me, not the other way around. If you want to go home, then go." He turned to head into his house.

She pushed past him, stomped indoors, and slammed onto the sofa. Max took the sofa opposite, making it feel too much like the way this whole stupid thing started.

He leaned forward, as if hearing him clearly would convince her of whatever it was he wanted her to do. "It's a terrific itinerary. Boston— where we can shout, 'Bill Buckner!' as we pass Fenway Park. Salem, where we can do witch stuff. Rockport—our favorite spot in New England—for some time on the beach, and you know how much you love *Helmut's* strudels. Then back down to Fall River—Lizzie Borden!— then on to the Long Island Sound to Mystic, then up the Hudson to Sleepy Hollow…"

Her face was fierce. "In other words, do *all* the cliched monster stuff."

"And other things. The strudels. Bill Buckner. Of course, we don't have to get off at the stops." He tapped the toe of his shoe, tat-tat-tat, on the scuffed linoleum. "There's plenty to do on board."

"Please tell me we won't be drowning in pumpkin spice."

"We won't be drowning in pumpkin spice."

Despite herself, Cecelia laughed, then sighed. "When does it leave?"

"October 7th."

She stood. "Giving me plenty of time to recover from my dating fiascos."

He beamed at her.

"Oh, don't get cocky." Her voice held a warning note. "I may jump ship at any of the ports—*or* leap overboard."

"Nah, just turn into a bat and fly home."

She leaned forward to kiss his cheek. "I'm not mad anymore," she whispered, "but I'm still staying at my place until then."
~~~~~

"Sure, sure; see you on October 7th."

Cecelia nodded, even though she was certain the cruise would be its own kind of hell.

~~~~~

Kedric stood on the dock and gazed up at the cruise ship. If this was a small boat, he'd hate to see what a large one looked like.

The Witchy Maiden. Hmmmm … weird name for a cruise ship, but then Kedric had never taken a cruise, so what did he know?

"Let's go! Let's go!" Aunt Viv exclaimed as she came up behind him. "The fun starts *on* the boat. Not on the dock."

Kedric trudged behind her and his mother. Why did he agree to this trip? He remembered telling his mother he should look for a wife in Iceland. A trip to Iceland sounded really good about now.

The cacophony of voices, footsteps, music, and the rumbling ship engine made Kedric wince. He hoped things would settle down once everyone was on board. There would be no relaxing otherwise.

They were directed to their cabins, which were all located in the stern — the back — of the ship. Kedric hoped for a balcony. After spending weeks in Aunt Viv's condo, he wanted someplace where he didn't feel closed in.

~~~~~

Cecelia looked at the other women on the dock and had one thought: what is wrong with people nowadays?

Once again, every woman had carefully curled locks of hair over their shoulders and too much makeup and baby-doll dresses and stiletto pumps. For a *riverboat* cruise? She'd gone casual.

Then she saw the name of the ship, twisted her face into a ferocious glower, and grunted.

"Exactly what," Max said from behind her, "are you objecting to now?"

"Everything, Dad. Is there one thing that isn't cliched?"

He stepped around to look in her eyes. "You can back out, hon."

"No." She tried not to sigh for the umpteenth time since this all started. "You paid for me, and there's no refund, right?"

"Nope. But if you *really* wanna back out…"

She shook her head.

"Good, because you loved the Day-Line, right? This is so much more."

"The Day-Line was a trip up the Hudson and back. No kitsch."

"No, but the *Witchy Maiden* has fantastic shipboard activities. You'll love 'em. Promise."

He was tapping a finger — tat-tat-tat — against the dock railing just like he'd tapped his toe when he'd first brought this up. A nervous tic Cecelia knew too well.

What was he hiding now?

~~~~~

"I'd rather just go to my cabin," Kedric said.

Vivan grabbed his arm. "Nonsense. This is what's done when the ship leaves port. You will stay here and do *bon voyage*. Unless you'd rather curse the trip?"

Kedric rolled his eyes. He didn't believe in curses, but he didn't notice anyone else heading for their cabin, so he stayed. Viv air-kissed his cheek. "It's fine, darling. You'll see."

The horn sounded, causing everyone around Kedric to shriek in delight. Confetti fell in mass quantities as the ship slowly pulled away. The captain must have loved the sound of the horn, because he blew it five or six more times. The vibration shook Kedric's body and made him feel slightly nauseated.

As Aunt Vivian and his mother stood at the rail and waved and blew kisses to the crowds on the dock, he backed slowly away, one smooth step at a time, until he stood behind everyone. He resisted looking to his left and right. He didn't want to see who else might be as uncomfortable as he. He didn't want to see any of the enthusiasm. He just wanted to get to his cabin, order a stiff drink, and sit on his private balcony. No music, no confetti, no people.

That was his idea of a vacation.

~~~~~

Cecelia actually liked the whole sail-away thing: the confetti and cheers and especially the sound of the ship's horn. Or she *did*. Now it was just more kitsch, complete with music and drinks and what the cruise director called "plenty of fun."

Max yelled along with everyone else and caught handfuls of confetti to fling down at the people yelling back from the dock, but Cecelia headed inside. Now, while the crowds were here, was the perfect time to explore. She could see what she'd gotten herself into and maybe find *something* worthwhile.

~~~~~

Finally, Aunt Viv gave Kedric permission to go to his cabin. "Aren't you and Mother coming?" he asked when Viv started to walk away after handing him his cabin information and key.

"Not yet," she answered. "I want to show Roxana around the ship."

"Okay."

He watched a minute as Viv strolled away before he thought, *Show Mother around the ship? Has she been on this cruise before?* Then he
~~~~~

remembered her saying she had done a witch hunt reenactment, so he assumed it was this ship. With a sigh, he turned and followed the directions to his cabin.

The room was very small, but attractive and clean. He saw his suitcase had been delivered, too. Good.

After changing into shorts, a t-shirt and flip-flops, he called room service and ordered a bottle of Pinot Noir and a cheese plate. It arrived in five minutes. He carried it out to the balcony, sat in a chair, and poured himself a glass.

This was going to be a fine vacation. And he determined that he was not going to let Aunt Viv make him get involved in any activities. He had packed two novels and a copy of *Power Vamps*, and he had plenty of cash, along with his card. All he needed was his room and balcony.

But after half an hour, he felt cramped. Drat. He decided to take a walk around the ship. Check out the dining room. Viv raved about the food. He'd check out the dinner menu, too.

As he walked past the bed he noticed a paper on his pillow. Puzzled, he picked it up. He felt his face flush as he read the list:

Bingo For Brides
Gambling for Grooms
Vamps Date
Cards for Courtship
Witchhunt for Wives
Hexes for Husbands
Shuffleboard for Sweeties
Zesty Bites — Hungry for Love

Kedric crumpled the paper into a tight ball. "I am going to kill her."

~~~~~

Every time Cecelia went on vacation, even now that she was older, she raced around the hotel, cruise ship, whatnot, to see the amenities. Were there vending machines? What kind? Game rooms? Swimming pool? Restaurants?

She visited each deck now, but because she'd vowed to take part in *no* activities, she didn't look at the signs before any of the event spaces, lounges, or theaters — not even the menu at main dining room. Then she turned a corner and found a huge glass-walled kitchen... or, kitchens.

Three mini kitchens all in a row, a bank of seats like a judging stand, and someplace for an audience. She moved closer and saw the sign at the entrance: *Zesty Bites — Hungry for Love*.

Where had she heard that before? Then she read the text underneath. "Each of our three couples have their own state-of-the-art kitchen in which to prepare their dishes in our Couples' Cook-off Competition. First prize is a Golden Spatula and, we hope, *love*."
~~~~~

She felt her face grow hot as she glanced at the *Witchy's Weekly* she'd stuffed into her pocket and read what other "activities" this ship had.

That's precisely when Cecelia remembered where she'd heard of *Zesty Bites*. She screeched one thing. "*Dad!!!!!*"

~~~~~

Kedric brooded in his room. He refused to come out after he confronted his aunt and mother.

"It *is* a cruise to the Salem Witch Hunt Reenactment!" Viv insisted. "But it's also a dating cruise."

"You don't have to do any of the activities," his mother put in.

Disgusted, Kedric marched back to his room and locked the door. He ordered room service for dinner, and after realizing Aunt Vivian could talk to him from her balcony, ate his dinner inside.

He turned on the TV, hoping for a news channel or something where he could check his stocks, but there was the on-board itinerary channel, the love song channel, the romance movie channel, and a cooking channel.

The cooking channel looked to be the most innocuous, but even that only showed couples cooking together.

So, off the TV went.

He tried reading *Power Vamps*, but it didn't hold his attention.

He ordered a pitcher of Bloody Marys and a slice of cheesecake, but when it got there, he didn't want it.

What to do? He could get off the ship in Boston and take an Uber back to Viv's condo. They would be at that port soon. It wasn't a long way. He nodded. It was a good plan.

Satisfied, he poured a glass of the Bloody Mary.

He started awake at a loud perky voice coming from the TV. Hadn't he shut that thing off?

This is Judy, your Activities Director! There's a change in our schedule. Tomorrow night, October 8th, the Draconid Meteor shower will be peaking, and because we're going to have clear skies, we're crossing our Boston shore excursion off the schedule and taking full advantage of the perfect weather and this epic event. It's the closest Earth will be to it for the next twenty years! The captain will be taking the ship out to sea so the glare of the city lights from the shore won't hinder our viewing.

Normally, we love a full moon on our October cruises, but not this week. The Draconids are best seen in the evening, right after nightfall, which is the opposite of most meteor showers, which are more clearly seen in the early morning. So, no sleeping in! Haha!

The crew of The Witchy Maiden *encourages you to find a date for this stunningly beautiful spectacle of nature. And be sure to check out our special menu for the occasion!*
~~~~~

~~~~~

Kedric was thankful he had packed black sweats and shirt. It would help him to stay unnoticeable in the shadows when he crept out to find a hiding place. He would normally be thrilled to watch a meteor shower, but not on this ship.

On October 8th, just before the Draconids were set to begin, Kedric slipped out and searched for a hiding place. He didn't have much time before Mother and Aunt Vivian would be pounding down his door. Vamps were waking up all over the ship. He nodded and smiled at those he passed, trying not to act like he was up to something.

Room after activity room were packed with people. Finally, he came to the room with the mini kitchens. It was empty and dark. Perfect!

He looked over both shoulders before opening the door. The room surprised him. While it was empty, he could smell the faint aromas of cooking: garlic, smoke, blood. His stomach growled. Drat. He didn't think about bringing something to eat.

Then he heard a faint sound. The door opened and someone came in. Where could he go? Nowhere. Kedric had been caught.

He slowly turned around. Then he gasped.

"You!"

~~~~~

Because the food and drinks were there, everyone watching the Draconids gathered on the left—port side—of the ship. Cecelia could still see it from where she hunkered down on the starboard side. Most people, she knew from past cruises, never stayed on deck, and for an October cruise, there was a terrific reason why. It was freezing. But Cecelia, who refused to participate in a blessed thing, stubbornly stayed, almost invisible in her Mets black "alternate" hoodie and sweats.

She'd hoped she could stay there until dawn, then sleep during the at-sea day before that night's stop at Salem, where she would take the T to Boston and then Amtrak it to New York. But no, it quickly got too cold even for her

Sighing, she strode indoors. No need to tiptoe; she hadn't seen Max since their raucous blow-up about the "tricking me onto the Love Boat" thing. But where to hide? She'd already seen Skye Lafreniere twice, and thought she'd spotted Robb-with-two-B's.

The room where they held *Cards for Courtship* was boisterous; she didn't know what that involved and didn't care. She power-walked down one deck and grinned. Blessedly, totally silent. And that stupid *Zesty Bites* place? Also blessedly silent. She stepped inside.

"You!" someone said.

Cecelia choked. It was Gorgeous Right Eyebrow Guy.

Well, if he raised either eyebrow to her now, she'd rip them both off.

~~~~~

Cecelia said one thing, "I came here to be alone."

Eyebrow-Guy responded, "*I* came here to be alone."

"Then leave. Find someplace else."

"No, I was here first. You find someplace else."

"Oh." Scorn made Cecelia's voice jagged. "Such a gentleman you are."

"Whatever happened to ladies first?"

She nearly let out a "Grrrr" and totally wanted to rip off his eyebrows *without* his raising them first, but she crossed her arms and stood her ground.

Giving out a mock-girl-y squeak and a foot-stamp, he crossed his arms and stood his ground.

They stayed like that for several seconds before they started laughing.

"I guess there's room for both of us," Eyebrow-Guy said.

Ugh. She didn't want to talk to him. She wanted to jump overboard. At least it was dark enough that she didn't know if he was lifting that eyebrow when he talked. Maybe if she didn't answer, he'd get the picture.

He pointed to the seats across the room. "Well, um, I'll go over there. If that's okay."

Cecelia folded her arms tight. She would not be drawn into conversation.

"I wonder how long they'll watch the meteor shower?" he asked.

Shut up! she wanted to scream at him.

"The last one I watched was so amazing, I sat outside for hours. I'd be out there watching tonight if I wasn't on this cruise."

Before she could stop herself, she asked, "Why?"

"Because I'd rather watch them alone. I'm just here for a quiet vacation. At least, that's what I thought I was doing, but—"

So, he *wasn't* looking for love? Cecelia couldn't believe it. But before she could ask how he ended up on this cruise, the door opened and the activities director charged in and snapped on the lights. Following her were a horde of people, including Max.

"Weren't the meteors glorious?" Judy-the-cruise-director chirped. "But it's time for our next game. I have a schedule to keep! Get in here, everyone! *Zesty Bites — Hungry for Love* starts now."

~~~~~

Cecelia's first thought was *Get out immediately!* But it wasn't easy to push toward the exit with so many people streaming into the room. Even Eyebrow-Guy—who'd obviously had the same idea—couldn't make headway.

"All right; fine; I'll be part of the audience," she muttered as she shoved someone aside and reached the theater-style seating area. Eyebrow-Guy, still trying to elbow his way from the room, finally gave up and took the upholstered seat next to her.

"I guess he who hesitates is lost," Max whispered from the row behind.

"Do not even," she growled.

Meanwhile, Judy, flanked by three people who looked like celebrity chefs, stated the rules of the game—a cooking competition where couples were randomly paired off "in our sincerest hope," she chirped, "that as many of you as possible find everlasting love."

"What other kind is there?" Eyebrow-Guy muttered and despite herself, Cecelia glanced at him. "For us *everything* is—"

"Everlasting. I get it." And she tried to hide her smile.

"To start off the fun," Judy exclaimed, "we're drawing three couples' names—six total—from this golden chafing dish. And because I *know* you're all super-excited to start, here are the first two names now!"

Before Cecelia could say, "Ugh!" Judy pulled out a slip of paper.

"Cecelia Ignarra, come on down!"

What? Why? She hadn't—!

"Kedric Blackthorne, come on down!"

Eyebrow-Guy jerked and grunted

What? *Him???* Cecelia hadn't even entered her name in this stupid thing and somehow she ended up with him?

He whirled around and shouted, "Aunt Viv!"

Cecelia turned to see where he was looking but caught her father's eye instead. From the grin on his face, she knew he'd entered her name.

And from the sick look on Eyebrow-Guy's face...

"Let me guess." Cecelia's voice was lethal. "That Aunt Viv person entered *your* name."

He nodded. "And if she wasn't undead..."

Judy clapped her hands twice. "Chop-chop, lovebirds! Come on down!"

"Do we have a choice?" Cecelia asked Eyebrow-Guy, er, Kedric.

His response was a deep sigh.

They "came on down."

~~~~~

Kedric stood almost at attention next to his "partner," Cecelia. He
~~~~~

felt conspicuous in his black sweats while everyone else was dressed for dating. He glanced at Cecelia. She was in black sweats, so at least he wasn't alone.

Chirpy Judy was gushing over couple #3's outfits.

What was he going to do? He loved good food, but he didn't know much about cooking. He never had to. Not with Oleg whipping up delicious concoctions. Not with all the wonderful restaurants he'd visited worldwide.

Cecelia leaned toward him. "Do you know anything about cooking?"

He gave a slight shake of his head.

"Great," she muttered.

"You?" he whispered back.

"I do. I love to cook. So, I guess you'll have to follow my lead."

Kedric shrugged.

"And now, the rules!" Judy was back at the mic stand. "This competition consists of three courses. Appetizer, dinner, and dessert. Special drinks *must* accompany them. The theme is *Romantic Dinner*. Do *not* give us a typical human dinner."

The crowd chuckled.

"I mean it!" Judy squealed. "I know many of you like dating humans, but *this* is a cruise for vampires, so, give us a delectable vampire dinner."

Kedric felt himself start to sweat a little. He hardly ever sweated! What was happening?

"We'll start with the appetizer course. You'll have twenty minutes, after which you'll be judged. The best app will earn a bonus for the next round. We're giving you *carte blanche* with this round, so get creative!"

~~~~~

Cecelia had to ground herself to work with someone as gorgeous as Kedric.

Kedric? Well, at least it wasn't "Tybalt." But the ever-present Skye Lafreniere worked at the next kitchen with a gal wearing the typical mini-dress and stilettos.

No! No distractions!

No time.

~~~~~

Twenty minutes? Was that enough time to prepare an appetizer and drink?

Cecelia stiffened beside him. "Twenty minutes?" she whispered. "That's it?"

Uh oh.

Before Kedric could think of his favorite appetizer, Judy rang a bell, and the other two couples sprang into action.

Cecelia punched him on the shoulder. "Come on!"

"Where? What? Don't we need to figure out what we're doing?"

But she had charged into the pantry with the others and grabbed items, throwing them into a basket.

"Kedric!!" she hollered. "Get over here!"

He must be in a nightmare. *Wake up, wake up!* he told himself.

"*Kedric!*"

He hustled to her.

"Snap out of it! Do you want your Aunt Viv to put your name in something else?"

That broke him out of his stupor. "What am I supposed to do?"

"Think of a drink!"

"But what are you making?"

"Little neck clams in a blood orange gastric."

Clams, clams. What goes with clams? He usually had wine or brandy.

"Get going!" she shrieked over her shoulder as she ran back to their workstation.

He went to the alcohol and wine section. He could hear Chirpy Judy commenting on what the couples were doing, but he tuned her out. As much as he wanted to walk out, what Cecelia said about Aunt Viv stuck in his head. If they did well in this competition, perhaps Viv and Mother *would* leave him alone.

Let's see, he'd been on so many dates in the last two months. What drinks had they had with dinner? That first horrible date with Cloris came to mind. She drank tequila. He shook his head. Several women enjoyed Amaretto. Too sweet for his taste. A Bloody Mary? Maybe?

He grabbed the vodka and tomato juice then ran to the produce. Celery, of course, but what would make it special? Different? He scanned the pantry shelves. There were jars of pickled vegetables like onions, but that didn't feel right. His hand rested on a jar of capers. That might work! He grabbed it and a bottle of Tabasco and Worcestershire and a tin of seafood seasoning.

After dumping all his stuff on the table and trying not to bump into Cecelia, he ran to the shelves of glassware. He chose a tall, slender, clear glass that would show off the redness of the drink.

"How are you doing?" he asked Cecelia, who was definitely flushed as she set sea green oval plates in front of her. And like before, he noticed how lovely her otherwise plain face became when that happened. *Stop it. Stay focused!*

"We have three minutes," she barked. "Get those drinks made! Three of them. There are three judges."

Holy bloodbath, three glasses? He hustled back to the glassware, grabbed a pitcher, two more glasses, and a strainer. Into the pitcher went ice, vodka, tomato juice, and the spices. He dropped a few capers into the bottom of the glasses, strained the drink into them, and looked. They needed something.

"Thirty seconds!" Judy sang out.

The celery! He tore three stalks off the bunch and plunked them into the glasses.

"Time's up!"

~~~~~

The three vampire judges, who all looked to be at least five hundred years old, were persnickety, to say the least. Kedric was thankful he and Cecelia weren't selected to be judged first.

"Are judges always like this?" he whispered out the corner of his mouth.

Cecelia didn't respond.

Too bad it wasn't a contest where they could be eliminated with the first course. That would be a relief.

The male judge, Kedric couldn't remember his name, was some kind of celebrity vampire chef from Brazil. The dude was especially picky. To the point of ridiculousness, in Kedric's point of view. But when he spit out the chicken neck Skye WhatsHisName made, Kedric almost laughed out loud.

Cecelia jabbed him in the ribs.

Finally, it was their turn.

"Tell us what you made," chirped Judy.

Cecelia nodded to the judges. "Tonight, for the appetizer round, we have Little Neck Clams in Blood Orange Gastric, paired with a Caper Spiced Bloody Mary."

Hmmmmmm. Kedric was impressed with her poise.

The judges began their tasting. No one spoke for a minute. They just ate. Kedric itched to ask Cecelia if this was normal.

Vampiress judge #1 was the first to put down her fork. "When I first heard your description, I thought this was a classic choice, which is to say, boring. But the gastric had an excellent balance of sweet and sour. Although I tasted something different I can't place."

The second vampiress spoke up. "I know! I just couldn't stop eating. You'll have to tell us your secret ingredient!"

Kedric glanced at Cecelia, who was smiling slightly. Again, he thought how lovely she looked in this setting.
~~~~~

Then the picky dude interrupted. "The clams were good, but the drink! I've never had capers and seafood seasoning in a Bloody Mary. Well done."

"Thank you for your feedback," Judy said. "We'll give them time to compare notes. Contestants, you can sit down. The judges will be back soon."

Five minutes later, the judges came back to their seats.

"Have you decided?" Judy asked.

"We have," the male vampire said.

"Ooooh, this is the exciting part," Judy exclaimed. "Who has won the advantage for the next round?"

"Cecelia and Kedric!"

What? They won? Kedric felt like he couldn't take a deep breath. Cecelia hugged him while he stood there like a lump.

That Skye guy sneered at them.

"Congratulations!" Chirpy Judy shouted over the exuberance of the audience.

Kedric made the mistake of looking at his mother and Vivian. Mother was clapping, but Vivian looked pompously self-satisfied. He looked away from his aunt and saw Cecelia's father cheering and dancing a little at his seat.

He stole a glance at Cecelia. Seemed like he was doing that a lot tonight. He had to get ahold of himself. But she didn't look upset. Just slightly flustered.

"And now, while the stations are being cleaned, I'll announce Cecelia and Kedric's advantage," Judy piped. "Everyone quiet down! Cee-cee, may I call you that? And Keddy? Your advantage is a five-minute consultation on what you're going to prepare for the main course. Keep in mind the two required ingredients are blood and purslane."

The audience immediately started talking among themselves. The other two teams were told to sit on the benches across the room.

Cecelia and Kedric went to a bench on the opposite side.

"What's purslane?" Kedric asked as soon as they sat.

~~~~~

"Don't you know *anything* about cooking?" Cecelia fumed.

"I..."

"Purslane is... No, no time. What's your drink idea?"

"I..."

"Crud. Okay, rare tuna's very red; and purslane... is red, too! Cool. Okay, blood, blood. What can I do with...?"

"What about a sauce with blood?"
~~~~~

"Not cooked; it won't be red. But if we schmear it…. No, I gotta *transform* it. With what? *And what's your drink idea???*"

"I'll think of something!" He darted to the pantry.

"Make it romantic," Cecelia mumbled. "How? Aaargh!" Then, amazingly, "Got it!"

And she got to work.

When she next glanced at the clock: one minute left.

"Girl, get plated." She grabbed three white rectangular plates.

As she put on the final touches, Kedric set his drinks down.

Huh.

"Nice!"

Then Judy cried, "Time!"

~~~~~

Cecelia faced the judges. "Our entree is a very-rare yellowfin tuna set on a shmear of venison blood which is drizzled with Fresno pepper oil. If you cut a piece of the tuna and drag it through the oil and blood, it combines to create a delightfully rich sauce that perfectly compliments the fish. And on the side: steamed purslane stalks with brown-butter, cherry tomato, and garlic sauce."

"Tell us about the drink," Judy enthused.

Kedric stepped forward. "Blood-moon rising cocktail consisting of Pinot Noir, a splash of Prosecco, and a honeydew melon ball on the rim of the glass to represent the full moon."

They aced this round, too.

Cecelia glanced at the audience. Max, Kedric's Aunt Viv, and some random woman, were deep in conversation. *Deep in conversation.*

What the heck did that mean?

~~~~~

The dessert round started off disastrously for the third couple, Jarek and Pearl. One of them knocked over a bowl of blueberries, and they both dropped to their knees and started to count them. They never got their dessert finished.

"Huh," Cecelia said to Kedric. "I thought vampires being compelled to count was a myth."

"Me, too."

Skye and his partner made the tragic mistake of not wearing gloves when they cut up passion peppers, the strongest aphrodisiac known to vampires. Within minutes, they were rolling on the floor making out.

Gross, Cecelia thought.

So, she and Kedric won the dessert round with their molten red velvet cake and coffee with Sambuca, whipped cream, and red sanding sugar.

As the confetti descended and the cheers rose, during what Cecelia could only call being swept up in the moment, she and Kedric kissed.

And it was *nice*.

However, as they walked back to her cabin—he insisted on accompanying her—the doubts began.

This is the way it always starts.

But maybe this time…

No! You know how it finishes.

But you like this one. And *maybe* this time, *he* will…?

They passed the bar where disco music (ugh!) blared and Max was… what? Crazy-madly-deeply in conversation with Random Woman?

"Who *is* that?" Cecelia cried just as Kedric said, "Looks like your dad met my mother."

"Your…???"

Oh, no.

Cecelia, you've really done it this time. You've fallen in love with the man who might become your brother.

~~~~~

Kedric leaned down, hoping Cecelia would allow him to kiss her. Sure, they'd kissed after they won the competition, but that felt spur-of-the-moment. And public. He wanted to see how he felt with a more intimate kiss.

She allowed him. He didn't want to linger too long, but it was a struggle to pull back after a few seconds.

"Thanks," he said.

"For what?"

He shrugged. "For the competition. It turned out to be really fun. I had no idea. I'd even do it again."

She gave him a small, sad smile.

"Are you okay?" he asked. Did he do something wrong? Say something wrong?

"I'm okay. Just tired." She turned to unlock the door. "Good morn."

"Good morn."

He stood and looked at her closed door for about fifteen seconds, then walked slowly back to his cabin. Once inside, he stood on the balcony and watched the sunrise, although he was careful to not stand in the full force of the sunrays. Another hoax about vampires was that sunlight killed them. It didn't, but it could weaken them.

As he watched the water start to reflect the yellow-orange light, he ruminated over the evening. As much as he grieved and missed Patricia, Cecelia made him feel something he never felt with his last wife, even
~~~~~

though he hadn't realized it. He smiled when he pictured her turning into a general at the beginning of the cooking competition, then, even though it was a short time, they turned into a team. She made him laugh. And her face, which he first thought plain until she flushed, well, no more did he think that. She was in her element while cooking, and that assurance changed her whole demeanor.

He searched his feelings again, trying to figure out how she made him feel. When he turned from the sunrise and went into his dark room, he could name it.

She made him feel like he had come home.

~~~~~

Kedric opened the balcony door and breathed in the night air. He felt almost giddy with anticipation. "I'm going to ask Cecelia to breakfast with me," he said to the stars. He noticed the ship had pulled into the Salem port. "And doing the re-enactment with her could be fun, too."

He tried not to run to her cabin door, instead setting a quick pace quite unlike himself. How could he have changed so much in just one night?

He smoothed his hair and knocked on her door. No answering call came. He knocked again. Silence. *Maybe she's already in the dining room.*

But the dining room was mostly empty. Kedric frowned as he sat at a table by the buffet. A waiter brought him coffee. As Kedric stirred a splash of brandy into it, Cecelia's father came into the room. Kedric jumped to his feet. "Sir..." he started.

"Max," he said. "I'm Max Ignarra, Cecelia's father."

Kedric shook his hand. "Kedric Blackthorne. But I guess you know that from last night's competition."

Max signaled the waiter, who brought coffee for him. "Yep. What a night, huh?"

Kedric grinned. "Sure was." He took a sip from his cup. "I was looking for Cecelia."

"Well, that's the thing. She's gone."

"Gone? What do you mean?"

"Dunno. She poked a note under my door." Max looked dreadfully unhappy. "Said she had to leave, that she'd take the train home from Salem, not to worry, she'd explain later..." He sighed. "Sorry, kiddo. That's all I can tell you."

Kedric stared into his coffee, shock paralyzing his voice. Max drained his cup. "I really am sorry. Wish I could tell you more."

"Sure," Kedric managed to get out.

Max left the room. Kedric pushed his cup away. What was he going to do now?
~~~~~

~~~~~

Kedric shifted in his first-class seat. He forgot how long the flight from Australia to New York took.

For three solid months he had tried to forget Cecelia. From gambling in Monaco's Monte Carlo to walking the Great Wall of China, to hunting rabbits and feral pigs with the Aboriginal people, nothing had helped to remove her from his thoughts.

Enough. He was going to find her.

Twenty hours later, he was banging on Max Ignarra's door.

~~~~~

"I'm sorry, Kedric, I don't know where she is," Max said. "I'm worried, too. I've asked everyone I know. Checked the usual spots Cee-Cee would go when upset. She's vanished."

"She'll come home," Roxana said from the couch. "I'm sure she will."

His mother and Max had become almost inseparable since the cruise.

Kedric paced. "What if something happened to her?"

"Nothing has happened. The *Noctem Nostra* would have told me." Max put a hand on Kedric's shoulder to stop his pacing. "How about you stay here a while, kid? We're going to be family soon. Let's get to know each other, huh?"

"Family? When did *that* happen?"

Mother wiggled her left hand. "About a month ago. We would have told you, but *you* had vanished."

Kedric hung his head. "Sorry."

Max laughed. "No worries. You're here now. Have something to eat. We can make more calls tomorrow."

"No. Thank you," Kedric said. "I think I'll take a walk."

He kissed his mother on the cheek and shook Max's hand. "Congratulations. I assume Aunt Viv is planning the wedding?"

Mother smiled. "Of course."

He wandered for miles with no destination in mind. Then, at two o'clock in the morning, he stood at the corner of First Ave and 58th Street. He looked up. There it was. The first place he had seen her face.

Stoker's in Sunset Park.

~~~~~

Cecelia was tired of hiding and even more tired of living in fear.

"Never be afraid," her mother had always said, and *Moms* sure hadn't been.

Besides, what was Cecelia afraid of? Being hurt again? Or being real?
~~~~~

She'd never felt more alive than in the short time she'd spent cooking with Kedric Blackthorne.

Sure, she'd always been a great cook, but who was that drill sergeant, that powerful woman, who blitzed the competition? Kedric brought that person out. Hadn't he? Whether it was working together or just being with him, she'd radiated confidence. She wanted to be that Cecelia.

But mostly she wanted Kedric.

He was different from the other guys. No ego. A gentleness.

Also, he was a good kisser.

During her three months at Moms' childhood home in Vilnius, Cecelia had gotten fifty-zillion (unanswered) texts from Max, but she'd read enough to know that he and Kedric's mom were an item.

For her first three nights back in New York, she sat at "her" table in *Stoker's*, eating but not enjoying their miso soup, because she couldn't think of anywhere else he might be. Tonight, swallowing her soup and pride, she fumbled for her phone and dialed.

"Dad, do you possibly know where...?"

Her hand went limp, and the phone thunked onto the table.

Kedric had just entered *Stoker's*.

"Cee-Cee?" Max's voice blared from the phone. "Baby? That you?"

Cecelia licked her lips, *staring* at Kedric.

And then, as if sensing that stare, he looked her way.

"Dunno," her dad's voice went tinny, like he'd turned away from his phone. "She just stopped speaking. No, shh! That's why I'm tryin' to *listen*..."

Kedric's gaze was anxious, questioning, hopeful...

Cecelia looked smack dab at him and raised her right eyebrow.

The End

CHILDREN OF THE NIGHT, SINGING SWEETLY
An Enchanted Castle Archives Story
A Belladonna Tale
Michelle L. Levigne

"We have a problem." Eyesallova, the primary magic mirror in the enchanted castle, sounded more disgusted than worried.

'Na was just finishing up lessons for the day. One of the drawbacks of attending classes through the magic mirror web with other magically talented girls around the world was that her table with her books, papers, inkwell, and the mirror, Scripta, sat in the mirror room on the third floor of the enchanted castle. That was where her parents, Lady Ashlyn and Lord Zared conducted much of their business, helping to unravel magic-based problems throughout the world. 'Na overheard quite a lot that she was very sure her parents and the kings, queens, prime ministers, viziers, and powerful enchanters around the world didn't think a girl of twelve, or any age, actually, should hear. Not until she was an adult and thoroughly trained in magic to assist her parents. Overhearing all that otherwise off-limits communication taught her quite a lot about magic, and the many ways people could totally mess up what should have been simple spells or repeatedly activate curses through stupidity and selfishness.

'Na knew better than to turn her head away from Scripta. Master Windyport might have looked like a sleepy, fuzzy old darling, but he noticed everything. And what he didn't notice, his mirror, Schmendrake, did. Paying attention was vital as he gave his students their research assignments during their class break. Three of the kingdoms where the many girls lived were having three- and five-day holidays, so it just made more sense to halt classroom meetings altogether, rather than force the girls to scramble to catch up with everyone when their holidays were over. That didn't mean they wouldn't have some sort of work to keep them busy and out of trouble, as Master Windyport said. Fortunately, his independent research assignments were always fascinating and entirely enjoyable. 'Na struggled to hear what Eyesallova was telling her parents while writing down her assignment.

Finally, Master Windyport intoned his farewell blessing over the girls, and the images in the magic mirror filling the entire wall in front of 'Na's study table started to fade and vanish. Now she could think about what she had just heard.

Angry panic shot through her.

King Ruprick was on his way to the enchanted castle. His traveling party was due to arrive by dinnertime.

Rathelshiffen, Ruprick's kingdom, sat on the southern border of the enchanted forest. Or more accurately, when the enchanted forest stopped drifting through time and space, it had settled on the northern border of Rathelshiffen. King Ruprick had been a difficult neighbor ever since, first trying to trick Ashlyn into marrying him, then trying to trick 'Na's parents into betrothing her to his son, Prince Ruprick.

"You did a very good job, 'Na," Scripta said, as she stacked her books and neatened her worktable. "I've received several requests from your classmates for a copy of your essay. May I send it?"

'Na agreed absently as she listened to her parents and Eyesallova discussing what the defensive spells at the border of Rathelshiffen and the enchanted forest had uncovered.

"This is more dastardly than the last attempt," Eyesallova said. Her surface flashed, her normal swirls of purple, blue, and green magic sparkles becoming images of various old, battered books and all sorts of coins, rings, and chains that glowed with ripples of ugly green and orange magic.

'Na fought down a queasy feeling in her stomach. If King Ruprick was carrying all that magic, then he was coming to the enchanted castle to make trouble. Whether he was going to use that magic to attack or to pretend to be helpful and turn it all over to her parents to lock it away for safekeeping, that didn't matter. King Ruprick was always a problem.

"He's carrying all those magical books and artifacts?" Lady Ashlyn said.

"No, that's the image from the inventory created by Scholar Terwilliger when he and his team finally unlocked that particularly problematic doorway under Ickbullion Castle, and found the Dockdon annex of the enchanters' library."

"That's not on the list of library annexes we're trying to track down," Lord Zared said.

"That's an annex that was deliberately locked away and all memory expunged from the official records. Everything in that library annex is problematic and troublesome, and most sensible enchanters and scholars agree it should remain lost." The mirror sighed. "The defensive spells have only identified four specific artifacts so far, but the suggested results of their combined magic all lead to the same thing. He's going to try to trick you into a betrothal. Again."

'Na barely managed to muffle a yelp of dismay. She almost used some very nasty words she had heard Melvin the monster hunter and several other old friends of her father use. Words that had earned them some rather vicious scolding from Lady Ashlyn and half the castle's mirrors.

'Na had never met Prince Ruprick, but her mother assured her that every Ruprick looked like the one before him. A clear-cut example of how the exterior often contradicted the interior. Thanks to the enchanted forest once residing in a slower time stream, Lady Ashlyn had encountered several King Rupricks since becoming lady of the enchanted castle. Every Ruprick down through history had been trying to gain control of the enchanted castle. Marrying into the family was just the most recent, and most repeated, tactic for that.

As she listened to her parents and Eyesallova and several more mirrors discuss how to neutralize King Ruprick's stolen magic, 'Na decided that since she was nearly twelve, it was high time she participated in her own defense. She had helped her parents solve magical puzzles, starting when she was only six years old. While her pet dragon had left the castle, that didn't make her helpless.

'Na got up, pushed her chair in to the table, and exchanged farewells with Scripta. She listened to her parents discussing what defensive charms to activate as King Ruprick approached the castle.

Why couldn't they just gather up some nasty magic from the castle's storage rooms and zap King Ruprick once and for all?

Once she was out of the mirror room, 'Na ran, along the gallery on the third floor, to the residential wing of the castle. She blinked back a few tears when she thought about Smedley's reaction if he was here to face down King Ruprick. Her dragon friend had been gone five months now, learning how to be a dragon, how to control his fire and learn to fly now that his wings had grown large enough to support him. Those five months felt like forever.

Smedley would have defended her. He would have threatened King Ruprick, or at least he would have been very rude, making all sorts of obnoxious noises until their unwanted guest got upset and stomped out of the castle. Before he left the enchanted castle, his wings had started growing at an inconvenient rate, leading to accidents. They might even be large enough to let him fly by now, but that did her little good since he wasn't anywhere near the castle.

Still, flying was a good idea. How long would it take to ransack the storage rooms under the castle and find a spell that would let her fly?

The problem with using any of the magic in the vast, expanding storage rooms under the castle was that so many of those spells were either broken or worn out or in a bad mood, they couldn't be relied on to work properly. Or more importantly, if the spell gave her wings or changed her shape into a flying creature, it might refuse to turn off and let her return to normal.

Still, that was the first part of the answer to dealing with King Ruprick and another attempt to betroth her to his son:

Get out of the castle.

If she wasn't anywhere in sight when King Ruprick arrived, he couldn't use any of his stolen magic on her or her parents. She understood enough of magic to know that it had to attach to her in some way, even if the magic was aimed at her parents. She needed to be out of the castle. Far away from the castle.

Twenty minutes later, she had changed into her sturdiest trousers and boots and jacket, made for exploring the enchanted forest. So, she was ready to run, but as her father often said, running was useless if she didn't have somewhere specific to run to or a plan of what to do when she got there.

'Na thought about her friends in the werewolf tribe. The boys loved adventures, and they would protect her. Maybe they didn't have any clue yet what natural werewolf magic any of them had inherited, but they would help her hide, and if necessary, they would fight off King Ruprick's magic with their teeth.

The trick was getting to the werewolf village, surrounded by their defensive magic, without King Ruprick using that stolen magic to detect her presence in the forest. Chances were good some of that nasty stolen magic had a tracking spell, to find her, maybe befuddle her mind so she didn't know what she was doing until she was in his clutches.

But what if she didn't travel through the forest to get to her friends?

The enchanted castle grew to accommodate all the broken, tired, rebellious, and outright wonky magic that her parents brought inside to keep it from causing trouble or being damaged further. Every few months, a new room budded off the castle to expand the library, or a new storage room appeared in the underground warren of tunnels. Just two months ago, a new underground corridor had opened up into a series of tunnels that, as far as her parents' explorations could tell, ran under the entire enchanted forest. Her father speculated that the tunnels were the residue of all the digging and dragging the castle had done over the centuries as it wandered through the enchanted forest. That was before he had risked his life and anchored it, partly by accident, and partly in furious desperation.

Her parents had put up huge, magically bound doors over the mouths of those tunnels, to keep all sorts of burrowing or just plain nosey and inquisitive creatures from getting into the lower levels of the castle. They didn't have as much time as they wanted to explore those tunnels. There was always some sort of magical emergency taking their family away from the castle on long trips, or else one royal envoy or scholar after another came to ask for help with magical problems or to search the library for magical research.

However, on one occasion when a fierce snowstorm had kept their family delightfully isolated in the castle for three straight days, they had explored down one branch of the tunnels to find a clearing just on the edge of werewolf territory.

'Na dashed down the hall out of the residential wing and down the central staircase to the main doors of the library. The front room had a map room. She didn't bother closing any of the doors behind herself as she dashed into the library and between dozens of rows of shelves and worktables and into the map room. When she asked the big central map on the wall of the map room to show her the charted arms of the tunnels, a clear diagram appeared over a map of the enchanted forest. She stared hard at it, trying to burn the image into her head, memorizing all the turns to keep her on the path that led to the clearing in werewolf territory. Then she ran for the closest door down to the underground levels of the castle.

"Where are you going? Don't you know you have visitors coming?" a shimmery little voice asked from straight overhead.

'Na looked up at the chandelier in the receiving area of the castle, between the main doors and the central staircase. It was made entirely of mirrors, to reflect light, and also let the castle's mirrors see from every angle. No one could sneak around the castle without being seen, their actions watched. The voice was Chatelaine, the housekeeper mirror who oversaw the housekeeping breezes and looked after guests.

"It's King Ruprick," 'Na said, and kept moving.

"Him? Why all the fuss, setting up dinner in the large dining room?"

"Eyesallova suggested distracting and tangling him with protocol. I'm getting out of the castle so he can't try some nasty new magic."

"Good thinking. But did you tell your parents what you're doing?" Chatelaine asked.

"No. Chatty, will you—"

"Go," the mirror said, and chuckled. "Do you know where you're going?"

"The werewolves." 'Na reached for the handle of the door.

"Good idea. Why are you going downstairs?"

"The new tunnels." 'Na didn't wait for the mirror's reaction. She yanked the door open and ran as fast as she could, taking two steps at a time, down the curving stairs.

She took the wrong turn three times before she found the massive, magically bound doors that guarded the tunnels under the forest. In the back of her mind, a clock seemed to tick, warning that King Ruprick and his nasty stolen magic were getting closer to the castle every second. The farther away she was before he focused some of that magic on finding and trapping her, the better.

Later, she decided that was why she didn't realize something felt ... not quite right as she ran down the tunnels. She was in a hurry. Her mother always warned her that when she felt rushed, she needed to slow down and think twice as hard to make sure she was on the right path.

She kept taking wrong turns, and that frustrated her, so she didn't notice until too late that the light filling the tunnel looked slightly odd. She came up the spiral stone stairs into a gloomy clearing that smelled of moss and damp stone and wriggly, slimy things, mixed with copper and iron. It smelled like blood, but not good blood. The werewolf village smelled of blood quite often, but it was a warm smell that promised a full stomach. The werewolf elders marked all their territory with pungent flowering herbs through all the seasons. She couldn't smell anything like that. Even discounting how weak her nose was, compared with werewolf noses, even in human form, 'Na knew she should smell the boundary markers.

Besides, the clearing by the werewolf village lay open to the sky, to let the sunlight and moonlight in. This place dripped with wet-smelling moss on the ground, creeper moss garlands in the trees, and all sorts of vines with black leaves. Sundown was still two hours away, but this place felt like it was always the darkest part of the night, when the moon hadn't risen high enough to spill silver light through the gaps in the forest canopy.

How had she gotten so lost?

She crouched down to present as small a target as possible. There were times when moving was dangerous, and times when sitting utterly still was even more dangerous, but she had no idea which time this was.

'Na had the awful feeling she would have been smarter to stay home and face King Ruprick.

She turned to go back to the tunnel, but the opening at the base of the tree where she had come above ground had vanished.

All right then, if she couldn't go back the way she came, then she had to call for help and pray really hard that she was close enough to werewolf territory for her friends to hear. And she would pray really hard for A'theosius to keep her safe until she was found.

"Please, please," she whispered, then closed her eyes and took a deep breath. She tipped her head back and dropped her jaw to create that hollow place at the back of her throat and widen her sinuses, and she howled.

The sound seemed to sink into the moss carpeting the ground and trunks and tree limbs.

'Na tipped her head back and howled again, aiming the sound away, on ground level, rather than trying to penetrate the thick, unfriendly canopy overhead.

Her voice echoed back to her. Faint and kind of muffled, but it echoed, meaning somewhere to her right, there wasn't as much moss and wetness and dark, creeping shadows. 'Na whispered a prayer, asking A'theosius to keep her safe and help her make the right choices, then she set off, following her ears.

Every fifty steps, she paused and took a deep breath and howled. Then she listened hard, following the gradually strengthening echoes of her own voice.

The fourth time she inhaled, she nearly choked. The air tasted different. Better. She smelled the spicebush that marked the werewolf territory boundaries at this time of year, predominantly cinnamon and anise. And an undercurrent of garlic. Why garlic? 'Na howled harder and louder, making her eyes ache and her temples pound from the effort. Then she kept moving, following her ears and her nose.

Something whispered through the trees overhead. She caught glimpses of strands of tangled, knotted, green-black moss swaying, just the slightest bit. She couldn't really be sure in the thick darkness.

Shadows flickered between the tree trunks, behind her and to the right. 'Na knew better than to stop and turn to look, because if anything or anyone followed her, they would know she sensed their presence.

If she wasn't imagining all this.

Another shadow flickered among the trees ahead of her on the left.

'Na wished she was imagining all this.

Something hissed, behind her on her left. She inhaled on her fiftieth step and let out the loudest, lowest, most furious howl she had ever offered to the sky during her visits to the werewolf village.

"It won't do you any good, little wolf," a scratchy kind of voice said from overhead.

'Na knew better than to look straight up. She kept moving until she was out from under that especially mossy, drippy, crooked branch where a thick shadow crouched. Then she turned and looked up, and kept her feet pointed where the echoes of her howl came through clearest and strongest.

"Oh, don't be cruel," another voice said, coming from the moving, skinny clump of shadows ahead of her to the left. This one was smooth and kind of sweet, in a sad, droopy kind of way. "She's going to be utterly miserable if you frighten her at the very start of her life with the nightborn. Who wants a miserable little bride?"

"No!" 'Na skittered away three steps before she could stop herself. "I ran away because I don't want to get married. You can't make me!"

She clamped her mouth shut to keep from wailing. Nightborn was the name the vampires gave themselves. She had ended up in vampire territory. Or maybe not entirely? Did that garlic smell mean she was in the borderland between the two territories? She knew there was an ongoing feud between the werewolves and vampires, and the werewolves marked the boundary between them with garlic. Her parents thought that was a rather cruel trick. Most vampires were allergic to garlic, the kind of allergy where once they tasted it, they wanted more, and kept eating, despite sneezing and scratching and their faces and tongues swelling up.

"Well, no, we won't, but your father will," a third, male voice said. It was one of those thick, jolly voices. The kind of voice a man had when he always got what he wanted and didn't care how many people were hurt or cheated or unhappy, because he was the most important person in the entire world.

"No, he won't." 'Na swallowed down the urge to tell them just what kind of damage her father would do to them. Her father was the disenchanted prince, Lord Zared who had smashed dozens of spells created by the Purple Sky magicians.

"Yes, he will. He has to. It's the only way to make peace between our clans, little wolf. It's just too bad there are so few girls born to your people," the woman vampire said.

'Na choked on a strange feeling she suspected was laughter. The vampires thought she was a werewolf?

Was she in more trouble, or less trouble, than if they knew she was Lady Belladonna of the enchanted castle?

"That's why you can't have her," a tight, young, tenor voice said.

The shadows split apart and six young wolves leaped forward to surround 'Na. A seventh figure somersaulted forward and landed in a crouch in front of her. Rolf, nephew of the werewolf clan leader, stood up and spread his arms, putting himself between 'Na and the vampire man who stepped forward and flicked open the shutter on a lantern. Silvery-purple light spilled out slowly, like it was syrup, slow to touch his features.

He was dressed all in black, navy blue, and dark red, all sharp angles as if there was nothing but skin covering his bones, and even his elegant clothes couldn't cover it.

"It's the only way to make peace between our people," the vampire woman said. She stepped into the slowly expanding pool of light from the lantern. Her pale skin looked blue and her eyes were violet, glowing gems. Instead of the usual flowing sleeves and skirts of most vampire women 'Na had seen, she wore trousers and knee-high boots and a sleeveless shirt, all in sleek, glossy black. Ebony and diamond bands covered her arms from wrists to above her biceps.

"We had peace until your folk broke it," Rolf said. The young werewolves surrounding him and 'Na growled and bared their teeth as they crouched down, poised to leap forward.

"Is that the story they tell you?" The third man laughed from his perch in the branches overhead.

"Doesn't it make you wonder why our leaders want peace with the werewolves?" the first man said. "Do we want to be friends and allies with creatures who ignore facts and the truth?"

"It doesn't matter what they want, or what we want," the woman said. "I've been waiting thirty years now to do my duty and take one of their leaders as mate, but they won't give up one of their daughters in return." She held out her hand to 'Na. "There's nothing to be afraid of, little wolf girl. It's not like they'll force you to become a vampire. Just like your werewolf kin won't force me to become a werewolf. We just need to formalize our friendship."

She offered a smile that would have been quite nice except for the fangs that poked out when her lips stretched just a little too thin. Those fangs were longer than werewolf fangs.

"What's wrong with your glamour, Lividia?" the man in the tree snarled, when 'Na just stood there, staring back at the woman, and the fur on her werewolf friends stood up so stiff and straight they were twice as wide as normal.

"I'm not using my glamour," the woman snapped, her smile vanishing for a few seconds.

"Use it and get the wolf brat under our power."

The largest werewolf cub lurched up onto his hind legs and shifted to human in just a few seconds. He grunted as he tugged his clothes straight, and 'Na almost laughed. Her werewolf friends didn't quite have the magic down right, that let them stay clothed when they were in wolf shape.

"It won't work," the werewolf boy snapped, and stomped for

emphasis. "You can't glamour Nana, 'cause she's full of magic."

"Shut up, Rollo," Rolf growled.

"Well of course, we all are," the first man said. "That's what it means to be nightborn and were kin. Magic is part of what we are." He came forward a few more steps and went down on one knee. "That's why we need to work together. I know your parents probably tell you that the folk in the castle keep things nice and friendly here in the enchanted forest, but can we really be sure?"

"It's a lot safer here in the forest than other places in the world. Even in Vanyltransia," 'Na said.

"What does she know?" the man in the tree said with a sneer. "She's just a cub."

Several of the werewolf cubs let out sharp, rapid barks of wolf laughter.

"Shut up!" Rolf growled, even louder.

"What gave you that idea?" the first vampire man said. "About it being safer here?"

"My Mama said so," 'Na said.

The man in the tree laughed, an ugly, mocking sort of sound. The woman glared at him and her eyes seemed to flash with a light of their own for a moment. He went silent and sort of stiffened before falling out of the tree.

"How does your mother know this is true?" the woman, Lividia, said. She came a few steps closer, until the two werewolf cubs closest to her growled, baring their fangs, and crouching down closer to the ground.

"She invited the vampires and werewolves to come live here, before the forest was anchored."

"'Na, don't," Rolf said. His voice cracked like he was going to cry.

"Your mother?" The first man smiled and got back up to his feet and came closer.

The cubs moved closer to 'Na and Rolf and growled, soft and low.

"'Na, as in Belladonna?" He licked his lips. His tongue was very red in the shadows and blue lantern light, and his teeth were very long and glowing white. They looked sharp enough to cut the shadows and make them bleed. "Lividia, my dear—"

"No," Lividia said.

"No, what?"

"No, I won't put a glamour on the girl." She stepped closer to the children.

"Just think what we can do, once we have a claim on the enchanted castle through the girl," he said, his voice low and sounding so friendly, with laughter bubbling through it.

"Just think what kind of war you'll ignite," Lividia snapped.

She flung up her hands. Light sparked from her fingertips. 'Na threw herself at Rolf, fully expecting all of them to get zapped with vampire magic and taken prisoner.

Rolf turned around and caught hold of her and kept turning, putting his back to the woman.

The light died. The first man dropped his lantern. The blue light sparked as the lantern hit the stony ground and cracked. Then it died.

"I can only hold them for so long," Lividia said. "Urmur has been exercising his magic and growing stronger." She spread her arms and made a shooing motion. "Go, children, before they break free. Run to safety!"

Rolf caught hold of 'Na's hand and raced back the way he had come. The cubs leaped ahead, silent in the darkness. Rollo was the last to shift back to wolf, and he kept close to 'Na's heels.

'Na looked back once, to see Lividia standing there in the clearing, silvery-purple sparks dancing on her fingertips, throwing handfuls of sparks at the two men sprawled on the ground.

She had time to wish for the wolf mask her mother wore, when she became the Beastly Beauty. Just a few seconds to wish she could turn to wolf and go on all fours and run like the wind with her friends.

Then suddenly the entire forest turned dark purple, streaked with red. she couldn't breathe and the ground reached up to slam against her.

When the silver faded, she lay in a heap with the cubs. 'Na took a shallow breath, because she couldn't take a deep breath with Keeyo's hindquarters on her belly. Her mouth tasted awful.

"Well, well, well, what do we have here?" a creaky sort of voice whispered. It made the dark, red-streaked purple dome surrounding them ripple.

'Na lay as still as she could. Maybe whoever had that nasty voice wouldn't see her under the cubs. They held very still, too. Were they scared or preparing to leap into battle? Usually she liked playing with her friends in wolf shape, holding still for minutes at a time, waiting for someone to slip, get a cramp, make the first move, and then everyone exploded into action.

This wasn't a game, though.

"You're being very rude, Lady Belladonna. You will answer me," the creaky voice snarled.

He could see her, even under the cubs.

Even worse, he knew who she was. 'Na hated her full, formal name. Usually when someone used it, that meant she was either in a very stiff, fancy, formal situation and had to wear her fanciest clothes, or she was in deep trouble.

Sometimes, when her parents faced someone especially arrogant or rude or demanding or threatening, they deliberately increased the trouble, just to force their opponent into a mistake. Could she do that?

She would talk like her classmate, Circe-Beth. Several of their teachers had been so flustered at the girl's attitude that everyone had to do things her way, they got flustered and made mistakes. Could she fluster this man into mistakes?

"Why do I need to tell you what you already know?" she said.

Rolf snorted, his mouth falling open in wolf laughter. He nudged Keeyo, who finally got off 'Na's stomach.

"You need to tame that sassy mouth of yours, little girl," the voice snapped, and the dark red streaks in the dome seemed to pulse, growing brighter, then thickening.

"You're not my papa, so you can't tell me how to behave."

"Oh, but I can make you my little girl, very easily, and then you'll have to obey me." He chuckled.

"No, you can't."

'Na shivered a little as she sat up, because she had the awful feeling this voice could do exactly what he said. She wasn't sure how he could do that, because she already had parents. She knew that children without parents could be adopted and get new parents.

Would he have to kill her parents to do that?

"You're in vampire territory. Haven't you figured that out by now?" He tsked several times. It was a strangely dry sound. Usually when people tsked at 'Na, they sort of spit.

"But the tunnel was supposed to take me—"

"My, have I been deceived? Have my spies lied about your magical sensitivity?" He tsked again. 'Na wanted to slap him.

One nice thing about being angry was that she had less room in her belly to be afraid.

"Surely, if you're as full of magic potential as everyone has said since before you were born, you should have sensed that the tunnels have changed. Urmur has been very busy, expending his very limited magical strength to take control of those tunnels under the forest. That's how you ended up here, in the barrier lands between the werewolf and vampire tribes."

"Is he the one who fell out of the tree?" Rolf asked, his voice very rough, having just shifted shape from wolf to boy.

"No, that was his brother, Hempho." The nasty voice let out a loud sigh. "Good help is so hard to find nowadays …"

"And even harder, once the rest of the tribe hears how you tried to break the peace accords, yet again, with the werewolves and the enchanted castle," a familiar baritone voice said.

A spot in the dome brightened and lost the red streaks, bulging inward.

"No! Go away. This is my triumph. You'll not interfere," the nasty voice snarled, ending on a shriek as the bulge in the wall turned lavender, then pale blue, and a man's shape appeared in silhouette inside it.

"Again, were you going to say? And I don't think this is anywhere near a triumph." The bulge turned transparent and the man became visible.

"Uncle Morris!" 'Na cried and jumped up to run to him.

At least, she tried to jump up. Her feet and bottom seemed glued to the ground.

"He's another vampire," Rolf said in a growling sort of whisper.

"Yeah, but he's the leader of the vampires," she said.

"Not for long!" the nasty voice shrieked. "When I forge the blood oath on that stupid little girl—"

"You mean *force* the blood oath?" Morris strolled over to where the werewolf boys and 'Na crouched on the ground. "Sorry, you can't. Only one blood oath with a vampire per customer."

"What are you yammering about now, you imbecile?" the nasty voice snarled.

Morris held out his left hand to 'Na. A star-shaped mark on his wrist lit up green, and an answering star-shaped mark on her right wrist glowed into life.

"No! It's not fair! You already have a blood oath with her? Why didn't you tell anyone? We could have used it to take over the castle long ago!"

"That's exactly why I didn't tell anyone. The blood oath was to get Lady Belladonna safely through vampire lands, back home to the enchanted castle. And to repay a huge debt I owed her mother from decades ago." Morris pulled 'Na to her feet.

Her legs stuck to the ground for a few heartbeats, and she took a deep breath, expecting something to hurt. There was a feeling like a popping soap bubble all over her.

"Help your friends up," Morris said.

'Na kept her grip on his left hand and reached out her left hand to Rolf, who held out his free hand to Keeyo. Each werewolf shifted to boy and reached for the boy next to him, until all the werewolf boys were free and standing on their own feet. Meanwhile, the nasty voice snarled and muttered and said things in a language 'Na didn't understand.

"Such language, and in front of innocent children," Morris scolded, shaking his head. He winked at 'Na.

The werewolf boys laughed. Then as one person, they tipped their heads back and howled.

The nasty voice let out a shriek of pain that made the dome shake. The red streaks turned pink and splintered into smaller streaks, running in crazy zigzags all through the dome. Morris staggered and pressed his free hand to his ear, but he smiled, baring his fangs.

"Keep singing, children. Sing until the dome shatters!"

The younger boys hesitated, but Rolf nodded to them and took a deep breath and flung his head back. As he raised his voice to the dome overhead, he shifted back to wolf. The other boys followed suit. 'Na joined them, until Morris went to his knees, pressing both hands over his ears. She yanked her hand free of Rolf's and twisted around to hold Morris upright. A gasp escaped her when she saw blood trickling through his fingers, coming from his ears. He smiled at her.

"It's all right," he said, his voice a groan broken by breathless little gasps.

"But—"

"Don't let them stop until—" He gasped, arching his back, as the dome let out a chiming, off-key shriek and suddenly purple shards of magic fell around them. Morris wrapped his arms around her and tucked her underneath him. All his muscles tightened, bracing for a heavy blow. 'Na closed her eyes.

Nothing happened.

'Na opened one eye, then the other. Ordinary nighttime gloom surrounded them, not the eerie purple streaked with red and black. She twisted her head enough to see past Morris's sheltering arm. Bits of glittering, fading purple melted into the mossy ground around them. She had to shout to be heard over the continued howling.

Morris collapsed, twisting sideways to keep from pushing her down to the ground. Then the cubs stopped howling. They gathered around, their faces solemn as they morphed back into boys.

"How come his blood smells funny?" Keeyo whispered.

"He's a vampire, stupid," Rollo whispered back.

Morris chuckled, broken instantly by coughing. He pulled himself upright on his knees and wiped his bloody hands on his jacket, then wiped his face clean with his palms.

"I'm sorry. You shouldn't have had to see that."

"Necessary, I think," a deep, howling sort of voice responded out of the shadows behind their little group.

Rolf caught his breath and stood up straight, then slowly turned as Arrasmus, his uncle, leader of the werewolf tribe, stepped into the pale moonlight that had replaced the poisonous purple magic light. Eyes gleamed in the darkness, among shapes that hinted at a large number of wolves who stayed in the darkness of the trees. The boys all took a step or two back, putting Rolf between them and his uncle.

"They came to help me," 'Na hurried to say.

It only now occurred to her that her call for help had gotten her friends into trouble. By entering the vampire-held territory to help her, the boys had broken one of the stringent rules of the werewolf tribe.

"Yes, we know. Sangruel wanted us to know what he was doing. He was so busy keeping us busy, he didn't see Master Morris arrive and start unraveling his spells." A chuckle escaped Arrasmus and his grim expression relaxed for a few seconds. "He had no idea what was going on." Then his face broke into a grin, and he chuckled. "We're only teasing, when we complain about the roughness of your voices when you join the community howls, but we never dreamed they could shatter vampire magic."

The boys all flinched and winced and several blushed.

Arrasmus held out his hand to Morris. "We owe you a debt of gratitude. You encouraged them to howl, even at the price of pain. I admit we have been far more skeptical than is justified, when your elders ask for peace. This is proof enough for me that the rebels among you are causing the problems, and your nightborn do want peace."

"I didn't intervene for the sake of the peace accords," Morris said. He looked at Arrasmus's hand, then at the last streaks of blood on his hand and held it out to the werewolf leader. "I intervened because of the blood bond I made with Belladonna, and the debt of friendship and peace I owe her mother. But if this night will help bring friendship between our people, then I am glad."

The werewolf leader nodded slowly, his expression stern as he studied Morris's face. He raked a thick fingernail across his palm to draw a thin line of blood and held his hand out. Clasping hands mixed the blood of the two men, vampire and werewolf.

An entirely wicked, yet somehow amused grin lit Morris's face when the two men ended the clasp. "Would you do me a favor, and loan me some of your boys? Let them stay in our village while they practice their singing? I can think of several among our elders who need … shall we say … further incentive to agree to the accords and seal it with their blood oaths."

Arrasmus grinned, baring his teeth. Both men laughed, a soft, rumbling sound.

"Does this mean we aren't going to get hung up by our tails?" Keeyo whispered.

"You're all in trouble, just not as much trouble as you could have been," Arrasmus said. "We're going to have to do something about those tunnels under the forest, if they can be warped so easily and detoured. Your parents were rather concerned, when they asked us to watch for you, and you didn't appear in the clearing."

"Am I in trouble?" 'Na said. She had the awful feeling that asking Chatelaine to tell her parents what she was doing wasn't the smartest tactic. If she had told her parents her plan, they would have checked the tunnel and sensed Urmur's warping magic at work.

"I don't know." The werewolf leader winked at Morris. "Your father's words were, 'Tell Belladonna to get home right away.'" He chuckled when she groaned.

Her parents only used her full name when she was in deep, deep trouble.

The End

SECRETS IN THE SHADOWS
Lindsi McIntyre

A thick white mist had settled across the valley, enshrouding the town like a veil. Viviana leaned against the door of the car, letting her cheek rest against the cool glass. Swirls of lacey vapor whipped across the other side as if beckoning her to leap from the moving vehicle. Wishful thinking.

There was no escape.

"Listen here, Viv." The pamphlet Mami was reading rustled. "Radelesca House has three different gardens."

"It's the middle of autumn," Viviana replied. "What good is a garden? Everything will be dead."

Mami sighed. The silence between them was loaded. Heavy with their unspoken secrets. Tati reached for the dial and turned up the radio. His finger tapped the steering wheel absently to the tempo of the old classical song coming out of the speakers.

The little hatchback tilted as they started up the mountainside. Tati threw the shift into a higher gear. The engine rattled at the sudden demand for more power, but the little car sputtered through. The mist thinned as they reached higher elevation.

Viviana looked out over the valley. The little town they'd spent the morning driving through was covered in white. Only the thatched rooftops of the cottages and the shingles of businesses in the square peeked out. Chimney smoke mingled with the moisture in the air and produced thick lines of smog.

Dark, wide trunks materialized by the side of the curving road. Dull reflectors affixed to a rusted railing flashed in the muted morning light. It wasn't only the mist that held the afternoon sun at bay; the trees towered overhead, their branches spread wide over the man-made path through their forest, as if declaring sovereignty over the land.

They reached even higher and each turn they twisted around sent a small pile of the loose gravel shifting beneath the tires. The radio crackled. Static replaced the music. Tati hit the switch, turning off the noise. Still, no one spoke. What was there to say? They already knew she didn't want to go to Radelesca House for the fall semester. And they'd made it clear that what she wanted didn't matter.

Miles up the mountain, far out of sight of the town, the road peaked over a hill and leveled out onto a massive plateau. There, a castle rose into the sky. Viviana sat up, despite herself.

Grey, stone walls punctuated by lines of brown and pink looked like they'd been carved out of the mountain itself, especially at the back where several sections pressed into the cliff side. Smooth lines made up squares and rectangles, fitted together in a series of blocks. Rooms that would have been molded hundreds of years before.

Dark pink shingles covered sections of the rooftop. A single turret stood high above the rest, its sharply sloped edges leading down to four points that jutted out sharp as spears. Windows dotted the side of the turret where the staircase would presumably be.

A wall had been carved or built along the front of the castle. It sat lower than the roof but tall enough to keep out invading forces. A gate had been fitted into the wall, complete with a drawbridge that sat open to welcome visitors.

Viviana couldn't deny the sight of the structure inspired awe. She quickly leaned back against the door. Her parents didn't need to know that, though. If they could keep their secrets, she had every right to keep hers.

The hatchback shook as it drove over the lowered drawbridge. More of the castle came into view. The courtyard acted as a driveway, leading them in a wide circle around the castle grounds. In the center sprawled an elaborate, though lifeless, garden complete with a large empty granite fountain.

On the right side of the courtyard stood a stable, once—no doubt—the home of many prized horses. It had since been converted into a garage.

As they passed, Viviana noticed half a dozen vans parked to one side. In the back, tucked away in the shadows, someone had parked a limousine. Who would drive a limousine on a mountain?

The garage vanished as Tati maneuvered to the front of the castle. Stone steps easily four people wide led up to a set of double doors just as broad. They were made of dark wood, most likely harvested from the mountain's own forest.

The car gave a *screech* as Tati threw it into park. He twisted the key to shut down the engine. Then sighed. "Well. Here we are."

Viviana peered up at the castle's front door. A bead of heat sparked to life somewhere beneath her rib cage. So, this was the place they'd chosen to abandon her for the next four months. She'd be "home" just in time for Christmas. Whatever that meant. She pressed her lips together as the urge to scream built up inside her lungs.

A heavyset woman with a bright smile emerged from the castle.

Her gaze landed on the little hatchback with a genuine twinkle. She waved excitedly. "Yoohoo. Mr. and Mrs. Balan? Is that you? How good to see you've made it." She started down the steps, her smile never wavering.

Viviana wondered what her parents had told the school. Probably that she was excited to become a student. She'd be willing to bet real money they hadn't mentioned she had said, in no uncertain terms, that she hated the idea with every fiber of her being.

Her parents practically jumped out of the hatchback. Mami didn't even wait for Viviana to open her own door. "Come on, Viv," her mother said, holding the door wide as if Viviana were a feral cat that might scratch if she got too close. "Time's wasting."

Viviana inched her way out of the back seat and slowly walked a few feet away from the car. The door slammed behind her, sealing her fate. She pulled in a deep breath, then sighed dreadfully. "My chest hurts."

"Huh? Oh, that's just the altitude." Tati pulled two large bags out of the trunk and slammed the top closed with his elbow. "You'll get used to it."

"Like I have a choice."

Tati sighed, a sound she was quickly becoming used to hearing from her parents. At least it was better than the yelling they tried to hide behind the paper-thin walls of their house. Barely.

"Listen, Jitterbug. I know this isn't exactly what you had in mind for finishing off the year. But it'll be for the best in the end." He looked ready to say something else. Viviana wondered if he was finally about to be honest with her.

Mami cleared her throat as if in warning. And Tati frowned back at her before turning back to Viviana. He forced a smile and said, "Parents need vacation time too, you know."

All of a sudden, she didn't care about holding the heat back. It radiated out of her chest and her breath fogged the air as the word slipped out.

"Liar."

Her father looked down at her in surprise. "What?"

"You're a liar." She glared up at him, ignoring the way he flinched at her stare. "You're not going on vacation. You're going to talk to the lawyers. You're getting divorced and you don't want me around to remind you of the inconvenience of the life you're ripping apart."

Her mother froze, hands clutching the pamphlet for the school, her face growing pale.

Her parents exchanged a look, as if trying to figure out which one had let the cat out of the bag before they could drown it. No doubt they relished having *another* thing to fight over.

Viviana threw her hands wide and tilted her head to the side. "What was the plan exactly? Come and pick me up in December and say, 'Surprise! We got divorced. Don't worry. Nothing in your life is ever going to be the same but *we're* happy and that's what matters.' Or did you bother to think about *me* at all?"

Tati straightened his shoulders. "I will not tolerate disrespect, young lady. Our business is our business and it'll stay that way."

"Riiight. Your business. It doesn't have anything to do with me. Not gonna affect *me* at all. Guess that answers my question."

"Enough." He set her luggage down with a thud. One of them toppled, landing with a spurt in the mud. "Now. You have two choices. You can try to enjoy your time here at a real life castle in the beautiful countryside, making new friends at a once-in-a-lifetime opportunity. Or, you can be miserable. It's up to you. But you're staying here until your mother comes to pick you up in December."

Viviana sneered. "Only Mother's coming? Not even trying to hide the abandonment anymore, huh?"

For a brief moment her father seemed shattered by what she'd said. Then Mami stepped in. "Some things are only for adults to sort out, Viv. You'll understand when you're older."

"I'm sixteen, not six. I understand just fine."

For a moment they stared at her, as if the fury she felt were battering them body and soul. Then her father's eyes shuttered. "Have a good time at school, Viviana." He spun on his heel and strode back toward the old family car. "Come on, Ailina." Her mother's head dropped but she followed after him, leaving Viviana standing alone in the middle of the lot as the woman from the castle bustled onto the scene.

"Heavens. Where are they headed off to in such a hurry?"

"They're just running from their responsibilities." Viviana made sure her voice was loud enough for her parents to hear in their hasty retreat. Mami looked back sadly as she opened the car door, but Tati was quick to say something that made her drop into the front seat.

"Don't worry, dear," the woman said.

The doors of the car slammed shut, and the engine sputtered to life. Gravel flew as her parents headed back for the drawbridge.

"They'll be back in a few short months. Time'll fly by. You'll see."

"It might be better if they didn't," Viviana replied. Nothing would be the same either way.

The woman placed a frigid hand on Viviana's shoulder and spun her to face the castle. "My name's Mahtilda, but everyone just calls me

Tilly. I'm the nurse and unofficial welcoming committee. Don't worry about your bags." She pointed to the steps where two women in starched black uniforms with aprons wrapped around their waists were hurrying toward them. "The staff will gather them up and take them to your room. Now, let's go meet our other newcomer."

Tilly hurried her toward a group of people huddled beside a rusty old van on the far side of the steps. They spoke in hushed, yet nearly frantic tones, their faces serious as the grave. The woman was motioning with her hand as if giving detailed instructions to a boy in his mid-teens. Lecturing him on how to behave while at school, perhaps? He didn't look happy with what his mom had to say. He opened his mouth.

"But I could help—"

They shut up mid-conversation as Viviana came within earshot. It was the kind of quick silence people did when they had something to hide. Viviana studied the three of them pointedly, her curiosity piqued.

"Yoohoo. Hello, Harker family. I'm Mahtilda. Tilly for short."

The mother stepped forward. "Hello, Tilly." The women shook hands. "I'm Sorinah Harker. We spoke over the phone."

"Of course. Sorinah. Such a pleasure to meet you. Did you have a good trip up?"

They chattered as Viviana studied the woman, the man, and finally the boy. At first glance they seemed normal. Boring even. Just a small family saying good-bye at the start of the semester. Until she spotted the knife tucked into the father's boot.

It was hard to see at first because the wood had been shaped flat and dyed the same color as the man's pants. Then, as if she were reading through a book of optical illusions, others started to take shape. One in his other boot. Several hidden along his belt. And, if she guessed correctly, there was at least one strapped to his side, hidden beneath his oversized coat.

Viviana studied the mom again. Yep. She had them too. And, even though the boy didn't have any on him that she could detect, Viviana could see the indents in his boots where they could go. He also had empty loops on his belt. Identical to the ones on his parents' clothing.

The boy cleared his throat. Viviana looked up, her gaze slamming into his. He smirked and raised an eyebrow. And Viviana realized where he thought she'd just been staring. Face burning, she quickly looked away.

It wasn't illegal to own knives. Especially out in the countryside in the mountains where bears and wolves were always looking for a quick meal. But the way they hid them seemed intentional.

Viviana sidled a step away and, when no one seemed to notice, stood on tiptoe, trying to see inside the van. The grime-covered windows made the task difficult. But then… What was that? In the front seat. *Whoa.* It was a cellular phone. Viviana moved a step closer for a better look. She'd only ever seen them in adverts in newspapers. They were expensive and their brick-like size made them impractical for most people. Why would a family driving such an ugly van have one? A bag bulging at the sides sat beside the phone. What was that sticking out of the top? A pole of some kind…

Viviana flinched as the boy suddenly stepped in front of her. It was clear from the position he took that he was purposely blocking her view. She lifted her gaze to meet his as she dropped back onto the heel of her foot with a soft thud. He smiled brightly, too brightly, considering the look of irritation she knew must be on her face.

"Hey." He stuck out his hand. "Name's Luca. Some place they got here, huh? I wasn't sure what to expect when my parents told me about the castle grounds, but now I'm pretty excited to go exploring."

"Viviana." She replied with an equally friendly smile, though she made sure he knew hers was phony. "And great work at your distraction. No really. *Not* super obvious at all."

He blinked as she took hold of his hand and shook it firmly, his smile melting into confusion. For a minute, she relished her victory. Then, to her surprise, he laughed. The adults stopped talking to glance over at them. Victory lost, Viviana let her hand drop along with her expression.

"There now," Tilly said. "Already making friends." She smiled brightly at Viviana, then shifted the ray of cheer back to Luca's parents. "Shall we begin the tour?"

"Unfortunately," Sorinah replied, "we can't stay." She exchanged a look with her husband. "We need to be back in town for an important appointment. It's very time-sensitive."

Why did all grownups think they were so clever? Especially when it was always so obvious when they lied. An *appointment*? Please. She didn't know what they were actually going to do, but she knew it wasn't that simple.

"Oh. Well, we're sorry not to have you, of course. But we understand, don't we kids?"

"You bet," Luca replied. He smiled at his parents. "I'll see you guys in a few months."

Sorinah stopped long enough to kiss her son's cheek. "Be safe."

Viviana lifted a brow. That sounded ominous.

His father gave Luca's shoulder a squeeze. "We'll be seeing you, son."

The two climbed into the beat-up old van while Luca pretended to casually move around to wave as they left, effectively blocking Viviana's attempts to sneak a peek into the vehicle when they opened the doors. She glared at him as the doors shut. He smiled her way and motioned to the castle as the van roared to life.

"Ladies first."

She snorted and headed for the steps as the van peeled out of the courtyard. Let him keep their secrets, for now. All secrets eventually came to light. It was only a matter of time.

~~~~~

Two hours later, Tilly and Luca dropped Viviana off at her room in the girls' wing of the castle.

"Dinner is at eight o'clock sharp," the nurse said. "In the great hall. You remember? That's a good girl. Don't be late."

Viviana forced a smile as Tilly hurried Luca away to show him to the boys' wing. She sighed heavily when the woman was out of sight. She did *not* remember. Not exactly. Tilly was not the most organized tour guide. Dozens of times she'd "remembered" things to show them, dragging them back the way they'd already come and turning down different hallways until Viviana felt hopelessly lost. They'd probably walked several rooms multiple times, but each one looked so similar she wouldn't have been able to say which. She was more confused about the layout of the castle now than she'd been when the tour had first started.

With another sigh, Viviana turned to inspect the room she'd be staying in for the next four months. And groaned. Sure it was big, but seven cots lined each wall. Fourteen beds. Which meant at least fourteen girls would be sharing the room with her. One set of windows let light in along the far wall, mirroring the doorway. It was simple, sparse and utterly dreary.

She spotted her luggage at the foot of one bed and considered unpacking. But the large clock at the end of the hallway behind her chimed. Half past six. Considering how big the castle was, she'd be late for dinner if she didn't leave right away.

Her footsteps echoed against the wooden floor as she left the room and headed in what she hoped was the direction of the great hall.

~~~~~

Viviana was hopelessly lost. She'd long given up trying to find the great hall on her own. Now she would settle for finding anyone, a student, a teacher, a member of the staff. *Anyone* who could show her where to go.

Every hallway looked the same, every staircase identical to the last. The electric lights buzzing along the walls barely made a dent in the shadows that kept her company. Her head hurt. Her stomach was growling. She wondered how long it would take anyone to notice she was missing, and if they'd find her body before she'd turned to bones. A soft sound caught her attention. The mumble of distant voices.

"I'm saved." She laughed, rushing to catch up to whoever was speaking.

She turned down one corner then ran to the next. The voices grew closer. Clearer. They no longer echoed but came from one solid direction.

"Have you found everything to be to your satisfaction, Count?"

"Indeed. The promised contributions are well in order. And your hospitality has been most appreciated."

Viviana stopped. A strange chill raced across her skin. The shadows were deeper here, like a physical thing waiting to swallow anyone foolish enough to come close. She peered into the next hallway instead of rushing in. Someone had pulled heavy curtains across the windows, blocking out the natural light. One stray sunbeam cut across the floor up ahead. A single point of gold in the abyss.

A man stood before an open doorway further down, speaking to someone inside. Even in the dark, Viviana could see the thin, white hair covering his head. He leaned heavily on the cane clutched tightly in his right hand.

"Excellent." The old man shifted, his cane scraping against the floor. "Then the ceremony will proceed as planned."

"Agreed. By this time tomorrow, you'll be a brand new man, Radelesca."

A twisted smile marred the old man's face as he turned away from the door. Viviana pressed herself into the wall, concealing herself in the shadows. His cane struck the floor as he walked. *Thump.* And his bad foot dragged. *Scrape. Thump. Scrape.* The man inched past her hiding spot. He limped down the hallway until he was out of sight.

"Hello, there little one," a voice called from the darkness.

Terror unlike anything she'd ever experienced seized Viviana. Cold. Solid. Final. Some instinct warned her to be still. To hide. Her chest burned. But she couldn't risk the breath begging to escape her lungs. Utterly afraid to move, she forced her eyes to shift until she could see the person speaking.

A shadow loomed just beyond the thin beam of sunlight—a man, with bright red eyes. His thin lips split into a smile, revealing razor sharp fangs.

"Come here, little one. Don't be afraid."

Pain lanced through her skull, dragging the air out of her lungs with an audible gasp. Suddenly, her body was no longer frozen. With a cry she spun away and sprinted from the specter as fast as she could go, heeding the instinct that screamed at her to run. Run. Run!

A chuckle haunted her retreat.

~~~~~

Heart pounding and gasping for air, Viviana sprinted through the castle, blind with terror until she nearly trampled two girls walking out of the library. She flung her arms wide as her momentum tried to drag her into them. The girls screamed.

They stared at each other. Then the girls gave an awkward laugh.

"Are you okay?" one of them asked. "You look like you've seen a ghost."

"Um. I—"

"It's these hallways," the other interrupted. "During the day it's not so bad. But at night? Ugh." She shivered dramatically. "They give me the creeps. I never walk around alone after the sun goes down."

"I *know*!" the second cut in. "Everything looks alive in the dark. Like the shadows are gonna jump out and grab you." She smiled at Viviana. "Don't worry, though. You'll get used to it. You're the new girl, right? They let us know you'd be coming. We were just about to head to the great hall for dinner. You should join us."

Viviana let out a little chuckle, still fighting to get her heart rate back to normal and her breathing under control. "Thanks. I was more than a little lost. I thought I'd be late for sure." She didn't know how far she'd run, but her legs shook as she followed the girls toward the great hall.

A wave of heat washed over her. Now that she was back in the central part of the castle, where the electric lights burned strong and she wasn't alone, she felt stupid. No wonder the man in the hallway had laughed as she'd run away. He wasn't some flesh-eating shadow monster. He was just some guy visiting the school to help with some kind of ceremony. He probably thought she was an addlebrained ninny.

The great hall was already packed with students. Boys and girls wandered about, chatting, laughing and occasionally picking seats at the five long tables stretched perpendicularly across the floor. The faculty had gathered at the table on the raised platform where the lord and his family would have sat for meals. The girls she'd followed disappeared into the crowd as Viviana hung back, overwhelmed.

"Hello there," a voice whispered close to her ear.

Viviana jumped.

"Whoa, jumpy." Luca studied her face and his smile vanished. He held out his hands as if calming a scared animal. "Sorry. I didn't mean to scare you. Are you okay?"

"I'm fine." Viviana flinched at the harsh sound of her own voice.
~~~~~

"Yeah. Sure. You sound *great*."

She glared up at his stupid grinning face. She much preferred being the one to point out other people's lies and didn't appreciate him turning it around on her. She opened her mouth to put him back in his place when a loud *clang* ripped through the room, silencing those gathered within.

A broad, angry looking man holding a bell spoke from the end of the platform. "Please be seated."

"Barnaby Fiffe," Luca leaned in to whisper as they filed with other kids toward a table. "Apparently, his family has worked with the Radelescas for decades. He and the headmaster have been friends since childhood. And both have lived here their whole lives."

They reached a table where knives and forks had been laid out just like an expensive restaurant.

"You've sure learned a lot about this place in only a few hours," she said.

He shrugged. "I have an inquisitive mind." He grinned. "It's one of my many charms."

She scoffed. "Many?"

They selected chairs. Viviana was both irritated and a little grateful he'd picked the seat next to hers.

A thud echoed through the platform and out across the nearly silent room. Viviana stiffened. *Thud. Scrape. Thud. Scrape.* Her chest tightened as if it might collapse in on itself. Her face and hands grew cold.

"Hey," Luca murmured. "Are you okay?" His eyes widened as he watched her.

"Yeah," she forced out, determined not to make a fool of herself twice in one day. "I'm fine." And, to prove she wasn't scared, she deliberately turned toward the sound of the man limping his way across the platform.

When she saw him, all the terror rushed out of her at once. He was just an old man. White hair. Wrinkled face. Glassy grey eyes. He walked with a pronounced limp, leaning heavily on a black cane topped with a mother of pearl handle. It was definitely the same man she'd seen before but now, under the harsh lights of the chandeliers hanging above, he looked frail and sickly and so far from a threat that she nearly laughed at how absurd her earlier reaction to him had been. He even sat like an old man, slowly lowering himself into the chair at the center of the high table with the help of Barnaby Fiffe.

Luca relaxed; probably relieved she hadn't passed out. "You really are jumpy tonight."

Viviana couldn't exactly argue the point. Luckily, she was saved from having to respond when the staff started bringing plates out to the students. The goat was tender and the potatoes were mashed to perfection. The hot food settled in her belly and chased away the last of the chill that had been clinging to her. She even managed to participate in the conversation with the kids around her as dinner went on. Finally, she leaned back in her chair, rubbing her stomach.

"Full?" Luca grinned.

Viviana laughed. "Yep. I didn't expect dinner to be so good. I'm glad I didn't miss it."

"Why would you miss it?" He scraped his fork against his plate.

"I got lost earlier. Everything looks the same here. Oh. Hey, you know a lot about this place now. What's the ceremony that's happening tonight?"

Luca froze, a fork full of mashed potatoes hovering near his lips. "What?"

Viviana shrugged. "It's just something I overheard earlier. When I was lost. Radelesca mentioned something about a ceremony to some man." She rubbed her neck, remembering the cold that had wrapped around her like a snake.

Slowly, he set down his fork as if trying to appear casual. His tone was full of forced indifference as he asked, "What kind of ceremony?"

She frowned. Why did he look like he was about to be sick? "I don't know. They just said the ceremony would proceed as planned because the *contributions* were all in order. I figured he meant they'd paid for something—"

Luca grabbed her by the shoulders. "What man?"

"Hey!" Viviana tried to pull away, but his grip dug into her skin. "What man?"

"I don't know," she said, suddenly aware people were staring at them. She lowered her voice. "Some creepy guy staying in a room deeper into the castle. How would I know who it was?"

Abruptly he stood, leaving her gaping up at him as his face drained of color. "I—I just remembered. I need to call my parents." He turned a shaky smile on those seated at the table. "Does anyone know where I can find a phone?"

"The only one we have is in the nurse's office," a boy across from them replied.

Luca spun on his heel and strode away from the table.

"They only let us use it in emergencies," the boy yelled. Luca ignored him.

Viviana frowned. Then she jumped out of her seat and followed him out of the room.

~~~~~

"What do you mean, the phone isn't working?" If Luca looked pale before, he was downright ghostly now. Viviana looked between him and Tilly, wondering if she should try to find somewhere for him to sit down.

"I'm sorry, dear," Tilly replied. The nurse had come out of the dining room to find them waiting by her office, unable to enter the locked room. Though, to Viviana's surprise, Luca had given a valiant effort in trying to pick the lock with two long pieces of metal he'd pulled out of his pocket. "There was some sort of issue with the lines. It seems Barnaby discovered the damage earlier today. It won't be fixed for quite a while, I'm afraid."

"Is there any way to get down the mountain? Please. It's an emergency."

Tilly blinked. "N—no. I'm sorry. Not without a good explanation and permission from Headmaster Radelesca."

Luca ran his hands through his hair. "That won't work."

Tilly smiled brightly and placed her hand on Luca's shoulder. "Now now. Let's not fret. I know it can be intimidating staying overnight in a new place. But a little homesickness is to be expected. Why, not so very long ago phones hadn't even been invented yet and kids everywhere spent days, even weeks at a time without speaking to their parents. And everything was fine. Don't you worry. You'll feel right as rain after a good night's sleep."

Luca forced his pale lips into the facsimile of a smile. "I'm sure you're right."

Viviana waited until the nurse had walked away before spinning to face the boy. "What the heck was that all about?"

But he wasn't listening.

He ran his hand absently under his chin as he paced in circles in front of the nurse's office. "They'll need to be outside. Somewhere nearby but close to soil." He snapped his fingers. "The eastern field. Past the old chapel. It's the only place that makes any sense for them to dig."

"Dig what? Is this still about the ceremony?"

He flinched as if he had forgotten she was there. He stared at her, eyes wide. Then, whatever he was feeling was shuttered away behind the fakest smile she'd ever seen. "What? No. Of course not. I was just—" He waved. "Blathering. It's nothing."

Viviana snorted. "Seriously. You expect me to believe—"

"Shut it, Viviana. You'll mind your own business if you know what's good for you."

Her mouth hung open as she watched him storm away. But her shock quickly transformed into a raging fury. How dare he talk to her
~~~~~

like that? He was so obviously up to something it was a joke for him to try to cover it up now. She'd show him. She was going to find out exactly what this ceremony was and expose what everyone was hiding.

~~~~~

Storm clouds had swooped into the valley and rapidly made their way toward the mountain where Radelesca House sat. Lightning flashed in their depths and distant thunder rumbled, threatening a drenching. Viviana shivered at the chill in the air and slid deeper into her winter coat. The fur-lined collar tickled her cheeks as she huddled into the cloth. It was not the kind of weather someone wanted to be out in. And yet, there she was, making her way across the back garden of the estate toward the eastern gate where Tilly had pointed out the lush green field on the other side of the castle.

She must be insane.

Her feet sank into the loamy earth as she stepped through the gate. The field stretched out before her, dark and still. A building stood halfway across, a pointed steeple rising from its roof. The chapel. It blocked her view of the grassy area beyond. She made her way there, hoping to catch a glimpse of something worth risking hypothermia for.

Had anyone else been dumb enough to come out with that storm building on the horizon? She'd just about convinced herself to go back inside when a rock skittered across the ground behind her. A black form slammed into her, knocking her to the ground and the air from her lungs. Viviana opened her mouth to scream, knowing no sound would come out but desperate for help, as her attacker threw her onto her back.

Luca knelt over her; arm extended overhead, hand clutching a long stick with a sharp pointed end. The fierce scowl marring his face melted into shock, which then transformed into rage. "What are you *doing* here?"

"Get--" the word slipped out of her battered chest as a whisper. She forced her lungs to fill with precious oxygen. "Get off of me."

"Go back inside. Now." He let go of her and shifted so his weight didn't pin her anymore.

Viviana jumped to her feet. "No."

"You have no idea what you're getting involved in."

"Then tell me."

They glared at one another.

"You wouldn't believe me," he said.

"Try me."

He turned to walk away. "Go back."

Viviana snorted and started after him.

He spun in a fury. "I should tie you up and stick you in a bush
~~~~~

somewhere."

"You do, and I'll scream my head off. Then we'll see what good all your whispering and sneaking around will do."

"Fine! But if you slow me down, I'm leaving you behind. I don't have time to babysit some stupid girl who doesn't know how to mind her own business."

She rolled her eyes. "Riiiight. I'm really scared."

"The fact that you're not scared is the reason you don't belong here."

Viviana watched him walk away with a frown. He actually seemed to believe there was something dangerous going on. Ridiculous. They were just at some silly school in the countryside.

Somewhere in the distance an owl hooted. Viviana hurried to catch up to him. A shiver coursed through her body just as she reached his side.

"Seriously, Viviana. You should go back." Luca frowned.

She hoped the frown she returned to him was as deep and pointed as his. "Not a chance."

He sighed. "You're just being stubborn."

"Says you," she replied. "You'll miss your chance to do whatever you're doing out here if you keep worrying about me."

He cursed. "Fine. But you'll regret it."

She rolled her eyes.

With a shake of his head, he moved the sharpened stick to his left hand, then reached for his belt, and whipped out a knife. She jumped at the sudden appearance of the deadly weapon. "Here. Take this."

She looked from the six-inch-long blade to his impassive face. Yet she still felt the need to ask, "Are you serious?"

He leaned forward, his brow furrowed and teeth clenched. "Take it. Or I *will* tie you up and leave you behind. No one is going up against what we're about to face without a weapon."

She raised her hands in surrender. "Okay. Okay. Jeez." Gingerly she wrapped her hand around the blade's wooden grip. Then she noticed he wasn't wearing the same clothes he'd had on at dinner.

His new ensemble was entirely black. Black shirt. Black jacket with a black fur lining. Slim black pants were tucked into calf-high black leather boots. Even the leather belt around his waist was black.

But the black knives tucked into those boots and along that belt truly caught her attention. Along with the knife he'd handed her, he had six others in sheaths along his belt, plus one tucked into each boot at his calf. Just as she'd suspected, he had the same set as his parents. There were also four flasks hanging from his belt.

As they walked, she glimpsed another belt strapped around his chest. She couldn't see what he carried on that belt, as his jacket covered it, but considering the arsenal he had visible, she imagined he carried something fairly deadly.

Viviana was about to ask what exactly he expected to find when she heard the sound of metal striking dirt somewhere further into the field. Luca motioned downward with his hand and crouched low to the earth. She mimicked his movements, only hesitating briefly as he dropped onto his belly and crawled toward the sound. Cold moisture seeped into her clothes as she crawled beside him. The ground sloped upward. Mud oozed beneath her fingernails. A bolt of lightning flashed across the sky. The storm had caught up with them.

Luca reached the top of the small hill first. Viviana joined him. On the other side, concealed from view of the castle, a man stood over a long rectangular hole in the ground. He wielded a shovel with cold precision, heaping mounds of dirt into the hole from a large pile of mud stacked beside it. Lightning flashed, illuminating the grizzly scene. With a jolt, Viviana realized it was none other than Barnaby Fiffe, and he was filling up a grave.

But it wasn't Barnaby or even the morbid task he was in the middle of that seized her attention. It was the man standing nearby. Tall. Cloaked in darkness. Eyes shining red above a fanged smile.

And staring right at their hiding spot.

In the next flash of lightning, the figure was gone.

A shadow shifted just out of view to the right. Viviana froze. Her eyes darted to the side, even while her body refused to move. The man stood on the hill beside them, only yards away. His eyes gleamed, boring into her like hot pokers. He wasn't wearing the cloak anymore. Now he stood, bare from waist to shoulders.

Slowly he stretched out his arms. No. They were wings. Massive leathery batwings stretched out behind him. His hands stayed by his side, his fingers tipped with claws that looked razor sharp.

Her hand shot out, clutching Luca's sleeve. But the warning was trapped behind her clenched teeth. It was right there. Her fingers burned as Luca jumped to his feet, yanking his sleeve from her grip. "Run, Viviana."

Viviana watched in horror as he jumped over her and ran.

Right at the monster.

A bolt of lightning split the sky above them. Viviana got up on her knees as Luca raised the sharpened stick above his head. His shout rang out over the field. The monster lifted one arm to block the weapon, and with the other, he struck Luca in the chest, hurling him back toward

Viviana.

The boy landed in front of her with a thud. His breath rushed out of his lungs on impact with an audible grunt. He rolled to his side, gasping. He had dropped his stick. He looked up at her from the mud, his eyes narrowed in pain.

"Run," he gasped. "Get to the chapel."

The shadow creature leapt into the air, wings extended.

"Look out," Viviana screamed.

Luca grabbed something from his waist and whipped around with more force than she would have thought him capable of. Silver flashed out of his hand, gleaming as lightning flashed, and buried itself in the creature's chest. It let out a terrible, animalistic shriek and lost balance as its wings collapsed. With a thud, it struck the ground and rolled back down the hill toward Barnaby and the grave.

Luca was back on his feet. He turned back toward the castle and grabbed her arm as he passed by. "Run, Viviana. Now!"

The two sprinted back the way they had crawled only moments before.

Now, they were the prey. And the heavy beat of wings on the air proved their pursuer wasn't about to let them get away.

They were a hundred yards from the chapel. Then fifty. Pale silver light illuminated their path and cast a winged shadow over them. It stretched, getting bigger. Closer. The light vanished. A hiss cut through the air at her back. Its breath tickled her neck. Viviana and Luca crashed to the ground beneath its weight as the sky opened up, unleashing rain.

Luca screamed as the monster sank its fangs into his shoulder. Thunder rumbled, drowning out the sound. Mud coated Viviana's face as she squirmed beneath the monster's weight. The three thrashed on the ground as it raised its head. It aimed those fangs at Luca's neck again. The spread wings trapped her alongside him so that she couldn't get away even as the monster focused its attack on the boy. Her hand brushed against Luca's waist as she tried to help him fend off the deadly fangs. A knife. She yanked it from the holster with a violent twist.

Then plunged it into the monster's side, just below its arm, deep into its ribs.

Its scream pummeled her eardrums, but she held on to the knife, forcing it deeper into the sickly pale flesh. With another shriek, it pulled away from her, ripping the knife out of her hand as it darted into the air. The flesh of her palm burned as she struggled to sit up. Luca hesitantly rose to his knees. A line of dark liquid slipped across his face, mixing with the mud and rain. Viviana made it to her feet first. This time she grabbed his arm. Urged him on.

"Up. Luca. Get up. We're almost there."

Their boots sank into the mud as they ran. Rain poured into Viviana's eyes, blurring the outline of the chapel as they approached. Lightning flashed then faded into darkness, leaving her disoriented. She felt the rumble of the thunder in her chest. And above it all, she heard the beat of wings in the air. Getting closer. And closer.

Viviana threw herself at the door of the chapel. With a splintering sound, it gave way. She fell into the sanctuary with a cry, with Luca right behind her. She watched the door in horror as the creature loomed outside with wings outstretched.

Luca threw his weight against the door, slamming it shut. Viviana curled into a ball, covering her head with her arms. There was no way that little piece of wood would keep that massive beast out. It was going to crash through and kill them where they sat.

"Easy," Luca said. "It can't follow us inside. This is holy ground."

Slowly, as the door stayed in one piece, Viviana uncurled. A heavy thud came from the other side.

"Come now, children." The voice crackled in a way that was not quite human. "Don't be afraid. Open the door."

Luca spun toward her, placing himself in front of the door as if to stop her. "Don't listen to it."

Viviana clutched her head as pain ripped through her skull. "Why would I listen to it?" The pain was bad but not unbearable. She might not know what that thing was, or why its voice made her head hurt, but she knew one thing for certain. Opening that door meant death.

"You…you don't feel…compelled to open it?" he asked.

She looked at him like he was insane. "No. And you better not either."

The creature hissed. "Very well then, children. I'll leave you to cower in your little hole." Its laughter slithered into the room like winter frost. "Perhaps we'll meet again someday. For now, I have other business to attend to. But don't worry. I'll be sure to come again if you change your minds." The door rattled as air beat against it with each flap of leathery wings.

Then the only sounds left were the rain, the wind, and the heavy breathing of the two hiding inside.

Viviana stared at the door for what seemed like ages. "Do you think it's really gone?" she whispered, watching Luca move by the flashes of the lightning slipping through the boarded-up windows.

Luca sat heavily, back pressed against the door with a grunt. "Doesn't matter. We can't risk going back out there. I've lost the element of surprise and without that, there's no way I can take it down by myself." He groaned as his hands gingerly prodded his right shoulder. "We'll stay put till the sun comes up. Then…" He shook his head. "Then, I don't know."

Viviana glared at him from where she sat huddled in the aisle between the pews. "What was that thing?"

"A vampire. Surely you've heard of them."

She stared at him for a long moment. "Vampire."

"My parents are back in town. Waiting."

"Your parents left you up here to fight that thing by yourself?" she interrupted.

"What?" he asked, genuinely offended. "No! They left me up here to fight him on *their* own. The plan," he grabbed the side of his jacket and tried to pull it off his injured arm with a grimace, "was to wait in town for him to pass through. To ambush him."

Viviana inched to his side and helped pull the jacket off. He gave her an appreciative half-smile.

"They tried to act like they needed me up here to investigate Radelesca's involvement with the vampires," he said. "But the truth is they wanted me out of the way. They left me here to *protect* me." He groaned as she pulled the leather free of his body. "Obviously, they didn't expect him to already be tucked away in the castle. All of our intel suggested he was still miles away. When you mentioned a ceremony and a creepy man, I knew we'd been tricked. My best bet was to try calling them…"

"But the phone lines were down," she added.

He gave a stiff nod. "Probably intentional. It would really put a damper on things if someone were to call for help once Radelesca rises and starts feeding."

"Whoa. Hold on." She raised her hands, still clutching his jacket, and shook her head. "How is Radelesca involved? Why is there a vampire *here*? And who are you people? Chasing vampires. Carrying around *stakes* like any of this is normal."

He chuckled despite the way he held his body so his right side wouldn't come into contact with the door behind him. "Well, it is normal. For me. It's sort of the family business."

Viviana wrapped her arms around her chest and sat back heavily against the wall, so that she faced him with her best no-nonsense look. "Explain."

He smiled, then rubbed mud off his cheek with the back of his left hand. "Basically, my family has been hunting vampires since…well. Since, forever. It all started with Jonathan Harker, my great-great-great-grandfather." He fiddled with his belt until he'd pulled a vial the length of his hand free of the leather. "Back then, almost no one knew about vampires. They killed any witnesses, so they did a pretty good job of keeping themselves a secret. But their leader, Count Dracula," he pulled the cork stopper out of the vial with his teeth, "got weirdly obsessed with someone in England. Went all the way there to try and get her. It was a huge deal. That's how my ancestor and his friends got dragged into it. Anyways, they killed off the original Dracula. But unfortunately, his subordinates had a plan for that." He poured a thick liquid from the vial into his hand and then slipped his palm under his shirt at the shoulder. He hissed and closed his eyes.

Viviana waited as he held his hand over the wound. He took deep breaths until his face relaxed. He pulled his hand free, opened his eyes and caught her watching him with eyebrow raised. He lifted his hand to show her his palm. "It's a coagulant. Vampires have venom in their fangs that makes the blood thin. It helps them feed."

She made a face at him, and he chuckled. "Yeah. Not my idea of a five star meal either."

"So," she prompted. "The other vampires had a plan and…"

"And they just gave his title to someone else. They picked a new vampire, the next strongest presumably, to inherit the lands, castle, name, everything. If any humans in the area noticed, they didn't say anything." He pulled a roll of gauze out of his belt and unrolled a strip of bandage. "Unfortunately, the vampires learned from their mistake. And ever since then, Dracula's castle has been nearly impenetrable. The elite vampires living there are practically untouchable. But there's one exception." Luca wadded the bandage into a square and shoved it beneath his shirt and over his wound. He paused again to catch his breath.

"They have one fatal flaw," he said through gritted teeth. "Dracula is the only vampire allowed to turn other humans. Thanks to that, they don't procreate very fast. Other, weaker vamps are left outside the castle to fend for themselves until they can prove worthy to join the upper echelons, but as far as we can tell, they aren't allowed to turn anyone. Dracula's enforcers will even kill any who try. It's one of the ways they've stayed hidden for so long."

Luca looked at the strip of bandage in one hand and the patch he'd made in the other as if wondering how he'd tie the strip around his shoulder without dropping both.

Viviana scooted toward him and waved. "Here. Let me."

He studied her for a moment and then handed her the strip. With a slight shift, he turned so that his injury was closer to her. She could see the patch of bandage pressed to his wound through the lacerated fabric of his shirt.

"But," he said through a hiss as he held his arm at an angle so she could wind the cloth around his shoulder, "that also leaves them vulnerable in a way. Because they need access to fresh blood and *that* means needing contact with the outside world. They wouldn't last long without initiating new recruits every couple of years. So they find semi-influential people who are willing to trade their humanity for immortality, and those people provide access to possible victims once they've been turned into vampires. And in order to turn them, none other than Count Dracula himself visits the area."

"So your parents came all the way here to catch him while he was out of his castle?" She finished tying off the cloth.

He leaned back against the door with a sigh. "Yep."

"That's insane."

He chuckled. "One of the only reasons the vampires bother being so secretive is because of people like my parents. Without us hunting them down, they'd have taken over the world long before technology would have advanced enough to stop them. They can manipulate people's minds." He slipped a finger beneath a chain she hadn't seen before and pulled it away from his neck, exposing the small piece of wood dangling from the necklace. "This protects me from the influence…" His eyes flew open, and he studied her face intently.

She squirmed. "What?"

"Are you sure you didn't feel compelled to open the door? Earlier. When it was talking to us."

Viviana snorted. "Not at all." She rubbed her temples, remembering the sudden pain stabbing through her head. "But I did get a wicked headache. *Both* times it talked to me."

His brow wrinkled. "It talked to you before?"

She nodded. "In the hallway. After I heard about the ceremony. It tried to get me to walk toward it." She chuckled mirthlessly. "Instead, I ran away as fast as I could. I guess my instincts were right all along."

"You're very lucky, Viviana," he said flatly. "Most people would not have survived an encounter like that with a vampire."

A burst of wind battered the walls of the chapel. Viviana shivered.

Luca ran a hand through his hair and stared at the ceiling. "You must have a natural immunity. It happens every once in a while. Though I'll be honest," he smiled at her, "you're the first I've ever met."

Viviana turned so that she was sitting beside him and settled deeper into her coat, not that it did much good, soaked as it was. "So. Radelesca is probably one of those new recruits they need."

"Yep," he sighed. "And I've failed to stop him from turning. In another hour or so, he'll claw his way out of the mud and kill his first victim."

"Wait." She stared at him as his meaning became clear. "You mean to tell me that it was Radelesca they buried in that grave?"

"His corpse, anyway," he replied.

"What? How? Why?"

Luca smirked. "Which question would you like me to answer?"

"All of them," she huffed.

"It's a bloody, nasty affair. That ceremony you asked about? It's how they turn people. The short version is, Dracula lets his initiate drink some of his blood and then kills and drains them. Then they're buried in a hole without a casket. So it's easier for them to dig their way back out once they wake up, see?"

"Oh yeah. Sure. Perfectly reasonable."

IIe laughed, then flinched as his injury rubbed against the door. "Don't make me laugh. It hurts. At any rate, once the initiate claws his way back up to the surface, the transformation is complete. He's a vamp. And hungry."

She fought to breathe. "The kids? In the school?"

His lips thinned into a frown. "Yeah. Most likely. Though, I'm sure the plan was to carefully pick people who wouldn't be missed. Unfortunately, for both Dracula and us, while newly risen vampires are weaker than old ones, they're also ravenous and drunk with power. They lack even the most basic self-control. But, there's no point in worrying about that now. There's nothing we can do."

Viviana looked away, staring across the room at nothing in particular. "My parents are getting divorced." She didn't know why she said it. Maybe because it was so normal, so different from fanged monsters swooping out of the sky to drink people's blood.

He was quiet for a long moment. "I'm sorry to hear that," he finally said softly.

His tone was gentle, sympathetic. Not at all judgmental, despite the odd change in topic. It didn't annoy her the way she thought it would. His sympathy. She shrugged. "It happens. Right?" She scooted until she was more comfortable and sighed. "The really annoying thing is that they decided to keep it a secret. They made up this whole trip as an excuse to get it all done behind my back. Like what? I wasn't supposed to notice that one of them had moved out when I got home?" She laughed dryly. "My parents wanted *me* out of the way too. But at least yours did it for your own good. Now I'm gonna get eaten by a vampire."

He nudged her side with his. "Don't say that. We aren't beat yet."

She scowled at the deep shadows surrounding them. "I hate secrets.

Especially the bad ones."

"Wait. Is *that* why you followed me out here? Because I wouldn't tell you what was going on?"

She glared at him. "Well, you have to admit, it was pretty crucial information."

He smirked. "Happy now? You know all about vampires and you're freezing your butt off out here with me instead of being tucked away warm in bed."

"Yes. Actually. Better out here knowing what's coming than back in bed, trussed up like a pig in a blanket waiting to be eaten. At least they can't get in *here*. You should have told everybody. At least they would have had a chance."

Luca shook his head. "I wish I could have, but they wouldn't have believed me. Even with evidence, which I didn't have, by the way, most people aren't as accepting of all this as you've been. And I couldn't risk word getting back to Radelesca or Dracula. Once I knew he was here, the only chance any of us had was to kill him before he realized there was a threat. I did try to call for reinforcements. Remember?"

"Yeah," she murmured. "You didn't take Tilly up on the offer to ask Radelesca for permission to drive you into town because you couldn't tell him why you needed to go there. Right?"

"Exactly. There were just too many things that went wrong. Too many mistakes were made. But telling people was absolutely out of the question." Viviana was shocked to see tears glittering in his eyes. "No matter how much I wanted to save everyone, the odds were against me from the start."

She reached for his hand. It wasn't much comfort, but she couldn't leave him like that. Alone. "And tomorrow?"

He held her hand in return and replied, "We'll have to wait and see."

They sat that way in silence as the storm raged outside the chapel walls.

<center>~~~~~</center>

Something landed on the roof with a clatter, startling Viviana from a light and fitful sleep. She sighed as it started chirping. Just a bird.

Sunlight filtered through the cracks in the boarded-up windows, crisscrossing the pews, illuminating the dust dancing in the air. Clearly, no one had used the building for a while. Viviana lifted her hands and grimaced at the layer of dirt coating her palms. Between that and the mud she could feel stuck in her hair, she was filthy. Then she laughed.

Better filthy than dead.

"What's so funny?" Luca's voice was grainy from interrupted sleep.

156

Viviana smiled as she watched him uncurl slowly from his spot on the ground. He was obviously not a morning person. "Just happy to be alive."

"For now," he said. Her smile faded. He looked at her and flinched. "Sorry."

They both got up, moving stiffly. Sunlight flooded the chapel as Luca opened the door.

Viviana squinted as she stumbled outside, shielding her eyes from the bright morning light. "So. What now?"

"Now," he said, "we go take stock of the damage."

Together they walked back toward the castle, circling around the east side until they'd made it back to the front gate so they could stay in the sun as long as possible. Viviana searched the area as they gingerly passed over the drawbridge.

"It's quiet," she said. "Is that a good thing?"

"Maybe," Luca replied. "Maybe not. I'm inclined to guess not. Let's go to the garage. Our best bet is to get out of here before they notice us. If we move fast, we can drive down the mountain and get back here with reinforcements before the sun goes down."

"But we don't have the keys."

He smiled. "I know how to start a car without one."

She shook her head. "Is that a typical vampire hunter skill?"

"Yes, actually." He laughed.

They reached the garage, and Luca's smile vanished. He cursed as Viviana wandered from one van to the next aimlessly. Someone had gutted every single one of the vehicles. .Ripped whole sections of the engines out. She looked back at Luca grimly.

"Can you fix them?"

"Before the sun goes down? Not a chance."

Viviana let her gaze wander, feeling despair settle behind her eyes in the form of tears. But wait. She did a doubletake. Then walked the length of the garage again to be sure. It was gone.

"Luca, look. The limousine is gone."

"What limousine?"

"There was a limousine here yesterday," she said, getting excited. "That had to be what the Count used to get here. Who else would have brought a limousine up a mountain? If it's gone, that means he's gone. Right?"

Luca did not share her relief. "He might be gone. But what about Radelesca?"

Her hopes plummeted. "I just thought. Since you said newly turned vampires are weaker..."

"No. You're right," he replied, running a hand through his hair. "It's better that Dracula is gone. Besides." He smiled ruefully. "Maybe my parents will catch him while he makes his way through town after all. Just on the way out, instead of on the way in." Luca drew a knife and walked back out of the garage.

"Where are you going?" Viviana asked, running to catch up with him.

"Inside the castle. If there's even a chance I can stop Radelesca, I have to take it."

She grabbed him by the arm and pulled him to a stop. "Are you crazy? You can't fight that thing alone. You said so yourself last night."

"No. I said I couldn't fight Dracula alone. Radelesca is a newly *turned* vampire. Weaker."

"Ravenous. Drunk with power. Lacks all common sense."

He grinned. "You were really listening, huh?"

"Yeah. And what I heard was, fighting is pointless."

"Fighting against a monster is never pointless, Viviana."

Tears burned her eyes. "But you could die."

He smiled and wiped away a stray tear that slipped down her cheek. "If I don't go, other people *will* die. It's a risk I have to take." He motioned for the drawbridge. "You should run. Head down the mountain. With Dracula fleeing back to his castle, and Radelesca distracted by the people inside, you have a solid chance of getting safely back to town. Here, take this." He offered her another knife to replace the two she'd used.

But she shook her head. "You need it. You're running out."

"*Take* it, Viviana. You might need it if you startle a bear or something." His look was kind. "And don't worry about me, okay? I have done this before, you know."

She clutched the knife in both hands and watched him disappear into the castle.

Viviana hesitated at the bottom step. Then, she ran after him, letting the darkness of the castle swallow her once more.

Luca spun toward her, fury contorting his face. "Seriously? Do you have a death wish?"

"I could ask you the same question," she whispered back. "Do you really think I can just head back on my own and pretend I don't know what's going on?"

He cursed, eyes wide, shifting from the door to the depths of the castle and back again as if considering whether to finish what he'd started or force her back outside. Viviana held up a hand to end his internal debate. "I'm not going, Luca. And that's the end of it. I won't let you fight that thing by yourself. Can you honestly tell me you'd have a better shot at killing it without me here?"

"Fine," he said with a sigh. He turned back to the task at hand. "But stay close. And stay quiet. No matter what you see. This isn't going to be pretty."

The first body lay just beyond the threshold of the foyer. Lifeless eyes stared out of a startled face beneath messy hair and a frilly white cap that had been knocked askew. Blood stained the woman's pale throat and splattered across her apron. Viviana forced back bile as she took in the sight. But she didn't scream. She was proud of herself for that.

They crept deeper into the castle, moving from room to room carefully. They found one body. Then another. But there was no sign of Radelesca. They made it past the great hall and were halfway to the library Viviana had stumbled across the night before when they heard a crash from inside. They exchanged a look, faces grim, then inched toward the door. Viviana hung back as Luca leaned against the wall and snuck a look inside.

He pulled back and whispered, "He's in there. And he's not alone. Last chance to run."

Viviana squeezed the handle of her knife until her knuckles turned white. "Not a chance," she replied, proud that her voice didn't shake.

"All right," he said. "Follow me." Crouching low, he slipped through the door. Viviana followed, heart pounding out a rapid rhythm. A small group of students had gathered in the library. They stood haphazardly around the room staring off into the distance as if in a trance. None of them seemed to notice as Luca and Viviana moved between them, making their way across the floor.

Someone had pulled the heavy curtains over the windows, blocking out the sun. But on the far side of the room, beneath the harsh glare of the electric lights, stood Headmaster Radelesca.

He looked nothing as he had before. His thinning white hair was now long and dark. His skin, while pale, was free of wrinkle or sunspot. He stood tall and sure on both legs, cane discarded. Monstrous wings stretched out from his shoulders and fell to the ground like a cloak. And his arms, now corded with muscle, were wrapped tightly around Nurse Mahtilda as his mouth pressed roughly against her neck. A trickle of blood seeped from the corner of his lip and slipped down the side of her throat. Her bright face was quickly losing color. Viviana knew they didn't have much time.

Apparently, Luca felt the same way. Suddenly he stood and charged the once old man with a flask from his belt in hand. Water sloshed from the top and doused the vampire. The stench of burning flesh filled the air even as Viviana opened her mouth to ask Luca if he were crazy. Why had he used water instead of his knife?

But Radelesca screamed like a wounded animal and lurched away, shooting into the rafters. Tilly fell to the ground with a sickening thud. Their quarry flailed against the ceiling, defying gravity, then crashed to the ground by the windows. Luca stalked forward, knife raised to attack.

"Children, to me," Radelesca hissed. "Grab them. Hold them still."

Viviana flinched at the sound of his voice. Dozens of footsteps echoed through the room as the students gathered around were galvanized into action. Luca held up his knife but hesitated. She guessed his dilemma: they were innocent. So how could he use it against them? Hands latched onto his sleeves. His jacket. Even his legs. He tried to fight them off, but they didn't falter.

Viviana ran, dodging the grasping hands of her dead-eyed pursuers. The bookcases and tables helped, getting in the way, but she was running out of room. The wall of curtained windows rose to block her escape. A line of slack-jawed, shuffling teenagers closed in from behind.

"The Count warned me about you hunters and your talismans," Radelesca said as he slowly made his way toward Luca. Relishing his victory. Luca glared up at him defiantly as the headmaster's hand wrapped around the chain at his neck and ripped it off with a metallic snap. "Without these, there will be no one who can stop me."

Luca's eyes glazed. His stiff muscles loosened.

Viviana watched in horror. "Luca. No."

Radelesca spun to face her. "You're next, my dear."

She stumbled back into the curtain, her legs growing weak under his glaring red stare. The movement pushed the fabric aside, releasing the tiniest beam of sunlight into the room. Radelesca hissed as the light passed across his path, falling just short of touching his clawed toes.

Of course. Her eyes widened. The sun.

It seemed Radelesca realized the threat as soon as she did.

"Grab her!"

The students charged forward, but Viviana had already spun so she could grab fistfuls of the curtains. Their combined weight knocked her to the ground, but she clutched the material for dear life. Something gave, then ripped. And the drapes and fixtures crashed down on top of her with a thud that buried her in heavy cloth.

Radelesca screamed.

Then everything was still.

Quiet.

And much too dark.

Viviana pushed against the cloth, but she couldn't find the way out. Desperation mounting, she clawed and pulled and twisted and fought against the weight of the curtains. When she felt hands grabbing at her through the fabric she screamed and fought even harder, kicking wildly at her attacker.

"Viviana, stop. It's just me."

Her frantic movements stilled. "Luca." Her voice broke as she called his name.

"Hold on." He pulled at the curtains. "I'll get you out."

"Where's Radelesca?" She blinked as sunlight flooded her vision, stinging her eyes.

"See for yourself," he replied as her eyes adjusted.

She followed his pointing finger to a pile of grey ash heaped on the floor where Radelesca had been standing. "Really?" Her breath came out in a sob. "It's over?"

"Yeah. It's over. Thanks to you."

Viviana threw her arms around his neck and laughed as sunlight streamed in through the windows, gold and pure. A testament that the long night had finally passed.

The End

EYES FULL OF STARS
Cortney Manning

Quincey Morris cocked his grade-A plasma revolver and aimed between the blood-red eyes of the Vampire outlaw.

"I'll warn you one last time, Dracula. Leave this planet and its people in peace, or I *will* do what I must."

Faster than thought, the Vampire's arm twitched, and red light flared across Quincey's vision.

"Quince!" A woman's shriek pierced his ears, and he turned his head in time to see her pale face etched in horror before he stumbled to his knees in the dirt. Pain seared against his chest, but a single thought cascaded through his mind, filling his very being: *At least I got to see my Lucy one last time.*

Twelve Hours Earlier

Twin moons set on the horizon as Quincey Morris stepped from the platform of the space-train back onto his home world, Eastseaxe. Mist curled around his boots, and he breathed deeply, savoring the rich, loamy scent of the planet that raised him. He tilted his hat to cast an attentive glance at his employer.

"Anything else you need, Mr. Helsing?"

"Thank you, Morris. Could you stop by the Whitby Mercantile on your way into town and check the prices of their crescent wheat? If it's not too pricey, perhaps we could use some on our next trip to soothe the cattle I buy today, especially if I'm lucky on my deal with Mr. West."

Quincey fought back the urge to shrink into himself like a disobedient child at the mention of the wealthy mayor's name and turned on his heel instead.

"Yessir, Mr. Helsing. Mayor West is a wealthy man and knows a fine prospect when he sees one. I'm sure we'll need all the wheat we can get."

"Thank you, lad." Mr. Helsing's heavy hand clapped down against his back, and he felt the man hesitate. Quincey glanced over to see his careworn face crinkled in empathy. Try as he might, Quincey couldn't pull himself away from that warm gaze. "I know you don't ask for holidays often, Quince, and it's been a good four years since you've first joined me here on my travels. So..." His voice held the traces of his Aurebean accent, one he often masked when making deals and trading cattle between the wealthy businessmen of great planets. But now his words were for Quincey alone, and they came straight from the heart. "Good luck today, son. I can't help but think that if Mr. West recognizes a fine prospect, then his daughter just might, too."

Quincey managed to pull his gaze away at last and straightened the lapels of his coat. "Thank you, kindly, Mr. Helsing," he muttered, though he knew in his gut it was all too late for that.

Four years was a long time for a body to live away from home and the folks one loved. Not that Quincey had known many friends in his youthful years on Eastseaxe, but as he strode down the lanes to Main Street, he was struck by the strangeness of it all.

The planet had not changed per se, with its dusty roads, colorful facades, and wooden boardwalks, but something felt different... Perhaps it was Quincey himself.

Glancing in the window glass, he caught his frame and profile. The moon-eyed, scrawny lad of eighteen had been replaced by a confident man with strong arms, wide shoulders, and a self-assured gait.

Few pedestrians lined the streets, but he tipped his hat to each as they swept by. He recognized a few, but none focused on him. Instead, their eyes were trained on the ground as they scurried to and fro.

Strange. Quincey squinted in the light of the rising sun and felt a cool line of sweat trickle down his back. He'd seen so many places in the past four years, but he did not recall his home planet feeling so... timorous.

With a steadying shrug of his shoulders, he trained his eyes on his destination: Whitby Mercantile, purveyor of goods and bastion of gossip. Helsing may have sent Quincey for wheat, but Quincey hoped to find something just as valuable in old Mr. Whitby's shop: news.

A bell jingled overhead as Quincey swung open the shop door. Memories assaulted him like dust. His mind flickered through them: Mr. Whitby keeping a sharp eye on him and the other boys from the orphanage, wealthy gentlemen and ladies with shiny silver buttons on their coats, a sunshiny girl twirling in delight when Quincey gave her his hard-won lemon drop, and then the same girl, a few years older, chatting animatedly with the banker's son.

Quincey shook his head and wondered if Art had taken over his father's bank. He'd always been good with sums and figures. Smart and dainty Lucy with her dictionary of fancy words had always been drawn to lads with brains, or rather *they* had been drawn to *her*, like bees to honey.

"Mornin', sir," came Mr. Whitby's voice from behind the counter.

Quincey nodded as he stepped nearer to the rotund man whose appraising eyes skittered over his broad shoulders and wide-brimmed hat down to the revolver holstered at his hip. No recognition lit his face. Instead, he gave a slow swallow. "Don't see many strangers 'round here no more."

Quincey frowned. Eastseaxe may not have been the busiest of planets, but surely Whitby Mercantile would still see its fair share of honeymooners, adventurers, and cattlemen. He flicked a glance around the store, neatly kept with fabrics, candies, and other odds and ends... but a little dingier than he remembered.

"I'm here on business," Quincey explained, but the shopkeeper's attention had already strayed nervously to the wide glass of his windows, so he added, "for Mr. Abraham Helsing." The warmth of pride heated his chest as Mr. Whitby's body straightened. The name of Quincey's employer was well known and respected among the planets of this sector and always certain to bring some level of respect, no matter what planet they berthed in.

"Mr. *Helsing*?!" the shopkeeper exclaimed, slapping his wide palm on the counter. "The Aurebean cattle-baron-turned-merchant, Mr. Helsing?!"

Quincey allowed the corners of his mouth to lift in a smug grin as a new light gleamed in the miserly shopkeeper's eyes.

"You're one of *his* cowboys? I've heard of the deals he's made with those Aurebean steers and horses of his and that he had a new breeding scheme brewing that could make a pretty penny. I'd love to learn more." Mr. Whitby eyed him expectantly, but Quincey merely lifted an eyebrow.

The man guffawed. "Understood, your lips are sealed as the grave. I'll be happy to help you, Mr. —"

Quincey bit back a grimace and left his name unspoken in the empty air. Instead, he detailed exactly what kind of wheat he and Mr. Helsing would need.

Surely it could do no harm to savor this bit of approbation from someone from his past without having to watch that consideration fade behind the distaste of recognition.

The shopkeeper laid out several catalogues and began discussing figures when a crash shattered from the backroom like glass and marbles spilling across the floor.

The man cursed beneath his breath and bade Quincey peruse the options while he handled the disaster.

No sooner had the man ducked through the doorway, muttering

with each step, when another sound met Quincey's ears. Soft, creeping footsteps. Someone who needed to sneak up on him couldn't have anything good in mind. He kept his eyes on the pages as he flicked through them lazily but kept one hand resting on the plasma revolver at his hip as someone crept up behind him from around a tall aisle.

"Quincey!" a semi-familiar voice cried.

He released his hold on the weapon and braced his feet to steady himself as a small, feminine form darted forward and wrapped both arms around him, tight as a whip.

"Little Mina Murray!" Quincey scooped the young girl in a hearty embrace and spun her about the room before setting her down with a grunt. He may have gotten stronger in the past four years, but the orphanage headmaster's young daughter, who'd once followed him like a lost sheep, had grown several inches at least. "Why, you're almost a young lady now, little lass," he exclaimed, grinning down at the girl's freckled face and tugging gently at one of her long braids. As much as he'd enjoyed the brief respect of Mr. Whitby in honor of his employer's name, he found himself much more delighted to be recognized at last by one of the few he'd always considered a friend.

The girl ducked her head shyly, and Quincey glanced suspiciously from her to the door the shopkeeper had just passed through. "You rascal of a girl! Did you somehow cause that mess?"

"No," she began, but a red blush blossomed over her cheeks as a mischievous twinkle lit her brown eyes behind her spectacles. "But I *may* have asked Johnny to do it."

Quincey recalled the lawyer's lovelorn son who had hung on Mina's every word, much like Quincey himself had once mooned over a different girl, one with hair like sunlight...

He shook his head and gave Mina his sternest look, but she just held up a hand before he could protest. "It was the only way I could think to get my dearest friend all to myself, and I'm sure Pa will pay Mr. Whitby for the damage. But were you truly going to act like a stranger here? Did you even plan to say hello to Pa and me?" A sheen of tears covered her eyes and stabbed Quincey with guilt.

"Me? Forget my best girl?" He tapped her chin playfully, making her laugh. "Never."

She peered up at him from behind the wire rims of her glasses. "Not even after all your adventures?"

"Not even then," Quincey promised.

She gnawed on her bottom lip, the pout fading. "But surely you saw so much!"

"That I did." Quincey chuckled and began regaling her with tales of the lovely vistas, waterfalls, and giant cities with proper gentlemen and fancy ladies wielding lacy parasols and proper manners. Her nose wrinkled at that, so he switched to the endless depths of space itself and the high-speed interstellar locomotive cutting through the galaxy on the power of stardust and scientific ingenuity.

"I learned a lot about cattle, too. My boss, Mr. Helsing hopes to breed his finest Aurborean cattle with some of the larger star-crested steers here. He hopes the new crossbreed will have more meat on their bones and a gentler temperament."

Mina, who had leaned her elbow on the counter, did not seem as impressed with this as Mr. Whitby would have been. Instead, her gaze locked onto his holster. "Did you learn how to shoot, too?"

"Ah yes." Quincey patted the weapon at his hip. "I may not be the fastest draw, but I've learned a thing or two about plasma revolvers, and this one's gotten me through some real tight patches."

Her eyes lit up, and she leaned forward again. "I bet you're real good at shooting. I remember you had a knack for knife throwing." Her expression turned sulky as her arms crossed over her chest. "But you never kept your promise to teach me how to do it." She sighed, staring wistfully at the revolver again. "I doubt Pa would approve of you teaching me to use a gun, would he?"

Before Quincey could think of an appropriate response, the girl raced on to her next question. "Have you ever really needed to use it, then?"

Quincey grinned at her exuberance. Mina might not be the perfect young lady by society's standards, but the lass certainly knew how to keep a soul on their toes, and her curiosity was boundless. In that aspect, she reminded him of clever Lucy, who, despite being the picture of ladylike refinement, still indulged in her passion for scholarly pursuits. He inhaled deeply, pulling his focus back to the conversation at hand.

"On occasion," he admitted. "Mostly against ver-bears or direwolves that threatened the cows, but—" He leaned conspiratorially closer. "On occasion, I've had to be ready for outlaws."

Her jaw dropped. "Really?"

Quincey nodded. "Outlaws are always a threat on our ventures, especially from one planet to another. I've even seen Vampires on the run from the law."

At that, her face paled, drawing into sharp contrast every little freckle. She darted a quick glance around the room and toward the window as if his words had the power to summon dark forces. Even her posture transformed from that spirited force of nature into a subdued child.

Quincey frowned. He had not meant to frighten her. Indeed, he had thought nothing could perturb this indefatigable young girl. Perhaps it would be best not to regale her with any further tales of that strange blood-drinking race from Vampira with their superhuman strength and speed. He would certainly not tell her of his early close encounter with Vlad Dracula himself. The audacious outlaw had evaded lawmen by ducking with his crew into a passing starship after taking over the planet of Sylvenia and draining first its animals and then its humans of their blood. Even Quincey shivered at the thought of all that criminal had done. He had seen Sylvenia after the Vampires had their way with it, and he would not wish those atrocities on anyone.

For a moment, he stood deep in the memory, hearing only the sounds of Mr. Whitby muttering and sweeping glass and marbles from the back room.

"We've seen things here, too," Mina whispered in a voice so faint he barely heard her. "The planet's not the same as when you left it."

Quincey frowned, wondering if he could have misheard her. Outside, a passerby caught his eye, scurrying quickly down the street. Thoughtfully, he turned his gaze back to the girl who now distracted herself with the catalogues on the counter. True, the town appeared far less bustling than before, with a far more strained atmosphere. But surely nothing truly harmful could have happened here in the time since Quincey left. Surely no one here had been in danger.

Mina's bowed head and shift in posture declared her intent to speak no more of her cryptic words, but an icy dread slipped through Quincey's veins, gripping his heart. He reached one hand up to the medallion he wore on his chest, half-hidden beneath his lapel. It had been a gift from Lucy, from the time before he had left Eastseaxe, and her, behind. Surely, she was safe and well. Quincey glanced at Mina again. Perhaps he could ask her about Lucy instead. He cleared his throat, unsure how to make the question seem natural, not too obvious as to reveal the feelings that still lay rooted deep inside his heart.

His fingers felt the tiny gems flecked over the medallion's silver-colored metal like stars.

This is for you, Quince, Lucy had whispered, *because I've never met another dreamer like you, with all the stars of the sky caught in your eyes.*

His chest tightened again, and he could not help but wonder...

"I should be back out with you momentarily, sir," came Whitby's voice from the back room, pulling Quincey's mind back to the present. "My humblest apologies for the wait. Please do give a holler if you have any questions."

"I will," Quincey called back and noticed Mina staring narrow-eyed at the medallion he still touched at his chest.

"You still wear that?" she asked.

Her tone held no accusation or judgement, but Quincey still found himself replying by rote, as he always had to the other boys at the orphanage, "I never take it off. It's a real hero's medal and old, too, made from a metal strong enough to deflect a plasma bolt. They used to make armor like that." He paused and lowered his fingers slowly before asking in the most casual tone he could muster, "I wonder, how is Miss West? Or… perhaps she is Mrs. Holmwood by now?"

Mina's nose crinkled beneath her round glasses. "No, she's not Mrs. Holmwood, but she could've had her pick of suitors."

"Oh?" Quincey aimed for an air of nonchalance.

Mina skipped away from the counter to a shelf with a rack of moontossers instead. It seemed her previous unease had now been forgotten, or perhaps she had simply hidden it beneath a mask.

Still, Quincey almost thought he saw her fingers shake as she spun one of the toys in her hand and explained in a tone nearly as nonchalant as his own. "Miss West has had many suitors like Art Holmwood. Even serious old Dr. Seward fell in love and asked for her hand when he was treating Lucy's Ma." Mina's chin did not lift, but her eyes flicked up toward his face several times as she spoke, as if gauging his reaction.

Quincey swallowed. In truth, the news of suitors was not surprising at all. Miss West had been the belle of the town, and charming and intelligent to boot. A man like him, even a cowboy as he was now, had never really stood a chance with her. That was why he had left to begin with, to prove himself, and make himself worthy—

"I half-thought Miss West might marry the old doctor, if only just to keep him from looking sad," Mina joked.

Quincey smiled. "Miss West has always had a big heart. That lass would care for an adder if it needed her help—and charm him, too."

"Well…" Mina stretched out the word as Quincey waited expectantly, his heart thudding.

"Miss West actually is engaged now, but not to Mr. Holmwood. In fact… her wedding is tonight at midnight." The air escaped Quincey's lungs, and for a moment he could not breathe as Mina held out the fabric of her pinstriped lavender skirt. "Why do you think I'm all dressed up like this?"

Quincey's chest burned like wildfire, but his mind urged him to keep his face unchanged. He had known this would be the case. A lass like Lucy could have her pick of suitors, and she had clearly made her choice.

"I'm supposed to meet Pa at the West mansion today," Mina

continued, though Quincey only heard her voice as if through a fog. "Pa is meeting with the mayor before the wedding, and I'm supposed to come, too. You should join me."

"W-what?" Quincey stuttered. "No, Miss West would not want me there. I'd be nothing but a stranger to her and her groom."

Mina shot him a skeptical look over the rims of her glasses. "You really think Miss West of all people could forget *you*? "

"Mina," Quincey urged, "please, I can't—"

"Please, Quincey!" She darted forward to grip his wrist in earnest eagerness. "I know you won't be here long, and Pa would want to see you, too." Mina paused, then gave his arm a gentle squeeze. "Think of this as a real goodbye. Please, Quincey?"

~~~~~

Quincey stood in the library of the West mansion, his hat clutched awkwardly in his hands and considering if he dared sit on the frilly little chairs in his dusty trousers and coat. The servants had offered to show him and Mina to the drawing room, but Mina had insisted the library would be better for meeting Lucy. Staring up at the rows upon rows of books, Quincey couldn't help but agree. From the scent of leather-bound tomes to sunny wallpaper and dainty chairs, this room was clearly the domain of Miss Lucy West. Though Quincey wondered at the heavy cloths curtaining every window. He had noticed the same dark shrouds in every room they passed, transforming the otherwise lovely home into a crypt of sorts.

He tugged at the collar of his shirt and strove to ignore the sweat gathering on his back and the cowardly urge to flee before Lucy had a chance to appear.

"She should be here soon." Mina flopped onto one of the fancy chairs without a care for its white fabric.

"You should be more careful, Mina." Quincey shot her a disapproving glance as she propped the heel of one boot against a nearby table leg.

"Caution killed the cat." She waved a hand dismissively, and Quincey felt a chuckle loosen his anxious frame.

"I don't think that's how the saying goes."

She shrugged, and Quincey marveled at her boldness. He straightened his spine. He could do with a dash of her temerity. He may not have come to Lucy's home to steal her from her wedding and claim her as his own, but he had still determined to see this meeting through. When she walked through those doors, he would hold himself straight, look her in the eyes and not be ashamed of who he was. As Mina had said, it would be a final goodbye. He'd get the closure he needed before
~~~~~

setting off on a new path—hurting, but hopefully wiser. For no one could call Quincey Morris a coward, even in affairs of the heart.

Just then, a young woman peeked her head in, and Quincey's stomach dropped to his boots before he realized it was a maid with a feather duster. The moment she spied him and Mina, her eyes grew wide, and she scrambled from the room, her dustpan scattering dust behind her.

Quincey blinked at the empty doorway. "Mina, is it just me, or is everybody here acting a bit... strange?" He nodded where the servant had so recently stood.

The girl shrugged, and it seemed that uneasy mask had returned to her face. "Oh, everyone's on edge these days." Her voice drifted down to a whisper. "Especially when Lucy's fiancé is around."

Quincey spun his full attention to Mina and matched her volume, though a shout would have better matched his nerves. "Why would that make a difference? Just who exactly is he?"

Mina leaned forward in her seat, glancing about the room for any hidden ears. "He showed up in town half a year ago with a crew of his own and quickly set up shop here. The adults don't like to tell me things, but I know they were at the gambling houses a lot and made some big deals. They carry fancy guns, too. Nobody wants to cross them."

The unease built in Quincey's chest like steam in a pot, and he silently fingered the medallion half-hidden under the lapel of his coat. Exactly what kind of man had Lucy chosen for herself? And why?

Unable to tolerate the confining shadows of the room, Quincey stepped to the window and pulled back the heavy curtains. Mina flinched in her seat, and Quincey raised an eyebrow.

"So why does Miss West want to marry this man?"

Mina's gaze skittered between the window and the open doorway. "Mayor West asked her to. Since her fiancé just made himself sheriff, folks have been saying it's a good match." Mina leaned closer toward where Quincey stood, her voice barely audible. "But I think Mr. West owes him something big, and this was the only way not to lose it all. Besides, everybody in town does what the sheriff's posse says now, anyways." Now that she had gotten started, the words spilled from her mouth, faster and faster, and her placid mask fell away to reveal more of the fear Quincey had seen before. "We might as well not even have a mayor. I even heard Pa tell Johnny's papa that they're going through all the best cattle awful fast."

Quincey tightened his grip on the curtains, his mind not comprehending her ominous words. "Going through?"

"For the blood of course," she explained, her tone far too even for the words she spoke.

Quincey felt his Adam's apple bob as he swallowed slowly. "Blood?"

"Do you truly think the white parasol's the best choice, Jane?" A feminine voice came from the hall before Mina could answer, and Quincey's attention swiveled to the open door. "I believe I left it in the library after my wa—"

"Miss," a servant called. "You have guests—"

A delicate lady drew to a stop in the entryway, causing the white trim and needlework of her blue dress to swirl about her like foam on a silken wave. Her white-gold ringlets swept around her face beneath a wreath of orange blossoms, and her rosy lips parted in a warm-hearted smile.

"Quince!" she exclaimed in a melodic voice that struck every chord in his soul.

He dropped the curtains and bobbed his head in a reverent nod. "Hullo, Miss Lucy."

~~~~~

The memory flashed through Quincey's mind as vivid as the woman standing before him. It had been the last day he saw her before he left.

He had met her by their favorite pond, and she'd brought her newest book to read aloud while they shared a simple picnic. The day had been pleasant, though they could no longer race through the fields as they once had, not with her longer hems and graceful bearing.

Of course, he had not told her about the meeting he had with her father. Sitting across from that tall and formidable man in his imposing office, shame had weighed his spirit as he recalled the man's words: "You can't keep coming here whenever you please. A penniless lad like you could never be worthy of my Lucy. I've tolerated her youthful charity toward you and the other orphans, but a time comes when a man must think of his daughter's prospects, her future! And someone like you could never share a part in it."

Thinking of that encounter, Quincey had gritted his teeth and impulsively slipped his hand over hers. She had smiled, and his heart had nearly stopped. He couldn't tell her what he planned to do, where he was going, or what he hoped to achieve.

He certainly couldn't ask her to wait for him as he tried to make a name for himself.

So he had settled instead for tracing his thumb over the back of her hand. She had startled for a moment, then leaned her head against his shoulder and continued reading. Her sweet scent of expensive perfume
~~~~~

and book bindings had tickled his nose and accelerated the thud of his heart in his chest.

He had stared down at the golden light of the sun dancing through the strands of her silken hair.

Yes, he could never let her know that this would be his goodbye—either forever or until he could become a man worthy of such lovely light in his life.

~~~~~

Lucy stepped closer, her movements cautious and disbelieving. "Quincey," she repeated. "Is it truly you?" A sheen of tears flooded her eyes as her fingers lifted slowly toward his face.

Part of Quincey longed to reach for her hand, or even lean into that tempting touch, drawing her close into his embrace, but her blue and white gown and wedding wreath held him back. He had come back too late.

"Miss West." Quincey bowed his head over her hand and pressed a gentle kiss to her knuckles before deliberately forcing himself to let her go.

Disappointment and isolation tightened her features, not unlike the faces of the few pedestrians he'd seen wandering the streets of Eastseaxe, and fear gripped his chest. The shift in the demeanor of the townspeople and overall unease had been one thing, but now this expression from his lively Lucy, too? Now he knew for certain. Something was wrong in Eastseaxe.

"Honestly, the gall!" boomed a commanding voice from down the hall. "To demand so much cattle for so little a reward! And you were going to give it to him? *My* inheritance."

A thud shook the walls of the house, followed by a grunt.

"All I own is to be Lucy's." The voice Quincey recognized as the mayor's, but weak and rasping.

Lucy's eyes widened again, and she moved toward the doorway, but Quincey raced past her, placing himself between her and any unseen threats. There in the hall, he spied a stranger who suspended Mayor West by the throat with unnatural strength and then dropped him to slide down the wall.

Shock stiffened Quincey's limbs, yet he would have raced to the mayor's side if not for the sudden touch of Lucy's fingers slipping around his elbow, warning him and holding him back.

"And all that's hers is to be *mine*," the stranger yelled. The bottom of his frock coat whipped around with the swiftness of his movement as he gripped the mayor again and shook him. "That is the arrangement we made. It belongs to me. You all belong to me now."
~~~~~

"Sir!" The accented tones of Mr. Helsing joined the fray, and Quincey noticed him holding up Quincey's old friend and Mina's father, Mr. Murray, whose white knuckles showed above his hawthorn cane. "The mayor only meant to increase your holdings by doing business with me. Surely—"

Quincey's heart thudded like a drum, and he feared the irate stranger would turn on his employer next. Instead, the clanking of metal against stone clattered down the hall, and all eyes swung to Lucy's servant, Jane, who stood clutching the missing white parasol and staring in horror at the brass statue she had toppled in her haste.

"You! Clumsy oaf!" The stranger swept down the hall then, and Quincey made out his features at last: a strong, aquiline nose, sharp cheekbones, a swooping mustache, and the longest incisors he had ever seen.

He inhaled sharply, his blood chilling with horror as the realization sunk in. This was no stranger. He knew this man, if man he could be called. He'd seen him once, fleeing the imperial lawmen, and laughing with his band of Vampire outlaws.

Too stunned to move, Quincey watched as the monster stalked toward the servant, his long, dark coat billowing behind him. As if observing through a thick fog, Quincey barely registered the Vampire's hand, lifted in rage, or graceful Miss Lucy shooting past him to stretch herself like a shield between the monster and her maidservant.

"Please, Vlad," she begged, laying a gloved hand on his forearm. "It's my fault. I sent her to find my—"

The outlaw's frame twisted, and his raised fist shot toward the new target. Quick as lightning, Quincey dove between them and felt the heavy blow crack against his shoulder instead of hers. Pain seared down his arm—pain that he'd gladly take for Miss Lucy any day.

Her worried yelp sounded behind him as if she could feel the smarting bruise of that punch. Quincey's blood boiled hot now as he wondered if it was an injury she'd sustained before.

"What's this?" the Vampire thundered. "Another stranger in my home?"

Quincey squared his shoulders, meeting him gaze for gaze. They were roughly the same height, but the Vampire's eyes flashed an unnatural hue of red.

"I'm no stranger here," Quincey spat, "though I can't say the same for you."

"You dare—" the Vampire began, but Quincey cut off his words by pressing closer.

"*I* dare? What gives *you* the right to storm about the mayor's home, inflicting damage and threatening its inhabitants?"

"Quincey." Helsing's voice came from down the hall, tinged with warning.

"Ah," the monster swiveled his head between them. "So you're here with the trader. I knew I didn't recognize you from my new town. What are you, his valet?" The Vampire brushed his sleeves as if flicking away any dirt he could have picked up from their encounter. "No matter. You're clearly lacking either brains or knowledge. You'd best retreat now with all your limbs still intact."

He licked his long fangs, but Quincey fingered the gun at his hip.

"And why should I leave? What right have you to be here and impose your will on the people?" From the corner of his eye, he saw Lucy glance up sharply from where she knelt beside her maid.

The Vampire appeared a bit more cautious now, taking in Quincey's strong build and holstered weapon.

"Why," he answered slowly, in a sinuous voice, "the right of a son-in-law and groom." One of his arms swept grandly toward Lucy, and she rose obediently, gracefully even, but with gritted teeth, her flashing eyes downcast. Quincey tightened his grip on his gun as the monster flung a casual arm about her waist, drawing her far too close. "And as the new sheriff of this planet."

"Sheriff?" Quincey scoffed. "I know exactly who you are, Vlad Dracula, and I doubt you came by that title fairly, nor could the imperial lawmen of the galaxy be aware of this little game you're playing. It would be wise for you to leave this planet now."

The calculating red eyes flickered between Quincey and Lucy as if he could sense how every muscle in Quincey's body longed to rip her from his grasp.

Slowly, deliberately, the Vampire pressed his face into Lucy's white-gold hair, never pulling his gaze from Quincey. Lucy did not whimper but held herself very still. "And if I don't leave? After all, I'm feeling mighty comfy and would hate to abandon my new bride."

"Then the imperial forces would have to be informed."

A low chuckle fell from the Vampire's crimson lips. "Surely you don't think you could leave this planet or send a message without my crew stepping in. After all, we take rabble-rousers very seriously here. Can't let them go just anywhere they please doing anything they like." His finger traced the bare skin between Lucy's glove and sleeve, and she inhaled sharply.

"I must insist that you let Miss West go."

The Vampire's eyes flared in triumph, and Quincey realized he'd revealed his hand too soon.

"Give up my bride?" the Vampire crooned, and the fingers of his free hand lifted to trace the veins of her throat. "I think not. Nor do I think you'll use that gun of yours while she's in this house, so close to her loving groom."

Quincey's blood pounded but he bit back his anger. A sinister grin lit up the monster's face, and a memory tickled the corner of Quincey's mind. It was something he'd heard about this famed outlaw who never backed down from a challenge.

"Then do not face me here," Quincey proposed.

The Vampire lifted a single black brow. "What exactly are you suggesting?"

"A duel. You and I on the Main Street, time of your choice." Quincey held his breath, hoping this opponent would take the dare.

His nostrils flared. "Very well. Just after sundown, and before the wedding. That's when we'll meet." The Vampire grinned widely, revealing every sharp tooth. "Prepare to meet your Maker, boy."

~~~~~

"I'm sorry, Mr. Morris." Mina stood, wringing her hands in the lavender skirt of her gown.

"What's got you so formal now, little miss?" Quincey asked, bending to meet her eyes. They stood together with her father in the fading light of evening on the boardwalk in front of Whitby Mercantile. Just up the road, in the painted saloon, he could hear the Vampire posse carousing.

"I pushed you to this." The girl sniffed. "I urged you to meet Miss West even though I knew you'd want to protect her — no, *because* I knew you'd want to protect her. I was just so excited to see my brave friend again. I thought you could help her, me, all of us." Her hands gestured desperately around them, and tears streamed down her cheeks. "But I've only put your life in danger!"

"Miss Mina." Quincey gripped her shoulder with as much comfort as he could offer. "I'd put my life at risk a thousand times if it meant I could keep you and Miss Lucy safe."

The girl threw her arms around his neck. "Oh, Quince! You were always a real hero."

Stunned warmth filled Quincey's chest, and he cleared his throat. Luckily, at that moment, Mr. Murray motioned for them to step into the shop where Mr. Helsing stood. The older gentlemen had managed to use Mr. Helsing's one-way transmitter to reach out to an old friend in the imperial police force. Apparently, the Vampires had long since taken control of telecasters and the post office, limiting what information could get out, so this would likely be their only shot to call for help. Quincey
~~~~~

wiped his sweaty palms across his trousers. They could only hope help would find them soon. After a quick conversation with the two men and making sure they and the girl had tucked themselves safely with Mr. Whitby behind the counter, Quincey stepped out of the store.

His boots clipped across the wooden boardwalk before hopping down into the dirt.

There in the distance, beneath the silver light of two full moons, he spied Dracula, his Vampires lining the porch of the saloon. Miss Lucy stood there, too, wrapped protectively in her father's arms. Quincey swallowed. He certainly hoped she wouldn't have to watch him die tonight.

Both Dracula and Quincey stepped across the hard-packed dirt. Neither had appointed seconds. It was just the two of them on the road with a sea of onlookers peering from behind locked doors and barred windows.

They stopped about ten paces apart, each fingering the air above their weapons.

With deliberate intention, the Vampire drew his gun but did not fire, not yet.

Quincey swallowed, not knowing what game the monster played. After a moment, he drew, too, and they began circling each other, shifting closer.

"Well, little man, are you prepared to die?"

Quincey Morris cocked his grade-A plasma revolver and aimed between the blood-red eyes of the Vampire outlaw.

"I'll warn you one last time, Dracula. Leave this planet and its people in peace, or I *will* do what I must."

Faster than thought, the Vampire's arm twitched, and red light flared across Quincey's vision.

"Quince!" A feminine shriek pierced his ears, and he turned his head in time to see a pale face etched in horror before he stumbled to his knees in the dirt. Pain seared across his chest, but a single thought cascaded through his mind, filling his very being: *At least I got to see my Lucy one last time.*

Then he fell in a heap on the packed dirt road. His breath caught in his throat, but his mind still whirled. *How?* He wondered until he remembered Lucy's medallion on his chest. *Strong enough to deflect a plasma bolt, indeed.*

Footsteps circled him once more, and Quincey forced himself to move as little as possible, taking stock of his situation. The plasma revolver had disappeared in his fall, so his only advantage could come from playing dead.

Carefully, he shifted one arm to reach for the sheath on his belt.

A kick thudded against his boot, and he heard the Vampire cock his gun again.

Instantly, Quincey flung himself upward, knocking Vlad back with the element of surprise. Before he could recover, Quincey's knife had already sliced through the air. Years of practice had made his aim true, and shock registered on the Vampire's face as he stared down at the object spearing his chest before tumbling down into the dirt.

For the span of a minute, no one stirred.

Then all at once, the world lit up with blaring beacons and resounding sirens. Dozens of starships flooded the sky. The imperial lawmen had arrived.

Chaos ensued as Vampires fled the saloon's porch and the emboldened townsfolk chased them down the streets, some with pitchforks, kitchen pots, and knives.

But Quincey knelt in the dirt, breathing heavily and staring into the empty eyes of his foe.

Then two pairs of arms wrapped around him, stealing his breath again.

Mina's hug knocked him to his back, and he found himself staring up at Lucy's halo of gold-white curls. Her rosy lips formed an O of surprise to find herself suddenly draped across his chest, but then she wrapped her arms around his neck before he could rise. Salty tears streamed down her face as she planted a sweet kiss against his lips. Quincey's eyes widened, and she started to draw back, but he pulled her closer.

After a few moments, both long and far too short, they separated, and he watched as she self-consciously sat beside him. He rose, too, but kept one arm cradled about her waist, afraid to let go and still dazed by her kiss.

No one but young Mina seemed to notice them among the chaos of starships, sirens, and outlaws. She blushed furiously and tried to concentrate on the cluster of lawmen handcuffing outlaws down the street amid the jubilant shouts of the townsfolk.

Quincey blinked at the flashing lights but could not keep his eyes away from the woman he loved.

"My dear, dear Quincey!" she exclaimed, squeezing his hand in hers. "You can't know how glad I am to see you, to touch your warm and living hand. How did you do it? How are you still alive after taking a plasma shot to the heart?"

A smile tugged at Quincey's lips as he lifted his free hand to reveal the medallion on his chest. He winked. "I'm always safe when carrying you in my heart, love."

"Oh dear." She sniffed, and a fresh tear traced down her cheek like a glimmering star. "And here I thought you'd forgotten all about me while I waited here for you year after year, turning down suitor after suitor until Papa put his foot down, and Vlad forced his suit. I only agreed to marry him because that fiendish devil threatened to take blood from more than just the cattle. I thought if I agreed, then he'd let the people on Eastseaxe be… "

Quincey felt spellbound, staring into her silver eyes. "You were waiting… for me?"

"Of course I was!" She teasingly swatted a palm against his chest. "Whyever did you leave me for so long?"

Quincey felt himself shrinking sheepishly beneath her unyielding gaze. "To make myself worthy." He rubbed the back of his neck uncomfortably. "It was ridiculous, really. A cowpoke like me could never deserve a high-class gal like you."

"Banish the thought!" she exclaimed before gripping the lapels of his coat in both her hands. "You, Quincey Philip Morris, were always worthy in my eyes. You always were and always will be, Quince."

The flashing lights and shouts around them jumbled Quincey's thoughts. "Is that why you've never married? After all these years?"

"Oh, Quincey Morris!" She heaved a sigh and leaned her head against his shoulder. "Didn't you know? I don't care what anybody else thinks, even Papa. I could only have room in my heart for one man, and he's a cowboy with stars in his eyes."

The End

MOTION PICTURE US TOGETHER
Jim Doran

Tyrone Ruby toed the oblong package on the floor of his massive foyer as he stroked his goatee. The two-foot-long, white box with a red ribbon scraped against the pristine marble floor, the fabric-rustling sound originating from inside the container. Who had delivered this present, and how had they slipped inside? And the most important question of all: Who had tripped the alarm? Tyrone wanted answers, not excuses, and he wanted them now.

He shifted his attention to his phone and replayed the footage. He couldn't believe his eyes, yet he was no stranger to inexplicable occurrences. The macabre ruled his life. As evidence, the posters hanging on the walls of this elegant and spacious foyer depicted the coming attractions of zombie apocalypses and monstrous sea creatures. Fantasies for the wider populace to make them afraid for two hours. But Tyrone was never scared.

Thumbing the phone, Tyrone spoke into it. "Charles, come here."

"Yes, sir."

Seconds later, the eight-foot-tall steel reinforced doors opened inward, revealing a dim glow on the horizon. A man marched inside, adjusting the collar of his uniform. Though the newcomer was four inches taller and three inches wider than Tyrone, his hands trembled as he approached. The security officer spotted the oblong box at Tyrone's feet and then returned his focus to his employer.

Tyrone's voice had all the warmth of a torture rack. "Charles, who am I and what do I do?"

The man exhibited a puzzled expression. "You are Tyrone Ruby, executive of Keyz Motion Pictures, sir."

"Quite right. And who are you?"

"I'm Charles Fenton, your chief security officer."

"Indeed. And the first of my cardinal rules about packages is…?" Tyrone raised an eyebrow.

Charles spoke as if reading off a manual. "All packages without your signature will be rerouted to a clearing location, away from the mansion. As you've mentioned, you have many enemies."

"Three for three." Tyrone edged the item of discussion closer to

Charles with his shoe. "Now, tell me how this delivery came to be in my foyer? In particular, how did the courier sneak through my gate and front door into this room to deliver it?"

Charles glanced at the object on the floor. "You say someone delivered it, sir?"

"I did. We have security footage. Let's review it."

Tyrone held up his cell and showed the feed to Charles. The video showed the security officer himself at the gate, speaking with a young, blonde woman courier. Charles was waving his hand as if to send her away, and then he grimaced. He hunched over and then straightened up. The courier reached out to him, but Charles lifted his hand. He then snatched the parcel from her grasp.

Charles' eyes shifted to Tyrone's. "I didn't do this. It isn't me."

"Keep watching," commanded Tyrone.

The footage switched to the front door, where Charles entered a code into a keypad. He set the box on the ground and used both hands to open the massive door. Shuffling forward, he entered the foyer and set the container on the marble floor, keeping the doors open. Straightening his shirt as if done with this task, the security officer turned and left the mansion, closing the door.

Charles bit his lip. "I can't account for my actions, sir. I suspect someone has hacked the video and—"

"Nobody has hacked the video," interrupted Tyrone. "The box has been sitting here for the last twenty minutes. Five minutes ago, someone tripped the alarm in this very room, bringing this anomaly to my attention. Charles Fenton, what were you doing then?"

"I was patrolling the grounds." Charles paled. "I don't regularly look at my watch, but I keep an eye out for trespassers."

"You're dismissed. I'll pay you for today, but nothing further."

Charles' hands curled, his thumbs rubbing the backs of his fingers. "Sir, I have a wife and children, and my wife is on medical leave. Give me a chance to find the courier, and I will force her to explain. She must have hypnotized me."

"Indicating a weak mind," snapped Tyrone. "What did she promise you? Sex?"

Charles shook his head and opened his mouth.

"I don't want to hear your impossible excuses." Tyrone leaned toward the larger man. "If you want to keep your job, then I suggest you open this package. I'll watch from the safety of the bunker."

Tyrone stuttered. "Y…you suspect the item inside is dangerous?"

"I do. Make your decision. Open it or leave the premises immediately."

Charles squared his shoulders. "I'll open it."

"See that you do." Tyrone turned around. "Wait until I reach the bunker."

Three minutes later, Tyrone observed a hapless Charles kneeling beside the box. He had already untied the red ribbon and placed it on the floor. Tyrone spoke into his cell. "You may now open it."

The mansion owner observed Charles' lips moving. Perhaps a useless prayer, calling to his worthless God for protection. He needn't have bothered. Tyrone knew what lay inside. Who delivered it and why was his primary concern.

Carefully, Charles lifted the lid and peeked inside. He placed the covering on the floor, then peered at the security camera in the room. "It's flowers, sir. Lavender, I think."

"Lilacs, you idiot," mumbled Tyrone. Then, he addressed the guard. "Show me the flowers so that I may see them."

Charles did as instructed. Tyrone observed that he didn't react to the flora. He could cross off contact poison.

"Remove them and the box from this house, immediately," said Tyrone. "You may keep your position here but understand that I'm watching you closely. As a penalty for today, you are dismissed until tomorrow without pay."

"Understood, sir."

Charles exited with the package while Tyrone sat back in his chair. He had detected the flowers through the box's cardboard. His olfactory sense exceeded any typical human's sense of smell. Ordinary lilacs weren't any concern to him. But who had sent them and why disturbed him.

Tyrone growled. His original questions remained, and he was no closer to the answers. He was one frustrated vampire.

<div align="center">~~~~~</div>

Tyrone and other vampires received no rest when lying in their coffins during the day. The truth was that the undead did not rest the same as the dead. They were eager to rise. Being cheated out of half of their day was infuriating.

Vampires didn't move their bodies while lying on their native soil. However, while they were physically still, their minds remained active. Tyrone's thoughts continued to dwell on the events of the day. Rivals were at work. Rivals, plural, not a *single* rival. He was the king of the undead, after all. They had imposed their will over the weak-minded Charles. Or had they? His instincts told him to consider alternatives. Charles had quite a strong sense of self that Tyrone would have trouble bending. Who were these adversaries who had, pardon the expression, peed in his coffin?

In the middle of his brooding, Tyrone's eyes snapped open. His disquiet transformed into shock. An outside presence had just now placed an object on his coffin, transmitting an effect he hadn't experienced in years. Someone had set a wild rose branch on the top of his burial container.

The vampire of vampires was trapped.

Tyrone had been careful to keep certain vampire legends from the public. Yes, the stake, the holy water, and the religious symbols were all common knowledge. But he worried how a hunter could use nature against him. Running water or mistletoe affixed above doorways prevented him from crossing. Worst of all, he could not rise from his coffin if a hunter placed a vine of wild roses on top of it.

Tyrone could be trapped here for a long time if the roses were fresh.

The alarms went off in his house. Excellent, Charles could capture the invaders, and Tyrone would then be free to punish them himself. He had instructed Charles to remove anything on top of the funeral containers in the basement. Once his security officer came —

And then, Tyrone remembered. He had dismissed Charles. He would have to wait for his employee to return tomorrow and discover Tyrone and his brides — ahem, "escorts" — weren't about. Charles would find the roses.

Seconds later, his resting quarters moved. The trespassers were transporting the coffin! What was their plan? He would wait. He hadn't lived hundreds of years without knowing how to be patient. And when they removed the rose — and they would, the fools always did — he would strike.

~~~~~

Time meant nothing to a vampire. However, Tyrone was impatient for his captors to remove the rose. They hadn't displaced the flower while loading it onto what sounded like a truck from its rear, rolling door. Strange, the whirring tires and the belching muffler reached his sensitive ears but nothing from his abductors. Tyrone's heightened sense of smell couldn't detect them again as they transported his coffin from the vehicle to another location. This place had an overbearing chemical odor.

He plotted for hours after the motion ceased, preparing for someone to free him. When the moment came, he still couldn't sense anyone outside. No matter. Time to strike.

Lightning-fast, Tyrone thrust off the lid of his coffin and rose, leaping to his feet. Rage radiated from him like heat from a furnace. He would kill anyone he encountered, no matter who they were. His desire
~~~~~

for revenge knew no bounds.

He halted, finding himself alone in a most unusual cell. Silver bars stretched between a concrete ceiling and floor. Although silver was distasteful, the metal was not a repellent. However, water trickled down the bars. The water emerged from holes next to the bars and swirled around the silver in a helix fashion. His ten-by-ten prison had four walls of running water. The movie producer was still trapped.

The room surrounding his cell had cinder block walls and was apparently outfitted for scientific study. It contained tables of chemicals, cabinets with hazard signs on some of the doors, and a hazmat suit hanging on a coat rack. A circular fan powered down nearby. The appliance must have blown off the roses.

In the back of the room, Tyrone spied a surgical table and smaller cages for animals. Every item in the area belonged in a lab except for one item from his castle. To one side lay another coffin, holding one of his brides. On top of the casket was a rose and a long wooden peg sticking into the container where the chest of the occupant would be.

Where was he?

Tyrone didn't have to wait long to find out. A door opened, and a man wearing a servant's dress coat and black trousers stepped into the room. His top button was undone, and his white shirt was stained with blood. His shoes made the scuffling noises of a hesitant gait as he headed for the cell. The servant's most unusual physical trait caught Tyrone's attention.

The man was headless.

For once, Tyrone was speechless.

How was this creature alive? The top of his neck—arteries, veins, vertebrae and throat—were exposed. Everything pulsed, but nothing spewed outward. The servant's blood pumped without escaping!

A deep, wavering voice addressed him. "Mr. Dracula, I presume."

And then Tyrone—Dracula being his more famous identity—realized the words came from the headless man. He blinked, too stunned to reply.

The man lifted a sheet of paper and appeared to be reading from it. "Once, a mighty count. Emigrated to London, causing a stir there. You then came to America in the 1920s. You settled in Hollywood and became a producer of shlock films. You have spread your—abilities—to others."

"How are you alive?" asked Dracula.

"I could ask you the same thing. However, I'm not asking the questions." The man lowered his voice to a whisper. "I suggest you do what she says. She may do worse to you than what she did to me."

Dracula moved toward the flowing water in a blur, stopping millimeters from its border. The man stepped back, and his arms came up to shield his missing head. Curious, if he didn't have one.

The vampire curled his fingers into claws. "Who do you mean? Who is *she*?"

"He means me."

This new voice originated from the headless man's right, near a table of test tubes, but nobody stood there. It had a commanding, feminine timbre, filling the room.

Whoever *she* was, she must be in gaseous form. Dracula was confronting an ancient creature. He could count on one hand the number of vampires who had mastered turning to air, only one of whom resided in the United States. How had she mastered the transformation and kept her voice?

"Camilla?"

"God, no." The voice came from the left of where it first spoke. "Camilla lives in Missouri. She's a far cry from Hollywood."

Footsteps walked toward the center of the room. Dracula could hear this woman but not see or smell her. The lack of a scent bothered him as much as his inability to view her. His heightened sense of smell allowed him to hunt with greater precision than his eyesight, an advantage he often used.

What sort of creature was this woman?

But he would not be afraid. He was the legendary Dracula. He was a deity to the human vermin, playing with them as a child played with ants. He extinguished their lives or let them go free as he pleased.

The count adjusted his voice, employing a tone to captivate his subjects. "Who do you think you are?"

At first, no one answered. Then, the headless figure spoke. "She is Gloria, a genius and a scientist. She—"

"Not another word, Oscar," Gloria interrupted.

Ah, the movie producer now had their names, but her resistance disturbed him. Few could withstand his power of persuasion. True, those with incredible faith in a benevolent power and others with a particular type of dementia could ignore his commands. In general, lording over the mentally ill, like Renfield, was easy unless...

Unless they, too, thought they were gods. He would show her. Only one god could rule this filthy town, and his name was Dracula.

Gloria moved, and the count's acute hearing picked up her footsteps behind the headless man, Oscar. He stiffened as if someone had put a hand on his shoulder. With the servant's, or perhaps lab assistant's, reaction, the count concluded the nature of the people confronting him. Genius. Scientist.

Dracula narrowed his eyes. "You are invisible, aren't you?"

Gloria's voice originated from the other side of Oscar. "Not merely invisible. You couldn't smell me, either. Those canine-sharp receptors in your nose have failed you, haven't they? I blocked the roses' scent when I put them in with the lilacs."

Dracula should have searched the box, not leaving it to Charles.

"And I injected your guard with a serum to put him in my control for a few minutes." The lady snorted. "Don't you think the less intelligent are beneath us? I determine what others do as well as what they see or smell."

"Once she blocks touch, you could call her senseless," said Oscar.

Gloria chuckled. "Terrible pun, Oscar. Another quip like that, and I'll kill you."

Oscar's body trembled. Her warning didn't sound like an idle threat.

Gloria moved away from Oscar, closer to the bride's coffin. "I have mastered the senses except touch. If I choose, I could also block the sounds I make. However, I need you to hear me, big-time producer. Tell me, why haven't you made an Invisible Woman picture?"

How ridiculous. "I have no patience for people who ask me inconsequential questions."

"Inconsequential?"

Enough! He must escape. Again, he used his power of influence. "Release me."

The vampire put all his will in the two words. Nobody spoke for a heartbeat, and then Gloria laughed at him. "As if, Dracles. Don't you understand the situation you're in? I suppose I ought to draw you a picture. I have a visible companion, Kitty, who does my dirty work. Kitty engaged people to become my subjects. She recruited Oscar for me. Didn't she, Oscar?"

Oscar wrung his hands.

"I rewarded him through experimentation until I made his head invisible. Unfortunately, my little Kitty cat bait accidentally attracted a large dog a few days ago. Perhaps I should say, she tempted a wolf."

Dracula had met the skinny blonde in a bar. He recalled thinking she would make a nice trophy for his basement mausoleum. Was her name Kitty? Who knew? Who cared? How vain these women were. Didn't they realize it was an honor to become his bride?

"I want her back, Dracles. She's not dead, yet. Tell me how to reverse the process, and you go free. I'll imprison you again, of course, and leave you for the rose to wilt. Alas—to let you know, the back of my hand is against my forehead — I'll have to forgo my movie career. But my higher pursuit in science must come first."

Impudent worm of a woman. Dracula had her now. This Kitty was the chink in her armor. He would drive a bargain with her. But first, make Gloria desperate. Negotiating with the upper hand was always best.

"The process is irreversible," Dracula lied. "Once she has my blood in her, she must die and rise, serving only me."

He expected the scientist to plead for her companion. She would beg for any solution, and then he would strike a concession. Perhaps, he would convert Gloria to be one of his brides.

Dracula spotted a massive roque mallet rise next to the other coffin. Now, he remembered. He had placed the new girl, Kitty, in this cast-off container of the dead. The wooden pole sticking out from the top was the stake. Gloria was lifting the mallet, using theatrics on him. She was pretending she was going to kill her singular bargaining chip. Did she take him for a fool? Did she honestly —

The mallet whipped around and swung down, striking the stake, driving it into the coffin. A high-pitched female voice screamed and called out for mercy. In response, Gloria repeated her actions twice, and then the mallet floated to the table. Not once did the tool hesitate or waver.

For the first time in his long life, Dracula pondered his vulnerability. But the thought vanished after it crossed his mind. So, bargaining for Kitty's life wasn't the opportunity he had first assumed. Nevertheless, *he* was the alpha dog here, the star of this little stage play. He hadn't risen to his station by being a coward or a fool. This Gloria creature had killed a bride. His most recent convert was nothing but a possession. But this invisible woman took his trinket from him. And for killing her, Gloria would pay.

Oscar's hands flew to his missing head. "I liked Kitty."

Gloria stepped next to Oscar, and he cringed.

"There, there, my pet," said Gloria. She directed her following sentence to Dracula. "You upset my servant. How dare you, Dracles?"

"Stop calling me that name!"

Gloria's footsteps indicated she was moving to an empty table. "You're kind of grumpy, aren't you? Are you still angry that the Transylvanian Twist is number two?"

She was deranged, flitting from subject to subject, and unaffected by killing a companion. Gloria's voice held no remorse. He admired her ruthlessness but also knew it to be a weakness. The vampire had to find a way to use her callousness against her.

"Now, let's talk," said Gloria. "Mano-to-monster. We can still make a deal. You're a producer of some note."

Of some note? The impudence!

"Hollywood loves making monster team-up films. Why not make a picture of the Invisible Woman meeting Dracula? An offering with us both is sure to be a bonanza."

Was she serious? Did a promise to make a movie ensure his freedom?

"Come on," Gloria sang-songed. "Why should the Frankenstein monster have all the fun? He and the Wolfman have hogged the spotlight for too long."

This conversation was the definition of insanity. She had a Mensa intellect, superior to the average human's, and a little girl's interest in movies? She was absurd. To escape, he, Tyrone Ruby, should say he'd consider such a proposal. Yet, this sounded like begging in Dracula's ears. He didn't *beg*. The simpletons in the village, the prostitutes in London, the homeless in Los Angeles—they begged. He was an aristocrat with wealth, power, and influence. Dracula didn't answer to an underling's demands.

"The Invisible Woman was a ridiculous picture the studios made when it had run out of ideas. The film was B-grade filth, better lost to time. Placing an invisible character alongside me is an insult."

Dracula paused for a breath. Oscar whispered, "She's toying with you. Play her game."

He? Play along? He would not.

"I will not ask you another time." Dracula squared his shoulders and commanded Gloria with all his power of influence. "You will release me immediately."

A silence filled the lab. Gloria broke it.

"I'm tired of you."

The vampire heard a *thwip* before his chest collapsed inward with an agony he had never experienced in his existence. He stumbled backward as his hands grasped his chest and encountered an invisible piece of wood. Gloria had shot him with a wooden crossbow bolt.

Dracula couldn't end this way. He would choose the time when he would leave this world.

Yet, the disintegration process started. Dracula's body rapidly decayed, and his hands transformed to dust first, the soot-like pieces drifting to the floor.

Oscar said, "No wonder they didn't make an Invisible Woman Meets Dracula. With him in it, it would have—"

Oscar choked, his neck tightening.

"I warned you about puns, my pet. But I'll be merciful for now and cut off what could have cost you your life. Haven't we had enough death today?"

Death? Yes, Dracula was dying. In a cage, no less.

Oscar coughed, and Gloria spoke next to him. "I do regret killing him, though. He may have known if others like him existed. As a scientist, I would like to meet them."

Dracula's legs were gone. His torso and head lay on the floor, transforming into ash.

"Other vampires?" asked Oscar.

"I'm over bloodsuckers. No, let's talk monsters. Do other monsters exist?"

Dracula was dying, but perhaps this scientist could help him. Reverse the process. He tried to call out to her, but it was too late. A strangled cry emerged from his lips.

"Perhaps," said Gloria, "I don't need to find them. With Kitty gone, I need a new companion. But why recruit when you have my genius?"

Only Dracula's head remained. His eyes blurred.

Oscar crossed his arms. "Who are you thinking of?"

Gloria spoke the last words the king of the vampires heard on Earth. "One of the Frankenstein models. I could repurpose Kitty. Watch out, Oscar. Here comes the Bride."

The End

SUBSTITUTIONS
Etta-Tamara Wilson

If you're reading this, then something has gone horribly wrong. I found out about a few things I probably shouldn't have, and I tried to deal with them. It seems likely I made the wrong choice. If you could fix my mistakes, that would be very helpful. I'm still not sure what it was that I did wrong, or what I missed, so I'm going to have to write it all down here so you can be the judge. Maybe you can do a better job of solving the problem than I did.

I should start from the beginning. My name is Jack Morris. I'm a research tech for Exeter Industries, a small but innovative company that specializes in the development of experimental blood substitutes. It's the company's goal to eventually make the need for mass blood drives after disasters unnecessary. I joined the company right after I graduated from university, intending to work on my master's part-time, drawn to the generally flexible schedule and decent pay, but then found that the work was far more interesting than I expected. Sure, I'm restricted mostly to the repetitive "grunt work," but I work arm-in-arm with the scientists who will change the world, looking over their shoulders—from a respectful distance—as they save humanity from the consequences of our distressingly common refrain of "hey, watch this!" It was over a year after I started there before I realized that I'd forgotten to finish the paperwork to start my master's program. So, I'm taking a gap year... "years" now, I guess. I'll get around to it eventually.

I'm off topic. Sorry. Anyway, since I'm trying to save this in an off-site folder and the video function can sometimes be a bit... uh... "problematic," I'll include transcripts below any attached videos, just in case. In light of what I'm doing tomorrow, it might be a good idea to provide any proof I have for "reasonable explanation" purposes.

I was just starting my fifth year at Exeter when everything changed. We had been making great progress on an artificial emergency blood substitute using donated blood, when the rumors began about a potential hostile takeover of the company. It wasn't something that was unheard of—even small research labs are expensive places to run, and for-profit companies aren't really known for patience when it comes to seeing results—but our company was owned by Peter Westin. He'd started the company twenty years ago after his daughter had died of blood loss following a nasty car accident. Finding a successful solution to the blood crisis became his passion in life. His reaction to the news was rumored to be quite, uh, *loud.*

The meeting was meant to be a secret, so naturally, everyone knew by the lunch break. Several of us decided to gather in the far corner of the cafeteria for the meal, hoping that Kate—a minor secretary for the executive office suite—would be there today. She wasn't a particularly popular woman, normally, but if anyone had been in that meeting that we could reach, it'd be her. She was usually a chatty girl when she had some sort of juicy tidbit to wave to the masses, so maybe we could get something interesting out of her.

By the time we got to the lunchroom, the woman in question was seated in a chair at the far end, surrounded by a sizable crowd of curious assistants and lab techs. She'd already worked herself up to full steam, waving her hands in the air in wide gestures as she spoke, her voice carrying a considerable distance away from the group. We hurried over, hoping to at least hear some of it before her enthusiasm called down the attention of the higher ups and the party dispersed.

"So, I'm sitting there, trying to do my job, while ignoring the fact I can hear yelling through the door at the end of the hall. It seemed to go on forever. Eventually, the door opened and the guy just came strolling out of the office looking like someone had just insulted his mother, all tight-lipped and tugging non-existent wrinkles out of his suit. He glared back at the open door, gave me the coldest side-eye I've ever seen, and stomped over to the elevator. Mr. Hennesey came out a moment later and told me to call down and warn security to escort him out of the building before Mr. Westin had the man bodily ejected by force."

"He wasn't a friendly sort, that's for sure. Tried to argue the entire time we were walking him out." Robert Murnau nodded thoughtfully. He was my favorite security guard, sociable and easy-going, while not as hung up on the rules as some of the others. He was usually assigned to a patrol around the first floor, which doesn't include an extended presence in the cafeteria. If I had to guess, this was going on the time sheet as "investigating a possible disturbance in the employee lounge area."

Kate nodded. "I don't understand what he hoped to achieve. I could hear a little through the door, but most of it was muffled and what I could hear made no sense. It really irritated Mr. Westin, though."

I elbowed my way closer to the center. "What was the bit you heard clearest?" We were a bunch of smart people; maybe we could puzzle it out. Kate just looked at me and raised an eyebrow.

"I could only hear what Mr. Westin yelled. 'It's not for sale!" and 'Get out!' were the two clearest statements."

I crossed my arms. "So, then the rumors of a company wanting to buy us were true? Who was it?"

"The business card he presented for the meeting said *The Strongmore Group.*"

"Strongmore? Isn't that a private equity firm? What do they want, the company or the product?" If the former, our jobs might be at risk. Companies like that bought and cannibalized other companies. Our jobs were at stake here.

Kate shrugged. "I couldn't tell. I never heard the visitor."

"It was the company as a whole." A quiet voice piped up from the back of the crowd. The crowd startled and pulled away from the source of the voice, revealing Thomas Hennesey, the newest member of the executive suite. "Not that it matters. Mr. Westin is issuing a statement company-wide in the morning. He has no intention of selling his company to a group focused almost entirely on short-term profits." He looked around the group. "Are you all still eating your lunch, or have you finished already?"

The group scattered into tiny clusters, spreading across the lunchroom. Robert quickly backed up and slid partly out of sight behind a pillar, pulling out his security notebook from his pocket and trying to look busy. Kate sighed at the loss of her audience and began picking at the remains of her lunch, visibly put out by the loss of attention. Hennesey turned in her direction. "Do you really think it wise to repeat what happens in the upper offices in the lunchroom, Miss Swales?"

She tilted her head and squinted at him. "Do you think Mr. Westin cares that the employees know that he tossed out someone for being impertinent, Mr. Hennesey? He's always been the type to brag about that fact, not hide it. Besides, I'm his secretary. He's not gonna fire me, when he needs me to do everything for him."

"You're *a* secretary, not *his* secretary." Hennesey nodded. "And that's no excuse. Mr. Westin's not exactly a young man. He won't always be the owner of the company. A future owner might not be so lenient about that sort of indiscretion."

Kate shrugged. "I'll deal with that when I come to it. And you should learn to relax. You're rarely out of the office except to grab your lunch, nowadays. It's not healthy to be so cramped up. Get out of the office sometimes. You never know, maybe even your dour attitude can attract someone interesting." She downed the last of her drink, ignoring the expression he leveled in her direction. She shifted the dishes she had used back onto a nearby empty tray and stood. "I should get back to my desk now. I have work to do." She turned away from the table and sashayed out the door, leaving her lunch tray behind. Hennesey sighed.

"So, we've nothing to worry about, then?" I asked. "Because the approval inspections are right around the corner, and you know how chaotic things get during those. I'd rather not get surprised when I'm trying to finish the documentation for the new line." The final approval for the beginning of the second clinical trials was in only a month, and I'd been working on the documentation from the first trials for half a year now. The chaos of a sale, especially if it was a hostile takeover or the beginnings of a corporate equivalent of a fire sale, had the potential to permanently derail one of the most promising projects we'd ever worked on. I really wasn't looking forward to that.

Hennesey smiled and patted my arm. "Like I said, don't worry about it. When I left him, Westin was fuming about the guy's audacity. Everything is fine. Enjoy your lunch and head back to work." He nodded and turned to leave, pausing next to Robert. "When you're done, please put Miss Swales' tray away before you resume your patrol."

Robert nodded, his face an interesting shade of pink. As Hennesey walked out of the room, Robert peered at me and widened his eyes dramatically, shoved his notebook in his jacket pocket and mimed loosening his collar. I rolled my eyes at his antics. The company prided itself on its company atmosphere, bragging online about the relaxed "family-like" relationships between employees. As long as everything got done, inspections passed, products launched without a problem, and no one caused issues, this intermission wouldn't risk Robert's neck.

With a grin, he swept up the abandoned tray and dropped it at the return window. I waved farewell to him as he left the room to resume his duties, and I went to fetch my delayed lunch while I still had time to eat it, trying my best to put the news out of my mind.

~~~~~

When I was a child, I believed that bad thunderstorms were an indication of impending disaster, like nature was unsettled on my behalf about upcoming drama. I grew out of it as I matured. In hindsight, the fact we had a massive thunderstorm that evening has caused me to rethink my stand. Can the approach of terrible events cause disastrous weather?

I do wonder now just how much Hennesey knew about what happened in that meeting. Mr. Westin didn't post a notice at the end of the next day, as Hennesey said he would. The CEO didn't even come into work that day. The boss stayed out of the office for weeks, despite the looming product deadline. Nervous exhaustion, we were told. Once he did return, it was to half-days. He was distracted, and his heart no
~~~~~

longer seemed to be in the work.

In the end, almost a month after the meeting, a public statement was made about what happened, but it didn't contain what everyone thought it would. Contrary to Hennesey's reassurance, due to his ongoing exhaustion and newfound anemia issues, the stalwart Mr. Westin had decided to sell his company. The Strongmore Group would be our new boss, after the inspections. For all of us, the clock was now ticking. The question was, where would we all end up?

~~~~~

As it turned out, I didn't actually have time to worry about the sale. With only weeks to go until the government inspectors arrived to look over the product for preliminary approval, and putting the final polish on the paperwork, I was already up to my ass in alligators at work. So the news I got when I arrived one morning, only a couple of days before the inspection, was most unwelcome.

"What do you mean, I have to meet the new boss? I'm swamped!"

The head scientist on the project, and my immediate supervisor, Dr. Vincent Paxton, looked unimpressed. "This man has spent a massive amount of money to buy the company. We know he wants the product, but if we want to keep our jobs, we need to roll out the red carpet. He needs to know that we have the company and his best interest in mind. Otherwise, we're all out on the street. I don't know about you, but I'd rather not be trying to find a new job in this economy."

"Can't someone else do it?" I put my hands on my hips, resisting the urge to flail them in frustration. "I still have to finish the final edit on the documentation. It has to be ready for final inspection within the next three days. I just don't have time for this."

Dr. Vincent shook his head. "There's no one else available. We're already short staffed, with everyone else involved in prepping the lab. You're actually the only one we have that can take the time out. You're doing it. Make it work." He picked up a clipboard with a distressingly thick pad of printouts and flipped through it once. Pulling off the top few pages, he handed them to me. "It shouldn't be difficult. Just meet them, show them around the lab and answer any questions they might have about the facilities. Once you're done, bring them to me and I'll answer any questions they might have about our products. Nothing hard about it. By the way, you have about ten minutes until they arrive."

He ignored my flustered sputtering, waved a hand in dismissal and practically ran out the door to the back offices. Coward. I spent the next few minutes scanning the file he'd handed me. It wasn't anything significant, just a series of personnel profiles and a handwritten list with the word "agenda" written at the top. From the list, it looked like they
~~~~~

wanted me to lead the group through the labs they'd already prepped for inspections. I guessed they wanted to show them everything as sparkly new as possible. The idea kind of made me feel like a used-car salesman. Well, if selling them on the lab and its staff got me back to work faster, I'd do my best.

I was just finishing my read-through of the dossier when the door to the hallway opened. Robert strolled into the office, leading a small group of people whose attire indicated they were not in their normal element. They were shepherded by a trio of our security guards. My eye was drawn first to the three women, all of whom would give your average modeling agency a case of the vapors. Each one had a different hair color, but all three were dressed identically, in classy black suits. The brunette and the redhead immediately turned and began inspecting different aspects of the lab. The brunette headed for the floor plan bolted to the wall next to the door and the redhead showed interest in the contents of the nearest desk. The statuesque blonde pulled out a phone and scrolled down the screen for a moment, then turned to offer the device to an older gentleman who stood in the very center of the group. I glanced down at my file for a moment to confirm my suspicions. Although the profiles were missing their usual photos of the guests, the written description was more than enough. This was Stewart G. Harker III, CEO of the Strongmore Group.

Harker stood six feet tall and leaner than average, but possessed more grace in his movements than I would have guessed for someone with such long limbs. His features seemed almost washed out, his skin unusually pale for the average American. Absolutely no color at all tinted his high cheekbones or thin nose, and his lips were nearly non-existent. The only features that stood out were his eyes, which were a brown so dark they looked almost black in the low light of the office. With an impressively full head of snow-white hair and the neat white mustache, curled slightly on the ends, he reminded me of the professor from my English literature class. Or maybe a really good Arthur Conan Doyle impersonator.

Taller than the women by only a few inches, he nonetheless seemed to tower over his entourage. If I recalled correctly, my professor would have referred to him as having "gravitas." Personally, he made me a little uneasy. Probably not unexpected; after all, as the new owner, he had great power over my life. One bad move and my career was essentially over. The more I observed him, the less he looked like a professor and the more the man resembled a skeleton instead.

I shook off a momentary case of the willies and stepped forward, plastering the friendliest smile on my face that I could manage. "Hello,

Mr. Harker, welcome to Exeter Industries. My name is Jack Morris, I am a research assistant for the experimental products development division, and I'd be pleased to show you around." I automatically flicked my eyes down to take a look at Mr. Harker's visitor badge, stuttering to a stop when I noticed the ID only had a name. No photo, despite photos being mandatory for both visitor and staff IDs. "Aah... Was there an issue with our credentialing equipment? We might need to alter the tour, as we need the badges to get through the doors in some areas."

"No, the equipment was fine," Harker stepped forward and held out his hand for me to shake. "Please forgive an old man's eccentricities. I was raised by a nanny from eastern Europe, who believed that photographs capture the soul. To this day, getting my picture taken unsettles me, so I much prefer to avoid it whenever there are other ways to prove my identity."

I shook his hand, which was as cold as ice. A shiver went up my spine, but I fought it down. Older generations had quirks, like poor circulation and odd personality traits. It was fine.

"It's normally not allowed, for security reasons," I carefully dropped his hand and suppressed the urge to rub my palm on my pants leg. "Especially with an important inspection imminent. But you're the new boss, so we'll make an exception, just for you. Just try not to touch any of the surfaces on the tour. Everything has already been prepped for inspections, and it's in all our best interests to pass them."

Harker nodded, the three women behind him bobbing their heads like a flock of silent chickens. He turned and smiled faintly at them.

"I should introduce the group. These are my daughters: Elizabeth, Laura, and Christine." He swept his hand across the group, indicating the blonde, brunette and redhead in turn. Elizabeth nodded politely, clasping her phone in her hand like a lifeline. Laura smiled brightly, her eyes morphing into almost cartoon-like crescents, and she waggled her fingers at me before turning back to stare at the floor plan. Christine just grinned at me. She was trying to disassemble a stapler, for some reason. "They all serve as advisors and vice-presidents at Strongmore."

I nodded at the trio. "I'm charmed. I'd be happy to show you around and tell you anything I can about the labs. If you have specific questions about our products, though, it'll have to wait. I'll pass you on to the scientists when we're done. If you give me a moment, I'll have to go get the override keys, so we can begin."

Robert waved a card key in the air, catching my attention. "I've already got it right here."

"Very proactive of you. All right, that means we can start the tour. Please, come this way." I turned and swung a hand to indicate the entrance door to the lab proper, and we embarked on our tour of my home away from home. As I led them from room to room, I watched them carefully. They didn't seem like the type to take a firsthand interest in the daily workings of a company, especially one in the medical field. To be honest, they seemed more like the type to send an employee to run the company, while they went on cruises or attended star-studded fundraisers. At least the women, anyway. The father might have been more at home in a library. But all four of them showed a keen interest in the lab and facilities.

Laura spent much of the tour trailing behind the group, questioning Robert about the security system and how it could be improved. She seemed concerned about the existence of an override key, until he assured her that the key was kept in a secure location, accessible only to security and the executive suite. Christine, on the other hand, spent the tour with her hands clasped tightly behind her back, staring intently at all the samples and resources being used for the test products. She never asked any questions, but from what I could see, her lips were moving. It almost looked to me like she was counting things. At one point, we came across a rack of test trays holding dozens of blood sample testing tubes, and she just froze in place. Elizabeth had to pull her from the lab.

"Christine has a bit of a thing with counting anything she comes across," she told me as she steered her sister through the door into the next lab, Christine muttering numbers in a low undertone. "It's annoying, but manageable. On the plus side, she's really good at figuring out the details in every company we get involved in."

"Everyone has their strengths and weaknesses," I said, trying for the most sympathetic expression I could muster. "Do you maintain operations in a lot of the companies you all acquire?" If there was any time to try to suss out what their plans for the company were, it was now. Nothing ventured, nothing gained, no?

"Not many of them, no. Only the ones worth keeping." She narrowed her eyes and glanced at me from the side, one side of her lip raising slightly. "Was that you trying to fish for info on your company?"

I grimaced. I'd hoped my motives would be less obvious. I guess not. "Can you blame a guy, if you stood in my shoes?"

A faint chuckle sounded behind me. I turned to face Harker, who had been inspecting results pasted to a nearby whiteboard. "Don't worry, my young friend. I have big plans for both the product and the company as a whole. Your job is safe. None of you are going to escape me now."

That was… reassuring, if a bit of an odd way to put it. "That's wonderful to hear. I look forward to working with you. Is there anything you wish to ask about the lab?"

Harker clasped his hands behind his back and shook his head. "No, everything seems perfectly in order. We can always talk about improvements in efficiency and resource management another time."

I nodded. "Excellent. In that case, I'd be pleased to introduce you to the scientists, so you can get details on our upcoming product testing."

"I'd like that. Thank you."

I waved them through the door at the end of the labs and into the lounge where the primary scientists were waiting. I left them there, listening intently to the beginning of what looked to be a fairly long presentation, complete with slides. I was glad to be able to leave, as I knew from past experience that the doctors in charge of the labs could become very talkative. Dr. Vincent could take over the tour from here. I had paperwork to finish.

Slipping out the door, I nearly ran into Robert, who was waiting for the group just outside the lab. He raised an eyebrow at me. "'*None of you are going to escape me now*'? Really? Could they make it sound more creepy?"

"What can you do, they're rich. They can afford to be eccentric. Our jobs are safe, and I, for one, am grateful. We can ignore the occasional odd word choice. It's not like we'll have to deal with them regularly."

"True. A job search right now would be a bear. Managing the creepy professor is worth it to avoid that."

"Agreed. Anyway, Dr. Vincent has them from here, so I'm going to finish my tasks for the day. You waiting around?"

"Yeah. I have to escort them out, since they have incomplete IDs." He looked back at the door with a contemplative expression.

"As you wish. But just so you know, Doc just started a slide show presentation." I turned and slid through the door to the front office, my mind already turning to my own work. As the door slid shut, I could still hear Robert grumbling.

"A slide show? There goes the next hour."

~~~~~

Thankfully, the inspections went off without a hitch. The executives escorted the inspectors around and showed off our production, handing them the documentation. After a few weeks of answering increasingly difficult questions, we got probationary approval. The final approval likely wouldn't come in for a while, as the wheels of bureaucracy always turned slowly, but with probationary approval, we could at least plan the upcoming testing agenda.

At the suggestion of a few of the top brass—quietly endorsed by
~~~~~

Elizabeth—we also ended up scheduling a media day. Having a bunch of reporters running around the lab generally drove me up the wall, but a message, passed down from Hennesey to the company at large, said that we needed the attention. Stock prices needed a boost, he stated, and good press of the upcoming products would help. Well, I don't know that many of the reporters wrote much about the products, but they certainly wrote glowing reviews of the company and its new owner. From the amount of praise they heaped on him, you'd think he declared that he had cured cancer. Charisma worked wonders for stocks, apparently, as they did jump significantly. So, it was worth it. I just hoped that our blood substitute ended up being as promising as it looked right now.

Everything was just starting to look up for the company when people began dropping like flies. That should have been my first clue. The fact that most of the people from important company departments were seemingly immune to the illness should have been the second. Unfortunately, I didn't notice until it impacted me directly. I blamed burnout from the documentation grind.

The illness that passed through the entire company started out slowly. Most people blamed the excessive fatigue on the workload that everyone had to take on to pass the inspections. It was reasonable to expect that there would be some delay in recovery, as it took time to regain lost sleep. But three months later with no improvement, and an ever-increasing number of people gaining symptoms? Blaming it on the inspections became an exercise in wishful thinking. It was easier to blame the excessive workload, rather than consider other possibilities.

Mostly the lower status workers fell ill, as large portions of the security staff, cafeteria workers, interns and first year employees in the various departments seemed to be the first who came down with it. I actually lost two clerical assistants to the unknown issue, but neither I nor any of the other research assistants or doctors suffered from any symptoms. I attributed that to our robust safety protocols, and vitamin supplement smoothies Dr. Vincent pushed on everyone in the lab. No one in the executive suite fell ill either, but they had an amazing health care plan, so that didn't surprise anyone.

There was no evidence of a similar illness in the general population outside the company, and no one had reported any lab accidents. Things became far more concerning, though, when the entire nightly cleaning crew were found scattered unconscious around the building one morning. They were examined and found to have all blacked out simultaneously on the job the night before. The idea of a potential lab accident having been covered up could no longer be discounted. The building was put on lockdown to prevent any rumors from getting out, and everyone involved with the labs were interviewed while the buildings were thoroughly inspected. I spent a good five hours repeating to a series of ever-increasingly dour investigators that for the last three months, I had spent most of my time sorting the applications for the potential test candidates for the next round of clinical trials. I hadn't stepped foot in the lab proper since I gave the new CEO his initial tour.

They realized it likely wasn't lab-related when several affected members of the company were diagnosed with severe anemia. It should have been a relief to the company, as the ability to rule out a recent accident meant it was far less likely to harm the final approvals of the trials, which were expected any day now. Unfortunately, stress levels in the company as a whole were approaching dangerous levels, as the affected employees began to stay home. With increasingly fewer people at work, cracks began to show in the company. Everyone capable of doing so was working longer shifts, and in some departments, quality began to suffer. The most obvious issues appeared in the security staff.

Four months after the inspections, I was working late one night, typing up preliminary acceptance letters for the upcoming trial. I didn't normally do that. It was usually the work of the clerical assistants, but we'd lost another two in the last week. All of the research assistants were now having to pull double duty, doing both our regularly assigned tasks and typing up all of the chicken scratch that our supervisors usually piled on the support staff. They were just lucky we could read their writing. I was on my fourth hour of overtime, approaching midnight, when I saw the beam of a flashlight sweep across the windows in the hall. I pressed save on the letter I was writing and closed my laptop, turning toward the door just in time to hear a quiet knock. I quickly rose to my feet and approached the door, opening it to find Robert, looking down the hallway and sweeping his flashlight from side to side.

"Hey, Jack. Are you the only one working here tonight?" He looked back at me, but kept his flashlight fixed on a spot down the hallway. I nodded.

"Yeah, the rest of the lab staff went home hours ago. I volunteered to stay here and finish some letters. What's up?"

Robert sighed. "I was doing a patrol of the building. When I looked through the windows of the upper floors on this side, I thought I saw someone walking through the hallways. There's only a couple of badges signed in tonight: yours, mine, and a couple of people from the executive suite. None of them match the figure I saw."

I tilted my head to one side, intrigued. "Well, I haven't seen anyone since the rest of the lab went home. And I haven't met a stranger in weeks. What did you see?"

"It looked like a woman in a white dress, but I only saw her for a moment. When I tried to get closer to see more clearly, she just vanished. Like she'd turned to mist or something."

Sounded like Robert was working too much and starting to see things. I could relate. "Have you looked around? Found anything?""

"By myself? If there's someone actually here, company policy says I have to wait for backup."

"And?"

"The rest of the security team is either out with the plague or sleeping off triple-shifts. I've got no one on call. If anything happens, they told me to lock myself in the office and call the police."

"For a possible false alarm? That sounds like a lot of hassle. And paperwork."

Robert nodded. "Doesn't it, though? I can actually feel the hand cramp now."

The chances were highest that there was nothing there; he was just seeing things. After all, an intruder coming in a window or exit door would have set off the alarms, and the only other way in went right through the lobby security barrier. No one could get through without a pass. However, checking it out seemed like a great excuse to leave the lab, and I could use the disturbance as an excuse to head home for the night. I decided to go "mist lady" hunting. After all, a lady made of mist could always have come in through the ventilation openings.

"Well, I'll go with you and provide back-up. Let's go take a look, and make sure there's no one here," I said, trying to keep a healthy sense of humor.

Robert looked skeptical. "Are you sure?"

I nodded. "Absolutely. Lead the way.

The two of us crept silently through several floors of hallway and lab spaces, looking for anything unusual. Robert went first, his large flashlight gripped tightly in one hand, his phone in the other. I followed closely behind him, gripping a short broom handle I stole from a maintenance closet along the way, in case we ran into any particularly solid intruders. You could never be too careful, after all.

We were in the last hallway of the second building when we discovered the intruder. I was all set to tease Robert about seeing things when we passed the lab dedicated to the blood sample processing for all our projects. The lights were on, which was strange. This lab was nothing special, and the techs involved were some of the first ones to go home at night. The lab should have been dark for hours. I crept up to the little window set into the door and peered into the bright room.

Inside was Elizabeth, wearing a 1950s style vintage cocktail dress in a shade of antique white that seemed to glow in the lab lighting. Her sleek blonde hair was pulled back with a blood red ribbon, the only trace of color on her. I could see why Robert had been spooked. She looked remarkably out of place in the deserted lab, and for no reason I could determine, she was looking over a printout.

Robert tried to peer around me. "Well? What is it?"

"One of our new bosses. Apparently reading."

"Really? Why here?"

I shrugged and opened the door. The sound must have startled her, because Elizabeth jumped slightly and dropped the printout. She turned to look, her shoulders tense and eyes wide, biting her bottom lip on one side. She had remarkably sharp canines. I wondered if that was a family trait. When she saw us, she relaxed and let go of her lip.

"We're sorry to startle you, Miss Harker. We were doing a security sweep of the building and noticed the lights were on in here." I gestured to Robert, who was leaning in around the half-open door. He gave her a smile and a small wave.

She raised an eyebrow, one hand drifting over to the countertop, her fingertips settling on the top of the printout. "A research assistant is doing a security sweep?"

"We're a bit low on staff at the moment, and patrols need backup. Everyone is lending a hand where we're needed." I smiled at her, as reassuringly as possible.

"It'd really help if we could hire some more security staff, even temporarily. Right now, we're running ourselves ragged trying to cover everything," Robert piped up.

"That does sound like a problem. I'll pass the info on to my father and see what we can do."

I leaned over, trying to see what she'd been reading. Resource reports? "We're a little startled to see you in the labs, especially at this time of night. Is there something I can help you with?"

"Ah," she said, looking down at the abandoned file. "I was trying to get a grasp on how our current stockpile of supplies is being stored and used. My father has entrusted me with making sure all the projects have ample resources, while improving and streamlining the intake and usage of the blood supplies. I was working on gathering the data."

"At nearly midnight? By yourself, in a closed lab?"

Elizabeth shrugged. "I've always found I work best alone. And I'm an incurable night owl. Almost all my work is done at night."

"Normally, we restrict our work to the daylight hours around here. Saves on manpower. But you are one of the bosses, so I'm sure you can do as you like." I shrugged. "If you really want to work on our supply issues, though, you should talk to Agnes Billington. She's responsible for our inventory, storage, and supply chain management. She's the one that would know all the details. If you would like, come in sometime in the next couple of days and I can introduce you."

"I would like that. Thank you."

Robert stepped forward, finally clearing the door frame. "Miss, considering the time, will you be much longer? The building itself is already closed for the night, and I'll need to stay and escort you out when you're done. I'm supposed to be locking the doors and doing the night patrol since the regular employees have left the building."

Elizabeth pushed away the file and waved her hand. "Oh, I'm done for the night, I've done all I can without talking to an employee. We can head out now. I'm sorry for keeping you."

I stepped aside and gestured toward the door, falling in behind her as she walked towards the exit.

Robert raised his hand to stop her as she approached the door. "While we have you, Miss, I have to ask. You're not marked as having entered in the system logs, and I didn't see you go through the security checkpoint. How did you get in? Is there a flaw in the security system we need to address?"

Elizabeth reached into a pocket in her dress and pulled out an executive ID card, waving it in the air. "I was given this today. I came out through the checkpoint, so I don't know why it didn't register. I'll make a note to have the company look over the system for issues."

"That would be appreciated, Miss. This way."

After Elizabeth passed Robert, I quickly drew close to him. "So, is she who you saw? Is our new boss your mist lady?" I whispered.

Robert nodded. "Her dress and hair match what I saw. She was too far away for me to see her face. But what kind of boss comes in during the middle of the night to do inventory?"

"I don't know. An eager one? I don't really care, as long as he or she doesn't make me do it."

"That's fair."

Elizabeth's voice echoed from the dark down the hall. "Are you coming?"

Robert leaned out into the hallway. "Coming, Miss."

After a quick glance at the lab to make sure nothing looked amiss, I turned off the lights and closed the door, then accompanied Robert and our new boss out of the lab complex. It was time to go home; my bed was waiting.

~~~~~
~~~~~

Six months after the sale of our company, despite the ongoing plague ravaging our workforce, we received the news we'd been waiting for. The government inspectors had put a rush on our case due to the nature of our project, and we officially had approval to begin the second phase clinical trials. The executive branch immediately went out, had dinner, and took the weekend off. Dr. Vincent and the other project supervisors in the lab promptly threw a banger of a party. Anybody in the lab was invited to come, although it was a small group, as much of the clerical staff was still down with the as-yet undiagnosed illness, and the research assistants all had too much work to do to risk the hangovers. Half of the lab were still nursing their headaches when the other shoe dropped. Mr. Westin had apparently gone home from the dinner and gone to bed, but didn't get back up. The plague had just taken its first life.

The company was shut down for two weeks. The public was told that the employees were given leave in honor of a great man and his dedication to improving the lives of humanity. In reality, though, the executive suite had sent everybody home to have the building deep-cleaned in an effort to stem the spread of the contagion. Somehow, despite the illness, we had gotten our permissions and they weren't going to risk losing it because a bunch of employees got a little worn down.

Likewise, when the employees returned at the end of the two weeks, every employee—regardless of department—was put through an employer-sponsored health clinic. It wasn't anything terrible—your standard temperature testing, some eye, nose and throat tests, an overall check-up, and a general health questionnaire. It had been a while since I'd had one of those, and I was pleased to know that I had lost twenty pounds since my last one. I wasn't as pleased with the shots one of the nurses lined up to give me, though. The doctor running the clinic, a Dr. Polidori, had explained earlier that they intended to give us a few of the standard shots used in this sort of situation. I recognized the flu shot, and I understood the vitamin B shots, but the third shot wasn't anything I was familiar with. I waved to get Dr. Polidori's attention and gestured at the syringe the nurse was wielding. It held an unidentified bright red fluid.

"What is that?"

Polidori paused on his way past my station and stared at the syringe for a moment, then picked up the paper on the counter. "It's a new vitamin supplement being produced by your company. It's supposed to help you get your energy back."

"Made by my company? I didn't see anything like that go through the labs."

Polidori stared at me. "Do you see everything that goes through all of the labs?"

"Well, no, there are some dedicated special labs that I don't interact with. But I don't recall seeing anything about a new vitamin supplement on the product list in the company newsletter."

He shrugged. "It probably went through one of those special labs, and they just didn't tell you. Or maybe it had a different name. I don't know what to tell you. I was just ordered to give you the shots, and it has your company's name on it. You want to question the providence of one of your company's products, you can take that up with your boss. Now, do you want to take the shot, or do I tell your boss you declined and went home?"

I wasn't a fan of putting something I didn't recognize in my body, but this was a professional, and I did trust my company. If it was a product they made to help, then I had no problem with it.

"Just get it over with." I gritted my teeth as the nurse gave me the three shots in quick succession. I thanked him and rolled down my sleeve, collected my paperwork and headed into work.

Twenty minutes later, I had to admit, I felt like a new man. I had more energy than I'd had in weeks, and even my senses seemed heightened. The light was incredibly bright, the overhead fluorescents actually buzzed audibly, and I never realized before quite how sharp the scent of the antiseptic we used for sterilization was. The effects dulled after a few days, but if that was the side effect of that new supplement, then the company was about to make a fortune. It was powerful stuff.

After those physicals, the number of employees who missed work due to the unknown plague began to level off. People still got sick and the illness itself began to show up in the general population of the city around the company, but it was no longer severe. The executive suite opened a free clinic to the public, offering the vitamin supplement for a nominal fee, and the public cases of the plague were mild and abated after a few days. As for the blood supplement, we began clinical trials in earnest.

When Exeter had first started, Mr. Westin had instituted a protocol. The only way to react quickly to an unexpected issue with a new discovery was to have a fresh set of eyes constantly monitoring the tests. As a result, whenever we were working on a project and it entered a new phase of development, we switched out the observers for new ones, people who hadn't worked on that particular project. Each new group had the notes from all the others, so any patterns and deviations could be recognized, but new observers meant that things the previous group might have missed had a greater chance of being caught and noted. I hadn't been on an observation team for a while, and the clerks had returned, pale and perennially exhausted, but capable of doing their jobs again. As a result, after all the candidates were selected and the trial began, I was taken off my documentation duties and reassigned as one of the observers for this round.

I was bored within days. Things had been so hectic for the last six months that I had spent the entire time on high alert, and I guess I'd gotten used to it. The slower crawl of the observation trials felt like torture. I got so starved for stimulation that I began looking for other things to do during my down time. There wasn't much available, but I took anything I could manage to do from my workstation, which was how I found myself staring at the last six months of user logs for the labs. Staring, because I was looking at something... well, strange, to put it bluntly.

According to the logs, twice a week, every week, for the last six months, somebody had logged in to the labs in the middle of the night. They were always there for at least two hours, and they left well before any of the workers arrived. But the identity section of the log, which should automatically fill in from the user ID, was blank. The ID literally registered as "no such user." That shouldn't be possible. Security would never have made one like this.

I looked back at the dates. One of the dates where the "ghost user" was registered as having entered was the night we found Elizabeth in the lab. Her name was nowhere on the log at all. Just the "ghost user." Could it have been her ID? Why was it registered as nameless? And why would she be coming into the lab so often and in the middle of the night? She'd been working with Agnes during the day for months now. Did she still find it easier to work at night?

Well, first things first, figure out that ID. Luckily, this was on Friday, and just after four. Since it wasn't a crunch time in the project, it was that sweet spot in the day when most of the office staff had already packed up and gone home. I should have been able to find out *something* with a little digging. I picked up my phone and called down to Robert at the security desk. I told him what I found.

"Well, that's really strange. We have to physically enter name data in that section, and it won't let you print the card without something in that space. Someone had to manipulate the system in person, and they knew what they were doing. Let me look over the system for a little bit, and I'll see if I can find anything. What was the first date our 'ghost' showed up?"

"May 20th. The night we found the new boss in the lab."

I could hear the keyboard clicking, then it abruptly stopped. "Really? Could she have seen the other user?"

I rubbed the back of my neck. "Or she *is* the ghost user. She doesn't show up on the log at all, not even from that night. I've no way of figuring it out for sure, though, not without seeing her ID card."

Robert resumed typing. "When I find the ghost ID, I'll also look up any other recent additions. Maybe I can find her card, figure out what's on it specifically, and the two of us can figure out why she doesn't show up."

"Do you think something is wrong?"

"Well, if nothing else, the lab security system isn't working like it's supposed to. That's a problem, especially since the building security is still not up to snuff."

"Still undermanned?"

"Finding competent help is hard, apparently. Anyway, let me do some digging, and I'll call you back."

While I waited, I was curious. What was the "ghost" doing in the lab? The log was connected to all the equipment in the lab, so there should have been some sort of indication. If it was Miss Elizabeth working on the supply chain by herself, a log-in request should have been in the lab computers. I checked them, but the log was blank. That was curious. If the "ghost" didn't use the computers, what were they doing? After a bit of digging through the spreadsheets, I found it on the logs for one of the bigger storage refrigerators in the lab. This particular one contained the storage bays for the medication being tested in the clinical trial. According to the log, the storage bays had each been opened for several minutes, one at a time. No identity was attached to the ID that opened the lockers, and no reason for the action was recorded on the log.

This was rather alarming. Normally, late alterations were only done by the head scientists in the project, and any manipulation of the test samples or medications by any other staff had to be done during working hours and under supervision. Undocumented contact with any part of the project at that hour of night could jeopardize the whole project. Who did this? Was it Miss Elizabeth? What was her motive?

As I sat and pondered, I realized that none of us knew anything about the new boss's background. We knew *The Strongmore Group* had a reputation for dismantling the companies they purchased, but I don't recall hearing anything about the owners themselves. Perhaps, I thought, it was time to correct that oversight. Normally, I would have waited until I got home to do any background research, since the company computers were monitored. It wouldn't look good on any sort of review if somebody caught me looking into our new CEO and his family. However, my internet at home was not nearly as good as the connection here, and I intended to take advantage of the superior bandwidth at my disposal.

I shouldn't have used my phone on the company wi-fi, but I did have an advantage in this case. My boss liked to throw loud parties for lab celebrations on company time. It wasn't really something he was supposed to do, but he did his job well, so the company turned a blind eye to the parties. Fortunately for me, all of his technical prowess seemed to be focused in the medical field, and he was all thumbs when it came to advanced technology. He couldn't find his way through the internet router if he had a map and a Sherpa. Tech support had gotten so annoyed with his constant calls that they sought out someone in the lab itself with the ability to act as his personal tech support. I was now one of the few assistants in the company with a set of limited computer admin credentials, and before every celebration, I had to link all of the sound systems to the router for his party music. I couldn't turn off the monitors on any of the lab computers, but I could attach equipment to the routers. Since the company didn't have any monitoring equipment on my phone, I linked my smartphone and began to search.

It turned out the new owners didn't have credentials of any sort. They barely had any records at all. The only evidence I could find was their names on the records of Strongmore, the women going back two decades, and their father going back to its founding in the 70s. There was no evidence of professional certification for any of them, no records of degrees from any universities, and no record of participation in any other companies. It was as if the entire family just appeared out of thin air when the private equity firm was founded. Mist woman, indeed. Who were these people?

As I sat there, contemplating the possibilities of a family with no history, my phone rang. I jumped a foot in the air and grabbed my chest, feeling as if my heart was jumping out of my chest and running a lap or two around the room. A quick glance at the screen told me that it was Robert, so I took a deep breath and answered. "Hey, what did you find?"

"None of them exist."

Was he looking over my shoulder? "What do you mean? Who doesn't exist?"

"Absolutely none of the new owners have an ID. I did a full scan, and there hasn't been a single card made with their faces or names in the system. I have no idea how they're getting in, but it certainly isn't with their own passes."

"That's peculiar. At least some of them have to be getting in. Miss

Elizabeth has been to the labs several times to work with Agnes. You and I both encountered her that night. If the ID she showed us didn't have her name and photo, what *was* on it?"

Robert's voice dropped. "I think I might be able to guess. The day before we found her in the lab, someone made four sets of IDs. These particular IDs were unusual, as they had no pictures, and the name section was filled in as '*no name available.*' You joked that it was a ghost ID, but according to the system, that's literally what it was. A ghost."

"Did you speak to the security guard who made it? What did he say about it?" At this point, our best clues would likely come from the person who dealt directly with the people the cards were made for. Maybe they dropped a clue about their intention.

"That's just it. According to the security logs, it wasn't made by any of the security guards."

I stared at my phone in disbelief for a moment, and then switched it to the other ear, "I thought it took a security guard to make those things. If it wasn't one of your guards, who made it?"

"Mr. Hennesey. from the executive suite. Evidently, he came down and filled them all out himself, and then took the finished cards back upstairs. We never even got to see who the cards ended up with. If you have any other questions, I think we're going to have to talk to him."

"Okay. I'll get back to you."

I looked at the clock. It was 5:30. Normally, the execs went home early, but there was always a possibility that somebody might be working late. I decided to risk it. It took three separate rounds of calls, but finally, someone picked up.

"Hello?"

It took me a second to recognize her. It was Kate, that gossipy secretary from the executive suite, but sounding far more withdrawn than I'd ever heard her before.

"Hey, it's Jack Morris, from down in the research labs. I'm sorry to bother you this late, but I was wondering if I could talk to Mr. Hennesey."

Kate cleared her throat. "Sure, if you can find him. But he's not up here, so…"

"He's gone home for the day already?"

"More like gone home for the year. I know I told him to relax, get out of the office and meet somebody, but I didn't expect him to take my advice to heart. He's rarely in the office anymore. He spends all his time hanging out with that redhead daughter of our CEO. How he's keeping his job, I just don't know, but I guess it helps to date the boss's daughter. Not likely to get fired, unless you piss him off."

Oh dear. "Well, I guess that rules out leaving a note and hoping I get called back. I guess I'll have to send him an email."

She sighed, and in the background, I heard the desk chair creak. "You're more likely to get him that way than anywhere else. He has been returning a few emails, but he hasn't been near his desk for memos in days."

"I'll do that, then. Thank you."

Kate hummed in response.

"While I'm on the phone, are you all right? You sound like it's been a rough day."

She huffed. "Yeah, I'm fine. I'm just fighting off the after-effects of a round of that blasted plague."

"I didn't know you caught that. It's hung on this long?"

Kate coughed. "No, actually. I managed to miss the illness when it was all the rage. It caught up to me a week or two ago. Nasty thing, too. I'm exhausted all the time, and I've apparently developed a bad case of anemia."

I raised an eyebrow at the news. "That sucks. I thought those shots were supposed to help prevent the thing from getting bad."

"You'd think. Unfortunately, two rounds of them haven't really helped me in the slightest." Kate sighed and then chuckled. "But on the bright side, the anemia seems to have given me the urge to bite people. Folks figured that one out pretty quick and now they don't bug me much. So, at least it's been pretty peaceful around here."

"There's always a silver lining somewhere."

"You just have to look hard enough. Say, what was it you wanted to ask Mr. Hennesey about? Is it anything I can help with? Maybe you won't have to wait for Mr. Reliable to get your answer."

Well, it was worth a shot. "Yeah, I just needed to ask Mr. Hennesey about a bunch of IDs he made a few months back. I needed to know who he'd given them to, I think one of them might actually affect my work a little."

"IDs? I don't know about any IDs. But all things considered, if he did anything, it was for one of those girls. The boss's daughters followed their father to the office on his weekly Saturday night visit just after they bought the company, and then they just started showing up throughout the week and hanging around Hennessy's office. They stopped after a few months, and now he's rarely here either. He just sort of follows Christine around, like a talking golden retriever. He does literally anything those women say."

Wow, sounded like Hennesey was toast. Wouldn't be the first time somebody had gone against the rules to gain favor with a love interest.

"What about Miss Elizabeth? Has she been in a lot?"

"The blonde? No, she only appeared the first day. She hasn't been back to the office since. I'm not even sure she's been in the company building."

Oh, that wasn't right. I'd seen her in the lab with my own eyes at least a dozen times over the last six months. Clearly, something was up, but who was involved? Was it just the daughters? What about Hennessy? Did Mr. Harker know? I doubted I could get any more information from Kate, so I decided to cut her loose. "Thanks for the info, Kate. That was actually very helpful. I'll send Hennessy an email, but if he doesn't get back to me, you have given me some things to think about. I'll let you go now. Have a good weekend."

"You too."

I quickly called Robert back. "Hennesey is incommunicado. Apparently, he's out of the office more often than he's in now. However, from what Kate said, the IDs were likely given to the Harker daughters."

"Well, three of them, at least. What happened to the fourth one? Given to the dad, or kept by Hennessy?"

"No clue. But I can tell you, whatever they're up to, we need to know what it is. They're monkeying with stuff in the lab, and it could endanger the company. Or worse."

"Worse? What do you mean?" Robert sounded worried.

"I tried looking the Harkers up. I couldn't find anything on them that predated 1975. And I do mean anything. It's like the family was invented the year they founded the company."

"Dang. Witness protection?" Clearly, Robert had seen far too many mafia movies.

"What family in hiding from anything currently dangerous would go create a multi-million-dollar company and make high-profile deals? If it's anything nefarious, I'm thinking it's closer to a 'running from my past' scenario. Maybe Grandpa did something he shouldn't, and they needed to change to get a fair deal. That sort of thing."

"Ah. Okay, that makes sense. And the stuff with the lab?"

"Industrial espionage?"

"Maybe. Regardless, what do we want to do about it?"

I thought for a moment. "Well, we don't know what they're truly trying to do. We also don't know if Mr. Harker knows what his daughters are up to. There's one way to get information on both: we go tell him ourselves."

Robert hesitated. "That seems kind of dangerous. If he knows, wouldn't the people telling him be at risk?"

I nodded. "Sure. That's why I'm going to have to take precautions.

For one thing, it'll just be me. If something happens, you can go to the police. I'll leave a detailed report of what we found so you can turn it over to them, if you need to. And second, I'll set my phone to record the conversation, and have it sent to the cloud. It can print a transcript of the video, so you'll know what happened."

Robert still seemed nervous. "All right. But are you sure? We could always just go to the police."

"All we have right now are suppositions, and a few random ghosts appearing where they shouldn't be. It could all just be nothing, or something that Mr. Harker needs to address personally to resolve it. We're not going to really know what we have until we ask."

"If you say so. When are you going to do it, so I can prepare?"

"Tomorrow night. Kate mentioned Mr. Harker keeps a regularly scheduled Saturday night office visit. If I come back tomorrow evening, he's likely to be in his office alone. Plus, that will give me time to set up my precautions."

Robert still didn't like the idea, but it wasn't like we had other options. So I bid him goodbye and headed home. I assumed he did the same. And so, you are all caught up. I have a suspicion that something is not quite right, but nothing is actionable at the moment. The only thing I can do is bring my questions to the attention of the top of the food chain and hope I'm not making a mistake.

Just in case Robert and his movie-inspired guess were closer to the truth than I was, and it really is a mob issue, I'm sending this file to my cloud server, and locking it in a protected folder. Robert should be able to figure the password out fairly easily. Someone please remember to feed my cat and erase the history on my computer before my mom sees it.

Thanks.
Jack Morris

<Error: "precaution_meeting.mp4" not found>

AI-assisted transcript follows:

[Video: An image of a set of mahogany double doors set into a beige wall. The image wobbles slightly as the pocket the device is propped up in moves with the owner's breath.]

Man: "Okay, I've got my camera on and automatically recording the video to my cloud server. Now to give it a little lead time for better editing...

[The same image as before as the person filming waits in silence. In the distance, a thunderstorm rumbles.]

Man: "Okay, that should be good enough. Now for help in the future audio cues: Testing, one, two, three, and clap.

[A set of hands rises into camera view, and as the man says the word *clap*, he claps his hands.]

Man: "To anyone who's watching this, my name is Jack Morris, and this video footage should be found with my document of evidence. If you know what I'm talking about, you know. If you don't, I'm not telling you where to find it."

[A piece of paper rises into frame. On it is written a date—November 08, 2025—and a time— 8:00 p.m. CST.]

Morris: This video is to document my attempt to inform Mr. Harker about some things I've discovered concerning illicit access to the labs, and the possibility that his daughters and/or at least one member of the executive suite may be involved in possible corruption. This video is being taken as a safety precaution in case Mr. Harker is involved. If he is uninvolved, or I remain unharmed, please delete this video.

[The paper drops. Morris begins walking toward the doors.]

 Morris: The secretary, Kathrine Swales, seems to be away from her desk, so all I can do is knock. Well, no time like the present. Here we go.

[Morris raises his hand and knocks on the door.]

Man, muffled: Come in.

[The door opens. Inside, an older man reads paperwork in a large but dimly lit office. The man is simply dressed in an old-fashioned dark suit, the jacket open to the waist, revealing the crisp white dress shirt. He looks up from his paperwork at Morris and smiles.]

Man: Ah, Mr. Morris. Welcome, my young friend. How can I help you this evening?

[Morris makes his way across the office. Reaching the desk, he sets down a pile of printed spreadsheets and takes a step back. The man seated at the desk looks down at the file, then reaches forward and sifts through it, before looking back up at Morris.]

Morris: Mr. Harker, sir, I'm afraid I have to bring some things to your attention, and they're not going to be easy to hear. I'm hoping there's a reasonable explanation for what I found, and that I'm just suffering from an overabundance of caution, but I felt you needed to know.

[Mr. Harker pulls his hands away from the pile and nods, settling back in his seat. A serious expression settles on his face.]

Mr. Harker: All right. What have you found?

[Morris's hand gestures at the folder of papers]

Morris: As you can see in that documentation, sir, someone has been accessing one of the labs responsible for holding the finalized samples that we intend to use in our clinical trial. They've been doing so twice a week for almost six months. I've checked the logs for these labs, and the person who checks in and manipulates the equipment has no registered name or profile in the security system. The time and lack of ID documentation makes it unlikely that it's one of the scientists responsible for the program, as they'd simply use their own IDs. This risks the accuracy of any results we get from the trials and endangers our ability to get the final approval we need to make these medications public.

[Harker leans forward again and rifles through the spreadsheets, a frown on his face.]

Harker: That is serious. Do you have any idea of who the person was who accessed the lab?

Morris: Not for certain, sir, but I have obtained information that a series of IDs with similar names and a lack of photos were created by Mr. Hennesey. He evidently gave them to someone, and a source I spoke to suggested that it was most likely one of your daughters. I give credit to this theory, as I personally encountered Miss Elizabeth in that very lab on the night of the first logged access. Miss Elizabeth was never noted in the logs as having entered. Instead, the log recognizes an unregistered user.

[Morris's hand taps an entry on the top spreadsheet, pointing to the unusual user data. Harker peers closely at it.]

Harker: That is disappointing. Do you have any idea what's been done in the labs?

Morris: No sir. Without the ability to test all the medications and all the affected lab equipment, we have no way of telling what—if anything—has been altered or corrupted. We will have to scrap the whole batch.

[Harker drops the spreadsheet and looks up at Morris.]

Harker: So the whole project would have to be canceled. The medication would never go out, at least not from this batch, and the project delayed. Perhaps indefinitely.

Morris: That is correct, sir.

[Harker looks contemplative for a moment, before switching his expression to 'resigned'.]

Harker: Thank you for drawing this to my attention. How did you discover this, when everyone else had overlooked it?

Morris: I was looking over the logs and noticed the odd log-ins at night. It made me curious. So I looked into it.

[Harker looks at him like he's had a bad day.]

Harker: Oh, human curiosity. One of the most inconvenient forces known to man.

Morris: Pardon, sir?

[Harker waves a hand in the air, waving away the question.]

Harker: Never mind. Tell me, you said a source told you. Possibly more than one. It'd be easier to document and handle the issues if I could talk to the sources myself. Can I please get the name of your source? Have you told anyone else about this?

Morris: I'm afraid I can't tell you that right now, sir. I haven't asked their permission, but until they give it, I am more than willing to relay sworn documentation as to what they saw or knew. And no, I've not told anyone else.

[Harker drops the spreadsheets on the desk and stands up, turning his back to the room.]

Harker: No need, then. I can figure it out on my own. You know, my young friend, one of the hardest things to do over my long life has been to find competent help. You are by far one of the more intelligent ones I've run into. I had actually been looking forward to the possibility of bringing you into the fold. But you're a little too observant. I'm not so sure it would work. I tried that before and it nearly killed me.

[Morris shuffles backward a step or two. The camera jerks, indicating nervous fidgeting. Harker crosses his hands behind his back.]

Morris: Sir?

Harker: One of the things you learn, Morris, is that the longer you live, the lonelier you get. I've never been truly alone, of course — it's hard to be truly alone when you always have a chattering trio of women following you around — but actually finding intellectual equals is so much harder than anyone ever tells you. I figured out long ago that I had to change my locations, to follow the worlds of industry and innovation, if I ever wanted to find people that were intellectually stimulating. I tried it once, making my way to England to live among the people of the late Victorian era. It was a foolish thing to do, as I was quickly caught and chased out by hunters. They even tracked me to my home and tried their level best to destroy me on my own doorstep. They nearly succeeded. They left me with my castle destroyed and my brides turned to dust in their crypts.

[Morris begins inching toward the door.]

Morris: I... I don't understand, sir.

Harker: Luckily, I had taken precautions that even that Dutch menace didn't know about. I wasn't even sure they would work. But as I lay in that coffin on the wagon top, stake and blade piercing my heart and neck, I knew I had no other choice. I took the leap. It was not ideal, but it was the only option. I followed the blood. I ended up with a usable form so underdeveloped that I had to sleep for years until he was finally old enough to bear me. Then I had to begin the long process of corrupting him until I could take over.

[Morris skirts around the visitor chair, slowly picking up speed. Harker reaches an open set of curtains over one of the many office windows and draws it closed.]

Morris: What?

Harker: It's what that old fool never understood about me. I am a monster, but that's not all I am. He called me a demon as an insult so many times, and he was far closer to the truth than he realized. His mistake was in not realizing that I wasn't tied to the body I possessed, just to the blood. By the time young Quincy grew old enough and corrupt enough for me to take over, mankind had forgotten that I was anything other than a fairy tale. They were far too focused on their new rationality, their new weapons, and their first Great War.

[Morris pauses. Harker walks to a second window, sliding those curtains closed as well.]

Harker: It was helpful to me, that war. So much hope and innocence lost, so much blood shed. After it ended and they sent the poor traumatized man home, he was ready for someone else to take over. He felt abandoned by everyone. And there I was, his oldest friend, the voice in his head, the only one who had never left him. With no solid voice he recognized in the other direction to plant his feet on, it was an easy takeover. Once I was in place, he went to sleep, and I was free to do as I pleased.

Oh, the look on that Dutch fool's face when I told him who his poor tortured godson had let in. It was incredibly gratifying. His sorrow when he realized how I'd survived, that the sacrifices the group had made all those years ago were wasted, made his death moments later so much sweeter. He died a far quieter death than the asylum doctor or the great lord did. Both of them retained more will to live. Didn't help them in the end, though. In honor of the spirit they showed, I reformed my brides using one of their daughters each. Laura and Christine are both a joy, far more emotionally stimulating than their predecessors ever were.

[Morris resumes inching toward the door. Harker continues around the room, aiming for the next window.]

Morris: Okay, so you're referring to your daughters as your brides, plural, and stated that they were adopted... from families you just admitted to murdering... I should leave.

[Harker stops in his tracks, looking at Morris with visible amusement.]

Harker: Nonsense, Morris. You can't leave now. It's far too late.

[Morris speeds up, aiming for the door.]

Morris: I won't tell anyone. I swear.

[Harker swings his hand in a wide arc toward the door and then resumes his march toward the final window. The mahogany doors rattle for a moment, and then the doorknobs click. Morris dashes toward them and grabs the handles, yanking on the doors to no avail. They're locked. And he's stuck.]

Harker: I've done so much this time around. This time, I made sure to move someplace with more future ahead of it than behind it. It was such a good choice, too. America's culture skyrocketed, and so did its businesses and economy. As those rose, so too did the opportunities I could take advantage of. It was just a matter of picking the right ones, dealing with the right desperate people. I didn't even have to change my name, as who would expect the businessman forming the new company to have come from the Edwardian era?

[Morris pauses mid-yank, turning back so the camera focuses on Harker.]

Morris: You're how old?

[Harker frowns at him, his hands on the newly closed curtains at the last window.]

Harker: That's rude, Morris. But if you must know, I was born in 1891. Well, reborn, anyway. Before that I was born in 1431. Before that, I was so many kings and emperors and leaders that I've lost count. I was anywhere a powerful man was inclined to trade the blood of innocents for power, going back millennia. It was my punishment from the beginning of time, I think, for reaching out for power that was not mine. I no longer recall when it began.

[Harker looks contemplative for a moment, then drops the curtains and waves the thoughts away with both hands.]

Harker: But how it started is unimportant. What matters right now is just that. The now. We were careful this time around, implemented so many rules. No snacking on anyone too much, keep the creation of thralls to a minimum, use the tools this marvelous new world gives us instead... It is amazing how well you people respond to large sums of money. Spread it around quietly and heavily enough in the right places and you can get all sorts of things: good public relations, positive news stories, dedicated people with the ability to apply pressure on, say, regulatory approval. In the end, we only had to enthrall that fool Westin. Made it easier to finish him off later, as well.

Morris: You haven't enthralled Hennesey?

Harker: Him? No. He's being controlled by something far more human. Although I wouldn't put it past Christine to have begun practicing her enthrallment techniques on him at some point.

Morris: Ah. I should have guessed that.

[Harker moves toward the visitor chair and turns it around, pushing it lightly in Morris's direction.]

Harker: Since you're not walking out of here, you should know, you were right. It was Elizabeth who was going to that lab every week. She told you the truth, she was operating on my orders. I gave her a task to do. Our final backup plan, in case someone ever figured out what we really were. Or in case that Dutch hunter inspired some other moron. And you're going to help me test the result.

[Morris slides down to sit on the floor, his knees drawn up to appear in the video.]

Morris: Please don't kill me.

[Harker laughs and leans back against the desk as he grins at Morris.]

Harker: Oh, my dear boy. I'm not going to kill you. That would be a waste. Not to mention how mad Elizabeth would be. She likes your face, you see. And dear Quincy is wearing so thin after so many years. We have decided to give him a rest.

[In the dim light, Harker's eyes begin to glow a faint red. Morris shivers and the camera shakes.]

Harker: Normally, this would be a lot harder. Let's see if our efforts have made it easier, shall we?

Morris: What... what are you doing?

Harker: Let's just call it "Moving."

[For a moment, both men's bodies become rigid, and the faint red glow expands to cover Harker and then Morris so it fills the camera lens. After a moment, it fades away, remaining only in Harker's eyes. The light quickly winks out, and his body crumples to the floor.]

Morris: Ah. That was... interesting.

[The camera moves to approach Harker's body and Morris's hands enter the view to check for signs of life.]

It took me a little while to find this. We had to go through all this documentation and sort through Morris's electronic services. Even after we eventually found it, we still had to figure out the password. Using the name of his cat was not the most clever thing, but it was very human. One of the things about people, you're very predictable. Usually.

So, clearly, it worked. I had my doubts when I sent Elizabeth in the lab every night to add small samples of our blood into the medicines. I mean, I knew it could *possibly* work, and it had a much greater chance of working as time went on, but it also felt a lot like giving up short-term safety for long-term possibilities. Now, I'm a very long-lived "man," but if there's anything that whole incident back in the day taught me, it's that you need a good backup plan. It was something I had discovered by accident. I took that desperate leap and tried to hide in the blood I had pushed into Mina. I discovered I couldn't take her over, She had too much faith, in both mankind and in God. But I could hide in that tiny amount of my blood she retained in the body of her growing child. Then it was just a matter of waiting.

It probably would have been a different outcome if the rise of atheism hadn't taken hold so strongly in the years after our battle. Take the gradual fall of faith and the particular nature of a rebellious child, and add in a war? Easiest takeover ever. Taking young Quincy for my form was the simplest part. After I exacted my revenge on the men who thought they had bested me at my castle, I hoped to take both of the Harkers back for my own. Both were under my control once, after all. I was willing to take them in again. Unfortunately, the strain of the previous encounter was too great. They both died before I could reach them. Quincy went to sleep permanently after that. The loss was just too much for him. It mattered not to me, as a sleeping companion just meant I had an easier time controlling the body.

The events of the past had taught me to hedge my bets, however. Nothing is guaranteed, not the continued presence of the Harkers, not my immediate success if attacked, not even the idea of still being around when my plan finally succeeds. So, I took precautions. I can chase the blood into different bodies if mine is damaged or abandoned. That's how it works. That's why we're lacing all the samples of the trial with it, so it spreads out to the general public, giving us all more options for a person-to-person jump. So, it stands to reason that it'd work in short-term medicines, too. See, I can be rational.

It turned out that to make it more effective, we had to increase the amount administered. By a sizable increase. It was a risk, putting so much blood into those "vitamin supplements" we gave out in the health clinics. Losing a lot of blood made all of us hungry and increased the chance we'd be caught. But it worked. Half the people we ran into throughout the average day smelled like they were already compatible, and no one seemed to realize what we'd done. We thought we'd gotten away with it. Finding out otherwise was a surprise.

It's over now, though. We cleared up the mess, although it took quite an effort. We had already needed to change out Quincy as he was starting to malfunction rather badly, and Morris clearly adapted well. He was not only ready, he was perfect. So I jumped. Quincy died not long after that night. At his advanced age, he couldn't sustain himself alone. He never even woke up. I do wonder where he went—heaven or hell. That's between him and God. I have no part in it.

I read through this report a time or two once we managed to retrieve it. I was surprised how little they managed to understand. It was all right there! Can no one put together a puzzle anymore? Anyway, we went through and cleaned up all of the mess. I let my dear "daughters" finish off Kate. Having a secretary who tells everyone the company business is bad for security, so I let them patch the hole. We'll figure out secretary issues later.

I considered letting them eat the security guard too. However, he seemed to come to us as a gift already wrapped, and it would be a waste to not use that. As it turns out, he was ridiculously easy to enthrall. All it took was a few simple commands, and the next thing you know, he's sitting in front of the police taking the punishment for the loss of Quincy. Lucky for him, it was considered a 'death by natural causes,' so he was released by the end of the day. I've decided to keep him. It's been too long since I had a Renfield, and one made from a security guard could come in handy.

Since "Quincy Harker" has now settled into a permanent repose, the CEO position is empty. After some discussion, I assigned Elizabeth to take over the company and run it until we can settle accounts. We'll give it a little time. I'll be seen walking around with Elizabeth wearing Jack Morris's face, build up a relationship, and rise up the ranks almost naturally. Eventually, I'll be able to step back into my role as CEO. This time, it will be with the first of my brides at my side, finally using her appropriate title.

This body is young, strong, and I will admit, he's quite handsome. Elizabeth was indeed furious with me at first, but once I explained the problem, she calmed down. She's just glad that we get to keep the young man. I haven't told her yet how much this one struggled. I tried to appease him, wiping his computer history as he asked—although I needed some help figuring that one out—and I gave his cat to the security guard. Strange little animals.

The cat, not the security guard.

Anyway, if it hadn't been for the blood connection, I'd have never taken over. I'm just glad it worked. I'll have to examine the results from the trial as time passes and see if a slower buildup might be able to overcome the barrier faith creates. Here's hoping! I'm also pulling this report off the cloud and storing it only on a thing Elizabeth called a "USB drive." We might need it later, she said, but it's too dangerous to leave available. In the meantime, I have to go talk to an insurance person who wants to interview Morris about the death of Quincy. Not sure what more there is to talk about, but the guy seemed interested. We need to live quietly and avoid attracting attention. So I guess I'm going to go talk to this "Frank Vaughn Stein" guy.

Wish me luck!

The End

FIT TO KILL
Darlene N. Bocek

*The trumpet shall sound
And the dead shall be raised
And the dead shall be rai — sed incorruptible.*

The urgent blast of a trumpet awakens me.

*The trumpet shall sound.
The dead shall be rai — sed
The dead shall be raised incorruptible.
And we shall be chan — ged.
And we shall be changed.*

It takes a moment to remember where I am. Where I should be.

I lie flat. My hands are crossed over my chest. The air around is a mix of damp and dust. Earthy.

My crypt!

And not a trumpet. It's the crypt door screeching open.

Beneath my fingers, my heart thumps inside me irregularly, weakly, not in time to the song in my head, but alongside it.

But my heart thumps! I'm alive again. The realization makes it speed up.

As my memory returns, so do the details of the music — an impeccable knowledge of this mental orchestra. My mind rejoices as my body comes to life again.

I have done it.

The triumphant oratorio joins all the trumpets my mind can muster, better than a live concert. Trumpets. Violins. Bass. That powerful acceleration of meaning and joy.

I have conquered death.

My body's most powerful muscle strengthens with each straining beat.

Thump. Pause. Pause. Whoosh. Pause. Pause. Thump. Pause. Pause.

Need to focus.

I count my heartbeats, causing them to repeat, over and over.

The song silences in the distance.

Thump. Pause. Whoosh. Pause. Thump. Pause. Whoosh.
Faster now. *Thump. Pause. Whoosh. Pause.*
Thump-whoosh. There we go.
Thump-whoosh. Thump-whoosh.
Thump-whoosh. Waking up.
Thump-whoosh. On my own.
Now where were we? Music.
The oratorio returns and I smile. At peace. Finally. True joy. Finally.
Under the command of my own power.

Behold I tell you a mystery.

My mouth moves along with the lyrics as my memory plays all instruments of the song with the power of a million-instrument conductor.

We shall not all die. But we shall all be changed.
In a moment.
In the twinkling of an eye.
At the last trumpet.

Thump-whoosh. Thump-whoosh.
I live again.
Beneath my hands are—I feel—jacket lapels. A shirt buttoned to the neck. No tie. But sharp collar buds.
My wrists? Cufflinks. I can feel the starch in my shirt. I am fit to kill.
I chuckle.
And it begins today.
All the naysayers? Wrong. Every one of them.
I glide my tongue across my teeth until I find it. One canine. Sharp and pointy. My heart adds a secondary *thump-thump* before the *whoosh*. And the other side? Yes. Two precious eye teeth, sharp as needles.
Alive. On my own terms.
The thrill of exultation rushes through me, like the drop and racing of a roller coaster.
I run my pointer finger over my lower teeth. My smile tightens. Four sharp teeth to grant this eternal life to others. They'll thank me someday.
Oh, precious new life. Precious new power.
I reach above me. Yes. Yes, above and under me are the concrete slabs, the beds of our family crypt. As expected. It took quite an investment to do it this way. But hey. What is a little money when you now own time for all eternity?

When no one can stop you.

My skin feels dry. Drier than I thought. As does my face. But never mind. It's certainly just from this excessively dusty crypt.

Lights. Camera. Action!

I open my eyes. All around is darkness. And dust. Lots of dust. *Billows of dust.*

That's from somewhere, too. Where have I heard that?

Fire and billows of dust.

Thump-whoosh. Thump-whoosh.

I've done it.

My heart soars in triumph.

And they all said it couldn't be done. When I smile, my special teeth pop out over my lips. I shake my head, almost unbelievingly. I really did it.

Ah. But first.

I pat my jacket pocket to find it. To find her. But she's not there.

Where is it?

I feel my tuxedo — *Thump-thump-thump-thump* — beginning to panic. *Aha.*

I relax. *There it is!*

Whoosh. Thump-thump.

A vial of the last payment.

Little Eveline.

Blond hair, brown eyes, a continual smile on her face, a bashful gleam in her eyes. The pastor's youngest daughter. I rub the vial with my thumb. Haven't needed her yet. But brought her…her strength…as backup. She was very special to me. The purest of the pure.

She hadn't wanted to give herself. They never do.

But what do children know of science? We all sacrifice something — one way or another — for humanity. Those girls and boys who made me…happen — they have served humanity. With me as the first of a new kind, we can finally all be free from mind-corrupting superstition, from all fear, from all oppressive religion. It can be done. And I am proof. The first fruit.

I kiss Eveline's vial and replace it into my vest pocket.

The song returns…

Behold I tell you a mystery. We shall not all die.

…reminding me of my duty. As I am proof.

I love this orchestra in my head. It almost echoes in the vault around me. Almost as if the universe is singing for me. *All hail!*

Again, I join my hands over my chest and feel my heart alive forever, *thump-thump* beneath them. Thumping with the rhythm of my new life. *Thump-thump-whoosh. Thump-thump-whoosh.* My deathless life. All power of life and death under my control forever. Mine.

I draw in another draught of the air from my crypt. No hurry when eternity is yours.

Time for action. Indirect light shines in from around the door.

Yes! Thrill of a life under control. Under my control. Fully, solely, completely autonomously mine.

I have done it.

Just as I expected. No. Even more than I hoped!

A bit more dust on my finger than I expected — I wipe that away. My consciousness is the first proof. The teeth are the second. My heartbeat. My singing soul. The vial.

My new life awaits just outside that door.

It's still closed. Hmm. Hadn't I heard it open earlier?

I cannot sit up on this shelf, so I roll myself out and my feet land on the floor. More dust puffs up around me. More dust than I'd have expected. I'll need to find a newspaper for the date. How long have I been out?

I thought it would be immediate — but it's been longer, for some reason.

The trumpet shall sound. The dead shall be raised. Incorruptible.

All on my own. I have done it. Here I am, incorruptible by my own initiative. No need for anyone else's assistance.

The power of an incorruptible life — belongs to me.

Outside sounds like the roaring of thunder. Rain. Some screeching. Like seagulls seeking a place to rest.

I brush off my clothing and lean against the slabs. No need to plan. It's all mine for the taking.

Get ready, World!

This power over death is like nothing I've ever felt. The fear is gone. What can man do to me? The dread, the ever-present question is proven wrong. The threat was unfounded. I have proven how to escape death. The greatest fear is under my foot.

And I can now invite others to join me with this power.

All it took was six children: Paulie, Charlotte, Emma, Mia, Riley, Greyson.

Seven with Eveline here. I pat her vial. Precious children. Thank you for this gift.

The process got easier. Paulie was the hardest. Figuring it out. Finding the adrenal gland — oxidizing the adrenaline. But one sip and I knew it would work. The gentler the child, the more powerful the compound. Which is why I saved Eveline for afterward.

Once the rain slows down, I'll explore my new world.

Like this, I'll fear nothing.

Beating death on your own terms fosters…a kind of powerful triumph. Immutable. Immortal.

They all said it had to be by the blood of…that Man.

I knew better.

When they pressed the issue, I took their children for my tests.

They all said we could only be raised from the dead by…His…power. By His blood.

What do they know?

I have proven them wrong.

I should go visit them. Show them what I've done. Ha!

I stand here today. Where are they? The vials their children granted me have shown the success of my research. Of my experimentation. Of my own wisdom. The mystery older than time itself. Answered — proven — by the blood of pure children.

I'll show you a mystery.
We shall not all die.
But we shall all be changed.
In a moment.
In the twinkling of an eye.

I rub my chin. Then cock my head. Wait.

That's not right. The sounds outside are not rain and seagull screeches. Those are bona fide screams. The scream of a human soul in terror.

I can almost taste it and grin in anticipation.

Then I set my hands on the crypt handle to pull it open, to enter my new life, to embrace my life of power immortal.

But the heavy door kicks in on me —

The joints open with the blasting, grating sound of a trumpet.

The powerful thrust shoves me back. I slam against the slab beds, struggling to gain my footing. To regain my breath.

Again the trumpet resounds. In my brain. All around me.

An all-consuming terror.

Wait.

Wait.

Something's wrong. Seriously wrong.

I block the light with my hand. Squinting to understand the movements beyond this dark crypt.

It's so bright. It hurts my eyes.

My ears. My eyes.

I don't understand.

He steps in.

A glowing being. Wings as wide as my crypt. Glowing gold like the sun viewed with naked eyes.

Who is this in my domain?

I raise my chin in challenge. My upper lip trembles with rage. I will chase him out. Prove who is strongest. I have earned this. It's mine.

But my mouth is shut. Fused at the teeth. Words cannot come. But I hiss. My soul hisses at this being.

The creature clamps his hand around my wrist. Good god. He has the strength of ten men.

But I am stronger. I press my heels into the dirt.

It makes no difference.

I cannot resist his pull because my feet no longer rest on the ground, no longer bound to the dust. He lifts me into the air and drags me out of the crypt.

No. I will not go with him.

Why is he here on this my greatest day? Let me go!

Aha. I will overpower him.

I seize my vial. *Oh, Eveline, this is why you're here.* I withdraw it from my vest. Pop the lid off with my thumb.

But the light being yanks the vial from my hand. He crushes it into pieces, then opens his hand before him. Out of his hand comes not remnants of liquid and glass. But a child.

Eveline. Whole. Smiling and laughing. Her hands are out at her sides and she is flying like a bird, spiraling, up, up into the sky.

How can this be?

She joins two others flying beings. My heart skips a beat. Her parents.

I tug my hand from the light being's grip, but he will not release me to fly like the others. I am chained to him by his grip of iron. We sail upward toward something.

Around me, everyone is in the air. Every single human from the surface of earth. From under the earth. From crypts. From the sea. The naysayers. The haters. The judgmental bigots.

They fly free, with hideous smiles on their faces, idiotic joy, hurrying with an inexplicable delight toward something I can't quite see.

I hiss at them, then an indignant screech echoes from my chest out at the universe.

Others, constrained like me, are pulled by the chain-grip of the beings of light.

All move toward the same destination.

What is happening? It makes no sense.

I squint to finally see through, out, around, beyond the bright beings.

When I see an army.

Thump thump thump thump their feet march on the skies. It wasn't thunder earlier. It was always this. It wasn't my heart earlier. It was always this. All those flying merge with the army, joining the progressing throng that moves across the sky.

My stomach tightens and I feel faint. Sick and frightened. Nauseous and terrified.

My fear is back.

The dread.

The anger.

The apprehension.

This is wrong. All wrong.

I fear to look more. But my guard stops mid-flight, directs me to look at the front of the assembly. The focal point of the universe.

I don't want to see.

I don't want to know.

It was not supposed to end like this.

But he says, "Behold," and my chin obeys him. My eyes obey him.

I see a man on a white horse.

Thump-thump-thump. This time it is my heart, horrified by truth. *Thump-thump-thump.*

I know who that is. *Thump-thump-thump.*

And my mouth must declare it.

The End

BLOOD ON THE THRONE
Deborah Cullins Smith

November 1558 — Hampton Court in London

Mary gazed out of the tall window. Moonlight on the roses looked unearthly, but her headaches had never allowed her to appreciate the gardens in sunlight. Pain used to slice through her head and stab her eyes like needles. It tortured her waking moments until she almost lost her mental capacity.

Thomas Cromwell, her one friend in this royal quagmire during her father's reign, had introduced her to her savior. She remembered his first visit.

1534 — Hatfield Palace in Hertfordshire

Thomas Cromwell removed his hat and swept a low bow. "My lady, may I present a visitor to our shores? This is Count Vladimir Dracula. He comes to your court from a small country far to the east of France."

Young Mary had few visitors. Her father's orders — and no one disobeyed Henry VIII. By keeping her isolated, he had hoped to make her more compliant to his will. But Mary was a true Tudor, strong-willed, stubborn, and as temperamental as any red-headed child ever born. Only in body was she ever weak. She hated this flesh that inflicted her with pain and made her live in darkened rooms for fear of the agony that sunlight often brought upon her.

Count Dracula was tall, and his features were finely chiseled, though his skin was so pale it was almost translucent. Dark curls framed a striking face with deep-set eyes and a narrow nose above tantalizingly full lips. He swept his cloak off with one hand while bowing low, elegance wafting from each graceful movement.

Mary felt a twinge of envy. She was tall for a young woman of twenty years, standing almost six feet. With her abnormal height, she had always felt awkward and gangly. Her mother had been the epitome of grace and beauty, and she never failed to remonstrate Mary to move more fluidly.

"Stand up straight, Mary." Queen Catherine's voice used to be uncharacteristically sharp when Mary disappointed her. "You are a princess of England. Yet you cower like a maid. Glide with your head erect. You do not need to stare at your feet to walk the halls of your own home."

I'm sorry, Mama, she thought. *I always wanted to make you proud. Yet I forever fell short.*

The Count rose to his full regal height, and his gaze seemed to look right through to her soul. Mary fell into those dark, penetrating eyes — felt herself swallowed by this man who seemed to know her every thought.

"Welcome to England, my lord," she said. She cleared her throat as the words seemed to crackle when they passed her lips. "My court is much smaller than that of my royal father, but I… I am grateful for your visit. We shall try to make you comfortable."

"You are most gracious, Princess Mary." His words flowed like a dark sonata and she felt each melancholy note, plucking the strings of her heart. His accent was heavy and indicated a Mediterranean flavor of the eastern European provinces.

Cromwell frowned as he leaned toward the Count. "Lady Mary, please. By her father's orders, we are not allowed…"

"But I am not an English subject, nor am I at the mercy of King Henry," Dracula interrupted smoothly.

Cromwell sighed and took a step back, leaving the Count to gaze upon Mary with an uncomfortable intensity. Her eyes shimmered with emotion. Few people had the temerity to stand up to her formidable father, even in his absence. But this man! Her curiosity rose.

"May I have my people show you to a room, sir? I'm sure you could use some time to rest after your long journey. But I will consider it my pleasure if you will dine with me this evening." Mary found the invitation coming out graciously. Something about the Count captivated her and gave her confidence and composure.

"It would be my honor, your Grace." Dracula bowed low. Mary nodded to one of her guards and he turned to lead the Count from the room. Dracula paused at the door and turned to face Mary. "Until later, my Princess."

The words, "my Princess," sent a shiver up Mary's spine. Thomas had turned to leave with the Count, but Mary's voice stopped him.

"Stay, Master Cromwell."

The door closed behind the Count and his guide. Cromwell waited, hat in hand.

"What a strange man you've brought to visit me," Mary said. "Tell me, Master Cromwell, what is your agenda? Is the Count looking to marry me? And is my father aware of this visit?"

"Not a suitor, my lady," Cromwell said, and his smile held a secret. "And no, your father does not know about the Count. In fact, I doubt he even knows Count Dracula is in this country."

Mary's eyebrows rose. "You take chances, Master Cromwell. Such audacity could land you in the Tower. You know my jailers here report to my father regularly."

"The Sheltons can hardly be called jailers, my lady," Cromwell objected.

"Jailers," Mary hissed. "What else do you call them when I am kept under lock and key? When I was kept from the bedside of my beloved mother when she lay dying? They are jailers."

Cromwell bowed his head, a concession to the truth of her words. Henry was a hard man, and he demanded complete submission from his children. Mary had never been able to acknowledge her mother's displacement as Queen of England, Henry's lawful wife, when he cast her aside for his mistress, Anne Boleyn. And when Henry married Anne and crowned her queen, Mary's fury knew no bounds. She would never bow to the strumpet, the usurper of her mother's position. The whore. As her punishment, she was banished from her mother's side to live with relatives of the new queen. Anne Boleyn's cousin, Lady Anne Shelton and her husband, Sir John, resided in the Hatfield Estate, and they kept a vigilant watch over the rebellious former princess. Henry seemed to find this necessary, lest her Catholic followers should rally to her side and try to overthrow his kingdom.

Cromwell's voice drew her back to the conversation. "I, too, serve your father, my lady. But I respected your mother and held her in high esteem. The current queen is... not working out well."

"Yet you helped to put her in my mother's place," Mary said, her chin raised defiantly.

"Yes, your Grace," Cromwell sighed, slipping into her forbidden title. "And I've lived to regret that. But it was what my King wanted at the time, and I was sworn to serve him in all things."

"So after years and years of helping my father lock me away, now you bring a very strange man to my doorstep." Her eyes narrowed. "Why?"

Cromwell paused and rubbed his brow with one hand. He shook his head ever so slightly and sighed deeply. "Because he asked me to. Count Dracula is... not someone you say no to."

Mary frowned. "Why would he want to see me?"

"I'm not sure, your Gra—my lady." He caught himself that time. Mary motioned for Cromwell to take a seat near her. He sat heavily in the wooden chair. "He is a very magnetic man," he explained slowly. "He asked very pointed questions about you. About your happiness — or lack of it." His smile was sheepish. "I found myself telling him things I would never speak of to anyone else. About Henry's harsh treatment of you, his cutting you from the succession, of your mother and her battle to save your place as Henry's first-born."

Cromwell leaned toward Mary and lowered his voice to almost a whisper. "The Count has assured me that he can help you regain your place at Henry's court, that he can ensure your place in history. He says he can make sure you are the next monarch of this country." He paused for a moment as Mary's face paled in shock. "There was something about his eyes," he continued. "I found myself believing him. My Princess, I believe he might hold your only hope."

Mary stared at Cromwell, speechless for many minutes. He held her gaze until she finally nodded. "But the Sheltons will inform my father of this visit, I'm sure of it," she hissed. "Then his life, as well as yours and mine, could be in jeopardy."

"I-I saw —" Cromwell swallowed hard. Mary had never seen him at such a loss for words. "I watched as the Count approached the door. Sir John was prepared to deny him entry, regardless of my own presence, but Dracula held the man's gaze, and suddenly, he was like clay in an artist's hands. His eyes glazed over. Dracula said, 'You will not tell anyone of my presence here, and you will allow me to visit undisturbed with the princess.' And Sir John mumbled, 'I will tell no one of your presence. You will visit Lady Mary undisturbed.' I felt shocked at this turn of events, but Dracula indicated I should say nothing. He did glare daggers at Sir John's use of your current title. But outside this door, the Count murmured that a will so dedicated to his sovereign would be harder to break down. Some of the King's orders — like the title of Lady, rather than Princess — will take time to change. If I understand the Count correctly."

"Well, dinner should prove to be interesting." She waved a hand in dismissal, and Thomas Cromwell rose and swept a low bow before leaving her to her tumultuous thoughts.

~~~~~

Dinner was indeed interesting. Dracula ate very little, but he regaled her with tales of his homeland, of battles so grisly and glorious, Mary felt herself propelled into a land she'd never seen or even heard of. When her servants removed their plates, Mary invited the Count to join her by the large marble fireplace. They settled into the padded chairs near the hearth.

"My dear Princess Mary," the Count began. "You've listened to me
~~~~~

prattle on about my country. Now I would like to hear about you." His eyes drilled into hers, reaching deep, probing, searching.

Searching for what? she wondered absently. "My own life is a shallow attempt to survive compared to the adventure you've experienced. It's like you've... lived ten lifetimes." She fumbled for the words then blurted them out, gesturing with both hands, then dropping them abruptly into her lap.

"Our experiences shape us, my lady," Dracula said gently. "And you are a fully formed, emotionally capable woman. Beautiful. Strong. One does not become such—" He hesitated, and she watched his lips with bated breath. "—an amazing human being without experiencing life. Whether those have been good days, or difficult days, painful ones or joyous ones, they shape you. You will be a remarkable queen someday."

Mary's shoulders sagged. "That may never happen, Count Dracula. My father disinherited me when he set aside my mother and married another woman. The crown will not come to me if Henry has his way."

"That must have been devastating for you, Mary." His voice was soft, compelling. Her name fell so naturally from his lips, she didn't even object to the familiarity. "Tell me about your mother."

Mary's smile became wistful. "She was beautiful, strong, a Spanish warrior. Her own mother had ridden into battle many times during her reign as Queen of Spain and wielded a sword as well as any man. After she and my father married, she was desperate to give Henry a son." Mary sighed. "That was never to be. But she still held her head high." She chuckled softly. "There is a family legend, though I have never known whether it was entirely true or not. Henry had sailed for France in some military campaign, leaving my mother as regent. She took that role very seriously. With Henry on the mainland, the King of Scotland decided it was a good time to invade. My mother called for the banners, and rallied troops. She was several months pregnant at the time, but she had armor made to accommodate her ..." Mary blushed, "...her girth. She rode at the head of the soldiers and gave a rousing speech about protecting their homeland from the barbarians of the north. They did not allow her to actually ride into the battle, though I think she might have been willing. But she had already lost a daughter and a son. She had to protect the child she carried."

Mary leaned her head against the back of her chair. Mother would scold her to sit up straight, but she wasn't here. And Mary's grief-filled memories wore away her strength.

"They defeated the Scottish invaders and killed King James IV. Her army commanders brought her the bloodied coat of the king. Here's where the legend comes in." She sat up, a twinkle in her eyes, and leaned forward ever so slightly toward the Count. "They say she asked for the head of James, that she might send it to Henry." Dracula chuckled at the image Mary painted. "Yes! Such audacity, you might think. Of course, her counselors talked her out of it, but that was the warrior in her. She settled for sending him the coat. I'm sure she wanted to prove to him that she was a worthy queen in his absence."

"And the child she carried then? Was that perhaps you, my lady?" Dracula asked.

Mary's face saddened. "No. That was three years before my birth. It was a son. Stillborn. Out of six children, I was the only one to survive."

"And I am so happy that you did." Dracula leaned forward and took her right hand between his icy cold fingers. Gently, he pressed his lips to her hand and looked deeply into her eyes. Mary felt the room tip and slide out of focus as his face loomed nearer to her. She closed her eyes, shook her head slightly, then opened her eyes to see Dracula pulling away and dropping her hand gently to her lap. He rose to his feet. "But you are weary, my Princess. I must leave you to rest. We can talk more tomorrow."

Mary felt the weight of her memories, and weariness consumed her. It came upon her quite suddenly, and she felt unable to move under the strange, dark eyes of her guest.

"Yes, I must rest," she repeated, her voice sounding dazed, even to her own ears.

~~~~~

The next morning, Mary felt sluggish, even though she had slept soundly. She had a dull headache and grimaced as she noted the rain spattering against the windowpane. Her maid, Bessie, held her thick auburn hair in one hand and gently pulled a brush through the heavy locks. Mary hated having her hair brushed, especially on days when she experienced the blinding pain. Every tug on her hair made the pain worse. But it would be scandalous to leave her hair down. Lady Shelton would report it to the King as wantonness, and he would have one more thing to scold her for. She gritted her teeth and endured the agony as Bessie twisted her hair into a figure eight on the back of her head and secured it in place. Her headpiece came next, and the bands on each side of her head felt like clamps, squeezing until she thought her brains might begin to leak out of her eyes. She waved away her maid and stood. Dizziness flooded her senses, and she swayed before sitting abruptly at her dressing table.

"My lady?" Her maid stepped forward, ready to catch her, should she fall.
~~~~~

"I'm fine," Mary snapped. "I just stood too quickly."

"Might I inquire…?" The maid hesitated.

"Yes? What is it?" Mary asked, pressing her fingertips into her eye sockets. If only the room would stop spinning.

"How did you get these two marks on your neck?" the girl asked.

Mary grabbed a hand mirror and examined her neck. "Where? What marks?"

The maid gestured to the right side, almost into the hairline behind her ear. Mary pushed back the thick black material of her headpiece. Frowning, she poked at the two small marks.

"I don't know. Perhaps an insect." Mary gazed at her reflection, then she dropped the mirror face down on the table and stood again. "It doesn't matter.

~~~~~

Count Dracula slipped Mary's hand in the crook of his elbow as they walked through the garden after dinner that evening. She smiled at the comforting gesture. Never had she grown so comfortable with a man in such a short amount of time. He appeared to hang on her words, listening intently, offering sympathy, amusement, righteous anger — whatever her soul needed at any given moment.

"You've spoken volumes about your mother, my dear Mary." He smiled at her, his eyes crinkling at the corners. "But what of your father? Master Cromwell has mentioned that you are — what is the word — estranged?"

Mary sighed. "Yes, he does not approve of my faith. You see, my mother was raised a devout Catholic. She remained loyal to the Church and to the pope until the day she died. But my father wished to put her aside so he could marry a younger woman. Someone who could still give him a son after my mother was no longer able." She shook her head in disgust. "His infatuation with that… that… trollop ruined our lives. My mother's and mine. The pope was unwilling to give him the dispensation to annul his marriage to my mother. Since he was determined to do as he wished, he cast aside the pope and the Catholic Church to get what he wanted. I don't even recognize him anymore."

"Was he always like this?" Dracula asked gently.

Mary paused for a few moments as they turned down another path between the rose bushes. "No, he wasn't. When I was quite young, he doted on me. He loved my mother. He respected and valued her opinions, her faith, her loyalty." Her voice grew wistful. "I remember how he loved to watch me dance or hear me sing. He'd show me off to all the ambassadors when they visited. He promised he'd find me an extraordinary match, someone to love me, as he loved Mother. He would
~~~~~

swing me up in his arms and laugh when I squealed with delight." She swallowed hard. "I adored my father then. He was my world."

"What happened to him?"

"I believe that Anne Boleyn is a witch. Somehow, she cast a spell over him, she seduced him with trickery and magic." Mary's voice turned to granite. "I hate the evil she has brought to my father and my country. Do you know she wore yellow when my mother died? Yellow! I'll never forgive her for taking my father's affection from me. I'm not even allowed at his court now. After she gave birth to my stepsister, Elizabeth, I was sent here to Hatfield. The Sheltons are relatives of that—" Mary tried to think of a socially polite term. "—that woman my father married. I'm supposed to be the servant of the child. The Sheltons are completely loyal to the trollop and my father, and they keep me under strict supervision at all times. My visitors are monitored, and I'm spied on continuously. I was not even allowed to see my mother on her death bed. It's all because of her—that woman. She has poisoned his mind."

"But why are you not allowed a visit with your father, dear one?" Dracula frowned. "Surely he has not cast you, his first-born, aside completely?"

"Yes, he has," Mary nodded miserably. "My name has been removed from the line of succession, and I am declared a bastard. I'm not even to be called a princess any longer, though I maintain that I *am* a Princess of England. I was born a princess, and I will remain one, no matter what that strumpet tells the court." Her chin jerked defiantly. Her voice softened ever so slightly. "I have tried to resent Elizabeth, my half-sister. And she was an obnoxious baby, screaming all the time. But now that she has reached the middle of her second year, she's a cute little thing." She smiled as she spoke of the child. "She's grown quite attached to me. How can I resist it when those plump little arms reach out for my affection?

"Did you know that my father has proclaimed himself head of the Church?" Mary walked beside the Count, her voice growing bitter again. "He has set himself above the pope! I'll never understand that. No one should be able to set themselves above the pope. He is God's representative on this earth."

"I have long felt that too much power is given the Church," Dracula said. "I myself do not credit the clergy as I used to. They have abused the privileges for centuries."

Mary stared in shock at the count. "But the pope—"

"—is just a man," he interrupted her. "You do not need him, dear princess. And he has done nothing for you or for your mother. Why defend him so vehemently?"

They walked in silence for several minutes. They stopped by a red rose bush, and Dracula's fingers caressed a bud as dark as a garnet, its petals opening slowly in the moonlight. Mary's hand dropped from his arm as he reached into the bush to break the stem. He presented the long-stemmed rose to her with a flourish.

"This flower, though exquisite, pales in comparison to your beauty, Mary." He drew closer as she took the flower with a trembling hand. She inhaled the intoxicating fragrance, then stared into his dark eyes.

She gasped as a thorn pierced her fingertip. The blood welling up looked black under the full moon.

"Allow me," Dracula whispered. He slipped her finger between his lips, and Mary gasped. Dracula pulled her close with one arm around her waist. His lips moved from her finger to her neck.

Mary remembered no more.

~~~~~

Mary found herself seated on a marble bench amid the roses, Dracula on one knee before her.

"My lady, are you well?" He patted her hand and peered into her face, concern—and something else, something Mary couldn't decipher—on his gaunt features.

"I—I don't' remember," she stammered. "Did I faint?"

"You fell against me, and did not respond, even when I called your name repeatedly."

She stared into his mesmerizing eyes.

"I've never fainted in my life," she murmured. "I don't understand."

"You will be fine, my lady," he reassured her, staring intently at her face. "It was only a momentary weakness."

"Y-yes, a momentary weakness," she repeated faintly.

Sir John and two guards hurried toward them, lanterns wavering in the darkness.

"Lady Mary, where are you?"

Dracula rose to his full height before Sir John and the men who flanked him, swords at the ready. "The Princess is not harmed. You will not lay hands upon her." His words rang out, and the men faltered, dropping their swords as they met the strength of his gaze. They stood, slack-jawed. Dracula waved his hands ever so slightly at the company and they froze in place.

"But, sir, she is not allowed outside after dark—"

Dracula cut off the objections as he lunged forward, grabbed Sir John, and bit into his neck with a ferocity that left Mary gasping in wonder. When he released the man, he turned back to see her reaction.
~~~~~

"The Princess is not harmed. We will not lay hands on her. She is perfectly fine." The words came out in a monotone, and her keeper swayed as he stared at—nothing at all.

"How did you do that?" she whispered, her eyes wide with wonder.

"I will teach you, Mary," he said, lifting her to her feet and wrapping her hand in the crook of his arm once again. "They will not accost you further. Nor will they report my visit to your father, King Henry." His voice rose slightly as he stared directly at Sir John.

"I won't report to King Henry..." the man's voice trailed off.

They entered the hallway, and Lady Shelton hurried toward them. Her plump face flushed bright pink as she raised a finger and opened her mouth to scold. When she noticed the Count, she shrank back against the wall, her face becoming a mask of terror.

"You will not berate Princess Mary for her evening walk, do you understand?" Dracula snarled at her, piercing her with his dark stare.

"I-I-I will not berate Princess Mary," she whimpered, cringing away from the Count's menacing figure. As she turned her face toward the wall, Mary noticed that the woman bore two marks on her throat.

"I have marks like that," she gasped. "Did you--?" She stared at her friend in shock.

"Yes, my Princess, I did," he said as she began to tremble. "But there is a difference. With you, I have shared my essence, my strength. I have opened a door for you, a door to the future, a door to power. With these peasants, I have made them slaves to my will. I promise I will never make a slave of you. I will raise you up in this country, until you ascend to the throne of England. You will be a monarch to be remembered forever."

Mary met his gaze. She raised her head, confusion mixed with triumph. She feared being overly optimistic, even though Dracula's confidence was contagious. "How can that be, when I've been cut from the line of succession by Henry? He hates me!"

"It will not always be thus, my Princess," Dracula said, taking her chin in his cold fingers.

"Are you here to broker a marriage with me?" she asked.

"No, dear Mary. That is not my plan. I simply want to help you take your place—your rightful place—as the Queen."

"What will you want in exchange for this power you offer?" Mary asked, her heart soaring with renewed hope.

"I will have a powerful ally in England, a woman equal to myself," he said.

"I believe you, Count Dracula," she stated. "What must I do?"

~~~~~

They talked late into the night. They heard the men stumble back into the manor, dazed and disoriented. But no one dared to intrude upon their discussion.

"We will rest at daybreak," the Count said as light began to climb over the horizon. "I must leave tomorrow evening when the sun sets. But I will return to you, Mary. And when I do, we will complete what we've begun."

"How will I manage without your strength to hold me up? Or your control over my servants?" she asked with a sad smile.

"My strength lives within you now, my dear. If ever your servants try to reprimand you again, simply stare into their eyes and say, 'Do as I command' — and they will do your bidding."

"Truly?" she asked.

"I will never lie to you." Dracula paused before adding, "Queen Mary." He rose from his seat, bowed low before her, then swept from the room as sunlight hit the window in a blaze of glory.

~~~~~

Lady Shelton bustled into the room as though the previous night had been nothing but a dream. "My lady, you've been awake all night?" She clucked her tongue in disapproval. "That Count may be charming and a nice distraction for you, but he's a bad influence, if I do say so myself."

"Shut. Your. Mouth." Mary said through gritted teeth, as she rose from her chair and pinned the stunned woman with a stare.

Lady Shelton tried to speak, but her lips wouldn't move, then her eyes went blank. She gulped, then stared at the floor and stepped back to allow Mary to pass. "Yes, my lady," she whimpered.

Mary swept past the woman and climbed the staircase to her bedroom, a triumphant smile on her face.

1536

Mary sat at her writing desk, a candle beside her though it was still daylight beyond her drape-covered window. Sunlight hurt her eyes more than ever since Count Dracula's departure. She could tolerate limited light if the day was overcast. The pain that used to come with rainy days had abated, but bright sunlight made her skin itch. Better a darkened room than discomfort. She picked up parchment and a quill.

My dear Count,
How I have missed you these past few months! So much has happened, I hardly know where to begin. I rejoice to tell you that my father's trollop is dead.

Yes, isn't that amazing? My father had her executed. The witch's spell is broken. My father married immediately, of course. The man has an insatiable appetite for feminine company. I wonder if he would have returned to my mother, had she lived. But we'll never know.

Since the execution of Anne Boleyn, Father has taken as his wife Lady Jane Seymour. She has a quiet spirit and is devout in my own faith. So, at least, that much pleases me. She has also taken up my cause to Father, and he has moved me to Hunsdon House and given me my own staff at last. My long-time companion, Susan Clarencius, has been allowed to return to me, and we are settled in quite comfortably. I did have to acknowledge Jane as his Queen, but she has been most gracious, so it was not a terribly vile task. Father still watches me like a hawk to make sure I am complying with his will.

I pretend to be subservient only to him, but long for the day you will return to set me — and my country — free.

Once again a Princess,

Mary

1537

My dear Count,

I long to see your face, my friend. Queen Jane gave birth to a son, calling him Edward. They have named me as godmother. While I am honored to be closer to my father again, it is a bit vexing to be godmother to the child who will take my place on the throne. While Edward lives, I am farther from the goals we discussed than ever. Sadly, the queen died shortly after giving birth. Poor little babe will never know what a kind mother he had. My father grieves more deeply than I've ever seen. After all, he came to despise my dear mother and almost rejoiced when she died, as her presence no longer made him look guilty. And he called for Anne's head, so he didn't grieve for her at all. But he did seem to love Jane deeply. I can almost feel sorry for him, in spite of the hellish existence I've lived through at his hands.

I remain your devoted,

Mary

1541

My dear Count,

The years pass, and still I cling to your promise that you will return. It has been seven long years since I last saw your face. I remember all that you taught me and still find our bond strong enough that my servants do my bidding without question. I know you have cautioned me against writing too often. We do not want our letters intercepted. And now I no longer have Thomas Cromwell to ensure my correspondence is not tampered with. Father had Master Cromwell executed last year. His death was a blow to me, for he was often my only friend in this world. That is, until you came into my life. But even that miracle came by Master Cromwell's hands. Poor Thomas negotiated another marriage for Father, but when she arrived, she was not to the great King Henry's liking. (Note my sarcasm.) Father cast her aside, I'm told, without even consummating the marriage. Her name was Anne of Cleves, and she came to England from Germany. I cannot help but rejoice a little bit, since she is one of those detestable Protestants. As I understand it, Father has named her 'sister' and allowed her to remain in England. As long as she lives quietly, I hope she will have no further influence upon the Church.

I felt I had to write and pour out my broken heart to you. For Henry has also killed my beloved governess, Lady Margaret Pole. Her son, Reginald, has been accused of treason, but no one seems to be able to drag him from Europe to England to face Henry's wrath. I fear that my dear Lady Pole has paid the price for her son's defiance. Will Henry continue to kill all the Catholics in this country until I am quite alone?

After Cromwell's death, I began to search for a trustworthy avenue for our correspondence. Eustace Chapuys has been the ambassador from Spain, and devoted confidante to both my mother (before her death) and to me. You may trust in his discretion.

Come soon, dear Count. I fear my own neck may be on the chopping block next.

Your loving,
Mary

1544

My dearest Count Dracula,
Finally! My father has rewritten the line of succession. Elizabeth and I have both been added — after Edward of course. But we have both regained our status at court. After that childish ninny, Katherine Howard, became Henry's fifth queen and just as quickly lost her head in 1542, Father remarried for the sixth time. Another Catherine, if you can imagine! She became queen in 1543, and so far, he has found no fault in her. She is a pleasant enough woman though, and I feel certain that she has been the one to convince Father to return Elizabeth and me to the succession. Whatever the reason, Father has not been well, and I think his reign is drawing to a close.

Come quickly, dear Count.

My future Queen,
I am coming soon. I will see you at the Palace at Greenwich.
D

1545 — Palace at Greenwich

Dracula's second visit to England proved to be quite different from his first. He spent long hours alone with Mary from evening to sunrise. There was no pretext of formality. Mary's training had begun in earnest. She still clung to her prayer times and her rosary, attending the small chapel near her chambers—the one place the Count would not enter with her. But slowly, he was convincing her to forsake faith for the promise of power. Mary learned to project her voice and her naturally strong will to bend others to do her bidding. She remained amazed at the success she continued to enjoy.

Could this be how my mother held such sway over her servants? She wondered about it often. *Mother's voice was instantly obeyed, even without the boisterous shouting and brutal physical duress used by Henry.*

Then the second phase of her training began.

Dracula had not marked her again after the first visit in 1534. The wounds had long since healed and disappeared, and no new ones sprang up from their sessions together. Mary told him that her headaches—a life-long struggle with pain—had not recurred in the last seven years, but the sensitivity to sunlight clearly remained.

"An unfortunate side effect of my condition," the Count said, his voice silky. "I assure you, the benefits will outweigh such small inconveniences. Darkened rooms during the day will be one of the disadvantages for a queen, but you will find alternatives. When you are queen, no one will dare to challenge your practices."

Mary's eyes blazed with growing desire for this future he promised.

"The next step is your—" Dracula paused "—transformation."

"Will it hurt? This thing you are going to do to me?" She tried to keep her voice steady. *I am strong; I am my mother's daughter, and I will be queen.*

"There is some pain involved as you change, but nothing you cannot endure." Dracula's gaze filled her vision, his eyes mesmerizing, compelling. "I must taste your blood again, my Princess. But only for a moment."

She nodded as he drew closer and lowered his mouth to her neck. She gasped and bit her lip as he gently filled his mouth with her blood. He drew back slowly. She swayed only slightly but did not experience the vertigo of her previous experiences. Nor did she forget.

He smiled approvingly. "Now this part will be a little harder for you, but it is necessary."

She nodded slowly. "I'm ready, Count."

He pushed his sleeve away from his wrist, baring the pale skin. Then he bit down hard. When his mouth came away from his wrist, she saw blood flowing from the wound. "You must drink," he said, raising his wrist level with her face.

"Drink? Your blood?" she gasped.

"There is power in the blood, my Princess. If you want my power, you must share my blood. It is not enough for me to simply feed on you. You must feed on me as well."

Mary stared, first in revulsion, then in fascination.

"Quickly, my lady," Dracula said, raising his arm closer to her lips. "My blood will thicken and stop flowing more quickly than your own will."

Gingerly, Mary closed her lips over the open wounds and closed her eyes. His blood seeped into her mouth, and she swallowed, tasting a sweet ambrosia on her tongue. When the flow began to ebb, she pulled away.

"That was not so bad, was it?" he asked her gently.

"No, surprisingly," she said, smiling into his pale features. "But what will happen to me now?"

"You will rest for the day, and tonight you will become Nosferatu — just as I am. We are creatures of the night, and we need blood to sustain our survival. Tonight, I will teach you to feed. And more importantly, when, where, and who to choose. Your hunger will be most fierce for the first thirty days, and whenever the moon is full. I will remain close as you adjust, mostly to help you control your new urges."

"My… urges?" she asked.

"You'll see what I mean when you rise from your bed tonight."

~~~~~

And see she did. The insatiable hunger would have forced her to drain every servant in her court, had Dracula not been there to help her control the thirst. Her hearing had become acute enough that she could hear the heartbeat of any person within five feet of her. She could see the blood pulsing in the vein at the neck or wrist of her servants and courtiers. She ran from Margaret's concerned expression because the urge to feast on her friend hit her so violently, she almost attacked the poor girl.

Dracula came swiftly at the sound of her running feet.

"Let us go for a moonlit stroll, my lady," he said, loudly enough to be heard. In a lower tone, for her ears alone, he added, "We should leave your home and hunt elsewhere in the countryside." Then he swept her out the door and down one of the many garden paths. He wore a dark cloak, and carried another over his arm, which he slipped around her shoulders as soon as they were far enough from the house to be hidden from view. "You will learn to disguise yourself when you venture out to
~~~~~

feed. You do not want any… casualties to be connected to you. And you will have to use the techniques I have already shown you to influence the memories of your servants, so they will swear you remained at home all evening. That will become essential to your survival."

Each night they roamed the countryside, always taking a new direction, and Mary fed on the populace. She marveled when her fangs suddenly lengthened with her first feeding. She was startled enough that she nipped her own tongue, and the taste of blood in her mouth nearly drove her crazy. She yanked the first young maid she saw in the village almost off her feet, dragging her away from the local inn, and draining her of blood in mere moments. When she dropped the girl and realized she was lifeless, her heart shrank from the corpse. But Dracula praised her for the strength and swiftness of the attack. Exhilaration followed, and they moved on to another victim.

"Remember this, my dear Mary," he said, keeping his voice low to avoid being overheard. "You will have to wait for people to step outside before you attack, or you will have to be invited into their homes. Another inconvenience of being what we are."

"How would I possibly be invited in?" she asked.

"You might plead for shelter," he said. "Or perhaps request aid — you fell from your horse and it ran from you. People will be far more trusting of a woman in distress than a man. You will learn you can cajole people into many things."

Her height — and the dark cloak — kept people from recognizing her, as no one could remember later if they were assaulted by a man or a woman. She even took to wearing a man's oversized shirt and the dark trousers of a tradesman, which further masked her gender. The first few victims were drained completely, leaving no witness to worry about, but she gained exceptional control after only a week. Dracula was well-pleased with her progress and praised her self-control. She basked in his approval, feeling more and more confident in her new powers. She held life and death in her hands. Gradually, she began making sure she feasted primarily on the non-Catholics of her area. Though she prayed less, and holding her rosary became increasingly painful to her, she could not throw away her rituals as easily as Count Dracula had seemed to do. But his contempt for organized religion slowly rubbed off on the Princess.

The pope did nothing as my mother lay dying, abandoned by her husband and kept from the company of her only child. What allegiance do I truly owe to the Church? Count Dracula has helped me more than the Church — or God — ever did. Those thoughts felt blasphemous at first, but gradually, she felt the dark power course through her soul. Soon, she abandoned the chapel altogether, never realizing that, as she changed, she could no longer step on holy ground.

Dracula returned to the mainland after only three weeks.

"I've seen strangers in town at night lately," he admitted to a forlorn Mary. "It may be that Henry has heard of a stranger near your home. We would not want him to suddenly arrive on your doorstep and demand to meet me himself. Killing the sovereign of any nation draws far more attention than we want to deal with." He raised her chin with one cold finger. "I will return when I hear the King is dead. I promise you, I will help you take your throne."

She kissed the hand that held her chin. "Thank you, Vladimir. You have changed my life more than I could have imagined. You will always be welcome in my realm."

January, 1547 — Whitehall Castle

Mary smiled as she thought of the many properties she held, due in part to her father's new generosity toward her, and partly because she had used a small portion of the influence Dracula had graced her with to "encourage" her father to grant her gifts to keep her happy. Young King Henry would have never been susceptible to those manipulations, but older Henry lived with unbearable pain from a leg wound, and his own overindulgences. Having the girth of a gorilla and an uncontrollable appetite had led to an obesity that rendered him almost crippled. He was much easier to influence as his health declined.

When she received the summons for a Christmas reunion, she got a good first-hand look at the king's declining health. It was more than a little shocking. His servants now used a makeshift harness to lift the King from floor to floor, always in secret, so as not to embarrass him. Then he was placed in a chair with wheels, and servants pushed him from room to room. For the rest of the day, he would visit with his children, preside over his courtiers, and bawl out orders — especially "bring more wine!"

Mary nodded to herself.

"It's time," she murmured, watching Henry lecture her half-brother, Edward from across the room.

Queen Katherine's voice had pulled her back to the present conversation. She returned to her chair in the circle of ladies. Elizabeth smiled from her seat beside their stepmother.

"Katherine just taught me a new embroidery stitch," she said, glancing up from the wooden hoop with a piece of fabric stretched over it. Mary admired the neat stitches, and the floral pattern emerging from

Elizabeth's needle.

A courtier scurried toward the ladies and whispered in Queen Katherine's ear. She nodded with the smallest sigh. Excusing herself, she rose and glided after the courtier to the king's chair. Mary watched her lean over Henry with a sweet concern on her face.

She really seems to care, Mary thought. *Though how she can bear to stand so close to the king is beyond me.*

The stench coming from the king's body was nauseating. Mary had cornered one of her father's physicians in the hallway soon after her arrival.

"What is that horrid smell? Does no one ever think to bathe the King?" Her gaze had pinned the physician in place. He obviously hesitated to discuss the King's condition, but she was a princess, after all. Quite possibly his sovereign someday, if anything happened to Edward. She watched those thoughts flicker across his face. She forced a little power into her stare, and his will crumpled before her.

"You are aware, no doubt, that King Henry fell from a horse many years ago and injured his leg," he began. She nodded, so the doctor continued. "He has often had ulcers from that wound, infection, pus — we've had to drain his wounds many times. But this time, it's worse. Nothing seems to stem the spread of these sores. So most of the … uh, odors… are from that. But he also loves his food too much. We've warned him over and over, but the gout only worsens as he gains more weight. We've begun to see boils on his body, mostly around his belly."

Mary's face remained impassive. She had swallowed hard, then nodded, forcing a look of concern to crease her forehead. "I—I feared as much, good doctor. Can you venture an opinion about…?"

"How long he'll live?" He had chuckled and shaken his head. "I have no idea. We've seen King Henry on what we thought was his deathbed so many times, I've lost count of them. He has a way of rallying each time, far beyond what we think a mortal is capable of. His will is extraordinary. Henry won't leave this earth until he's good and ready."

"Yes," Mary said, "his will has always been made of iron."

As the doctor strode away, Mary gazed at the door to Henry's bedroom. *Maybe it's time you are pushed off your throne, Father. And I have the power to do it.*

Before she could plan her attack, the King ordered Katherine and the girls to embark for Greenwich. The Queen pleaded to remain at his side, but Henry was adamant. The women did not need to see the King in a weakened state. As soon as he regained his strength, he would send for them. But as the women shared glances, Mary understood. They all knew Henry would not recover this time.

He was dying.

When they'd been at Greenwich for a month, Elizabeth and Katherine began to grow impatient for news from Whitehall.

"Why have we not received word from the King?" Katherine ranted, pacing between the large windows overlooking the courtyard. "We're only six miles from the royal palace. Can they spare no one to ride over here and tell me how my husband fares?"

"Maybe we should ride to the castle ourselves and ask," Elizabeth ventured.

"Nonsense," Mary said, more sharply than she'd meant. "If we dare to appear at the gates without Father's express permission, do you think he won't throw us in the Tower? Have you really not learned that about our father?"

Elizabeth shrank from Mary's words. Her own mother had dared too much and trusted that Henry would never harm her. That had been her death sentence. The child was all too familiar with Henry's volatile nature.

Katherine stopped pacing and sank into a chair by the fireplace. "Mary is right. We have no choice but to wait patiently for the King to call us home." She sighed and picked up an embroidery hoop and needle. Mary heard her whisper under her breath. "Please, Henry. Let me come home."

~~~~~

Mary stood below the windows of Henry's palace. Candles burned, and figures moved within the king's chambers, as she watched and waited. It was well after midnight before the lights began to dim, and movements ceased. Mary bent her knees and jumped, leaping from the ground to the second-floor balcony. She landed gracefully, her cape flowing around her slender figure. She wished Dracula had been here to witness it. Her first few jumps had not been as fluid, and she wanted him to see that she had practiced until she could land with hardly a sound.

She had ridden her horse the short six miles well after they had all retired to bed. Slipping from the castle was child's play with her vampiric powers, and she relished the freedom she now possessed. Getting into Whitehall undetected had been a little trickier, but a nip on the neck, a little sip of blood, and the gate guards lay like cast-off toys. She slipped through the shadows, then watched and waited. Mary couldn't wait much longer though. The sun would rise, and she would be trapped. It was imperative that she complete her mission, leave Whitehall, and sneak back into Greenwich before the sun rose. Before servants began to stir.
~~~~~

She quietly swung open the balcony door and slipped into her father's room. Since she had been admitted to his chambers several times over the Christmas holidays, the question of an invitation to enter was moot. She approached his bedside, staring at the bloated belly above his blankets, which had also been folded aside to keep them from rubbing against his wounded leg. Blood and pus trickled down his thigh and pooled on the sheets below his massive body. Henry's eyes opened slowly, confusion clouding his features, then recognizing her, wondering at her presence, and — was that affection on his face? Mary sat primly on a chair that sat conveniently beside the enormous canopy bed.

"Hello, Father," she said coldly. "I thought we might have a little chat. I've been wanting to talk to you, but then you sent me away so suddenly, I never got the chance."

"Not... well, daughter. Perhaps — perhaps another time? When... I'm better?" His words came out in gasps, fractured thoughts weaving in and out of his diminished mind.

"I'm afraid there isn't going to be another time, Father dear," she said, a small gloating smile curving her lips upward. "You see, I met the most remarkable man." Henry's eyes widened, then blinked, as if keeping them open took too much effort.

"It all... went by... too quickly, my daughter," Henry moaned. "Life is... so much... shorter than... I thought it would be." He gasped every few words, straining to fill his lungs with air. His pus-filled bulk weighed heavily on him as he lay on his back. "So many... regrets. So many... deaths... during my reign."

"How odd," Mary said with a malevolent smile. "My life will be very long indeed. And I won't have to murder over 70,000 people to hold my throne. You have a lot of blood on your hands, King Henry — blood on your throne." She practically spat his own name at him. "I hope I'm never as quick to destroy lives as you've been during your reign."

"What has... happened to you, Mary?" Henry gasped. "You've changed."

"Yes, in spite of you, I met a man with extraordinary gifts. He showed me how to access this power, and I want to tell you, Father, it's been an amazing experience."

Henry tried to speak, but words couldn't get past his lips.

"I thought about sharing these gifts with you, Father," she said, sighing with false regret. "But the biggest gift is — immortality." She watched his eyes widen and flicker again. "Yes, you could live forever. Isn't that incredible? But then you would continue to discredit our religion, disassemble the monasteries, and murder anyone who dares to disagree with you. I think it's time we had a new sovereign in England. What do you think?"

Anger tinged the king's features as he saw her rebellion unmasked. She no longer feared him, respected him, trembled in anticipation of his punishments.

"Of course, you are thinking that it won't be me. Edward will follow you." A grimace twisted Henry's mouth as she continued. "But Father—Edward is a child. Do you think he'll sit on the throne for very long? Oh, I'll allow him to reign for a couple of years. If he were to pass away too soon, I would fall under suspicion. But don't worry, Father. I'll send him to you before you know it."

She rose and approached his bed, staring into his angry eyes until his gaze became unfocussed and dazed. "You have no idea how distasteful this is for me, Father, But I will take no chances that you might rally and regain your strength yet again." She lunged forward and sank her teeth into his neck, tasting the bitter acid in his blood. Illness and disease had polluted his body, and she drained him until she felt the spark of life barely holding his soul to his physical form. "No, I'm not going to kill you, Father," she said, pulling back and wiping her mouth on her sleeve. "I'm going to leave you weak and dying. I will not make your end peaceful or pleasant. Enjoy these moments, for soon you will be in hell for all you've done to me and to my mother."

She cocked her head and studied the blank expression on Henry's face. "Any last words, Father?" She waited. Henry gurgled, his face pale against the pillow. "I thought not," she said, striding to the balcony. "Good-bye, Father."

And she jumped. She landed with a soft scrape of her boots against the cobblestones. Moving swiftly in the shadows to her horse, which she'd left tied to a tree outside the castle walls, she mounted and spurred the animal toward Greenwich Castle.

~~~~~

Just before dawn, word arrived by messenger.

The King was dead.

Susan's tear-stained face hovered over her, gently shaking her shoulder. She clutched a shawl around her shoulders over her nightgown, and wisps of hair escaped the white bonnet covering her hair. Mary sat up in bed and pretended to rub sleep from her eyes, when, in truth, she had only been back between the sheets for little more than an hour's time.

"Oh, my lady," Susan whispered. "Your father—King Henry—has passed on from this life. I am so sorry."

"Father is—" She paused. "Dead?"
~~~~~

"A courtier just arrived from Whitehall."

An anguished cry echoed down the hallway from Katherine's room. Elizabeth's voice soon joined her stepmother's grief. Mary gave her head a small shake. *I must pretend to grieve*, she thought.

"I just can't take it in," Mary said with a sigh. "We expected that this might happen, but Father always rallies." She tossed back the covers and rose. "Fetch my robe, Susan. I must join the Queen and my sister."

~~~~~

The women returned to Whitehall, and they clung to one another through the funeral and entombment of Henry. Then Edward's coronation became the focal point of the court. Through it all, Mary was forced to pretend her crippling headaches plagued her so she could remain in her darkened room during the daylight hours. Any crack in the drapes seared her eyes and made her skin sizzle. As soon as the crown was on Edward's head, she excused herself and returned to Framlingham Castle.

Dracula joined her within a fortnight.

"That child is insufferable," Mary snapped, as she paced before the fireplace. "King? He's a spoiled little boy."

"You need not spend time in his presence, Mary," Count Dracula said. He sat in a chair by the fire, watching her swish back and forth. "You have your own home now. Many of them, in fact."

"That's not the point, Vlad," she said sharply. "The throne is mine. I've waited all these years, and still you counsel me to wait longer? Do you know how Edward demeans my faith?"

"Why do you persist in defending the Catholic Church?" Dracula asked, raising his hands and slapping them down on the arms of his chair with a thud. "The power you possess did not come to you by way of the pope! Why do you persist in this blind faith?"

Mary stared at him, conflict flickering over her stern features. He was right, of course. But to abandon all faith? Everything she'd learned from her beloved mother?

"Maybe I should leave you to your precious faith," Dracula declared, rising to his feet. "Maybe the pope can help you gain the throne. Do you think he will bother with you?"

"No!" she cried, flinging herself against him. "Don't leave me, please. What will I do without you?"

"Will you listen to me?" Dracula asked, his voice like iron. "Will you heed my words, my plans for you? I have lived many lifetimes already. I will not waste efforts on a woman who cannot honor her commitment."

"I-I'll listen, Vl—" Her voice froze in her throat. "My dear Count
~~~~~

Dracula, I will heed you. Please don't leave."

His eyes narrowed, and he grasped her by the shoulders. "Have I not promised to help you take your throne?"

"Yes," she whispered, staring deep into his dark eyes.

"Do you believe me?" His gaze deepened, and Mary felt the room tilt.

"Y-yes," she stammered.

He released her arms and she stumbled backward, slumping into her chair.

"You. Must. Wait." His voice was low but filled with the power of his intensity. "You cannot kill Edward so soon after his coronation. Do you think the members of his Privy Council are fools? Do you not think they will blame you? You, who are the next in line? It's folly! You would risk everything."

"I'll wait," she whispered. "I understand, Count. Truly, I do."

Dracula relented, moving to sit in the chair opposite hers. "I know you are tired of waiting, my dear Princess. But look how far you've come! And your greatest hurdle—the death of Henry—is now behind you. I am so proud of you for controlling your impetuous nature. He was seen alive, though greatly weakened. If anyone had witnessed your visitation, or noticed anything odd, you are not connected to the King's death whatsoever. I know how greatly you were tempted to drain him completely."

Mary grimaced. "Actually, it was all I could do to feed on him at all. His blood was vile." She shuddered.

He patted her hand reassuringly. "A few short years, and Edward's reign can end. You have eternity, Mary. Remember that."

She nodded. "I will remember."

Christmas 1550—Hampton Court

Christmas with her family. How Mary had dreaded it. Religious holidays had become more and more uncomfortable since her transformation. She had finally been forced to put her rosary beads in a pouch she tied around her waist with a cord. Touching the silver cross caused her fingers to blister and burn. And when Count Dracula visited, she made sure the pouch remained out of sight.

She still sought Dracula's approval, though his comments about the faith of her mother rankled. She dared not voice her feelings for fear he could indeed desert her.

But this holiday visit with Elizabeth and Edward was the last straw. She could take no more, could wait no longer.

As she paced her chambers, a latch clicked softly behind her. She whirled, fangs extended, toward the intruder at her balcony door.

"Vlad!" She exhaled sharply as she hurried to draw him into a desperate embrace. "How did you know to come?"

"I felt your pain," he said, pulling back to stare into her eyes. "And I have servants in Edward's court who provide the occasional report." His smile carried a hint of conspiracy.

Mary covered her mouth to muffle her amusement. "You keep a spy in my brother's household? I should have known."

"Not only his household, my dear Mary. I have them in several courts in this land, including Elizabeth's."

Mary's eyes widened. She knew the Count was powerful, but she hadn't expected this.

His features sobered. "I have heard of Edward's rebuke after dinner. I knew you would need my support."

"The nerve of that child!" Mary raved. "He dared to reproach me for the faith of my mother. He all but attacked the Catholic Church. A boy of only thirteen winters would instruct me on matters of church doctrine? I am the daughter of Catherine of Aragon—"

"Please, Mary," Dracula interrupted her. "I grow weary of your defense of your precious faith. Have I not told you? Your power does not come from the church!"

A low knock on her chamber door cut them both off. Dracula moved swiftly to the balcony doors and slipped into the shadows.

Mary hesitated a moment longer, then strode over to open the massive oak door.

"Princess Mary, may I come in for a moment?"

Mary stared at the kind face of Thomas Cranmer, the archbishop of the Church of England. He was the last person she had expected to see at her door.

"Y-yes, of course, Bishop Cranmer," she said, stepping aside. "What brings you here so late in the evening?"

"I want to apologize for the King's unkind words after dinner," Cranmer began. "I know he was a bit overbearing, but I am sure he only wanted to ease any spiritual distress he feels you might be experiencing." His words became more halting as he watched her expression harden.

"I am not in distress," Mary said icily. "But I do not take my spiritual instructions from a child, either."

"King Edward only wants you to have the same peace of heart and soul which he, himself, has experienced." Cranmer paused, his gaze searching her face uneasily. "Princess Mary, is there any comfort I can give? You seem… different of late. I thought it concerned the death of your beloved father, but I sense a darkness surrounding you. May I help you find God's peace, your Grace?"

Mary wanted to lash out at the man. He read her too well. But if he said much more, she feared Dracula would sweep in and tear out his throat.

"I am fine, Bishop Cranmer," she said, forcing a civility into her words that she did not feel. "I find it… tiring to spend too much time with my family, though I love them."

"Perhaps you are spending too much time in solitude," Cranmer suggested. "Maybe I could convince Edward to let you linger after the new year—"

"No," Mary objected. She paused, then tried to smile warmly. "Please do not suggest that to my brother. I am more than ready to return home to Suffolk. I find it peaceful there." She pasted a wobbly smile on her face.

Cranmer's unease creased his face in a frown. "Princess Mary, are you quite certain?"

"Yes, I am," she injected smoothly. "I will be fine after a nice rest."

Cranmer seemed to debate his next words, and he chose carefully before speaking.

"My lady, you have suffered terribly over the past years. I know it may seem… acceptable to allow a certain amount of bitterness to reside in your heart. But it will only hurt you in the long term. I beg you to seek God's forgiveness and grace. Please don't slide into the sins of anger and resentment. It will be your undoing."

Mary gritted her teeth, careful to keep her fangs retracted.

"I appreciate your concern, Bishop, but I grow quite fatigued."

"Yes, of course." He hastened toward the door. "I am at your service, should you ever need prayer," he said as she ushered him out.

She leaned against the heavy oak and listened as his footsteps shuffled against the stone floors.

"You are right, Mary." Dracula's voice startled her. "It is time to end the boy's reign."

"Tonight?" she asked. "Before I leave for Suffolk?"

"Yes, but as you did with Henry. Do not drain him entirely. He must survive for a time. His chest is weak. If you weaken him further, his death will appear to be a natural progression."

As she crept to the King's bedchambers in the darkness of the early morning hours, she remembered his mother, Jane. She had been kindness itself to her and had encouraged her father to rekindle their relationship. She thought of Bishop Cranmer's words about resentment and bitterness. For the first time, she wondered if she was becoming as evil as they all seemed to think.

She slipped into the bedroom and listened to the rhythmic snores of the boy king.

He's only a child, she told herself as she drew near to the huge canopy bed.

A child who would rule over you. Dracula's voice in her head spoke clearly in that distinctive accent.

"You can't be so foolish as to still advocate allegiance to the pope, can you?" Edward's arrogant words taunted her memory. "That's unacceptable in my kingdom," he had continued.

Her own heated words, and Elizabeth's distress at their bickering, finally became too much.

It will never end, she thought. *The older he gets, the more like Father he'll be, until he finishes what Henry started and destroys every Catholic in this country.*

She leaned over Edward's sleeping form and sank her fangs into his neck.

November 1558 — Hampton Court

Mary turned away from the window overlooking the garden. Eight years had passed since that Christmas with her siblings. Edward had been a true Tudor. In spite of the poor condition of his lungs, he had lived another three years before succumbing to disease.

Of course, Edward had feared she would return England to the hands of the Catholics, so he had removed her from the line of succession again, naming their cousin, Lady Jane Grey, to follow him. But Mary's followers made short work of Jane Grey. Within ten days, Mary had the upstart imprisoned in the Tower.

Mary I was crowned by Thomas Cranmer at Baynard's House in August 1553. She remembered the sweet taste of victory, even as she saw the worried expression on the Bishop's face. He had known, hadn't he? Had suspected the darkness coiled in her soul.

She had released many of her old supporters from the Tower, men her father had locked away and left to rot. Thomas Howard, the Duke of Norfolk and Stephen Gardiner, the former archbishop before Anne's annihilation of Catholicism, were released and given prominent positions on her Privy Council.

Mary remembered the jousts that marked the celebration of her coronation. The blood spilled on the fields that day, combined with her own long-delayed success, made her thirst soar. On the pretext of consoling the wounded losers, Mary had slipped into the medical tents and sated her bloodlust, draining the men dry. It was assumed they'd succumbed to their injuries, but she saw suspicion in Thomas Cranmer's eyes. She replaced him with Stephen Gardiner. Cranmer and many other Protestant clergy were confined to the Tower and later burned at the stake. In all, she had signed death warrants on over 300 people.

"Still not quite as bad as my father," she murmured to the windowpane.

Marriage had not gone as Mary expected either. While she purged the country of those she called heretics, she entered a pact with Spain, which included marrying Philip—a cousin on her mother's side of the family tree.

After an uncomfortable pregnancy, Mary gave birth to a deformed monster of a creature, the product of her transformed state. Dracula had tried to warn her against pregnancy, knowing that a human and a vampire would not be able to make a "normal" child. When she saw the bat-like monster, she had shrieked like a banshee and then executed everyone who had witnessed the event.

Mary's mind had fractured that day. Philip left for a battlefield in France.

Dracula returned to England one last time.

~~~~~

The Count tucked Mary's hand into the crook of his arm as they wandered through the rose garden.

"Do you remember the first night we walked in a garden much like this one?" she asked.

"I remember every moment clearly," he said, patting her hand gently.

"I thought gaining the throne would be my life's goal. If only I could achieve that, my joy would be complete." She sighed. "How wrong I was. Nothing has turned out the way I planned." Mary looked up at the night sky. "I once told Henry that he had left blood on the throne. But what have I done? The very same thing. Maybe we Tudors were never meant to rule. One way or another, we all do the same things. We plot, we conspire, we bicker, and then we destroy those who would thwart our causes."

"I tried to warn you," Dracula said softly. "We have an eternity. This time as Queen of England is a mere blink of the eye compared to the life ahead of us. And blood will always be a part of our lives. We must have it to survive. But the burden of ruling need not consume you like it did your predecessors."

"I still can't quite grasp that," she said, leaning against his side as
~~~~~

they walked. "Eternity on this earth. Where will we go?"

"First we will have to execute your death," he said. Mary stopped in her tracks and stared. "No, no, my queen. You must pretend to die. Then we will be free of this country. Free of the crown, the religions, the ties that are choking the life out of your soul."

They resumed walking. "But you aren't doing this to be rid of me, are you?"

They paused beside a fragrant rose bush, and Dracula plucked free an exquisite bud on a long stem. Presenting it to Mary with a flourish, Dracula drew his arm around her.

"We'll be together forever. And you will be *my* queen."

1878 — Outskirts of London

"It's been more than three hundred years since I left England behind me," Mary said as she gazed out the window at the nocturnal activities of this current generation of commoners. "The Count whisked me away from the grief and resentments of my youth. We had many adventures, many battles, shared a lot of blood over those centuries."

She faced the lieutenants who had scouted ahead for her. They had served her well, earning their own immortality along the way.

"So tell me again. How did this happen? A mere mortal destroyed my Count, then she vanished? She's no longer anywhere in London? Nor the continent?" Her voice rose, the famous Tudor temper fully engaged.

"She was — is — more than a mere mortal, my queen." A handsome vampire stepped forward, top hat in hand, as he faced her wrath. "The Count passed a bit of his own powers to her."

Mary's breath exploded, and she wavered. "He did — what?" The malevolence in her voice shook the room.

"She did not turn completely, your Grace, but she did manage to retain many of Dracula's qualities. His speed, his strength, his ability to heal his own wounds —"

"How did this happen?" she shrieked again.

"We do not know," the vampire said, spinning his top hat in nervous hands. He bowed his head in deference to her. "But we have dealt her many blows, my queen."

"If she's still breathing, you have not battered her nearly enough yet."

The vampire flinched. "She was aided by Father Gallagher at the White Chapel Parish."

"Father Gallagher?" Mary slammed her right fist into her left palm.

"I remember him. Why is he not dead yet? He's been a thorn in our side for far too long. I want him destroyed."

"We think he sent Mrs. Harker to the American continent recently. We've sent agents to seek her location."

"Not good enough!" Mary bellowed. "She destroyed the man who created us all." She swallowed the lump in her throat, and her voice hardened.

"Find Mina Harker."

The End

MEET THE AUTHORS

Darlene N. Bocek is an award-winning author of YA Sci-fi. She is a pastor's wife living on a farm in Izmir, Turkey. She and her husband have a plethora of pets named after pop culture heroes, a son named after a sci-fi hero, two daughters practicing science-fact (dentistry), and a daughter studying to be an author. Her well-acclaimed first book, *Trunk of Scrolls*, was re-released last year. See her books and join her club at darlenebocek.com. (Editor's note: Darlene has also written for *Moonlight and Claws*, *Don't Go in the Water*, and *The Invisible Files* by Ye Olde Dragon Books!)

Jordan Campbell was born in California and moved to Maine when he was eleven. All through his childhood, Jordan had a book in his hand nearly continuously. Educated at the University of Maine, majoring in English, Jordan has had almost a dozen short stories published in the last three years. He is excited to bring his stories to the world. Jordan's first story for Ye Olde Dragon Books was *Neher, Demon of the River*, which was published in the third Classic Monsters Anthology, *Don't Go in the Water*.

Rosemarie DiCristo had lots of fun writing *Love Sucks*, especially since she could pretend things like Tad's Steaks, Avon's Buttercrunch lip gloss, the Hudson River Day-Line, Helmut's strudels, and that scrumptious chocolate mousse still exist. She's been a vampire fan ever since she ran home from school every afternoon to watch *Dark Shadows* on her friend Emily's color TV. Rosemarie is delighted to have another story published in one of Ye Olde Dragon Books' anthologies. She's also published short stories and rebuses for children in *StarLight* magazine and has published flash fiction in *Havok*. By the way, Rosemarie is absolutely *not* a Mets fan.

Jim Doran is a genre writer who enjoys transporting his readers into worlds of wonder, mystery, and danger. Whether it's the fairytale hijinks in his Kingdom Fantasy series or a centaur agent's daring adventures, Jim aims to entertain his audience with every word. His forthcoming YA horror novel, ***Forlorn Harbor***, will be published by Rowan Prose Publishing in 2026. Among his published shorter works, Jim has had six stories included in Ye Olde Dragon monster and fairy tale anthologies (always a thrill). If you enjoyed *Higpins* (in *Trouble Comes in Threes*), Rebecca Eidelweiss will be featured in the novel, ***DEED***, coming soon.

Pam Halter is an award-winning picture book, short story, and fantasy author. But she has a darker side. She spent many hours in high school watching any and all of the low budget horror movies TV had to offer. Every Saturday afternoon, anyone could find Pam watching the Dr. Shock show out of Philadelphia, which featured the delights of Bela Legosi, Lon Chaney, Boris Karloff, Vincent Price, Peter Lorre, and more. She wrote a research paper in 11th grade about Bela Legosi, Boris Karloff, and Vincent Price, complete with pictures she xeroxed at the public library. Her teacher did not appreciate that and gave her a B+. It was the only grade Pam ever argued, but the teacher didn't budge. It's Pam's belief the teacher was stilted in her creativity. She still has that report and is still proud of it. Pam had Count Dracula show up at her door to escort her to her bridal shower thirty-five years ago, so it was only natural her vampire story would go rom-com. Learn more about Pam at www.pamhalter.com

Michelle Levigne started writing for fanzines in college, while earning a bunch of useless degrees in theater, English, film/communication, and writing. Her first professional publication came from winning first place in the Writers of the Future contest in 1990. She has over 100 published books and novellas in SF, fantasy, cozies, and romance. Her Enchanted Castle Archives series started here in the fairytale and classic monster anthologies. Look for a middle-grade tie-in about 'Na and her pet dragon Smedley soon. A tea snob, she freelance edits for a living and terrorizes writers and readers through Mt. Zion Ridge Press and Ye Olde Dragon Books, as well as the storytelling podcast, Ye Olde Dragon's Library. For reasons she still can't figure out, she was named ACFW's Editor of the Year in 2025. Be afraid… be very afraid.

Cortney Manning resides in Florida but has always loved traveling the world. She holds a master's degree in Victorian Literature from the University of Glasgow and has a not-so-secret love of fantasy and fairy tales. In her free time, Cortney enjoys walking, drawing, and afternoon tea. Her flash fiction fantasy and mysteries can be found on Havok, and her novellas and short stories have been featured in several anthologies: *Five Poisoned Apples*, *The Depths We'll Go To*, *Casting Call*, *Tales from the Tower*, and *The Willow Tree Swing*. In addition, she has two published novels, *As Long as We Live* and *The Lord of Shadow and the Queen of Flames*. More information about Cortney and her writing, visit her website, https://cortneymanning.wixsite.com/author, or on Instagram @cortneymanningauthor.

Lindsi McIntyre is a linguaphile from Texas who hopes to use her words, both written and spoken, to bring glory to the Lord Most High. When not writing she can be found within the pages of a good book or watching the latest episode of her favorite TV shows and drinking way too much tea while doing both. You can check out more of her work on *Havok*, grab a copy of *Moonlight and Claws*, *Tales from the Tower*, *Who's the Monster*, *Tales from the Forest* (a Realm Award finalist), and *Perchance to Dream* anthologies from *Ye Olde Dragon Books*, or the *Wither and Bloom* anthology from *Twenty Hills Publishing*. Look for her award-winning novella, *Broken Pieces*.

Stoney M. Setzer lives south of Atlanta, GA. He has a beautiful wife, three wonderful children, and one crazy dog who has convinced himself that he is human. His previous contributions to the Ye Olde Dragons anthologies involve the citizens of Sardis County, Tennessee, and he has recently released these stories as a series of ebooks. He is also the author of the Wesley Winter trilogy and the *Zero Hour* short story anthology. He has had short stories featured in such publications as *Havok* and *Residential Aliens*. When he is not writing, he likes reading, drawing, and following the highs and lows of his beloved Atlanta Braves and Atlanta Falcons. Learn more at www.tinniepress.blogspot.com or on Facebook @ stoneymsetzerofficial.

Deborah Cullins Smith has been writing stories ever since she could hold a pencil, but she came to her actual career in writing rather late in life. In 2019, she published the trilogy, *The Last of the Long-Haired Hippies*, in a rapid-release timed for the 50th anniversary of Woodstock, which she covered in great detail in the second volume. CWG Press released **Shroud of Darkness, The Birth of the Storm,** and **Victoria's War** over a four-month period, a culmination of almost twenty years in development. Ms. Cullins Smith's first Mina Harker adventure, **Mina: Warrior in the Shadows**, won the 2022 Realm Award for Horror Novel. Her next novel will continue the saga of Billy the Kid, which she began in the anthology *Moonlight and Claws*, with the story *Habitations of Violence*, and continued in *Who's the Monster?* with the story *Phillippe*. Her love of historical research makes these books and short stories challenging, as she is devoted to maintaining as much historical accuracy as possible while sliding things sideways to suggest that a few characters might be more than we gave them credit for! (No disrespect intended.)

When **Jessica A. Tanner** isn't writing stories full of vivid characters and creatures, she enjoys a view of the Rocky Mountains, takes long walks, and hangs with her many critters. She is a member of the American Christian Fiction Writers (ACFW), Realm Makers, and Wolf Creek Christian Writers Network (WCCWN). Jessica has short stories published in several anthologies—for example "The Invisible Boy" which is in *The Invisible Files:* Classic Monsters Anthology #4 from Ye Olde Dragon Books and ties into "The Pale New Kid," along with several pieces published under the *Matter of Faith* column of the *Pagosa Sun's Preview*. Her first novel, **Sonji**, is a YA fantasy about a girl and her magical horse. Her recently released novella *Peaflower: a Princess and Pea Retelling* is a wholesome YA romance featuring a princess with a pet rat. To connect or learn more, please visit www.jessicaatannerauthor.com

A childhood spent obsessing over fantasy and role-play while haunting the landscape of Central Europe resulted in **Etta-Tamara Wilson** having a deep fascination with rarely told fairy tales. She's now preoccupied with reminding a whole host of fairytale characters to mind their manners and be patient, while she thinks up future adventures for them. When not writing, she's usually off learning new skills or dreaming of travel in lands near, far, or fictional. She has additional stories in *Tales from the Tower, Who's the Monster?, Don't Go in the Water,* and *Trouble Comes in Threes.*